DEATH AT THE BAR

Dame Ngaio Marsh, a tall, vigorous New Zealander, published her twenty-seventh novel in 1972—at the age of seventy-two. Her best-selling whodunnits are in the classic tradition of Dorothy Sayers and Agatha Christie.

Dame Ngaio, in common with many white New Zealand children, was given a Maori name. (The 'g' is silent.) It is a 'portmanteau' word which can mean 'light-on-the-tree', or a type of tree with a white flower which she describes as 'undistinguished'. It can also mean 'clever'.

Despite her enormous output, the writing of crime fiction is only her second love. The first is the theatre, and she developed the New Zealand public's interest in live theatrical performances almost single-handed. Now the University of Canterbury has a theatre named after her. Amost as splendid an honour as what she likes to call 'me damery'.

D1514437

Available in Fontana by the same author

Dead Water
Enter a Murderer
Died in the Wool
False Scent
A Man Lay Dead
Overture to Death
Death at the Dolphin
Clutch of Constables
Death in a White Tie
When in Rome
Spinsters in Jeopardy

NGAIO MARSH

Death at the Bar

FONTANA / Collins

First published 1939
First issued in Fontana Books 1954
Seventh Impression August 1973

Printed in Great Britain
Collins Clear-Type Press London and Glasgow

CONTENTS

CAST OF CHARACTERS

CHAPTER ONE

THE PLUME OF FEATHERS

I

As Luke Watchman drove across Otterbrook Bridge the setting sun shone full in his eyes. A molten flood of sunlight poured towards him through the channel of the lane and broke into sequins across Otterbrook waters. He arched his hand over his eyes and peered through the spattered dazzle of the windscreen. Somewhere about here was the turning for Ottercombe. He lowered the window and leant out.

The warmth of evening touched his face. The air smelt of briar, of fern, and more astringently of the distant sea. There, fifty yards ahead, was the finger-post with its letters almost rubbed out by rain, " Ottercombe, 7 miles."

Watchman experienced the fulfilment of a nostalgic longing and was content. Only now, when he was within reach of his journey's end, did he realise how greatly he had desired this return. The car moved forward and turned from the wide lane into the narrow. The curves of hills marched down behind hedgerows. There was no more sunlight. Thorns brushed the windows on each side, so narrow was the lane. The car bumped over pot-holes. The scent of spring-watered earth rose coldly from the banks.

"Downhill all the way now," Watchman murmured. His thoughts travelled ahead to Ottercombe. One should always time arrivals for this hour when labourers turned homewards, when lamps were lit, when the traveller had secret glimpses into rooms whose thresholds he would never cross. At the Plume of Feathers, Abel Pomeroy would stand out in the roadway and look for incoming guests. Watchman wondered if his two companions had got there before him. Perhaps his cousin, Sebastian Parish, had set out on his evening prowl round the village. Perhaps Norman Cubitt had already found a subject and was down on the jetty dabbing nervously at a canvas. This was the second holiday they had spent

9

together in Ottercombe. A curious trio when you came to think of it. Like the beginning of a funny story. "A lawyer, an actor, and a painter once went to a fishing village in Devon." Well, he'd rather have Cubitt and Parish than any of his own learned brethren. The law set too dead a seal on character, the very soul of a barrister took silk. And he wondered if he had failed to escape the mannerisms of his profession, if he exuded learned counsel, even at Ottercombe in South Devon.

The lane dived abruptly downhill. Watchman remembered Decima Moore. Would she still be there? Did the Coombe Left Movement still hold its meetings on Saturday nights, and would Decima allow her arguments with himself to end as they had ended that warm night nearly a year ago? He set his thoughts on the memory of the smell of seaweed and briar, and of Decima, trapped half-way between resentment and fright, walking as if by compulsion into his arms.

The hamlet of Diddlestock, a brief interlude of white-wash and thatch, marked the last stage. Already, as he slid out of the shadow of Ottercombe Woods, he fancied that he heard the thunder of the sea.

Watchman checked his car, skidded, and changed into low gear. Somewhere about here Diddlestock Lane crossed Ottercombe Lane, and the intersection was completely masked by banks and hedgerows. A dangerous turning. Yes, there it was. He sounded his horn and the next second crammed on his brakes. The car skidded, lurched sideways, and fetched up against the bank, with its right-hand front bumpers locked in the left-hand rear bumpers of a baby two-seater.

Watchman leant out of the driving window.

"What the hell do you think you're doing?" he yelled.

The two-seater leapt nervously and was jerked back by the bumpers.

"Stop that!" roared Watchman.

He got out and stumbled along the lane to the other car.

It was so dark down there between the hedgerows that the driver's features, shadowed both by the roof of his car and the brim of his hat, were scarcely discernible. He seemed about to open the door when Watchman, bare-headed, came up to him. Evidently he changed his mind. He leant farther

10

back in his seat. His fingers pulled at the brim of his hat.

"Look here," Watchman began, "you're a hell of a fellow, aren't you, bucketing about the countryside like a blasted tank! Why the devil can't you sound your horn? You came out of that lane about twenty times as fast as—— What?"

The man had mumbled something.

"What?" Watchman repeated.

"I'm extremely sorry. Didn't hear you until——" The voice faded away.

"All right. Well, we'd better do something about it. I don't imagine much damage has been done." The man made no move and Watchman's irritation revived. "Give me a hand, will you?"

"Yes, certainly. Of course." The voice was unexpectedly courteous. "I'm very sorry. Really, very sorry. It was all my fault."

This display of contrition mollified Watchman.

"Oh well," he said, "no harm done, I dare say. Come on."

The man got out on the far side and walked round to the back of his car. When Watchman joined him he was stooping over the locked buffers.

"I can heave mine up if you don't mind backing an inch or two," said the man. With large calloused hands he gripped the buffers of his own car.

"All right," agreed Watchman.

They released the buffers without much trouble. Watchman called through his driving-window: "All clear!" The man lowered his car and then groped uncertainly in his pockets.

"Cigarette?" suggested Watchman and held out his case.

"Very kind," said the man. "Coals of fire——" He hesitated and then took a cigarette.

"Light?"

"I've got one, thanks."

He turned aside and cupped his hands round the match, dipping his head with extravagant care as if a wind threatened the flame.

"I suppose you're going to Ottercombe?" said Watchman. He saw a flash of teeth.

"Looks like it, doesn't it? I'm sorry I can't let you through till then."

11

"I shan't be on your heels at the pace you travel," grinned Watchman.

"No," agreed the man, and his voice sounded remote as he moved away. "I'll keep out of your way. Good-night."

"Good-night."

That ridiculous little car was as good as its driver's word. It shot away down the lane and vanished over the brow of a steep drop. Watchman followed more cautiously and by the time he rounded the hill the other car had turned a farther corner. He caught the distant toot of a horn. It sounded derisive.

II

The lane ran out towards the coast and straight for Coombe Rock, a headland that rose sharply from the downs to thrust its nose into the channel. A patch on the hillside seemed to mark an inconsequent end to the route. It was only when he drew closer to this patch that a stranger might recognise it as an entrance to a tunnel, the only gate into Ottercombe. Watchman saw it grow magically until it filled his range of vision. He passed a roadsign "Ottercombe. Dangerous Corner. Change down," and entered the mouth of the tunnel. He slowed down and switched on his lights. Dank walls closed about him, the sound of his progress echoed loudly and he smelt wet stones and seaweed. Before him, coldly and inkily blue, framed in black, was the sea. From within, the tunnel seemed to end in a shelf; actually it turned sharply to the left. Watchman had to stop and back his car before he could get round. There, down on his left and facing the sea, was Ottercombe.

Probably the alarming entrance into this village has saved it from becoming another Clovelly or Polperro. Ladies with Ye Olde Shoppe ambitions would hesitate to drive through Coombe Tunnel and very large cars are unable to do so. Moreover the village is not too picturesque. It is merely a group of houses whose whitewash is tarnished by the sea. There are no secret stairs in any of them, no ghosts walk Ottercombe Steps, no smugglers' cave looks out from Coombe Rock. For all that, the place has its history of grog-running and wrecking. There is a story of a fight in the tunnel between excisemen and the men of Coombe, and there are traces of the gate that once closed the tunnel every night at sunset. The whole of Ottercombe is the property of an irascible eccentric who keeps the houses in good repair, won't let one of them to a strange shopkeeper and breathes venom on the word "publicity." If a stranger cares to stay in Ottercombe he must put up at the Plume of Feathers, where Abel Pomeroy has four guest rooms, and Mrs. Ives does the house-keeping and cooking. If the Coombe men like him, they will take him out in their boats and play darts with him in the evening. He may walk round the cliffs, fish off the rocks, or drive seven miles to Illington where there is a golf-course and a three-star hotel. These are the amenities of Ottercombe.

The Plume of Feathers faces the cobbled road of entrance. It is a square building, scrupulously whitewashed. It has no great height but its position gives it an air of dominance over the cottages that surround it. On the corner of the Feathers the road of approach splits and becomes a sort of inn yard, off which Ottercombe Steps lead through the village and down to the wharf. Thus the windows of the inn, on two sides, watch for the arrival of strangers. By the corner entrance is a bench, occupied on warm evenings by Abel Pomeroy and his cronies. At intervals Abel walks into the middle of the road and looks up towards Coombe Tunnel as his father and grandfather did before him.

As Watchman drove down, he could see old Pomeroy standing there in his shirt sleeves. Watchman flicked his headlights and Pomeroy raised his hand. Watchman sounded his horn and a taller figure, dressed in the slacks and sweater of some superb advertisement, came through the lighted doorway. It was Watchman's cousin, Sebastian Parish. Then the others *had* arrived.

He drew up and opened the door.

"Well, Pomeroy."

"Well, Mr. Watchman, we'm right down glad to see you again. Welcome to you."

"I'm glad to get here," said Watchman, shaking hands. "Hallo, Seb. When did you arrive?"

"This morning, old boy," answered his cousin. "We stopped last night at Exeter with Norman's sister."

"I was at Yeovil," said Watchman. "Where is Norman?"

"Painting down by the jetty. The light's gone. He'll be in soon. He's started a portrait of me on Coombe Rock. It's going to be rather wonderful. I'm wearing a red sweater and the sea's behind me. Very virile!"

"Good Lord!" said Watchman cheerfully.

"We'll get your things out for you, sir," said old Pomeroy. "Will!"

A tall fox-coloured man came through the doorway. He screwed up his eyes, peered at Watchman, and acknowledged his greeting without much show of enthusiasm.

"Well, Will."

"'Evening, Mr. Watchman."

"Bear a hand, my sonny," said old Pomeroy.

His son opened the luggage carrier and began to haul out Watchman's suitcases.

"How's the Movement, Will?" asked Watchman. "Still well on the left?"

"Yes," said Will shortly. "It's going ahead. Will these be all?"

"Yes, thanks. I'll take the car round, Seb, and join you in the bar. Is there a sandwich or so anywhere about, Abel?"

"We can do a bit better than that, sir. There's a fine lobster Mrs. Ives has put aside, special."

"By George, you're a host in a million. God bless Mrs. Ives."

Watchman drove round to the garage. It was a converted stable, a dark building that housed the memory of sweating horses rubbed down by stable lads with wisps of straw. When he stopped his engine Watchman heard a rat plop across the rafters. In addition to his own the garage held four cars. There was Norman Cubitt's Austin, a smaller Austin, a Morris, and there, demure in the corner, a battered two-seater.

"You again!" said Watchman, staring at it. "Well I'll be damned!"

He returned to the pub, delighted to hear the familiar ring of his own steps, to smell the tang of the sea and of burning driftwood. As he ran upstairs he heard voices and the unmistakable tuck of a dart in a cork board.

"Double twenty," said Will Pomeroy, and above the general outcry came a woman's voice.

"Splendid, my dear. We win!"

"So, she *is* here," thought Watchman as he washed his hands. "And why, 'my dear'? And who wins?"

III

Watchman, with his cousin for company, ate his lobster in the private taproom. There is a parlour at the Feathers but nobody ever uses it. The public and the private taprooms fit into each other like two L's, the first standing sideways on the tip of its short base, the second facing backwards to the left. The bar proper is common to both. It occupies the short leg of the Public, has a counter for each room and faces the short leg of the Private. The top of the long leg forms a magnificent ingle-nook flanked with settles and scented with three hundred years of driftwood smoke. Opposite the ingle-nook at the bottom angle of the L hangs a dart board made by Abel Pomeroy himself. There, winter and summer alike, the Pomeroys' chosen friends play for drinks. There is a board in the Public for the rank and file. If strangers to the Feathers choose to play in the Private, the initiates wait until they have finished. If the initiates invite a stranger to play, he is no longer a stranger.

The midsummer evening was chilly and a fire smouldered in the ingle-nook. Watchman finished his supper, swung his legs up on the settle, and felt for his pipe. He squinted up at Sebastian Parish, who leant against the mantelpiece in an attitude familiar to every West End playgoer in London.

"I like this place," Watchman said. "Extraordinarily pleasant, isn't it, returning to a place one likes?"

Parish made an actor's expressive gesture.

"Marvellous!" he said richly. "To get away from everything! The noise! The endless racket! The artificiality! God, how I loathe my profession!"

"Come off it, Seb," said Watchman. "You glory in it. You were born acting. The gamp probably burst into an involuntary round of applause on your first entrance and I bet you played your mother right off the stage."

15

"All the same, old boy, this good clean air means a hell of a lot to me."

"Exactly," agreed Watchman dryly. His cousin had a trick of saying things that sounded a little like quotations from an interview with himself. Watchman was amused rather than irritated by this mannerism. It was part and parcel, he thought, of Seb's harmless stagyness, like his clothes which were too exactly what a gentleman, roughing it in South Devon, ought to wear. He liked to watch Seb standing out on Coombe Rock, bareheaded to the breeze, in effect waiting for the camera man to say "O.K. for sound." No doubt that was the pose Norman had chosen for his portrait of Sebastian. It occurred to him now that Sebastian was up to something. That speech about the artificiality of the stage was the introduction to a confidence, or Watchman didn't know his Parish. Whatever it was, Sebastian missed his moment. The door opened and a thin man with untidy fair hair looked in.

"Hallo!" said Watchman. "Our distinguished artist." Norman Cubitt grinned, lowered his painter's pack, and came into the ingle-nook.

"Well, Luke? Good trip?"

"Splendid! You're painting already?" Cubitt stretched a hand to the fire. The fingers were grimed with paint.

"I'm doing a thing of Seb," he said. "I suppose he's told you about it. Laying it on with a trowel, I am. That's in the morning. To-night I started a thing down by the jetty. They're patching up one of the posts. Very pleasant subject, but my treatment of it so far is bloody."

"Are you painting in the dark?" asked Watchman with a smile.

"I was talking to one of the fishing blokes after the light went. They've gone all politically-minded in the Coombe."

"That," said Parish, lowering his voice, "is Will Pomeroy and his Left Group."

"Will and Decima together," said Cubitt. "I've suggested they call themselves the Decimbrists."

"Where are the lads of the village?" demanded Watchman. "I thought I heard the dart game in progress as I went upstairs."

"Abel's rat-poisoning in the garage," said Parish. "They've

16

all gone out to see he doesn't give himself a lethal dose of prussic acid."

"Good Lord!" Watchman ejaculated. "Is the old fool playing round with cyanide?"

"Apparently. Why wouldn't we have a drink?"

"Why not indeed?" agreed Cubitt. "Hi, Will!"

He went to the bar and leant over it, looking into the Public.

"The whole damn place is deserted. I'll get out drinks and chalk them up. Beer?"

"Beer it is," said Parish.

"What form of cyanide has Abel got hold of?" Watchman asked.

"Eh?" said Parish vaguely. "Oh, let's see now. I fetched it for him from Illington. The chemist hadn't got any of the stock rat-banes, but he poked round and found this stuff. I think he called it Scheele's acid."

"Good God!"

"What? Yes, that was it—Scheele's acid. And then he said he thought the fumes of Scheele's acid mightn't be strong enough, so he gingered it up a bit."

"With what, in the name of all the Borgias?"

"Well—with prussic acid, I imagine."

"You imagine! You imagine!"

"He said that was what it was. He said it was acid or something. I wouldn't know. He warned me in sixteen different positions to be careful. Suggested Abel wore a half-crown gas mask, so I bought it in case Abel hadn't got one. Abel's using gloves and everything."

"It's absolutely monstrous!"

"I had to sign for it, old boy," said Parish. "Very solemn we were. God, he was a stupid man! Bone from the eyes up, but so, so kind."

Watchman said angrily, "I should damn well think he was stupid. Do you know that twenty-five drops of Scheele's acid will kill a man in a few minutes? Why, good Lord, in Rex v. Bull, if I'm not mistaken, it was alleged that accused gave only seven drops. I myself defended a medical student who gave twenty minims in error. Charge of manslaughter. I got him off but—how's Abel using it?"

"What's all this?" inquired Cubitt. "There's your beer."

"Abel said he was going to put it in a pot and shove it in a rathole," explained Parish. "I think he's filled with due respect for its deadliness, Luke, really. He's going to block the hole up and everything."

"The chemist had no business to give you Scheele's, much less this infernal brew. He ought to be struck off the books. The pharmacopœial preparation would have been quite strong enough. He could have diluted even that to advantage."

"Well, God bless us," said Cubitt hastily, and took a pull at his beer.

"What happens, actually, when someone's poisoned by prussic acid?" asked Parish.

"Convulsion, clammy sweat, and death."

"Shut up!" said Cubitt. "What a filthy conversation!"

"Well—cheers, dear," said Parish, raising his tankard.

"You do get hold of the most repellent idioms, Seb," said his cousin. "*Te saluto.*"

"But not *moriturus,* I trust," added Parish. "With all this chat about prussic acid! What's it look like?"

"You bought it."

"I didn't notice. It's a blue bottle."

"Hydrocyanic acid," said Watchman with his barrister's precision, "is, in appearance, exactly like water. It is a liquid miscible with water and this stuff is a dilution of hydrocyanic acid."

"The chemist," said Parish, "put a terrific notice on it. I remember I once had to play a man who'd taken cyanide. 'Fool's Errand,' the piece was; a revival with whiskers on it, but not a bad old drama. I died in a few seconds."

"For once the dramatist was right," said Watchman. "It's one of the sudden poisons. Horrible stuff! I've got cause to know it. I was once briefed in a case where a woman took——"

"For God's sake," interrupted Norman Cubitt violently, "shut up, both of you. I've got a poison phobia."

"Have you really, Norman?" asked Parish. "That's very interesting. Can you trace it?"

"I think so." Cubitt rubbed his hair and then looked absent-mindedly at his paint-grimed hand. "As a matter of fact, my dear Seb," he said, with his air of secretly mocking at himself, "you have named the root and cause of my

18

affection. You have perpetrated a coincidence, Sebastian. The very play you mentioned just now, started me off on my Freudian road to the jim-jams. 'Fool's Errand,' and well named. It is, as you say, a remarkably naïve play. At the age of seven, however, I did not think so. I found it terrifying."

"At the age of seven?"

"Yes. My eldest brother, poor fool, fancied himself as an amateur and essayed the principal part. I was bullied into enacting the small boy who, as I remember, perpetually bleated: 'Papa, why is mamma so pale' and later on: 'Papa, why is mamma so quiet? Where has she gone, papa?'"

"We cut all that in the revival," said Parish. "It was terrible stuff."

"I agree with you. As you remember, papa had poisoned mamma. For years afterwards I had the horrors at the very word. I remember that I used to wipe all the schoolroom china for fear our Miss Tobin was a Borgian governess. I invented all sorts of curious devices in order that Miss Tobin should drink my morning cocoa and I hers. Odd, wasn't it? I grew out of it but I still dislike the sound of the word and I detest taking medicine labelled in accordance with the Pure Food Act."

"Labelled what?" asked Parish with a wink at Watchman.

"Labelled poison, damn you," said Cubitt.

Watchman looked curiously at him.

"I suppose there's something in this psycho-stuff," he said. "But I always rather boggle at it."

"I don't see why you should," said Parish. "You yourself get a fit of the staggers if you scratch your finger. You told me once, you fainted when you had a blood test. That's a phobia, same as Norman's."

"Not quite," said Watchman. "Lots of people can't stand the sight of their own blood. This poison scare's much more unusual. But you don't mean to tell me, do you, Norman, that because at an early age you helped your brother in a play about cyanide you'd feel definitely uncomfortable if I finished my story?"

Cubitt drained his tankard and set it down on the table.

"If you're hell-bent on your beastly story——" he said.

"It was only that I was present at the autopsy on this woman who died of cyanide poisoning. When they opened her up, I fainted. Not from emotion but from the fumes. The pathologist said I had a pronounced idiosyncrasy for the stuff. I was damned ill after it. It nearly did for me."

Cubitt wandered over to the door and lifted his pack.

"I'll clean up," he said, "and join you for the dart game."

"Splendid, old boy," said Parish. "We'll beat them to-night."

"Do our damnedest anyway," said Cubitt. At the doorway he turned and looked mournfully at Parish.

"She's asking about perspective," he said.

"Give her rat-poison," said Parish.

"Shut up," said Cubitt and went out.

"What was he talking about?" demanded Watchman.

Parish smiled. "He's got a girl-friend. Wait till you see. Funny chap! He went quite green over your story. Sensitive old beggar, isn't he?"

"Oh yes," agreed Watchman lightly. "I must say I'm sensitive in a rather different key where cyanide's concerned, having been nearly killed by it."

"I don't know you could have a—what did you call it?"

"An idiosyncrasy?"

"It means you'd go under to a very small amount?"

"It does." Watchman yawned and stretched himself full length on the settle.

"I'm sleepy," he said. "It's the sea air. A very pleasant state of being. Just tired enough, with the impressions of a long drive still floating about behind one's consciousness. Flying hedges, stretches of road that stream out before one's eyes. The relaxation of arrival setting in. Very pleasant!"

He closed his eyes for a moment and then turned his head to look at his cousin.

"So Decima Moore is still here," he said.

Parish smiled. "Very much so. But you'll have to watch your step, Luke."

"Why?"

"There's an engagement in the offing."

"What d'you mean?"

"Decima and Will Pomeroy."

Watchman sat up.

"I don't believe you," he said sharply.

"Well—why not?"

"Good Lord! A politically minded pot-boy."

"Actually they're the same class," Parish murmured.

"Perhaps; but she's not of it."

"All the same——"

Watchman grimaced.

"She's a little fool," he said, "but you may be right," and lay back again. "Oh well!" he added comfortably.

There was a moment's silence.

"There's another female here," said Parish, and grinned.

"Another Who?"

"Norman's girl-friend of course. My oath!"

"Why? What's she like? Why are you grinning away like a Cheshire cat, Seb?"

"My dear soul," said Parish, "if I could get that woman to walk on the boards every evening and do her stuff exactly as she does it here—well, of course! I'd go into management and die a millionaire."

"Who is she?"

"She's the Honourable Violet Darragh. She waters."

"She *what*?"

"She does water-colours. Wait till you hear Norman on Violet."

"Is she a nuisance?" asked Watchman apprehensively.

"Not exactly. Well, in a way. Pure joy to me. Wait till you meet her."

Parish would say no more about Miss Darragh, and Watchman, only mildly interested, relapsed into a pleasant doze.

"By the way," he said presently, "some driving expert nearly dashed himself to extinction againt my bonnet."

"Really?"

"Yes. At Diddlestock Corner. Came bucketing out of the blind turning on my right, beat me by a split second, and hung his silly little stern on my front buffers. Ass!"

"Any damage?"

"No, no. He heaved his pygmy up by the bottom and I backed away. Funny sort of fellow he is."

"You knew him?" asked Parish in surprise.

"No." Watchman took the tip of his nose between thumb and forefinger. It was a gesture he used in cross-examination.

"No, I don't know him, and yet—there was something—I got the impression that *he* didn't want to know *me*. Quite an educated voice. Labourer's hands. False teeth, I rather fancy."

"You're very observant," said Parish, lightly.

"No more than the next man, but there was something about the fellow. I was going to ask if you knew him. His car's in the garage."

"Surely it's not—hallo, here are others."

Boots and voices sounded in the public bar. Will Pomeroy came through and leant over the counter. He looked, not toward Watchman or Parish, but into a settle on the far side of the Private, a settle whose high back was towards them.

"'Evening, Bob," said Will cordially. "Kept you waiting?"

"That's all right, Will," said a voice from beyond the settle. "I'll have a pint of bitter when you're ready."

Luke Watchman uttered a stifled exclamation.

"What's up?" asked his cousin.

"Come here."

Parish strolled nearer to him and, in obedience to a movement of Watchman's head, stooped towards him.

"What's up?" he repeated.

"That's the same fellow," muttered Watchman, "he must have been here all the time. That's his voice."

"Hell!" said Parish delightedly.

"D'you think he heard?"

"Of course he heard."

"Blast the creature! Serves him right."

"Shut up."

The door into the private bar opened. Old Abel came in followed by Norman Cubitt. Cubitt took three darts from a collection in a pewter pot on the bar and moved in front of the dart board.

"I'll be there in a moment," said a woman's voice from the passage. "Don't start without me."

Abel walked into the ingle-nook and put a bottle on the mantelpiece.

"Well, souls," he said, "reckon we'm settled the hash of they vermin. If thurr's not a corpse on the premises afore long, I'll be greatly astonished."

CHAPTER TWO

ADVANCE BY WATCHMAN

I

THE bottle was a small one and as Sebastian Parish had remarked it was conspicuously labelled. The word "POISON" in scarlet on a white ground ran diagonally across on an attached label. It struck a note of interjection and alarm and focused the attention of the five men. Few who read that warning escape a sudden jolt of the imagination.

Parish said, "Mr. Watchman thinks you are a public danger, Abel. He's afraid we'll all be poisoned."

"I'm afraid he'll poison himself," said Watchman.

"Who, sir? Me?" asked Abel. "Not a bit of it. I be a mortal cautious sort of chap when it comes to this manner of murderous tipple, Mr. Watchman."

"I hope you are," said Cubitt from the dart board.

"You're not going to leave it on the mantelshelf, father?" asked Will.

"No fear of that, sonny. I'll stow it away careful."

"You'd much better get rid of it altogether," said Watchman. "Don't put it away somewhere. You'll forget all about it and some day someone will take a sniff at it to find out what it is. Let me take it back to the chemist at Illington. I'd very much like to have a word with that gentleman."

"Lord love you," said Abel, opening his eyes very wide, "us 've not finished with they bowldacious varmints yet, my sonnies. If so be they've got a squeak left in 'em us'll give 'em another powerful whiff and finish 'em off."

"At least," said Cubitt, throwing a dart into double-twenty, "at least you might put it out of reach."

"Mr. Cubitt has a poison-phobia," said Watchman.

"A what, sir?"

"Never mind about that," said Cubitt. "I should have thought anybody might boggle at prussic acid."

"Don't fret yourselves, gentlemen," said Abel. "Thurr'll be none of this brew served out at the Feathers Tap."

He mounted the settle and taking the bottle from the mantelpiece pushed it into the top shelf of a double cupboard in the corner of the ingle-nook. He then pulled off the old gloves he wore, threw them on the fire, and turned the key.

"Nobody can call me a careless man," he said. "I'm all for looking after myself. Thurr's my first-aid box in thurr, ready to hand, and if any of the chaps cuts themselves with a mucky fish-knife or any other infectious trifle of that sort, they gets a swill of iodine in scratch. Makes 'em squirm a bit and none the worse for that. I learnt that in the war, my sonnies. I was a surgeon's orderly and I know the mighty powers thurr be in drugs."

He stared at the glass door. The label "POISON" still showed, slightly distorted, in the darkness of the little cupboard.

"Safe enough thurr," said Abel and went over to the bar.

With the arrival of the Pomeroys the private bar took on its customary aspect for a summer's evening. They both went behind the counters. Abel sat facing the Private and on Cubitt's order drew pints of draught beer for the company. A game of darts was started in the Public.

The man in the settle had not moved, but now Watchman saw his hand reach out for his pint. He saw the callouses, the chipped nails, the coarsened joints of the fingers. Watchman got up, stretched himself, grimaced at Parish, and crossed the room to the settle.

The light shone full in the face of the stranger. The skin of his face was brown, but Watchman thought it had only recently acquired this colour. His hair stood up in white bristles, his forehead was garnished with bumps that shone in the lamplight. The eyes under the bleached lashes seemed almost without colour. From the notsrils to the corners of the mouth ran grooves that lent emphasis to the fall of the lips. Without raising his head the man looked up at Watchman, and the shadow of a smile seemed to visit his face. He got up and made as if to go to the door, but Watchman stopped him.

"May I introduce myself?" asked Watchman.

The man smiled more broadly. "They *are* false teeth,"

thought Watchman, and he added: "We have met already this evening, but we didn't exchange names. Mine is Luke Watchman."

"I gathered as much from your conversation," said the man. He paused for a moment and then said: "Mine is Legge."

"I'm afraid I sounded uncivil," said Watchman. "I hope you'll allow me a little motorists' licence. One always abuses the other man, doesn't one?"

"You'd every excuse," mumbled Legge, "every excuse." He scarcely moved his lips. His teeth seemed too large for his mouth. He looked sideways at Watchman, picked up a magazine from the settle, and flipped it open, holding it before his face.

Watchman felt vaguely irritated. He had struck no sort of response from the man and he was not accustomed to falling flat. Obviously, Legge merely wished to be rid of him and this state of affairs piqued Watchman's vanity. He sat on the edge of the table, and for the second time that evening offered his cigarette-case to Legge.

"No thanks—pipe."

"I'd no idea I should find you here," said Watchman, and noticed uncomfortably that his own voice sounded disproportionately cordial, "although you did tell me you were bound for Ottercombe. It's a good pub, isn't it?"

"Yes, yes," said Legge hurriedly. "Very good."

"Are you making a long visit?"

"I live here," said Legge.

He pulled out his pipe and began to fill it. His fingers moved clumsily and he had an air of rather ridiculous concentration. Watchman felt marooned on the edge of the table. He saw that Parish was listening with a maddening grin, and he fancied that Cubitt's ears were cocked. "Damn it," he thought, "I will not be put out of countenance by the brute. He *shall* like me." But he could think of nothing to say and Mr. Legge had begun to read his magazine.

From beyond the bar came the sound of raucous applause. Someone yelled: "Double seventeen and we'm beat the Bakery."

Norman Cubitt pulled out his darts and paused for a moment. He looked from Watchman to Parish. It struck

25

him that there was a strong family resemblance between these cousins, a resemblance of character rather than physique. Each in his way, thought Cubitt, was a vain man. In Parish one recognised the ingenuous vanity of the actor. Off the stage he wooed applause with only less assiduity than he commanded it when he faced an audience. Watchman was more subtle. Watchman must have the attention and respect of every new acquaintance, but he played for it without seeming to do so. He would take endless trouble with a complete stranger when he seemed to take none. "But he's getting no change out of Legge," thought Cubitt maliciously. And with a faint smile he turned back to the dart board.

Watchman saw the smile. He took a pull at his tankard and tried again.

"Are you one of the dart experts?" he asked. Legge looked up vaguely and Watchman had to repeat his question.

"I play a little," said Legge.

Cubitt hurled his last dart at the board and joined the others.

"He plays like the devil himself," he said. "Last night I took him on, 101 down. I never even started. He threw fifty, one, and the fifty again."

"I was fortunate that time," said Mr. Legge with rather more animation.

"Not a bit of it," said Cubitt. "You're merely odiously accurate."

"Well," said Watchman, "I'll lay you ten bob you can't do it again, Mr. Legge."

"You've lost," said Cubitt.

"Aye, he's a proper masterpiece is Mr. Legge," said old Abel.

Sebastian Parish came across from the ingle-nook. He looked down good-humouredly at Legge. "Nobody," thought Cubitt, "has any right to be as good-looking as Seb."

"What's all this?" asked Parish.

"I've offered to bet Mr. Legge ten bob he can't throw fifty, one, and fifty."

"You've lost," said Parish.

"This is monstrous," cried Watchman. "Do you take me, Mr. Legge?"

Legge shot a glance at him. The voices of the players

beyond the partition had quietened for the moment. Will Pomeroy had joined his father at the private bar. Cubitt and Parish and the two Pomeroys waited in silence for Legge's reply. He made a curious grimace, pursing his lips and screwing up his eyes. As if in reply, Watchman used that K.C.'s trick of his and took the tip of his nose between thumb and forefinger. Cubitt, who watched them curiously, was visited by the fantastic notion that some sort of signal had passed between them.

Legge rose slowly to his feet.

"Oh yes," he said. "Certainly, Mr. Watchman. I take you on."

II

Legge moved, with a slovenly dragging of his boots, into a position in front of the board. He pulled out the three darts and looked at them.

"Getting a bit worn, Mr. Pomeroy," said Legge. "The rings are loose."

"I've sent for a new set," said Abel. "They'll be here to-morrow. Old lot can go into Public."

Will Pomeroy left the public bar and joined his father. "Showing 'em how to do it, Bob?" he asked.

"There's a bet on, sonny," said old Pomeroy.

"Don't make me nervous, Will," said Legge, with a grin.

He looked at the board, poised his first dart and, with a crisp movement of his hand flung it into the bullseye.

"Fifty," said Will. "There you are, gentlemen! Fifty!"

"Three-and-fourpence in pawn," said Watchman.

"We'll put it into the C. L. M. if it comes off, Will," said Legge.

"What's the C. L. M.?" demanded Watchman.

Will stared straight in front of him and said, "The Coombe Left Movement, Mr. Watchman. We're a branch of the South Devon Left, now."

"Oh Lord!" said Watchman.

Legge threw his second dart. It seemed almost to drop from his hand, but he must have used a certain amount of force since it went home solidly into the top right-hand division.

27

"And the one. Six-and-eight pence looking a bit off colour, Mr. Watchman," said Abel Pomeroy.

"He's stymied himself for the other double twenty-five, though," said Watchman. "The first dart's lying right across it."

Legge raised his hand and, this time, took more deliberate aim. He threw from a greater height. For a fraction of a second the dart seemed to hang in his fingers before it sped downwards, athwart the first, into the narrow strip round the centre.

"And fifty it is!" said Will. "There you are. Fifty. Good for you, comrade."

A little chorus went up from Parish, Cubitt and old Abel.

"That man's a wizard."

"Shouldn't be allowed!"

"You'm a proper masterpiece."

"Well done, Bob," added Will, as if determined to give the last word of praise.

Watchman laid a ten-shilling note on the table.

"I congratulate you," he said.

Legge looked at the note.

"Thank you, Mr. Watchman," he said. "Another ten bob for the fighting fund, Will."

"Good enough, but it's straightout generous to give it."

Watchman sat down again on the table-edge.

"All very nice," he said. "Does you credit, Mr. Legge. I rather think another drink's indicated. With me, if you please. Loser's privilege."

Will Pomeroy glanced uncomfortably at Legge. By Feathers etiquette, the winner of a bet at darts pays for the next round. There was a short silence broken by old Pomeroy who insisted that the next round should be on the house, and served the company with a potent dark ale, known to the Coombe as Treble Extra.

"We'll all play like Mr. Legge with this inside us," said Parish.

"Yes," agreed Watchman, looking into his tankard, "it's a fighting fund in itself. A very pretty tipple indeed." He looked up at Legge.

"Do you know any other tricks like that one, Mr. Legge?"

28

"I know a prettier one than that," said Legge quietly, "if you'll assist me."

"I assist you?"

"Yes. If you'll stretch your hand out flat on the board I'll outline it with darts."

"Really? You ought to be in the sawdust ring. No. I don't think I trust you enough for that, you know. One would need a little more of Mr. Pomeroy's Treble Extra."

He stretched out his hand and looked at it.

"And yet, I don't know," he said. "I'd like to see you do it. Some other time. You know, Mr. Legge, as a good Conservative, I feel I should deplore your gesture. Against whom is your fighting fund directed?"

But before Legge could speak, Will answered quickly, "Against the capitalist, Mr. Watchman, and all his side."

"Really? So Mr. Legge is also an ardent proletarian fan?"

"Secretary and treasurer for the Coombe Left Movement."

"Secretary *and* treasurer," repeated Watchman. "Responsible jobs, aren't they?"

"Aye," said Will, "and it's a responsible chap that's taken 'em on for us."

Legge turned away and moved into the ingle-nook. Watchman looked after him. Cubitt noticed that Watchman's good humour seemed to be restored. Any one would have thought that he had won the bet and that it had been for a much larger sum. And for no reason in the world Cubitt felt that there had been a passage of arms between Legge and Watchman, and that Watchman had scored a hit.

"What about you, Abel?" Watchman asked abruptly. "Are you going to paint the Feathers red?"

"Me sir? No. I don't hold with Will's revolutionary ideas and he knows it, but us've agreed to differ. Does no harm, I reckon, for these young chaps to meet every Friday and make believe they're hashing up the laws and serving 'em out topsy-turvy—game in servants' hall and prunes and rice for gentry. Our Will was always a great hand for make-believe from the time he learned to talk. Used to strut about taproom giving orders to the furniture. 'I be as good as Squire, now,' he'd say in his little lad's voice and I reckon he's saying it yet."

"'You're blind to reason, father," said Will. "Blind—stupid and hidebound. Either you can't see or you won't. Us chaps are working for the good of all, not for ourselves."

"Right enough, sonny. A fine noble ideal, I don't doubt, and when you've got us all toeing the line with no handicaps and nothing to run for——"

"The good of the State to run for. Each man equal——"

"And all coming in first. Damn' queer sort of race."

"The old argument," said Legge from the fireplace, "and based as usual on a false analogy."

"Is it a false analogy?" asked Watchman. "You propose to kill private enterprise——"

"A chap," said Will Pomeroy, "will be as ambitious for the public good as he will for his own selfish aims. Give him the chance—that's all. Teach him to think. The people——"

"The people!" interrupted Watchman, looking at Legge's back. "What do you mean by the people? I suppose you mean that vast collection of individuals whose wages are below a certain sum and who are capable of being led by the nose when the right sort of humbug comes along."

"That's no argument," began Will angrily. "That's no more than a string of silly opinions."

"That'll do, sonny," said Abel.

"It's all right, Abel," said Watchman, still looking at Legge. "I invited the discussion. No offence. I should like to hear what Mr. Legge has to say about private enterprise. As treasurer——"

"Wait a bit, Bob," said Will as Legge turned from the fireplace. "I don't like the way you said that, Mr. Watchman. Bob Legge here is well-respected in the Coombe. He's not been long in these parts, ten months isn't it, Bob? But we've learned to know him and we've learned to like him. Reckon we've showed we trust him, too, seeing the position we've given him."

"My dear Will," said Watchman delicately, "I don't dispute it for a moment. I think Mr. Legge has done remarkably well for himself, in ten months."

Will's face was scarlet under his thatch of fox-coloured hair. He moved forward and confronted Watchman, his tankard clenched in a great ham of a fist, his feet planted apart.

"Shut up, now, Luke," said Sebastian Parish softly, and Cubitt murmured, "don't heckle, Luke, you're on a holiday."

"See here, Mr. Watchman," said Will, "you can afford to sneer, can't you, but I'd like to know——"

"Will!" Old Abel slapped the bar with an open hand. "That's enough. You'm a grown chap, not a lad, and what's more, the son of this house. Seems like I ought to give'ee light draught and lemonade till you learn to take a man's pint like a man. If you can't talk politics and hold your temper then you'll not talk politics at all. 'Be a job for you in Public here. 'Tend it."

"I'm sorry, Will," said Watchman. "Mr. Legge is fortunate in his friend."

Will Pomeroy stood and looked under his brows from Watchman to Legge. Legge shrugged his shoulders, muttered something about moving into the public bar, and went out. Will turned on Watchman.

"There's something behind all this," he said. "I want to know what the game is, Mr. Watchman, and damme, I'm going to find out."

"Did I hear something about a game?" said a woman's voice. They all turned to look at the doorway. There they saw a short fat figure clad in a purple tweed skirt and a green jersey.

"May I come in?" asked the Hon. Violet Darragh.

III

Miss Darragh's entrance broke up the scene. Will Pomeroy turned, ducked under the flap of the private bar, and leant over the counter into the Public. Watchman stood up. The others turned to Miss Darragh with an air of relief, and Abel Pomeroy, with his innkeeper's heartiness, intensified perhaps by a feeling of genuine relief, said loudly, "Come in then, Miss, company's waiting for you and you'm in time for a drink, with the house."

"Not Treble Extra, Mr. Pomeroy, if you don't mind. Sherry for me, if you please."

31

She waddled over to the bar, placed her hands on the counter, and with an agility that astonished Watchman, made a neat little vault on to one of the tall stools. There she sat beaming upon the company.

She was a woman of perhaps fifty, but it would have been difficult to guess at her age since time had added to her countenance and figure merely layer after layer of firm wholesome fat. She was roundabout and compact. Her face was babyish, and this impression was heightened by the tight grey curls that covered her head. In repose she seemed to pout, and it was not until she spoke that her good humour appeared in her eyes, and was magnified by her spectacles. All fat people wear a look of inscrutability, and Violet Darragh was not unlike a jolly sort of sphinx.

Abel served her and she took the glass delicately in her small white paws.

"Well now," she said, " is everybody having fun?" and then caught sight of Watchman. "Is this your cousin, Mr. Parish?"

"I'm sorry," said Parish hurriedly. "Mr. Watchman, Miss Darragh."

"How d'ye do?" said Miss Darragh.

Like many Irishwomen of her class she spoke with such a marked brogue that one wondered whether it was inspired by a kind of jocularity that had turned into a habit.

"I've heard about you, of course, and read about you in the papers, for I dearly love a good murder and if I can't have me murder I'm all for arson. That was a fine murder case you defended last year, now, Mr. Watchman. Before you took silk, 'twas you did your best for the poor scoundrel."

Watchman expanded.

"I didn't get him off, Miss Darragh."

"Ah well, and a good job you didn't, for we'd none of us have been safe in our beds. And there's Mr. Cubitt come from his painting down by the jetty, in mortal terror, poor man, lest I plague him with me perspective."

"Not at all," said Cubitt, turning rather pink.

"I'll leave you alone now. I know very well I'm a trouble to you, but it's good for your character, and you may look upon me as a kind of holiday penance."

"You're a painter too, Miss Darragh?" said Watchman.

"I'm a raw amateur, Mr. Watchman, but I've a kind of itch for ut. When I see a little peep I can't rest till I'm at ut with me paints. There's Mr. Cubitt wincing as if he had a nagging tooth, when I talk of a pretty peep. You've a distinguished company in your house, Mr. Pomeroy," continued Miss Darragh. "I thought I was coming to a quiet little village, and what do I find but a galaxy of the talents. Mr. Parish who's turned me heart over many a time with his acting; Mr. Cubitt, down there painting within stone's throw of meself, and now haven't we the great counsel to add to our intellectual feast. I wonder now, Mr. Watchman, if you remember me poor cousin Bryonie's case?"

"I—yes," said Watchman, greatly disconcerted. "I—I defended Lord Bryonie. Yes."

"And didn't he only get the mere eighteen months due entirely to your eloquence? Ah, he's dead now, poor fellow. Only a shadow of himself, he was when he came out. It was a terrible shock to 'um."

"Undoubtedly."

"'Twas indeed. He never had many brains, poor fellow, and it was an unlucky day for the family when he took it into his head to dabble in business. Where's Miss Moore? I thought I heard you speak of a game of darts."

"She's coming," said Cubitt.

"And I hope you'll all play again for I found it a great entertainment. Are you a dart player too, Mr. Watchman?"

"I try," said Watchman.

Footsteps sounded on the stairs.

"Here is Decima," said Cubitt.

IV

A tall young woman came into the room and stood, very much at her ease, screwing her eyes up a little in the glare of the lights.

"I'm so sorry if I've kept you waiting," said Decima Moore. "Good-evening, every one."

They all greeted her. There was a second's pause and then Watchman moved into the centre of the room.

"Good-evening," said Watchman.

She faced him and met his gaze.

"So you have arrived," she said. "Good-evening."

She touched his outstretched hand, walked over to the bar, and settled herself on one of the tall stools. She wore a fisherman's jersey and dark blue slacks. Her hair was cut like a poet's of the romantic period and was moulded in short locks about her head and face. She was good-looking with a classic regularity of beauty that was given an individual quirk by the blackness of her brows and the singular intensity of her eyes. She moved with the kind of grace that only just escapes angularity. She was twenty-four years of age.

If an observant stranger had been at the Feathers that evening, he might have noticed that on Decima's entrance the demeanour of most of the men changed. For Decima owned that quality which Hollywood has loudly defined for the world. She owned a measure of attraction over which she herself had little governance. Though she must have been aware of this, she seemed unaware, and neither in her manner nor in her speech did she appear to exercise conscious charm. Yet from the moment of her entrance the men when they spoke to each other, looked at her, and in each of them was the disturbance of Decima's attraction reflected. Watchman's eyes brightened, he became more alert, and he spoke a little louder. Parish expanded as if in a spotlight and he exuded gallantry. Cubitt's air of vague amiability contracted to a sharp awareness. Abel Pomeroy beamed upon Decima. Will, still flushed from his passage with Watchman, turned a deeper red. He answered her greeting awkwardly and was very much the solemn and self-conscious rustic.

Decima took a cigarette from Parish and looked round the taproom.

"Has the dart game begun?" she asked.

"We're waiting for you, my angel," said Parish. "What have you been doing with yourself all this time?"

"Washing. I've attended a poison party. I hope you didn't spill prussic acid about the garage, you two Pomeroys."

"You're not 'feared, too, are you Miss Dessy?" asked Abel. "A fine, bold, learned, female like you."

Decima laughed.

34

"A revolting picture," she said. "What do you think, Will?"

She leant across the bar and looked beyond Abel into the Public. Will's back was towards her. He turned and faced Decima. His eyes devoured her, but he said nothing. Decima raised her tankard and drank to him. He returned the gesture clumsily, and Cubitt saw Watchman's eyebrows go up.

"Well," said Decima suddenly, "what have you all been talking about? You're very silent now, I must say."

Before any of the others could reply, Watchman said: "We've been arguing, my dear?"

"Arguing?" She still looked at Will. Watchman drained his tankard, moved up to the bar, and sat on the stool next hers.

"Yes," he said. "Until Miss Darragh came in we did nothing else."

"And why should I stop you?" asked Miss Darragh. She slipped neatly off her high stool and toddled into the ingle-nook. "I've a passion for argument. What was it about, now? Art? Politics? Love?"

"It was about politics," said Watchman, still looking at Decima. "The State, the People, and—private enterprise."

"You?" Decima said. "But you're hopeless. When our way of things comes round, you'll be one of our major problems."

"Really? Won't you need any barristers?"

"I wish I could say no," said Decima.

Watchman laughed.

"At least," he said, "I may hold a watching brief for you." She didn't answer and he insisted: "Mayn't I?"

"You're talking nonsense," said Decima.

"Well," said Parish suddenly, "how about a Round-the-Clock contest to enliven the proceedings?"

"Why not, indeed?" murmured Cubitt.

"Will you play?" Watchman asked Decima.

"Of course. Let's all play. Coming, Will?"

But Will Pomeroy jerked his head towards the public taproom where two or three new-comers noisily demanded drinks.

"Will you play, Miss Darragh?" asked Decima.

"I will not, thank you my dear. I've no eye at all for

sport. When I was a child, didn't I half-blind me brother
Terence with an apple intended to strike me brother Brian?
I'd do you some mischief were I to try. Moreover, I'm too
fat. I'll sit and watch the fun."

Cubitt, Parish and Decima Moore stood in front of the
dart-board. Watchman walked into the ingle-nook. From
the moment when Will Pomeroy had taken up cudgels for
him against Watchman, Legge had faded out. He had taken
his drink, his pipe, and his thoughts, whatever they might be,
into the public bar.

Presently a burst of applause broke out, and Will Pomeroy
shouted that Legge was a wizard and invited Decima and
Cubitt to look at what he had done. The others followed,
peered into the public bar. A colossal red-faced man stood
with his hand against the public dart-board. His fingers were
spread out, and in the gaps between darts were embedded,
with others outside the thumb and the little finger.

"Look at that!" cried Will. "Look at it!"

"Ah," said Watchman. "So Mr. Legge has found another
victim. A great many people seem to have faith in Mr.
Legge."

There was a sudden silence. Watchman leant over the
private bar and raised his voice.

"We are going to have a match," he said. "Three-a-side.
Mr. Legge, will you join us?"

Legge took his pipe out of his mouth and said, "What's
the game?"

"Darts. Round-the-Clock."

"Round-the-Clock?"

"Yes. Haven't you played that version?"

"A long time ago. I've forgotten——"

"You have to get one dart in each segment in numerical
sequence, ending on a double," explained Cubitt.

"In fact," said Watchman very pleasantly, "you might call
it 'Doing Time.' Haven't you ever done time, Mr. Legge?"

"No," said Legge, "but I'll take you on. I'll be there in
a minute."

"Right. And if you beat me at this I'm damned if to-
morrow night I don't let you take a pot at my hand."

"Thank you," said Legge. "I'll remember."

CHAPTER THREE

FURTHER ADVANCE BY WATCHMAN

I

"The chief fault in Luke," said Sebastian Parish, "is that he is quite incapable of letting well alone."

Norman Cubitt tilted his hat over his eyes, peered from Parish to his canvas, and began to scuffle among his tubes of paint. He uttered a short grunt.

"More than that," added Parish, "he glories in making bad a good deal worse. Do you mind my talking, old boy?"

"No. Turn the head a little to the right. Too much. That's right. I won't keep you much longer. Just while the sun's on the left side of the face. The shoulders are coming too far round again."

"You talk like a doctor about my members—'*the*' head, '*the*' face, '*the*' shoulders."

"You're a vain fellow, Seb. Now, hold it like that, do. Yes, there's something persistently impish in Luke. He jabs at people. What was he up to last night with Will Pomeroy and Legge?"

"Damned if I know. Funny busines, wasn't it? Do you think he's jealous of Will?"

"Jealous?" repeated Cubitt. With his palette-knife he laid an unctuous stroke of blue beside the margin of the painted head. "Why, jealous?"

"Well—because of Decima."

"Oh nonsense! And yet I don't know. He's not your cousin for nothing, Seb. Luke's got his share of the family vanity."

"I don't know why you say I'm vain, damn you. I don't think I'm vain at all. Do you know I get an average of twelve drivelling letters a day from females in front? And do they mean a thing to me?"

"You'd be bitterly disappointed if there was a falling off.

Don't move your shoulders. But you may be right about Luke."

"I'd like to know," said Parish, "just how much last year's little flirtation with Decima added up to."

"Would you? I don't think it's relevant."

"Well," said Parish, "she's an attractive wench. More 'It' to the square inch than most of them. It's hard to say why. She's got looks, of course, but not the looks that usually get over that way. Not the voluptuous type. Her——"

"Shut up," said Cubitt violently and added: "I'm going to paint your mouth."

His own was set in an unusually tight line. He worked for a time in silence, stood back, and said abruptly:

"I don't really think Will Pomeroy was his objective. He was getting at Legge, and why the devil he should pick on a man he'd never seen in his life until last night is more than I can tell."

"I thought he seemed to be sort of probing. Trying to corner Legge in some way."

Cubitt paused with his knife over the canvas.

"Yes," he said slowly. "That's perfectly true. I thought so too. Trick of the trade perhaps. Counsels' curiosity. Almost one expected him to put his foot on the seat of a chair and rest his elbow on his knee. Now I come to think of it, I believe he did hitch his coat up by the lapels."

"Characteristic," pronounced Parish seriously. He himself had used these touches several time in trial scenes.

Cubitt smiled. "But he sounded definitely malicious," he added.

"He's not malicious," said Parish uncomfortably.

"Oh yes, he is," said Cubitt coolly. "It's one of his more interesting qualities. He can be very malicious."

"He can be very generous too."

"I'm sure he can. I like Luke, you know. He interests me enormously."

"Apparently, he likes you," said Parish. "Apparently."

"Hallo!" Cubitt walked back from his canvas and stood squinting at it. "You said that with a wealth of meaning, Seb. What's in the air? You can rest a minute if you like."

Parish moved off the boulder where he had been sitting, stretched himself elaborately, and joined Cubitt. He gazed solemnly at his own portrait. It was a large canvas. The figure in the dull red sweater was three-quarter life-size. It was presented as a dark form against the lighter background which was the sea and sky. The sky appeared as a series of paling arches, the sea as a simple plane broken by formalised waves. A glint of sunlight had found the cheek and jawbone on the right side of the face.

"Marvellous, old boy," said Parish. "Marvellous!"

Cubitt, who disliked being called 'old boy,' grunted.

"Did you say you'd show it in this year's Academy?" asked Parish.

"I didn't, Seb, but I will. I'll stifle my æsthetic conscience, prostitute my undoubted genius, and send your portrait to join the annual assembly of cadavers. Do you prefer 'Portrait of an Actor.' 'Sebastian Parish, Esq.' or simply 'Sebastian Parish?'"

"I think I would like my name," said Parish seriously. "Not, I mean, that everybody wouldn't know——"

"Thank you. But I see your point. Your press agent would agree. What were you going to say about Luke? His generosity, you know, and his apparently liking me so much?"

"I don't think I ought to tell you, really."

"But of course, you are going to tell me."

"He didn't actually say it was in confidence," said Parish. Cubitt waited with a slight smile.

"You'd be amazed if you knew," continued Parish.

"Yes?"

"Yes. Oh, rather. At least I imagine you would be. I was. I never expected anything of the sort, and after all I am his nearest relation. His next-of-kin."

Cubitt turned and looked at him in real astonishment.

"Are you by any chance," he asked, "talking about Luke's will?"

"How did you guess?"

"My dear, good Seb——"

"All right, all right. I suppose I did give it away. You may as well hear the whole thing. Luke told me the other day that he was leaving his money between us."

"Good Lord!"

"I know. I happened to look him up after the show one evening, and found him browsing over an official-looking

39

document. I said something, chaffingly you know, about it, and he said: 'Well, Seb, you'll find it out some day, so you may as well know now.' And then he told me."

"Extraordinarily nice of him," said Cubitt uncomfortably, and he added: "Damn! I wish you hadn't told me."

"Why on earth?"

"I don't know. I enjoy discussing Luke and now I'll feel he's sort of sacrosanct. Oh well, he'll probably outlive both of us."

"He's a good bit older than I am," said Parish. "Not, I mean, that I don't hope with all my heart he will. I mean—as far as I'm concerned——"

"Don't labour it, Seb," said Cubitt kindly. "I should think Luke will certainly survive me. He's strong as a horse and I'm not. You'll probably come in for the packet."

"I hate talking about it like that."

Parish knocked his pipe out on a stone. Cubitt noticed that he was rather red in the face.

"As a matter of fact," he muttered, "it's rather awkward."

"Why?"

"Well I'm plaguily hard up at the moment and I'd been wondering——"

"If Luke would come to the rescue?"

Parish was silent.

"And in the light of this revelation," Cubitt added, "you don't quite like to ask. Poor Seb! But what the devil do you do with your money? You ought to be rolling. You're always in work. This play you're in now is a record run, isn't it, and your salary must be superb."

"That's all jolly fine, old man, but you don't know what it's like in the business. My expenses are simply ghastly."

"Why?"

"Why, because you've got to keep up a standard. Look at my house. It's ruinous, but I've got to be able to ask the people that count to a place they'll accept and, if possible, remember. You've got to look prosperous in this game, and you've got to entertain. My agent's fees are hellish. My clubs cost the earth. And like a blasted fool I backed a show that flopped for thousands last May."

"What did you do that for?"

"The management are friends of mine. It looked all right."

"You give money away, Seb, don't you? I mean literally. To out-of-luck actors? Old-timers and so on?"

"I may. Always think 'there but for the grace of God!' It's such a damn' chancy business."

"Yes. No more chancy than painting, my lad."

"You don't have to show so well if you're an artist. People expect you to live in a peculiar way."

Cubitt looked at him, but said nothing.

Parish went on defensively: "I'm sorry, but you know what I mean. People expect painters to be Bohemians and all that."

"There was a time," said Cubitt, "when actors were content to be Bohemians, whatever that may mean. I never know. As far as I am concerned it means going without things you want."

"But your pictures sell."

"On an average I sell six pictures a year. Their prices range from twenty pounds to two hundred. It usually works out at about four hundred. You earn that in as many weeks, don't you?"

"Yes, but——"

"Oh, I'm not grumbling. I've got a bit of my own and I could make more, I dare say, if I took pupils or had a shot at commercial art. I've suited myself and it's worked out well enough until——"

"Until what?" asked Parish.

"Nothing. Let's get on with the work, shall we? The light's no good after about eleven."

Parish walked back to the rock and took up his pose. The light wind whipped his black hair away from his forehead. He raised his chin and stared out over the sea. He assumed an expression of brooding dominance.

"That right?" he asked.

"Pretty well. You only want a pair of tarnished epaulettes and we could call it 'Elba.'"

"I've always thought I'd like to play Napoleon."

"A fat lot you know about Napoleon."

Parish grinned tranquilly.

"Anyway," he said, "I'd read him up a bit if I had to. As a matter of fact Luke looks rather like him."

"The shoulders should come round," said Cubitt. "That's more like it. Yes, Luke is rather the type."

He painted for a minute or two in silence, and then Parish suddenly laughed.

"What's up?" asked Cubitt.

"Here comes your girl."

"What the devil do you mean?" demanded Cubitt angrily and looked over his shoulder. "Oh—I see."

"Violet," said Parish. "Who did you think it was?"

"I thought you'd gone dotty. Damn the woman."

"Will *she* paint me too?"

"Not if I know it."

"Unkind to your little Violet?" asked Parish.

"Don't call her that."

"Why not?"

"Well damn it, she's not very young and she's—well, she may be a pest, but she's by way of being a lady."

"Snob!"

"Don't be so dense, Seb. Can't you see—oh Lord, she's got all her gear. She *is* going to paint. Well, I've just about done for to-day."

"She's waving."

Cubitt looked across the headland to where Miss Darragh, a droll figure against the sky, fluttered a large handkerchief.

"She's put her stuff down," said Parish. "She's going to sketch. What is there to paint, over there?"

"A peep," said Cubitt. "Now, hold hard and don't talk. There's a shadow under the lower lip——"

He worked with concentration for five minutes, and then put down his palette.

"That'll do for to-day. We'll pack up."

But when he'd hitched his pack on his shoulders and stared out to sea for some seconds, he said suddenly:

"All the same, Seb, I wish you hadn't told me."

II

It was understood among the three friends that each should go his own way during the weeks they spent at Otter-combe. Watchman had played with the notion of going out in the dawn with the fishing boats. He woke before it was light and heard the tramp of heavy boots on cobble-stones and the sound of voices down on Ottercombe Steps. He told himself comfortably that here was a link with the past. For hundreds of years the Coombe men had gone down to their boats before dawn. The children of Coombe had heard them stirring, their wives had fed them and seen them go, and for centuries their voices and the sound of their footsteps had roused the village for a moment in the coldest hour of the night. Watchman let the sounds die away, snuggled luxuriously down in bed, and fell asleep.

He woke again at half-past nine and found that Parish had already breakfasted and set out for Coombe Rock.

"A mortal great mammoth of a picture Mr. Cubitt be at," said Abel Pomeroy, as Watchman finished his breakfast. "Paint enough to cover a wall, sir, and laid on so thick as dough. At close quarters it looks like one of they rocks covered in shell-fish, but 'od rabbit it, my sonnies, when you fall away twenty feet or more, it's Mr. Parish so clear as glass. Looking out over the Rock he be, looking out to sea, and so natural you'd say the man was smelling the wind and thinking of his next meal. You might fancy a stroll out to the Rock, sir, and take a look at Mr. Cubitt flinging his paint left and right."

"I feel lazy, Abel. Where's Will?"

"Went out along with the boats, sir." Abel rasped his chin, scratched his head, and re-arranged the objects on the bar.

"He's restless, is Will," he said suddenly. "My own boy, Mr. Watchman, and so foreign to me as a changeling."

"Will is?" asked Watchman, filling his pipe.

"Ah, Will. What with his politics and his notions he's a right down stranger to me, is Will. A very witty lad too, proper learned, and so full of arguments as a politician. He won't argufy with me, naturally, seeing I'm not his equal in the way of brains, nor anything like it."

"You're too modest, Abel," said Watchman lightly.

"No, sir, no. I can't stand up to that boy of mine when it comes to politics and he knows it and lets me down light. I'm for the old ways, a right down Tory, and for why? For no better reason than it suits me, same as it suited my forebears."

"A sound enough reason."

"No, sir, not according to my boy. According to Will it be a damn' fool reason and a selfish one into the bargain."

"I shouldn't let it worry you."

"'More I do, Mr. Watchman. It's not our differences that worry me. It's just my lad's restless mumbudgetting ways. You saw how he was last night. Speaking to you that fashion. Proper 'shamed of him, I was."

"It was entirely my fault, Abel, I baited him."

"Right down generous of you to put it like that, but all the same he's not himself these days. I'd like him to settle down. Tell you the truth, sir, it's what's to become of the Feathers that troubles me, and it troubles me sore. I'm nigh on seventy, Mr. Watchman. Will's my youngest. 'Tother two boys wurr took in war, and one girl's married and in Canada, and 'tother in Australia. Will'll get the Feathers."

"I expect," said Watchman, "that Will'll grow out of his red ideas and run the pub like any other Pomeroy."

Old Abel didn't answer and Watchman added: "When he marries and settles down."

"And when will that be, sir? Likely you noticed how 'tis between Will and Miss Dessy? Well now, that's a funny state of affairs, and one I can't get used to. Miss Dessy's father, Jim Moore up yurr to Carey Edge Farm, is an old friend of mine. Good enough. But what happens when Dessy's a lil' maid no higher than my hand? 'Od rabbit it, if old Jim don't come in for a windfall. Now his wife being a ghastly proud sort of a female and never tired of letting on she came down in society when she married, what do they do but send young Dessy to a ladies' school where she gets some kind of free pass into a female establishment at Oxford."

"Yes. I know."

"'Ess and comes home at the end of it a dinky lil' chit, sure enough, and husband-high; but speaking finniky-like and the equal of all the gentlefolks in the West Country."

"Well?" said Watchman.

"Well, sir, that's fair enough. If she fancies our Will

above the young sparks she meets in her new walk of life, good enough. I'm proper fond of the maiden, always have been. Good as a daughter to me, and just the same always, no matter how ladylike she'm grown."

Watchman stood up and stretched himself.

"It all sounds idyllic, Abel. A charming romance."

"Wait a bit, sir, wait a bit. 'Baint so simple as all that. These yurr two young folks no sooner mets again than my Will sets his heart, burning strong and powerful, on Decima Moore. Eaten up with love from time he sets eyes on her, was Will, and hell-bent to win her. She come back with radical notions, same as his own, and that's a bond a'tween 'em from the jump. Her folks don't fancy my Will, however, leastways not her mother, and they don't fancy her views neither, and worst of all they lays blame on Will. Old Jim Moore comes down yurr and has a tell with me, saying life's not worth living up to farm with Missus at him all day and half night to put his foot down and stop it. That's how 'twurr after you left last year, sir, and that's how 'tis still. Will burning to get tokened and wed, and Dessy——"

"Yes?" asked Watchman as Abel paused and looked fixedly at the ceiling. "What about Decima?"

"That's the queerst touch of the lot, sir," said Abel.

Watchman, lighting his pipe, kept his eye on his host and saw that he now looked profoundly uncomfortable.

"Well?" Watchman repeated.

"It be what she says about wedlock," Abel muttered.

"What does she say?" asked Watchman sharply.

"'Be shot if she haven't got some new-fangled notion about wedlock being no better than a name for savagery. Talks wild trash about freedom. To my way of thinking the silly maiden don't know what she says."

"What," asked Watchman, "does Will say to all this?"

"Don't like it. The chap wants to be tokened and hear banns read, like any other poor toad, for all his notions. He wants no free love for his wife or himself. He won't talk to me, not a word, but Miss Dessy does, so open and natural as a daisy. Terrible nonsense it be, I tells her, and right down dangerous into bargain. Hearing her chatter, you might suppose she's got some fancy-chap up her sleeve. Us knows better of course, but it's an uncomfortable state of affairs and

45

seemingly no way out. Tell you what, sir, I do blame this Legge for the way things are shaping. Will'd have settled down, he *was* settling down, afore Bob Legge come yurr. But now he've stirred up all their revolutionary notions again, Miss Dessy's along with the rest. I don't fancy Legge. Never have. Not for all he'm a masterpiece with darts. My way of thinking, he'm a cold calculating chap and powerful bent on having his way. Well, thurr 'tis, and talking won't mend it."

Watchman walked to the door and Abel followed him. They stood looking up the road to Coombe Tunnel.

"Dally-buttons!" exclaimed Abel, "talk of an angel and there she be. That's Miss Dessy, the dinky little dear. Coming in to do her marketing."

"So it is," said Watchman. "Well, Abel, on second thoughts I believe I'll go and have a look at that picture."

III

But Watchman did not go directly to Coombe Rock.. He lingered for a moment until he had seen Decima Moore go in at the post-office door, and then he made for the tunnel. Soon the darkness swallowed him, his footsteps rang hollow on the wet stone floor, and above him, a luminous disc, shone the top entry. Watchman emerged, blinking, into the dust and glare of the high road. To his left, the country rolled gently away to Illington; to his right, a path led round the cliffs to Coombe Rock, and then wound inland to Cary Edge Farm where the Moores lived.

He arched his hand over his eyes and on Coombe Head could make out the shape of canvas and easel with Cubitt's figure moving to and fro, and beyond a tiny dot which must be Sebastian Parish's head. Watchman left the road, climbed the clay bank, circled a clump of furze and beneath a hillock from where he could see the entrance to the tunnel, he lay full length on the short turf. With the cessation of his own movement the quiet of the countryside engulfed him. At first the silence seemed complete, but after a moment or two the small noises of earth and sky welled up into his consciousness. A lark sang above his head with a note so high that it impinged upon the outer borders of hearing and at times soared into nothingness. When he turned and laid his ear to the earth it throbbed with the far-away thud of surf against Coombe Rock, and when his fingers moved in the grass it was with a crisp stirring sound. He began to listen intently, lying so still that no movement of his body could come between his senses and more distant sound. He closed his eyes and to an observer he would have seemed to sleep. Indeed his face bore that look of inscrutability which links sleep in our minds with death. But he was not asleep. He was listening: and presently his ears caught a new rhythm, a faint hollow beat. Someone was coming up through the tunnel.

Watchman looked through his eyelashes and saw Decima Moore step into the sunlight. He remained still, while she mounted the bank to the cliff path. She rounded the furze-bush and was almost upon him before she saw him. She stood motionless.

"Well, Decima," said Watchman and opened his eyes.

"You startled me," she said.

"I should leap to my feet, shouldn't I? And apologise?"

"You needn't trouble. I'm sorry I disturbed you. Good-bye."

She moved forward.

Watchman said: "Wait a moment, Decima."

She hesitated. Watchman reached out a hand and seized her ankle.

"Don't do that," said Decima. "It makes us both look silly. I'm in no mood for dalliance."

"Please say you'll wait a moment and I'll behave like a perfect little gent. I've something serious to say to you."

"I don't believe it."

"I promise you. Of the first importance. Please."

"Very well," said Decima.

He released her and scrambled to his feet.

"Well, what is it?" asked Decima.

"It'll take a moment or two. Do sit down and smoke a cigarette. Or shall I walk some of the way with you?"

She shot a glance at the distant figures on Coombe Head and then looked at him. She seemed ill at ease, half-defiant, half-curious.

"We may as well get it over," she said.

"Splendid. Sit down now, do. If we stand here, we're in full view of anybody entering or leaving Ottercombe, and I don't want to be interrupted. No, I've no discreditable motive. Come now."

He sat down on the hillock under the furze-bush and after a moment's hesitation she joined him.

"Will you smoke? Here you are."

He lit her cigarette, dug the match into the turf, and then turned to her.

"The matter I wanted to discuss with you," he said, "concerns this Left Movement of yours."

Decima's eyes opened wide.

"That surprises you?" observed Watchman.

"It does rather," she said. "I can't imagine why you should suddenly be interested in the C. L. M."

"I've no business to be interested," said Watchman, "and in the ordinary sense, my dear Decima, I am not interested. It's solely on your account—no, do let me make myself clear. It's on your account that I want to put two questions to you. Of course if you choose you may refuse to answer them."

Watchman cleared his throat, and pointed a finger at Decima.

"Now in reference to this society——"

"Dear me," interrupted Decima with a faint smile. "This green plot shall be our court, this furze-bush our witness-box; and we will do in action as we will do it before the judge."

"A vile paraphrase, and if we are to talk of mid-summer-night's dreams, Decima——"

"We certainly won't do that," she said, turning very pink. "Pray continue your cross-examination, Mr. Watchman."

"Thank you, my lord. First question: is this body—society, club, movement, or whatever it is—an incorporated company?"

"What does that mean?"

"It means among other things that the books would have to be audited by a chartered accountant."

"Good Heavens, no. It's simply grown up, largely owing to the efforts of Will Pomeroy and myself."

"So I supposed. You've a list of subscribing members"

"Three hundred and forty-five," said Decima proudly.

"And the subscription?"

"Ten bob. Are you thinking of joining us?"

"Who collects the ten bobs?"

"The treasurer."

"*And* secretary. Mr. Legge?"

"Yes. What are you driving at? What were you at last night, baiting Bob Legge?"

"Wait a moment. Do any other sums of money pass through his hands?"

"I don't see why I should tell you these things," said Decima.

"There's no reason, but you have my assurance that I mean well."

"I don't know what you mean."

"And you may be sure I shall regard this conversation as strictly confidential."

"All right," she said uneasily. "We've raised sums for different objects. We want to start a Left Book Club in Illington and there are one or two funds—Spanish, Czech and Austrian refugees and the fighting fund and so on."

"Yes. At the rate of how much a year Three hundred for instance?"

"About that. Quite that, I should think. We've some very generous supporters."

"Now look here, Decima. Did you inquire very carefully into this man Legge's credentials?"

"I—no. I mean, he's perfectly sound. He's secretary for several other things. Some philatelic society and a correspondence course, and he's agent for one or two things."

"He's been here ten months, hasn't he?"

"Yes. He's not strong, touch of T.B., I think, and some trouble with his ears. His doctor told him to come down here. He's been very generous and subscribed to the movement himself."

"May I give you a word of advice? Have your books audited."

"Do you know Bob Legge? You can't make veiled accusations——"

"I have made no accusations."

"You've suggested that——"

49

"That you should be business-like," said Watchman. "That's all."

"Do you know this man? You must tell me."

There was a very long silence and then Watchman said: "I've never known anybody of that name."

"Then I don't understand," said Decima.

"Let us say I've taken an unreasonable dislike to him."

"I'd already come to that conclusion. It was obvious last night."

"Well, think it over." He looked fixedly at her and then said suddenly:

"Why won't you marry Will Pomeroy?"

Decima turned very white and said: "That, at least is entirely my own business."

"Will you meet me here to-night?"

"No."

"Do I no longer attract you, Decima?"

"I'm afraid you don't."

"Little liar, aren't you?"

"The impertinent lady-killer stuff," said Decima, "doesn't wear very well. It has a way of looking merely cheap."

"You can't insult me," said Watchman. "Tell me this. Am I your only experiment?"

"I don't want to start any discussion of this sort. The thing's at an end. It's been dead a year."

"No. Not on my part. It could be revived; and very pleasantly. Why are you angry? Because I didn't write?"

"Good Lord, no!" ejaculated Decima.

"Then why——"

He laid his hand over hers. As if unaware of his touch, her fingers plucked at the blades of grass beneath them.

"Meet me here to-night," he repeated.

"I'm meeting Will to-night at the Feathers."

"I'll take you home."

Decima turned on him.

"Look here," she said, "we'd better get this straightened out. You're not in the least in love with me, are you?"

"I adore you."

"I dare say, but you don't love me. Nor do I love you. A year ago I fell for you rather heavily and we know what happened. I can admit now that I was—well, infatuated.

I can even admit that what I said just then wasn't true. For about two months I *did* mind your not writing. I minded damnably. Then I recovered in one bounce. I don't want any recrudescence."

"How solemn," muttered Watchman. "How learned, and how young."

"It may seem solemn and young to you. Don't flatter yourself I'm the victim of remorse. I'm not. One has to go through with these things, I've decided. But don't let's blow on the ashes."

"We wouldn't have to blow very hard."

"Perhaps not."

"You admit that, do you?"

"Yes. But I don't want to do it."

"Why? Because of Pomeroy?"

"Yes."

"Are you going to marry him, after all?"

"I don't know. He's ridiculously class-conscious about sex. He's completely uneducated in some ways, but—I don't know. If he knew about last year he'd take it very badly, and I can't marry him without telling him."

"Well," said Watchman suddenly, "don't expect me to be chivalrous and decent. I imagine chivalry and decency don't go with sex-education and freedom anyway. Don't be a fool, Decima. You know you think it would be rather fun."

He pulled her towards him. Decima muttered, "No, you don't," and suddenly they were struggling fiercely. Watchman thrust her back till her shoulders were against the bank. As he stooped his head to kiss her, she wrenched one hand free and struck him clumsily but with violence, across the mouth.

"You——" said Watchman.

She scrambled to her feet and stood looking down at him.

"I wish to God," she said savagely, "that you'd never come back."

There was a moment's silence.

Watchman, too, had got to his feet. They looked into each other's eyes; and then, with a gesture that, for all its violence and swiftness suggested the movement of an automaton, he took her by the shoulders and kissed her. When he had released her they moved apart stiffly with no eloquence in either of their faces or figures.

51

Decima said, "You'd better get out of here. If you stay here it'll be the worse for you. I could kill you. Get out."

They heard the thud of footsteps on turf, and Cubitt and Sebastian Parish came over the brow of the hillock.

CHAPTER FOUR

THE EVENING IN QUESTION

I

WATCHMAN, Cubitt and Parish lunched together in the tap-room. Miss Darragh did not appear. Cubitt and Parish had last seen her sucking her brush and gazing with complacence at an abominable sketch. She was still at work when they came up with Watchman and Decima. At lunch, Watchman was at some pains to tell the others how he and Decima Moore met by accident, and how they had fallen to quarrelling about the Coombe Left Movement.

They accepted his recital with, on Parish's part, rather too eager alacrity. Lunch on the whole, was an uncomfortable affair. Something had gone wrong with the relationship of the three men. Norman Cubitt, who was acutely perceptive in such matters, felt that the party had divided into two, with Parish and himself on one side of an intangible barrier, and Watchman on the other. Cubitt had no wish to side, however vaguely, with Parish against Watchman. He began to make overtures, but they sounded unlikely and only served to emphasise his own discomfort. Watchman answered with the courtesy of an acquaintance. By the time they had reached the cheese, complete silence had overcome them.

They did not linger for their usual post-prandial smoke. Cubitt said he wanted to get down to the jetty for his afternoon sketch, Parish said he was going to sleep, Watchman, murmuring something about writing a letter, disappeared upstairs.

They did not see each other again until the evening when they met in the private taproom for their usual cocktail. The fishing boats had come in, and at first the bar was fairly full.

The three friends joined in local conversation and were not thrown upon their own resources until the evening meal which they took together in the ingle-nook. The last drinker went out saying that there was a storm hanging about, and that the air was unnaturally heavy. On his departure complete silence fell upon the three men. Parish made one or two halfhearted attemps to break it but it was no good, they had nothing to say to each other. They finished their meal and Watchman began to fill his pipe.

"What's that?" said Parish suddenly. "Listen!"

"High tide," said Watchman. "It's the surf breaking on Coombe Rock."

"No, it's not. Listen."

And into the silence came a vague gigantic rumour.

"Isn't it thunder?" asked Parish.

The others listened for a moment but made no answer.

"What a climate!" added Parish.

The village outside the inn seemed very quiet. The evening air was sultry. No breath of wind stirred the curtains at the open windows. When, in a minute or two, somebody walked round the building, the footsteps sounded unnaturally loud. Another and more imperative muttering broke the quiet.

Cubitt said nervously:

"It's as if a giant, miles away on Dartmoor, was shaking an iron tray."

"That's exactly how they work thunder in the business," volunteered Parish.

"*The business.*" Watchman said with violent irritation. "What business? Is there only one business?"

"What the hell's gone wrong with you?" asked Parish.

"Nothing. The atmosphere," said Watchman.

"I hate thunder-storms," said Cubitt quickly. "They make me feel as if all my nerves were on the surface. A loathsome feeling."

"I rather like them," said Watchman.

"And that's the end of *that* conversation," said Parish with a glance at Cubitt.

Watchman got up and moved into the window. Mrs. Ives came in with a tray.

"Storm coming up?" Parish suggested.

" 'Ess, sir. Very black outside," said Mrs. Ives.

The next roll of thunder lasted twice as long as the others and ended in a violent tympanic rattle. Mrs. Ives cleared the table and went away. Cubitt moved into the ingle-nook and leant his elbows on the mantelpiece. The room had grown darker. A flight of gulls, making for the sea, passed clamorously over the village. Watchman pulled back the curtains and leant over the window-sill. Heavy drops of rain had begun to fall. They hit the cobble-stones in the inn yard with loud slaps.

"Here comes the rain," said Parish, unnecessarily.

Old Abel Pomeroy came into the Public from the far door. He began to shut the windows and called through into the Private.

"We'm in for a black storm, souls."

A glint of lightning flickered in the yard outside. Parish stood up scraping his chair-legs on the floor-boards.

"They say," said Parish, "that if you count the seconds between the flash and the thunder it gives you the distance——"

A peal of thunder rolled up a steep crescendo.

"——the distance away in fifths of a mile," ended Parish.

"Do shut up, Seb," implored Watchman, not too unkindly.

"Damn it all," said Parish. "I don't know what the hell's the matter with you. Do you, Norman?"

Abel Pomeroy came through the bar into the taproom.

"Be colder soon, I reckon," he said. "If you'd like a fire gentlemen——"

"We'll light it, Abel, if we want it," said Cubitt.

"Good enough, sir." Abel looked from Cubitt and Parish to Watchman, who still leant over the window-sill.

"She'll come bouncing and teeming through that window, Mr. Watchman, once she do break out. Proper deluge she'll be."

"All right, Abel. I'll look after the window."

A livid whiteness flickered outside. Cubitt and Parish had a momentary picture of Watchman, in silhouette against a background of inn-yard and houses. A second later the thunder broke in two outrageous claps. Then, in a mounting roar, the rain came down.

"Yurr she comes," said Abel.

He switched on the light and crossed to the door into the passage.

"Reckon Legge'll bide to-night after all," said Abel.

Watchman spun round.

"Is Legge going away?" he asked.

"He'm called away on business, sir, to Illington. But that lil' car of his leaks like a lobster-pot. Reckon the man'd better wait till to-morrow. I must look to the gutters or us'll have the rain coming in through upstairs ceilings."

He went out.

The evening was now filled with the sound of rain and thunder. Watchman shut the window and came into the room. His head was wet.

He said: "It's much colder. We might have that fire."

Cubitt lit the fire and they watched the first flames rise uncertainly among the driftwood.

"The rain's coming down the chimney," said Parish. "Hallo! Who's this?"

The taproom door opened slowly. There, on the threshold, stood the Hon. Violet Darragh, dripping like a soused hen. Her cotton dress was gummed to her person with such precision that it might as well have melted. Her curls were flattened into streaks, and from the brim of her hat poured little rivers that rushed together at the base of her neck, and, taking the way of least resistance, streamed centrally to her waist where they deployed and ran divergently to the floor. With one hand she held a canvas hold-all, with the other a piece of paper that still bore streaks of cobalt-blue and veridian across its pulpy surface. She might have been an illustration from one of the more Rabelaisian pages of *La Vie Parisienne*.

"My dear Miss Darragh!" ejaculated Watchman.

"Ah, look at me!" said Miss Darragh. "What a pickle I'm in, and me picture ruined. I was determined to finish it and I stayed on till the thunder and lightning drove me away in terror of me life, and when I emerged from the tunnel didn't it break over me like the entire contents of the ocean. Well, I'll go up now and change, for I must look a terrible old sight."

She glanced down at herself, gasped, cast a comical glance at the three men, and bolted.

Will Pomeroy and two companions entered the Public from the street door. They wore oilskin hats and coats, and their boots squelched on the floor-boards. Will went into the bar and served out drinks. Parish leant over the private bar and gave them good-evening.

"You seem to have caught it in the neck," he observed.

"That's right, Mr. Parish," said Will. "She's a proper masterpiece. The surface water'll be pouring through the tunnel if she keeps going at this gait. Here you are chaps, I'm going to change."

He went through the Private into the house, leaving a wet trail behind him. They heard him at the telephone in the passage. He had left the door open and his voice carried above the sound of the storm.

"That you, Dessy? Dessy, this storm's a terror. You'd better not drive that old car over to-night. Tunnel'll be a running stream. It's not safe."

Watchman began to whistle under his breath. Abel returned and took Will's place in the bar.

"I'd walk over myself," Will was saying, "only I can't leave father single-handed. We'll have a crowd in, likely, with this weather."

"I'm going to have a drink," said Watchman suddenly.

"Walk?" said Will. "You're not scared of lightning, then. Good enough, and nobody better pleased than I am. I'll lend you a sweater and, Dessy, you'd better warn them you'll likely stay the night. Why not? So I do, then, and you'll find it out, my dear. I'll come a fetch along the way to meet you."

The receiver clicked. Will stuck his head round the door.

"Dessy's walking over, Dad. I'll go through the tunnel to meet her. Have you seen Bob Legge?"

"He said he'd be up to Illington to-night, sonny."

"He'll never make it. Has he left?"

"In his room yet, I fancy."

"I'll see," said Will. "I've told Dessy she'd better stay the night."

"Very welcome, I'm sure. Ask Mrs. Ives to make room ready."

"So I will, then," said Will, and disappeared.

"Walking over!" said Abel. "A matter of two miles it is,

from yurr to Cary Edge. Wonderful what love'll do, gentlemen, 'baint it?"

"Amazing," said Watchman. "Is nobody else going to drink?"

II

By eight o'clock the public tap was full and the private nearly so. Decima Moore and Will had looked in, but at the moment were closeted upstairs with Mr. Legge who had apparently decided not to go to Illington. Miss Darragh came down in dry clothes with her curls rubbed up, and sat writing letters by the fire.

Two of Abel's regular cronies had come in: Dick Oates, the Ottercombe policeman, and Arthur Gill, the grocer. A little later they were joined by Mr. George Nark, an elderly bachelor-farmer whose political views chimed with those of the Left Movement, and who was therefore a favourite of Will Pomeroy's. Mr. Nark had been a great reader of the Liberal literature of his youth, and had never got over the surprise and excitement that he had experienced thirty years ago on reading Winwood Reade, H. G. Wells, and the *Evolution of Man*. The information that he had derived from these and other serious works had, with the passage of time, become transmitted into simplified forms which though they would have astonished the authors, completely satisfied Mr. Nark.

The rain still came down in torrents and Mr. Nark reported the Coombe Tunnel was a running stream.

"It's a crying shame," he said, gathering the attention of the Private. "Bin going on for hundreds of years and no need for it. We can be flooded out three times a years and capitalistic government only laughs at us. Science would have druv a class-A highroad into the Coombe if somebody had axed it. But does a capitalistic government ax the advice of Science? Not it. It's afraid to. And why? Because Science knows too much for it."

"Ah," said Mr. Gill.

"That's capitalism for you," continued Mr. Nark. "Blind-stupid and arrogant. Patching up where it should pitch-in and start afresh. What can you expect, my sonnies, from a parcel of wage-slaves and pampered aristocrats that don't know the smell of a day's work. So long as they've got their luxuries for themselves——"

He stopped and looked at Miss Darragh.

"Axing your pardon, Miss," said Mr. Nark. "In the heat of my discourse I got carried off my feet with the powerful rush of ideas and forgot your presence. This'll be all gall and wormwood to you, doubtless."

"Not at all, Mr. Nark," said Miss Darragh cheerfully. "I'm myself a poor woman, and I've moods when I'm consumed with jealousy for anybody who's got a lot of money."

This was not precisely the answer Mr. Nark, who was a prosperous farmer, desired.

"It's the government," he said, "that does every man jack of us out of our scientific rights."

"As far as that goes," said P.C. Oates, "I reckon one government's as scientific as the other. Look at sewage for instance."

"Why?" demanded Mr. Nark, "should we look at sewage? What's sewage got to do with it? We're all animals."

"Ah," said Mr. Gill, "so we are, then."

"Do you know, Dick Oates," continued Mr. Nark, "that you've got a rudimentary tail?"

"And if I have, *which* I don't admit——"

"Ask Mr. Cubitt, then. He's an artist and no doubt has studied the skeleton of man in its present stage of evolution. The name escapes me for the moment, but we've all got it. Isn't that correct, sir?"

"Yes, yes," said Norman Cubitt hurriedly. "Quite right, Mr. Nark."

"There you are," said Mr. Nark. "Apes, every manjack of us, and our arms have only grown shorter through us knocking off the habit of hanging from limbs of trees."

"What about our tongues?" asked Mr. Oates.

"Never mind about them," answered Mr. Nark warmly, "do you know that an unborn child's got gills like a fish?"

"That doesn't make a monkey of it, however."

"It goes to show, though."

"What?"

"You want to educate yourself. In a proper government

58

the State 'ud educate the police so's they'd understood these deep matters for themselves. They know all about that in Russia. Scientific necessity that's what it is."

"I don't see how knowing I've got a bit of a tail and once had a pair of gills is going to get me any nearer to a sergeant's stripe," reasoned Mr. Oates. "What I'd like is a case. You know how it happens in these crime stories, chaps," he continued, looking round the company. "I read a good many of them, and it's always the same thing. The keen young P.C. happens to be on the spot when there's a homicide. His super has to call in the Yard and before you know where you are, the P.C.'s working with one of the Big four and getting praised for his witty deductions. All I can say is I wish it happened like that in the Illington and Ottercombe Riding. Well, I'd best go round the beat, I reckon Down the Steps and up again, is about all this drownded hole'll see of me to-night. I'll look in again, chaps."

Mr. Oates adjusted his helmet, fastened his mackintosh, looked to his lamp, and went out into the storm.

"Ah, the poor fellow!" murmured Miss Darragh comfortably from inside the ingle-nook settle.

"In a properly conducted state——" began Mr. Nark.

His remark was drowned in a clap of thunder. The lights wavered and grew so dim that the filaments in the bulbs were reduced to luminous threads.

"Drat they electrics," said old Abel. "That's the storm playing bobs-a-dying with the wires somewhere. Us'll be in darkness afore closing time, I dare say." And he raised his voice to a bellow.

"Will! Oi, Will!"

Will's voice answered from above. The lights brightened. After a minute or two, Decima and Will came downstairs and into the Private. Each carried an oil lamp.

"Guessed what you were hollowing for," said Will, with a grin. "Here's the lamps. We'll put 'em on the two bars, Dessy, and matches handy. Bob Legge's fetching the other, Dad. Ceiling in his room's sprung a leak and the rain's coming in pretty heavy. The man was sitting there, so lost in thought he might have drowned. I've fixed up a bucket to catch it, and told him to come down."

Will stared for a second at Watchman, and added rather

truculently: "We told Bob we missed his company in the Private, didn't we, Dess?"

"Yes," said Decima.

Watchman looked at her. She turned her back to him and said something to Will.

"Let us by all means have Mr. Legge among us," Watchman said. "I hope to beat him—all round the clock."

And in a minute or two, Mr. Legge came in with the third unlit lamp.

III

On the day following the thunderstorm, the patrons of the Plume of Feathers tried very hard to remember in some sort of order, the events of the previous evening; the events that followed Mr. Legge's entrance into the private taproom. For one reason and another their stories varied, but no doubt the principal reason for their variation might be found in the bottle of Courvoisier '87 that Abel Pomeroy had brought up from the cellar. That was after Mr. Gill had gone home, and before Mr. Oates returned from a somewhat curtailed beat round the village.

It was Watchman who started the discussion on brandy. Watchman apparently had got over whatever unfriendly mood had possessed him earlier in the evening and was now as communicative as he had been silent. He began to tell legal stories and this he did very well indeed, so that in a minute or two he had the attention of both bars; the patrons of the public taproom leaning on the bar counter and trying to see into the other room. He told stories of famous murder trials, of odd witnesses, and finally of his biggest case before he took silk. He did not give the names of the defendants, only describing them as the embezzling experts of the century. He had led for the defence of one of them and had succeeded in shifting most of the blame to the other who got, he said, a swingeing big sentence. He became quite exalted over it all.

Sebastian always said that his cousin would have made an actor. He was certainly an excellent mimic. He gave a character sketch of the judge and made a living creature of

60

the man. He described how, after the verdict, when the defendant's house was sold up, he had bought three dozen of brandy from the cellar.

"Corvoisier '87," said Watchman. "A superb year."

"Me cousin Byronie," said Miss Darragh, looking round the corner of her settle, "had the finest cellar in County Clare, I believe. Before the disaster of course."

Watchman started and stared at Miss Darragh in confusion.

"Dear me, Mr. Watchman," she said composedly, "what is the matter with you? Had you forgotten I was here?"

"I—it sounds very ungallant, but I believe I had."

"What brandy did you say, sir?" asked Abel, and when Watchman repeated mechanically, 'Courvoisier '87,' Abel said placidly that he believed he had three bottles in his own cellar.

"I picked 'em up when old Lawyer Payne over to Diddlestock died and was sold up," said Abel. "Half-dozen, thurr was, and squire split 'em with me. I think that's the name. It's twelve month or more since I looked at 'em."

Watchman had already taken three glasses of Treble Extra and, although sober, was willing to be less so. Parish, suddenly flamboyant, offered to bet Abel a guinea that the brandy was not Courvoisier '87 and on Abel shaking his head, said if it was Courvoisier '87, damn it, they'd kill a bottle of it there and then. Abel took a candle and went off to the cellar. The three men in the public taproom went away. Will Pomeroy left the public bar and came to the private one. He had shown little interest in Watchman's stories. Legge had gone into the ingle-nook where he remained reading a book on the Red Army in Northern China. Watchman embarked on a discussion with Cubitt on the subject of capital punishment. Soon it became a general argument with Decima, Cubitt and Parish on one side; and Watchman, dubiously supported by Mr. Nark, on the other.

"It's a scientific necessity," said Mr. Nark. "The country has to be purged. Cast out your waste material is what I say, and so does Stalin."

"So does Hitler if it comes to that," said Cubitt. "You're talking of massed slaughter, aren't you?"

"You can slaughter in a righteous manner," said Mr. Nark,

"and you can slaughter in an unrighteous manner. It's all a matter of evolution. Survival of the fittest."

"What on earth's that to say to it?" asked Cubitt.

"We're talking about capital punishment in this country aren't we?" Decima asked.

Throughout the discussion, though she had launched several remarks at Watchman, she had not spoken directly to him. In each instance Watchman had answered exactly as if the conversation was between those two alone. He now cut in quickly.

"*I* thought so," said Watchman. "My learned friend is a little confused."

"I regard it," Decima continued, always to Cubitt, "as a confession of weakness."

"I think it's merely barbaric and horrible," said Parish.

"Terrible," murmured Miss Darragh drowsily. "Barbarous indeed! If we can't stop men from killing each other by any better means than killing in turn then they'll persist in it till their dying day."

Cubitt, with some difficulty, stifled a laugh.

"Quite right, Miss Darragh," he said. "It's a concession to the savage in all of us."

"Nonsense," said Watchman. "It's an economic necessity."

"Ah," said Mr. Nark with the air of one clutching at a straw, "ah, now you're talking."

Abel came back with a bottle in his hands.

"There you are gentlemen," he said. "It's Mr. Watchman's brandy and no doubt about it. See for yourself, sir."

Watchman looked at the bottle.

"By God, you're right, Abel."

"This is magnificent," cried Parish. "Come on. We'll open it. Have you any brandy glasses? Never mind, tumblers'll do. It's a bit cold, but we'll humour it."

Abel opened the bottle.

"This," said Watchman, "is my affair. Shut up, Seb, I insist. Abel, you and Will must join us."

"Well, thank you very much, sir, I'm sure," said Abel.

"I'm afraid," said Decima, "that I really dislike brandy. It'd be wasted on me."

"What will you have then?"

"I'm sorry to be so tiresome, but I'd really rather not have a drink."

"My poor girl," said Watchman.

"Dessy'll have a stone-ginger with me," said Will Pomeroy suddenly.

"With me," said Watchman. "Eight brandies, two stone-gingers, Abel, and kill the bottle."

"Good Lord, Luke," expostulated Cubitt, "you'll have us rolling."

"None for me, thank you, Mr. Watchman," said Miss Darragh. "I'm afraid that I, too, am a Philistine."

"You'll have a drink, though?"

"I shall join you," said Miss Darragh, "in the non-alcoholic spirit."

"Six brandies, Abel," amended Watchman. "The first half now, and the second hereafter."

Abel poured out the brandy. They watched him in silence. The rain still poured down, but the thunder sounded more distantly.

Watchman took the first tot to Legge and put it on a table at his elbow.

"I hope you'll join us, Mr. Legge," he said.

Legge looked at the brandy and then directly at Watchman.

"It's very kind of you," he said. "As a matter of fact I've some work to do and——"

"'Let other hours be set apart for business,'" quoted Watchman. "To-day it is our pleasure to be drunk. Do you like good brandy, Mr. Legge?"

"This," said Legge, "is the vintage of my choice."

He took the glass and nursed it between those calloused hands.

"An exquisite bouquet," said Mr. Legge.

"I knew you'd appreciate it."

"Your health," said Legge and took a delicate sip.

The others, with the exception of Mr. Nark, murmured self-consciously and sipped. Mr. Nark raised his glass.

"Your very good health, sir. Long life and happiness," said Mr. Nark loudly and emptied his glass at one gulp. He drew in his breath with a formidable whistle, his eyes started from his head and he grabbed at the air.

"You'm dashed at it too ferocious, George," said Abel.

Mr. Nark shuddered violently and fetched his breath.

"It's a murderous strong tipple," he whispered. "If you'll pardon me, Mr. Watchman, I'll break it down inwardly with a drop of water."

But presently Mr. Nark began to smile and then to giggle, and as he giggled so did Cubitt, Parish and Watchman. By the time the first tot of Courvoisier '87 had been consumed, there was much laughter in the private bar, and a good deal of rather loud, aimless conversation. Watchman proposed that they have a round-the-clock competition on the dart-board.

Parish reminded him of Legge's trick with the darts.

"Come on, Luke," cried Parish. "If you let him try it on you, damme if I won't let him try it on me."

Mr. Legge was understood to say he was willing.

Watchman pulled the darts out of the board.

"Come on now," he said. "I'm equal to the lot of you. Even Mr. Legge. Round-the-clock it is, and if he beats me this time, we'll have the other half and he can do his circus trick with my hand. Is it a bargain, Mr. Legge?"

"If you're not afraid," said Legge indistinctly, "I'm not. But I'd like a new set of darts."

"Afraid? With a brandy like this on board, I'd face the devil himself."

"Good old Luke," cried Parish.

Abel fished under the shelves and brought up a small package which he clapped down on the bar counter.

"Brand new set o' darts, my sonnies," said Abel. "Best to be bought, and come this evening from London. I'll fix the flights in 'em while you play round-the-clock with the old 'uns. Bob Legge can christen 'em with this masterpiece of an exhibition."

He broke the string and opened the package.

"Come now, Mr. Legge," said Watchman. "Is it a bargain?"

"Certainly," said Legge. "A bargain it is."

CHAPTER FIVE

FAILURE BY MR. LEGGE

I

P.C. OATES had gone as far as the tunnel, had returned, and had descended the flight of stone steps that leads to the wharf from the right-hand side of the Feathers. He had walked along the passage called Fish Lane. flashing his lamp from time to time on streaming windows and doorways. Rain drummed on Oates's mackintosh cape, on his helmet, on cobble-stones, and on the sea that, only a few feet away, in the darkness, lapped at the streaming waterfront. The sound of the rain was almost as loud as the sound of thunder and behind both of these was the roar of surf on Coombe Rock. A ray of lamplight from a chink in a window-blind shone obliquely on rods of rain, and by its suggestion of remote comfort made the night more desolate.

Far above him, dim and forlorn, the post-office clock told a quarter past nine.

Oates turned at the end of Fish Lane and shone his light on the second flight of Ottercombe Steps. Water was pouring down them in a series of miniature falls. He began to climb, holding tightly to the handrail. If anyone could have seen him abroad in the night, lonesome and dutiful, his plodding figure might have suggested a progression into the past when the night-watchman walked through Ottercombe to call the hours to sleeping fishermen. Such a flight of fancy did not visit the thoughts of Mr. Oates. He merely told himself that he was damned if he'd go any farther, and when the red curtains of the Plume of Feathers shone through the rain he mended his pace and made for them.

But before he had gone more than six steps he paused. Some noise that had not reached him before threaded the sound of the storm. Someone was calling out—shouting— yelling. He stopped and listened.

"O-o-oates! Hallo! Dick! Di-i-ick! Oo-o-oates!"

"Hallo!" yelled Oates and his voice sounded very desolate. "Hallo! Come—back—here."

Oates broke into a lope. The voice had come from the front of the pub. He crossed the yard, passed the side of the house and the door into the Public, and came in sight of that front door. A tall figure, shading its eyes, was silhouetted against the lighted entry. It was Will Pomeroy. Oates strode out of the night into the entry.

"Here!" he said, "what's up?" And when he saw Will Pomeroy's face: "What's happened here?"

Without speaking Will jerked his thumb in the direction of the private tap. His face was the colour of clay, and one corner of his mouth twitched.

"Well, what *is* it?" demanded Oates impatiently.

"In there. Been an accident."

"*Accident.* What sort of a accident?"

But before Will could answer Decima Moore came out of the taproom, closing the door behind her.

"Here's Dick," said Will.

"Will," said Decima, "there's no doubt about it. He's dead."

"My Gawd, who's dead!" shouted Oates.

"Watchman."

II

Oates looked down at the figure on the settle. He had remembered to remove his helmet, but the water dripped off his cape in little streams. When he bent forward three drops fell on the blind face. Oates dabbed at them with his finger and glanced round apologetically.

He said, "What happened?"

Nobody answered. Old Pomeroy stood by the bar, his hands clasped in front of him. His face spoke only of complete bewilderment. He looked from one to another of the men as if somewhere there was some sort of explanation which had been withheld from him. Sebastian Parish and Norman Cubitt stood together in the ingle-nook. Parish's face was stained with tears. He kept smoothing back his hair with a nervous and meaningless gesture of the right hand. Cubitt's

66

head was bent down. He seemed to be thinking deeply. Every now and then he glanced up sharply from under his brows. Mr. Nark sat on one of the bar-stools, clenching and unclenching his hands, and struggling miserably with intermittent but profound hiccoughs. Legge, as white as paper, bit his fingers and stared at Oates. Decima and Will stood together in the doorway. Miss Darragh sat just outside the ingle-nook on a low chair. Her moonlike face was colourless but she seemed composed.

Watchman lay on a settle near the dart-board and opposite the bar. His eyes were wide open. They seemed to stare with glistening astonishment at the ceiling. The pupils were wide and black. His hands were clenched; the right arm lay across his body, the left dangled, and where the knuckles touched the floor they, like the back of the hand, were stained red.

"Well," repeated Oates violently, "can't any of you speak? What happened? Where's your senses? Have you sent for a doctor?"

"The telephone's dead," said Will Pomeroy. "And he's past doctoring, Dick."

Oates picked up the left wrist.

"What's this? Blood?"

"He got a prick from a dart."

Oates looked at the clenched hand and felt the wrist. In the third finger there was a neat puncture on the outside, below the nail. It was stained brown. The nails were bluish.

"I did that," said Legge suddenly. "It was my dart."

Oates laid the hand down and bent over the figure. A drop of water fell from his coat on one of the staring eyes. He fumbled inside the shirt, looking over his shoulder at Will Pomeroy.

"We'll have to fetch a doctor, however," he said.

"I'll go," said Cubitt. "Is it Illington?"

"Doctor Shaw, sir. Main road in, and the last corner. It's on the left after you pass police station. He's police-surgeon. I'd be obliged if you'd stop at the station and report."

"Right."

Cubitt went out.

Oates straightened up and unbuttoned his cape.

"I'll have to get some notes down," he said, and felt in

the pocket of his tunic. He stepped back and his boots crunched excruciatingly.

"There's glass all over the floor," said Will.

Decima Moore said, "Can't we—cover him up?"

"It would be better, don't you think?" said Miss Darragh, speaking for the first time.

"Can I——"

Will said, "I'll get something," and went out.

Oates looked round the group and at last addressed himself to Sebastian Parish.

"How long ago was this, sir?" he asked.

"Only a few minutes. It happened just before you came in."

Oates glanced at his watch.

"Half-past nine," he said and noted it down.

"Let's hear what happened," he said.

"But it's not a case for the police," said Parish. "I mean, because he died suddenly——"

"You called me in, sir," said Oates. "It's no doubt a case for the doctor. Leave it, if you wish, sir, till he comes."

"No, no," said Parish, "I don't mean that I object. It's only that your notebook and everything—it's so awful somehow." He turned to Abel Pomeroy. "You tell him."

"It was like this, Dick," said old Abel. "Mr. Legge here, had told us how he could throw the darts like a circus chap between the fingers of a man's hand stretched out on board. You heard him. Mr. Watchman, in his bold way, said he'd hold his hand out and Mr. Legge was welcome to have a shot at it. 'Twouldn't do no great damage, Mr. Watchman said, if he did stick him. Us all said it was a silly rash kind of trick. But Mr. Watchman was hell-bent on it."

"He insisted," said Will.

"So he did, then. And up goes his hand. Mr. Legge throws the first three as pretty as you please, outside little finger, a'tween little and third, a'tween third and middle. Then he throws the fourth and 'stead of going a'tween middle and first finger it catches middle finger. 'Got me,' says Mr. Watchman, and then—then what?" asked Abel.

"It was curious," said Miss Darragh, slowly. "He didn't move his hand at once. He kept it there, against the board. The blood trickled down his finger and spread like veins in a leaf over the back of his hand. One had time to wonder if the dart had gone right through and he was, in a way, crucified."

"He turned mortal ghastly white," said Abel.

"And then pulled the dart out," said Parish, "and threw it down on the floor. He shuddered, didn't he?"

"Yes," said Abel. "He shuddered violent."

"He always turned queer at the sight of his own blood, you know," said Parish.

"Well, what next?" asked Oates.

"I think he took a step towards the settle," said Parish.

"He sat on the settle," said Decima. "Miss Darragh said, 'He's feeling faint, give him a sip of brandy.' Mr. Legge said he looked ill and could he have lockjaw? Someone else, Mr. Pomeroy I think, said he ought to have iodine on his finger. Anyhow Mr. Pomeroy got the first-aid box out of the bottom cupboard. I looked for a glass with brandy in it but they were all empty. I got the bottle. While I was doing that—pouring out the brandy, I mean—Mr. Pomeroy dabbed iodine on the finger. Mr. Watchman clenched his teeth and cried out. He jerked up his arms."

She stopped short and closed her eyes.

Will Pomeroy had come back with a sheet. He spread it over Watchman and then turned to Decima.

"I'll take you out of this," he said. "Come upstairs to Mrs. Ives, Dessy."

"No, I'll finish."

"No need."

Will put his arm across Decima's shoulder and turned to Oates.

"I'll tell you. Mr. Parish, here, said Mr. Watchman couldn't stand the sight of blood. Father said something about iodine, like Dessy told you, and he got the first-aid box out of the cupboard. He took out the bottle and it was nearly empty. Father tipped it up and poured some on Mr. Watchman's finger and then got out a bandage. Then Dessy gave him his brandy. He knocked the glass out of her hand."

"Miss Darragh was just going to tie his finger up," said Abel, "when lights went out."

"Went out?"

"'Ess. They'd been upping and downing ever since

thunder set in and this time they went out proper for about a minute."

"It was frightful," said Parish rapidly. "We could hear him breathing. We were all knocking against each other with broken glass everywhere and—those awful noises. Nobody thought of the oil lamps, but Legge said he'd throw some wood on the fire to make a blaze. He did, and just then the lights went up."

"Hold hard, if you please, sir," said Oates. "I'll get this down in writing."

"But, look here——"

Parish broke off and Will began again.

"When the lights went on again we all looked at Mr. Watchman. He was in a kind of fit, seemingly. He thrashed about with his arms and legs and then fell backwards on settle, where he is now. His breathing came queer for a bit and then—didn't come at all. I tried to get doctor, but the wires must be down. Then I came out and called you."

Will turned Decima towards the door.

"If you want me, Father," he said, "I'll be up along. Coming, Dessy?"

"I'm all right," said Decima.

"You'll be better out of here."

She looked at him confusedly, seemed to hesitate, and then turned to Miss Darragh.

"Will you come, too?" asked Decima.

Miss Darragh looked fixedly at her and then seemed to make up her mind.

"Yes, my dear, certainly. We're better out of the way now, you know."

Miss Darragh gathered up her writing block and plodded to the door. Decima drew nearer to Will, and obeying the pressure of his hand, went out with him.

Legge walked across and looked down at the shrouded figure.

"My God," he said, "do you think it was the dart that did it? My God, I've never missed before! He moved his finger. I swear he moved his finger. My God, I shouldn't have taken that brandy!"

"Where is the dart?" asked Oates, still writing.

Legge began hunting about the floor. The broken glass crackled under his boot.

"If it's all the same to you, Abel," said Oates suddenly, "I reckon we'd better leave this end of the room till doctor's come. If it's all the same to you, I reckon we'll shift into the Public."

"Let's do that, for God's sake," said Parish.

Mr. Nark was suddenly and violently ill.

"That settles it," said old Abel. "Us'll move."

III

"Steady," said the doctor. "There's no particular hurry, you know. It's no joke negotiating Coombe Tunnel on a night like this. We must be nearly there."

"Sorry," said Cubitt. "I can't get it out of my head you might—might be able to do something."

"I'm afraid not from your account. Here's the tunnel, now. I should change down to first, really I should."

Cubitt changed down. "I expect you wish you'd driven yourself," he said grimly.

"If it hadn't been for that slow puncture—there's the turning. Can you do it in one in this car? Splendid. I must confess I don't enjoy driving into the Coombe, even on clear nights. Now the road down. Pretty steep, really, and it's streaming with surface water. Shameful state of repair. Here we are."

Cubitt put on his brakes and drew up with a sidelong skid at the front door of the Feathers. The doctor got out, reached inside for his bag, and ducked through the rain into the entry. Cubitt followed him.

"In the private bar, you said?" asked Dr. Shaw.

He pushed open the door and they walked in.

The private bar was deserted but the lights were up in the Public beyond, and they heard a murmur of voices.

"Hallo!" called Dr. Shaw.

There was a scuffling of feet and Will Pomeroy appeared on the far side of the bar.

"Here's doctor," said Will, over his shoulder.

"Just a minute, Will," said the voice of Mr. Oates. "I'll

trouble you to stay where you are, if you please, gentlemen."

He loomed up massively, put Will aside, and reached Dr. Shaw by way of the tap proper, ducking under both counters.

"Well, Oates," said Dr. Shaw, "what's the trouble?"

Cubitt, stranded inside the door, stayed where he was. Oates pointed to the settle. Dr. Shaw took off his hat and coat, laid them with his bag on a table, and then moved to the shrouded figure. He drew back the sheet and, after a moment's pause, stooped over Watchman.

Cubitt turned away. There was a long silence.

At last Dr. Shaw straightened up and replaced the sheet.

"Well," he said, "let's have the whole story again. I've had it once from Mr. Cubitt, but he says he was a bit confused. Where are the others?"

"In here, doctor," said Abel Pomeroy. "Will you come through?"

Oates and Will held up the counter-flap and Dr. Shaw went into the public bar. Parish, Mr. Nark and Abel had got to their feet.

Dr. Shaw was not the tallest man there but he dominated the scene. He was pale and baldish and wore glasses. His intelligence appeared in his eyes which were extremely bright and a vivid blue. His lower lip protruded. He had an unexpectedly deep voice, a look of serio-comic solemnity, and a certain air of distinction. He looked directly and with an air of thoughtfulness, at each of the men before him.

"His relations must be told," he said.

Parish moved forward. "I'm his cousin," he said, "and his nearest relation."

"Oh, yes," said Dr. Shaw. "You're Mr. Parish?"

"Yes."

"Yes. Sad business, this."

"What was it?" asked Parish. "What happened? He was perfectly well. Why did he—I don't understand."

"Tell me this," said Dr. Shaw. "Did your cousin become unwell as soon as he received this injury from the dart?"

"Yes. At least he seemed to turn rather faint. I didn't think much of it because he's always gone like that at the sight of his own blood."

"Like what? Can you describe his appearance?"

"Well, he—O God, what did he do, Norman?"

Cubitt said, "He just said 'Got me,' when the dart stuck, and then afterwards pulled it out and threw it down. He turned terribly pale. I think he sort of collapsed on that seat."

"I've seen a man with tetanus," said Legge suddenly. "He looked just the same. For God's sake, doctor, d'you think he could have taken tetanus from that dart?"

"I can't tell you that off-hand, I'm afraid. What happened next?"

Dr. Shaw looked at Cubitt.

"Well, Abel here—Mr. Pomeroy—got a bandage and a bottle of iodine and put some iodine on the finger. Then Miss Darragh, a lady who's staying here, said she'd bandage the finger, and while she was getting out the bandage Miss Moore gave him brandy."

"Did he actually take the brandy?"

"I think he took a little but after she'd tipped the glass up he clenched his teeth and knocked it out of her hand."

"Complain of pain?"

"No. He looked frightened."

"And then? After that?"

"After that? Well, just at that moment, really, the lights went out, and when they went up again he seemed much worse. He was in a terrible state."

"A fit," said Mr. Nark, speaking for the first time. "The man had a fit. Ghastly!" He belched uproariously.

"There's a very strong smell of brandy," said Dr. Shaw.

"It spilt," explained Mr. Nark hurriedly. "It's all over the floor in there."

"Where's the dart, Oates?" asked Dr. Shaw.

"In there, sir. I've put it in a clean bottle and corked it up."

"Good. I'd better have it. You'll have to leave the room in there as it is, Mr. Pomeroy, until I've had a word with the superintendent. The body may be removed in the morning."

"Very good, sir."

"And I'm afraid, Mr. Parish, that under the circumstances I must report this case to the coroner."

"Do you mean there'll have to be an inquest?"

"If he thinks it necessary."

"And—and a post-mortem?"

"If he orders it."

73

"Oh God!" said Parish.

"May I have your cousin's full name and his address?"

Parish gave them. Dr. Shaw looked solemn and said it would be a great loss to the legal profession. He then returned to the private bar. Oates produced his note-book and took the floor.

"I'll have all your names and addresses, if you please, gentlemen," he said.

"What's the use of saying that?" demanded Mr. Nark, rallying a little. "You know 'em already. You took our statements. We've signed 'em, and whether we should in law is a point I'm not sure of."

"Never mind if I know 'em or don't, George Nark," rejoined Oates. "I know my business and that's quite sufficient. What's your name?"

He took all their names and addresses and suggested that they go to bed. They filed out through a door into the passage. Oates then joined Dr. Shaw in the private bar.

"Hallo, Oates," said the doctor. "Where's that dart?".

"Legge picked the dart off the floor," Oates said.

He showed it to Dr. Shaw. He had put it into an empty bottle and sealed it.

"Good," said Dr. Shaw, and put the bottle in his bag.

"Now the remains of the brandy glass. They seem to have tramped it to smithereens. We'll see if we can gather up some of the mess. There's forceps and an empty jar in my bag. Where did the iodine come from?"

"Abel keeps his first-aid outfit in that corner cupboard, sir. He's a great one for iodine. Sloshed it all over Bob Legge's face to-day when he cut himself with his razor."

Dr. Shaw stooped and picked up a small bottle that had rolled under the settle.

"Here it is, I suppose." He sniffed at it. "Yes, that's it. Where's the cork?"

He hunted about until he found it.

"Better take this too. And the brandy bottle. Good heavens, they seem to have done themselves remarkably proud. It's nearly empty. Now where's the first-aid kit?"

Dr. Shaw went to the cupboard and stared up at the glass door.

"What's that bottle in there?" he said sharply.

Oates joined them:

"That, sir? Oh yes, I know what that is. It's some stuff Abel got to kill the rats in the old stables. He mentioned it earlier this evening."

Oates rubbed his nose vigorously.

"Seems more like a week ago. There was the deceased gentleman standing drinks and chaffing Abel, not much more than a couple of hours ago. And now look at him. Ripe for coroner as you might say"

"Did Abel say what this rat-poison was?"

"Something in the nature of prussic acid, I fancy, sir."

"Indeed?" said Dr. Shaw. "Get my gloves out of my overcoat pocket will you, Oates."

"Your gloves, sir?"

"Yes, I want to open the cupboard."

But when Oates brought the gloves, Dr. Shaw still stared at the cupboard door.

"Your gloves, sir."

"I don't think I'll use 'em. I don't think I'll open the door, Oates. There may be fingerprints all over the shop. We'll leave the cupboard door, Oates, for the expert."

CHAPTER SIX

INQUEST

I

THE Illington coroner was James Mordant Esq., M.D. He was sixty-seven years old and these years sat heavily upon him for he suffered from dyspepsia. He seemed to regard his fellow-men with brooding suspicion, he sighed a great deal, and had a trick of staring despondently at the merest acquaintances. He had at one time specialised in bacteriology and it was said of him that he saw human beings as mere playgrounds for brawling micrococci. It was also said that when Dr. Mordant presided over an inquest, the absence in court of the corpse was not felt. He sat huddled behind his table and rested his head on his hand with such a lack-lustre air that one might have thought he scarcely listened to the evidence. This was not the case, however. He was a capable man.

On the morning of the inquest on Luke Watchman, the third day after his death, Dr. Mordant, with every appearance of the deepest distrust, heard his jury sworn and contemplated the witnesses. The inquest was held in the town hall and owing to the publicity given to Watchman's death in the London papers, was heavily attended by the public. Watchman's solicitor, who in the past had frequently briefed him, had come down from London. So had Watchman's secretary and junior and a London doctor who had attended him recently. There was a fair sprinkling of London pressmen. Dr. Mordant, staring hopelessly at an old man in the front row, charged the jury to determine how, when, where, and by what means, deceased came by his death, and whether he died from criminal, avoidable, or natural causes. He then raised his head and stared at the jury.

"Is it your wish to view the body?" he sighed.

The jury whispered and huddled, and its foreman, an auctioneer, said they thought perhaps under the circumstances they *should* view the body.

The coroner sighed again and gave an order to his officer. The jury filed out and returned in a few minutes looking unwholesome. The witnesses were then examined on oath by the coroner.

P.C. Oates gave formal evidence of the finding of the body. Then Sebastian Parish was called and identified the body. Everybody who had seen his performance of a bereaved brother in a trial scene of a famous picture, was now vividly reminded of it. But Parish's emotion, thought Cubitt, could not be purely histrionic unless, as he had once declared, he actually changed colour under the stress of a painful scene. Sebastian was now very pale indeed and Cubitt wondered uneasily what he thought of this affair, and how deeply he regretted the loss of his cousin. He gave his evidence in a low voice but it carried to the end of the building, and when he faltered at the description of Watchman's death, at least two of the elderly ladies in the public seats were moved to tears. Parish wore a grey suit, a soft white shirt and a black tie. He looked amazingly handsome and on his arrival, had been photographed several times.

Cubitt was called next and confirmed Parish's evidence.

Then Miss Darragh appeared. The other witnesses exuded discomfort and formality but Miss Darragh was completely at her ease. She took the oath with an air of intelligent interest. The coroner asked her if she had remembered anything that she hadn't mentioned in her first statement or if there was any point that had been missed by the previous witness.

"There is not," said Miss Darragh. "I told the doctor, Dr. Shaw 'twas, all I had seen; and when the policeman, Constable Oates 'twas, came up on the morning after the accident, I told 'um all I knew all over again. If I may be allowed to say so it is my opinion that the small wound Mr. Watchman had from the dart had nothing whatever to do with his death."

"What makes you think, that, Miss Darragh?" asked the coroner with an air of allowing Miss Darragh a certain amount of latitude.

"Wasn't it a small paltry prick from a brand new dart that couldn't hurt a child? As Mr. Parish said at the time, he was but frightened at the sight of his own blood. That was my own impression. 'Twas later that he became so ill."

"When did you notice the change in his condition?"

"Later."

"Was it after he had taken the brandy?"

"It was. Then or about then or after."

"He took the brandy after Mr. Pomeroy put iodine on his finger?"

"He did."

"You agree for the rest with the previous statements?"

"I do."

"Thank you, Miss Darragh."

Decima Moore came next. Decima looked badly shaken but she gave her evidence very clearly and firmly. The coroner stopped her when she came to the incident of the brandy. He had a curious trick of prefacing many of his questions with a slight moan, rather in the manner of a stage parson.

"N-n-n you say, Miss Moore, that the deceased swallowed some of the brandy?"

"Yes," said Decima.

"N-n-n you are positive on that point?"

"Yes."

"Yes. Thank you. What happened to the glass?"

"He knocked it out of my hand on to the floor."

"Did you get the impression that he did this deliberately?"

"No. It seemed to be involuntary."

"And was the glass broken?"

"Yes." Decima paused. "At least——"

"N-n-n—yes?"

"It was broken, but I don't remember whether that happened when it fell, or afterwards when the light went out. Everybody seemed to be treading on broken glass after the lights went out."

The coroner consulted his notes.

"And for the rest, Miss Moore, do you agree with the account given by Mr. Parish, Mr. Cubitt and Miss Darragh?"

"Yes."

"In every particular?"

Decima was now very white indeed. She said, "Everything they said is quite true, but there is one thing they didn't notice."

The coroner sighed.

"What is that, Miss Moore?" he asked.

"It was after I gave him the brandy. He gasped and I thought he spoke. I thought he said one word."

"What was it?"

"Poisoned," said Decima.

And a sort of rustling in the room seemed to turn the word into an echo.

The coroner added to his notes.

"You are sure of this?" he asked.

"Yes."

"Yes. And then?"

"He clenched his teeth very hard. I don't think he spoke again."

"Are you positive that it was Mr. Watchman's own glass that you gave him?"

"Yes. He put it on the table when he went to the dartboard. It was the only glass there. I poured a little into it from the bottle. The bottle was on the bar."

"Had anyone but Mr. Watchman touched the glass before you gave him the brandy?"

Decima said: "I didn't notice anyone touch it."

"Quite so. Have you anything further to tell us? Anything that escaped the notice of the previous witnesses?"

"Nothing," said Decima.

Her deposition was read to her, and, like Parish and Cubitt, she signed it.

Will Pomeroy took the oath with an air of truculence and suspicion, but his statement differed in no way from the others, and he added nothing material to the evidence. Mr. Robert Legge was the next to give evidence on the immediate circumstances surrounding Watchman's death.

On his appearance there was a tightening of attention among the listeners. The light from a high window shone full on Legge. Cubitt looked at his white hair, the grooves and folds of his face, and the calluses on his hands. He wondered how old he was and why Watchman had baited him, and exactly what sort of background he had. It was impossible to place the fellow. His clothes were good; a bit antiquated as to cut perhaps, but good. He spoke like an educated man and moved like a labourer. As he faced the coroner he straightened up and held his arms at his sides almost in the manner of a private soldier. His face was rather white and his fingers twitched, but he spoke with composure. He agreed that the account given by the previous witnesses was correct. The coroner clasped his hands on the table and gazed at them with an air of distaste.

"About this n-n-n experiment with the darts, Mr. Legge," he said, "when was it first suggested?"

"I believe on the night of Mr. Watchman's arrival. I mentioned, I think, that I had done the trick and he said something to the effect that he wouldn't care to try. I think he added that he might, after all, like to see me do it." Legge moisted his lips. "Later on that evening I did the trick in the public taproom and he said that if I beat him at round-the clock he'd let me try it on him."

"What," asked the coroner, drearily, "is round-the-clock?"

"You play into each segment of the dart-board beginning at number one. As soon as you miss a shot the next player has his turn. You have three darts, that is three chances to get a correct opening shot, but after that you carry on, until you miss. You have to finish with fifty."

"You all played this game?"

Legge hesitated: "We were all in it except Miss Darragh. Miss Moore began. When she missed, Mr. Cubitt took the next turn, then I came."

"Yes?"

"I didn't miss."

"You mean you—ran out in one turn?"

"Yes."

"And then?"

"Mr. Watchman said he believed he would trust me to do the hand trick."

"And did you do it?"

"No, I was not anxious to do it, and turned the conversation. Later, as I have said, I did it in the public room."

"But the following night, last Friday, you attempted it on the deceased?"

"Yes."

"Will you tell us how this came about?"

Legge clenched his fingers and stared at an enlargement of a past mayor of Illington.

"In much the same circumstances. I mean, we were all in the private bar. Mr. Watchman proposed another game of round-the-clock and said definitely that if I beat him I should try the trick with the hand. I did win and he at once insisted on the experiment."

"Were you reluctant?"

"I—no. I have done the trick at least fifty times and I have only failed once before. On that occasion no harm was done. The dart grazed the third finger but it was really nothing. I told Mr. Watchman of this incident, but he said he'd stick to his bargain, and I consented."

"Go on please, Mr. Legge."

"He put his hand against the dart-board with the fingers spread out as I suggested. There were two segments of the board showing between the fingers in each instance." Legge paused and then said: "So you see it's really easier than round-the-clock. Twice as easy."

Legge stopped and the coroner waited.

"Yes?" he said to his blotting paper.

"I tried the darts, which were new ones, and then began. I put the first dart on the outside of the little finger and the next between the little and third fingers, and the next between the third and middle."

"It was the fourth dart, then, that miscarried?"

"Yes."

"How do you account for that?"

"At first I thought he had moved his finger. I am still inclined to think so."

The coroner stirred uneasily.

"Would you not be positive on this point if it was so? You must have looked fixedly at the fingers."

"At the space between," corrected Legge.

"I see." Dr. Mordant looked at his notes.

"The previous statements," he said, "mention that you had all taken a certain amount of a vintage brandy. Exactly how much brandy, Mr. Legge, did you take?"

"Two nips."

"How large a quantity? Mr. William Pomeroy states that a bottle of Courvoisier '87 was opened at Mr. Watchman's request and that the contents were served out to everyone but himself, Miss Darragh and Miss Moore. That would mean a sixth of a bottle to each of the persons who took it."

"Er—yes. Yes."

"Had you finished your brandy when you threw the dart?"

"Yes."

"Had you taken anything else previously?"

"A pint of beer," said Legge unhappily.

"N-n-n—yes. Thank you. Now where did you put the darts you used for this experiment?"

"They were new darts. Mr. Pomeroy opened the package and suggested——" Legge broke off and wetted his lips. "He suggested that I should christen the new darts," he said.

"Did you take them from Mr. Pomeroy?"

"Yes. He fitted the flights while we played round-the-clock and then gave them to me for the experiment."

"No one else handled them?"

"Mr. Will Pomeroy and Mr. Parish picked them up and looked at them."

"I see. Now for the sequel, Mr. Legge."

But again Legge's story followed the others. His deposition was read to him and he signed it, making rather a slow business of writing his name. The coroner called Abel Pomeroy.

II

Abel seemed bewildered and nervous. His habitual cheerfulness had gone and he gazed at the coroner as at a recording angel of peculiar strictness. When they reached the incident of the brandy, Dr. Mordant asked Abel if he had opened the bottle. Abel said he had.

"And you served it, Mr. Pomeroy?"

"'Ess sir."

"Will you tell us from where you got the glasses and how much went into each glass?"

"'Ess sir. I got glasses from cupboard under bar. They was the best glasses. Mr. Watchman said we would kill the bottle in two halves, sir. So I served half-bottle round. 'Twas about two fingers each. Us polished that off and then they played round-the-clock, sir, and then us polished off 'tother half. 'Least, sir, I didn't take my second tot. Tell the truth, sir, I hadn't taken no more than a drop of my first round and that was enough for me. I'm not a great drinker," said old Abel innocently, "and I mostly bides by beer. But I just took a drain to please Mr. Watchman. I served out for the rest of the company 'cepting my Will and Miss Darragh and Miss Dessy—Miss Moore, sir. But I left fair drain in bottle."

"Why did you do that?"

Abel rubbed his chin and glanced uncomfortably at the other witnesses.

"Seemed like they'd had enough, sir."

"This was before the experiment with the deceased's hand, of course," said the coroner to the jury. "Yes, Mr. Pomeroy. How much was in the glasses on the second round?"

"'Bout a finger and half, sir, I reckon."

"Did you hand the drinks round yourself?"

Abel said: "I don't rightly remember. Wait a bit though. I reckon Mr. Watchman handed first round to everyone."

Abel looked anxiously at Will who nodded. "'Ess, sir. That's how 'twas."

"You must not communicate with other persons, Mr. Pomeroy, before giving your answers," said Dr. Mordant darkly. "And the second round?"

"Ah. I poured it out and left glasses on bar," said Abel thoughtfully. "Company was fairly lively by then. There was a lot of talk. I reckon each man took his own, second round. Mr. Watchman carried his over to table by dart-board."

"Would you say that at this juncture the men who had taken brandy were sober?"

"Not to say sober, sir, and not to say proper drunk. Bosky-eyed, you might say, 'cepting old George Nark and he was proper soaked. 'Ess, he was so drunk as a fish was George Nark."

Two of the jury men laughed at this and several of the public. The coroner looked about him with an air of extreme distaste and silence set in immediately.

"Is it true," said the coroner, "that you have been poison-ing rats in your garage, Mr. Pomeroy?"

Old Abel turned very white and said, "Yes."

"What did you use?"

"'Twas some stuff from the chemist."

"Yes. Did you purchase it personally?"

"No sir. It was got for me."

"By whom?"

"By Mr. Parish, sir. I axed him and he kindly fetched it. I would like to say, sir, that when he give it to me 'twas all sealed up chemist fashion."

"N-n yes. Do you know the nature of this poison?"

"I do believe, sir, it was in the nature of prussic acid. It's not marked anything but poison."

"Please tell the jury how you used this substance and when?"

Abel wetted his lips and repeated his story. He had used the rat poison on Thursday evening, the evening of Watch-man's arrival. He had taken great care and used every pre-caution. A small vessel had been placed well inside the mouth of the rat hole and some of the fluid poured into it. The hole was plugged up with rags and the bottle carefully corked.

No waste drops of the fluid had escaped. Abel had worn old gloves which he afterwards threw on the fire. He had placed the bottle in a corner cupboard in the ingle-nook. It had stood alone on the shelf and the label, "Poison" could be seen through the glass door. Every one in the house was aware of the bottle and its contents.

"We have heard that the iodine was taken from a cupboard in the ingle-nook. Was this the same cupboard?"

"'Ess fay," said Abel quickly, "but 'twasn't same shelf, sir. 'Twas in a tin box in another shelf and with a different door, but same piece of furniture."

"You fetched the iodine?"

"So I did, then, and it was snug and tight in first-aid tin same as it always is. And, axing your pardon, sir, I used a dab of that same iodine on Bob Legge's chin only that evening and there the man is as fit as a flea to bear witness."

"Quite. Thank you, Mr. Pomeroy. Call Bernard Noggins, chemist of Illington."

Mr. Bernard Noggins could have been called nothing else. His eyes watered, his face was pink, his mouth hung open, and he suffered from hay fever. He was elderly and vague, and he obviously went in great terror of the coroner. He was asked if he remembered Mr. Parish's visit to his shop. He said he did.

"Mr. Parish asked you for a rat-poison?"

"Yes. Yes, he did."

"What did you supply?"

"I—er—I had no proprietary rat-bane in stock," began Mr. Noggins miserably, "and no arsenic. So I suggested that the fumes of a cyanide preparation might prove beneficial."

"Might prove *what*?"

"Efficacious. I suggested Scheele's acid."

"You sold Mr. Parish Scheele's acid?"

"Yes. No—I—actually—I diluted—I mean I added—I mean I produced a more concentrated solution by adding K.C.N. I—er—I supplied a 50% solution. Yes."

The coroner dropped his pen and gazed at Mr. Noggins, who went on in a great hurry.

"I warned Mr. Parish. He will agree I warned him most carefully and he signed the register—every formality and precaution—most particular. Full instructions. Label."

The coroner said: "Why did you make this already lethal fluid so much more deadly?"

"Rats," said Mr. Noggins. "I mean Mr. Parish said it was for rats, and that Mr. Pomeroy had tried a commercial rat-bane without success. Mr. Parish suggested—suggested—I should——"

"Should what, Mr. Noggins?"

"That I should ginger it up a bit as he put it." Mr. Noggins in the excess of his discomfort uttered a mad little laugh. The coroner turned upon him a face sickly with disapprobation and told him he might stand down. Dr. Mordant then addressed the jury.

"I think, gentlemen, we have heard enough evidence as to fact and circumstance surrounding this affair and may now listen to the medical evidence. Dr. Shaw, if you please!"

Dr. Shaw swore himself in very briskly and, at the coroner's invitation, described the body as it was when he first saw it. The coroner's attitude of morbid introspection increased but he and Dr. Shaw seemed to understand each other pretty well.

"The eyes were wide open and the pupils widely dilated, the jaws tightly clenched——". Dr. Shaw droned on and on. Parish and Cubitt who had remained in court both looked rather sick. Legge eyed Dr. Shaw with a sort of mesmerised glare. Will Pomeroy held Decima's hand and old Abel stared at his boots. Mr. Nark, who had expected to be called, looked alternately huffy and sheepish. A large bald man who looked as if he ought to be in uniform seemed to prick up his ears. He was Superintendent Harper of the Illington Police Force.

"You have performed an autopsy?" asked the coroner.

"Yes."

"What did you find?"

"I found the blood much engorged and brilliant in colour. I found nothing unusual in the condition of the stomach. I sent the contents to be analysed however and the report has reached me. Nothing unexpected has been found. I also sent a certain quantity of the blood to be analysed."

Dr. Shaw paused.

"N-n—yes?"

"In the case of the sample of blood the analyst has found

85

definite traces of hydrocyanic acid. These traces point to the presence of at least a grain and a half of the acid in the blood stream."

"And the fatal dose?"

"One may safely say less than a grain."

"Did you send the brandy bottle and the iodine bottle which was found under the bench to the analyst?"

"Yes."

"What was the result, Dr. Shaw?"

"The test was negative. The analyst can find no trace of hydrocyanic acid in either bottle."

"And the dart?"

"The dart was also tested for traces of hydrocyanic acid." Dr. Shaw looked directly at the coroner and said crisply. "Two tests were used. The first was negative. The second positive. Indications of a very slight trace of hydrocyanic acid were found upon the dart."

III

There was only one other witness, a representative of the firm that made the darts. He stated with considerable emphasis that at no stage of their manufacture did they come in contact with any form of cyanide and that no cyanic preparation was to be found in the entire factory.

The coroner summed up at considerable length and with commendable simplicity. His manner suggested that the jury as a whole was certifiable as mentally unsound but that he knew his duty and would perform it in the teeth of stupidity. He surveyed the circumstances surrounding Watchman's death. He pointed out that the only word spoken by the deceased, the word "poisoned" overheard by one witness alone, should not weigh too heavily in the minds of the jury. In the first place the evidence might be regarded as hearsay and therefore inadmissable at any other court. In the second there was nothing to show why the deceased had uttered this word or whether his impression had been based on any actual knowledge. They might attach considerable importance to the point that the post-mortem analysis gave positive signs of the presence of some kind of cyanide in the blood. They might, while remembering the presence of a strong solution of hydrocyanic acid in the room, also note the assurance given by several of the witnesses that all reasonable precaution had been taken in the use and disposal of the bottle. They would very possibly consider that the use for domestic purposes of so dangerous a poison was extremely ill-advised. He reminded them of Watchman's idiosyncrasy for the acid. He delivered a short address on the forms in which this, the most deadly of the cerebral depressants, was usually found. He said that since hydrogen cyanide is excessively volatile the fact that none was found in the stomach did not preclude the possibility that the deceased had taken it by the mouth. He reminded them again of the expert evidence. No cyanide had been found in the brandy bottle or the iodine bottle. The fragments of the broken brandy-glass had also given a negative result in the test for cyanide but they might remember that as these fragments were extremely minute the test in this instance could not be considered conclusive. They would of course note that the point of the dart had yielded a positive result in the second test made by the analyst. This dart was new but had been handled by three persons before Mr. Legge used it. He wound up by saying that if the jury came to the conclusion that the deceased died of cyanide poisoning but that there was not enough evidence to say positively how he took the poison, they might return a verdict to this effect.

Upon this hint the jury retired for ten minutes and came back to deliver themselves, as well as they could remember them in Dr. Mordant's own words. They added a shocked and indignant remark on the subject of prussic acid in the home.

The inquest on Luke Watchman was ended and his cousin was free to bury his body.

CHAPTER SEVEN

COMPLAINT FROM A PUBLICAN

I

"SUMMER," said Chief Detective-Inspector Alleyn moodily, "is a-comyng in and my temper is a-going out. Lhude sing cuccu. I find that the length of my patience, Fox, fluctuates in an inverse ratio with the length of the days."

"Don't you like the warm weather?" asked Detective-Inspector Fox.

"Yes, Fox, but not in London. Not in the Yard. Not in the streets where one feels dirty half an hour after one has bathed. Not when one is obliged to breathe the fumes of petrol and the body-odour of those who come to make statements and remain to smell. That creature who has just left us stank abominably. However, the case is closed, which is a slight alleviation. But I don't like summer in London."

"Ah well," said Fox shifting his thirteen stone from one leg to the other, "*chacun à son goût.*"

"Your French improves."

"It ought to, Mr. Alleyn. I've been sweating at it for two years now but I can't say I feel what you might call at home with it. Give me time and I can see my way with the stuff but that's not good enough. Not nearly good enough."

"Courage, Fox. Dogged as does it. What brought you up here?"

"There's a chap came into the waiting-room an hour ago with rather a rum story, sir. They sent him along to me. I don't know that there's much in it, but I thought you might be interested."

"Why?" asked Alleyn apprehensively.

"I nearly sent him off," continued Fox who had his own way of imparting information. "I did tell him it was nothing to do with us and that he'd better go to the local Super, which is, of course, what he'll have to do anyway if there's anything in it."

"Fox," said Alleyn, "am I a Tantalus that you should hold this beaker, however unpalatable, beyond my reach? What was this fellow's story? What prevented you from following the admirable course you have outlined? And why have you come in here?"

"It's about the Watchman business."

"Oh?" Alleyn swung round in his chair. "What about it?"

"I remembered you'd taken an interest in it, Mr. Alleyn, and that deceased was a personal friend of yours."

"Well—an acquaintance."

"Yes. You mentioned that there were one or two points that were not brought out at the inquest."

"Well?"

"Well, this chap's talking about one of them. The handling of the darts."

Alleyn hesitated. At last he said. "He must go to the local people."

"I thought you might like to see him before we got rid of him."

"Who is he?"

"The pub-keeper."

"Has he come up from Devon to see us?"

"Yes, he has. He says the Super at Illington wouldn't listen to him.

"None of our game."

"I thought you might like to see him," Fox repeated.

"All right, blast you. Bring him up."

"Very good, sir," said Fox and went out.

Alleyn put his papers together and shoved them into a drawer of his desk. He noticed with distaste that the papers felt gritty and that the handle of the drawer was sticky. He wished suddenly that something important might crop up somewhere in the country, somewhere, for preference, in the South of England and his thoughts switched back to the death of Luke Watchman in Devon. He called to mind the report of the inquest. He had read it attentively.

Fox returned and stood with his hand on the door.

"In here, if you please, Mr. Pomeroy," said Fox.

Alleyn thought his visitor would have made a very good model for the portrait of an innkeeper. Abel's face was broad, ruddy, and amiable. His mouth looked as if it had only just left off smiling and was ready to break into a smile again, for all that, at the moment, he was rather childishly solemn. He wore his best suit and it sat uneasily upon him. He walked half-way across the floor and made a little bow.

"Good-afternoon, sir," said Abel.

"Good-afternoon, Mr. Pomeroy. I hear you've come all the way up from the West Country to see us."

"I have so, sir. First time since Coronation and not such a pleasant errand. I bide home-along mostly."

"Lucky man. Sit down, Mr. Pomeroy."

"Much obliged, sir."

Abel sat down and spread his hands on his knees.

"This gentleman," he said, looking at Fox, "says it do be none of your business here, sir. That's a bit of a facer. I got no satisfaction along to Illington, and I says to myself, 'I'll go up top. I'll cut through all their pettifogging, small-minded ways, and lay my case boldly before the witty brains of those masterpieces at Scotland Yard.' Seems like I've wasted time and money."

"That's bad luck," said Alleyn. "I'm sorry, but Inspector Fox is right. The Yard only takes up an outside case at the request of the local superintendent, you see. But if you'd care to tell me, unofficially, what the trouble is, I think I may invite you to do so."

"Better than nothing, sir, and thank you very kindly." Abel moistened his lips and rubbed his knees. "I'm sore troubled," he said. "It's got me under the weather. First time anything of a criminal nature has ever come my way. The Feathers has got a clean sheet, sir. Never any trouble about after-hours in my house. Us bides by the law and now it seems as how the law don't bide by we."

"A *criminal* nature?" said Alleyn.

"What else am I to think of it, sir? 'Twasn't accident! 'Twasn't neglect on my part for all they're trying to put on me."

"Suppose," said Alleyn, "we begin at the beginning, Mr. Pomeroy. You've come to see us because you've information——"

Abel opened his mouth but Alleyn went on: "—information or an opinion about the death of Mr. Luke Watchman."

"Opinion!" said Abel. "That's the word."

90

"The finding at the inquest was death by cyanide poisoning, with nothing to show exactly how it was taken."

"And a proper fidgeting suspicioning verdict it was," said Abel warmly. "What's the result? Result is George Nark, so full of silly blusteracious nonsense as an old turkeycock, going round 't Coombe with a story as how I killed Mr. Watchman along of criminal negligence with prussic acid. George Nark axing me of an evening if I've washed out glasses in my tap, because he'd prefer not to die in agony same as Mr. Watchman. George Nark talking his ignorant blusteracious twaddle to any one as is stupid enough to listen to him."

"Very irritating," said Alleyn. "Who is Mr. Nark?"

"Old fool of a farmer, sir, with more long words than wits in his yed. I wouldn't pay no attention, knowing his tongue's apt to make a laughing-stock of the man, but other people listen and it's bad for trade. I know," said Abel steadily, " I know as certain-sure as I know anything in this life, that it was no fault of mine Mr. Watchman died of poison in my private tap. Because why? So soon as us had done with that stuff in my old stables, it was corked up proper. For all there wasn't a drop of wetness on the bottle, I wiped it thorough and burned the rag. I carried it in with my own hands, sir, and put it in the cupboard. Wearing gas mask and gloves, I was, and I chucked the gloves on the fire and washed my hands afterwards. And thurr that bottle stood, sir, for twenty-four hours and if any drop of stuff came out of it, 'twas by malice and not by accident. I've axed my housekeeper and the li'l maid who works for us and neither on 'em's been near cupboard. Too mortal scared they wurr. Nor has my boy Will. And what's more, sir, the glasses Mr. Watchman and company drank from that ghastly night, was our best glasses, and I took 'em special out of cupboard under bar. Now, sir, could this poison, however deadly, get itself out of stoppered bottle, through glass door, and into tumbler under my bar? Could it? I ax you?"

"It sounds rather like a conjuring trick," agreed Alleyn with a smile.

"So it do."

"What about the dart, Mr. Pomeroy?"

"Ah!" said Abel. "Thicky dart! When George Nark

don't be saying I did for the man in his cups, he be swearing his soul away I mused up thicky dart with prussic acid. Mind this, sir, the darts wurrn't arrived when us brought in poison on Thursday night, and they wurr only unpacked five minutes before the hijus moment itself. Now!"

"Yes, they were new darts, weren't they? I seem to remember——"

"'Ess fay, and never used till then. I opened 'em up myself while company was having their last go round-the-clock. I opened 'em up on bar counter. Fresh in their London wrappings, they wurr. Mr. Parish and my boy Will, they picked 'em up and looked at 'em, casual like, and then Bob Legge, he scooped 'em up and took a trial throw with the lot. He said they carried beautiful. Then he had his shot at Mr. Watchman's hand. They wurr clean new, they darts."

"And yet," said Alleyn, "the analyst found a trace of cyanide on the dart that pierced Mr. Watchman's finger."

Abel brought his palms down with a smack on his knees.

"'Od rabbit it," he shouted, "don't George Nark stuff that thurr chunk of science down my gullet every time he opens his silly face? Lookee yurr, sir! 'Twas twenty-four hours and more, since I put bottle o' poison in cupboard. I'd washed my hands half a dozen times since then. Bar had been swabbed down. Ax yourself, how could I infectorite they darts?"

Alleyn looked at the sweaty earnest countenance before him and whistled soundlessly.

"Yes," he said at last, "it seems unlikely."

"Unlikely. It's slap down impossible."

"But——"

"If poison got on thicky dart," said Abel, "'twasn't by accident not yet by carelessness. 'Twas by malice. 'Twas with murderacious intent. Thurr!"

"But how do you account——"

"Account? Me?" asked old Abel agitatedly. "I don't. I leaves they intellectual capers to Superintendent Nicholas Harper and a pretty poor fist he do be making of it. That's why——"

"Yes, yes," said Alleyn hurriedly. "But remember that Mr. Harper may be doing more than you think. Policemen have to keep their own counsel, you see. Don't make up your mind that because he doesn't say very much——"

"It's not what he don't say, it's the silly standoffishness of what he do say. Nick Harper! Damme, I was to school with the man, and now he sits behind his desk and looks at me as if I be a fool. 'Where's your facts?' he says. 'Don't worry yourself,' he says, 'if there's anything fishy us'll fish for it.' Truth of the matter is the man's too small and ignorant for a murderous matter. Can't raise himself above the level of motor licences and after-hour trade, and more often than not he makes a muck of them. What'll come to the Feathers if this talk goes on? Happen us'll have to give up the trade, after a couple of centuries."

"Don't you believe it," said Alleyn. "We can't afford to lose our old pubs, Mr. Pomeroy, and it's going to take more than a week's village gossip to shake the trade at the Plume of Feathers. It is just a week since the inquest, isn't it? It's fresh in Mr. George Nark's memory. Give it time to die down."

"If this affair dies down, sir, there'll be a murderer unhung in the Coombe."

Alleyn raised his brows.

"You feel like that about it?"

"'Ess, I do. What's more, sir, I'll put a name to the man."

Alleyn lifted a hand but old Abel went on doggedly.

"I don't care who hears me, I'll put a name to him and that there name's Robert Legge. Now!"

II

"A very positive old article," said Alleyn when Fox returned from seeing Abel Pomeroy down the corridor.

"I can't see why he's made up his mind this chap Legge is a murderer," said Fox. "He'd only known deceased twenty-four hours. It sounds silly."

"He says Watchman gibed at Legge," said Alleyn. "I wonder if he did. And why."

"I've heard him in court often enough," said Fox. "He was a prime heckler. Perhaps it was a habit."

"I don't think so. He was a bit malicious though. He

was a striking sort of fellow. Plenty of charm and a good deal of vanity. He always seemed to me to take unnecessary trouble to be liked. But I didn't know him well. The cousin's a damn good actor. Rather like Watchman, in a way. Oh well, it's not our pidgin, thank the Lord. I'm afraid the old boy's faith in us wonderful police has been shaken."

"D'you know the Super at Illington, Mr. Alleyn?"

"Harper? Yes, I do. He was in on that arson case in South Devon in '37. Served his apprenticeship in L. Division. You must remember him."

"Nick Harper?"

"That's the fellow. Devon, born and bred. I think perhaps I'd better write and warn him about Mr. Pomeroy's pilgrimage."

"I wonder if old Pomeroy's statement's correct. I wonder if he did make a bloomer with the rat poison, and is simply trying to save his face."

"His indignation seemed to me to be supremely righteous. I fancy he thinks he's innocent."

"Somebody else may have mucked about with the bottle and won't own up," Fox speculated.

"Possible. But who'd muck about with hydrocyanic acid for the sheer fun of the thing?"

"The alternative," said Fox, "is murder."

"Is it? Well, you bumble off and brood on it. You must be one of those zealous officers who rise to the top of the profession."

"Well, sir," said Fox, "it's funny. On the face of it, it's funny."

"Run away and laugh at it, then. I'm going home, Br'er Fox."

But when Fox had gone Alleyn sat and stared at the top of his desk. At last he drew a sheet of paper towards him and began to write.

"DEAR NICK,—It's some time since we met and you'll wonder why the devil I'm writing. A friend of yours has just called on us, Abel Pomeroy of the Plume of Feathers, Ottercombe. He's in a state of injury and fury and is determined to get to the bottom of the Luke Watchman business. I tried

94

to fob him off with fair words but it wasn't a howling success and he's gone away with every intention of making things hum until you lug a murderer home to justice. I thought I'd just warn you, but you'll probably hear from him before this reaches you. Don't, for the love of Mike, think we want to butt in. How are you? I envy you your job, infuriated innkeepers and all. In this weather we suffocate at C.1.

"Yours ever,
"RODERICK ALLEYN"

Alleyn sealed and stamped this letter. He took his hat and stick from the wall, put on one glove, pulled it off again, cursed, and went to consult the newspaper files for the reports on the death of Luke Watchman.

An hour passed. It is significant that when he finally left the Yard and walked rapidly down the Embankment, his lips were pursed in a soundless whistle.

CHAPTER EIGHT

ALLEYN AT ILLINGTON

I

SUPERINTENDENT NICHOLAS HARPER to Chief Detective-Inspector Alleyn.

"Illington Police Station,
"South Devon,
8th August.

"DEAR MR. ALLEYN,—Yours of the 6th inst. to hand for which I thank you. As regards Mr. Abel Pomeroy I am very grateful for information received as per your letter as it enabled me to deal with Pomeroy more effectively, knowing the action he had taken as regards visiting C.1. For your private information we are working on the case which presents one or two features which seem to preclude possibility of accident. Well Mr. Alleyn—Rory, if you will pardon the liberty—it was nice to hear from you. I have not forgotten that arson case in '37 nor the old days in L. Division. A country Super gets a bit out of things.

" With kind regards and many thanks,
" Yours faithfully,
" N. W. HARPER, *Superintendent.*"

Part of a letter from Colonel the Hon. Maxwell Bramming-ton, Chief Constable of South Devon, to the Superintendent of the Central Branch of New Scotland Yard.

" —and on the score of the deceased's interests and activities being centred in London, I have suggested to Superintendent Harper that he consult you. In my opinion the case is some-what beyond the resources and experience of our local force. Without wishing for a moment to exceed my prerogative in this matter, I venture to suggest that as we are already acquainted with Chief Detective-Inspector Alleyn of C.1., we should be delighted if he was appointed to this case. That, however, is of course entirely for you to decide.
" I am,
" Yours faithfully,
" MAXWELL BRAMMINGTON, C. C."

" Well, Mr. Alleyn," said the Superintendent of C.1., staring at the horseshoe and crossed swords that garnished the walls of his room, "you seem to be popular in South Devon."

" It must be a case, sir," said Alleyn, "of sticking to the ills they know."

"Think so? Well, I'll have a word with the A.C. You'd better pack your bag and tell your wife."

" Certainly, sir."

" You knew Watchman, didn't you?"

" Slightly, sir. I've had all the fun of being turned inside out by him in the witness-box."

" In the Davidson case?"

" And several others."

" I seem to remember you were equal to him. But didn't you know him personally?"

" Slightly."

" He was a brilliant counsel."

96

"He was indeed."

"Well, watch your step and do us proud."

"Yes, sir."

"Taking Fox?"

"If I may."

"That's all right. We'll hear from you."

Alleyn returned to his room, collected his emergency suit-case and kit, and sent for Fox.

"Br'er Fox," he said, "this is a wish-fulfilment. Get your fancy pyjamas and your toothbrush. We catch the midday train for South Devon."

II

The branch-line from Exeter to Illington meanders amiably towards the coast. From the train windows Alleyn and Fox looked down on sunken lanes, on thatched roofs and on glossy hedgerows that presented millions of tiny mirrors to the afternoon sun. Alleyn let down the window and the scent of hot grass and leaves drifted into the stuffy carriage.

"Nearly there, Br'er Fox. That's Illington church spire over the hill and there's the glint of sea beyond."

"Very pleasant," said Fox, dabbing at his enormous face with his handkerchief. "Warm though."

"High summer, out there."

"You never seem to show the heat, Mr. Alleyn. Now I'm a warm man. I perspire very freely. Always have. It's not an agreeable habit, though they tell me it's healthy."

"Yes, Fox."

"I'll get the things down, sir."

The train changed its pace from slow to extremely slow. Beyond the window, a main road turned into a short-lived main street with a brief network of surrounding shops. The word "Illington" appeared in white stones on a grassy bank, and they drew into the station.

"There's the super," said Fox. "Very civil."

Superintendent Harper shook hands at some length. Alleyn, once as touchy as a cat, had long ago accustomed himself to official handclasps. And he liked Harper who was bald, scarlet-faced, blue-eyed, and sardonic.

"Glad to see you, Mr. Alleyn," said Harper. "Good-afternoon. Good-afternoon, Mr. Fox. I've got a car outside."

He drove them in a police Ford down the main street. They passed a Woolworth store, a departmental store, a large hotel, and a row of small shops amongst which Alleyn noticed one lebelled "Bernard Noggins, Chemist."

"Is that where Parish bought the cyanide?"

"You haven't lost any time, Mr. Alleyn," said Harper who seemed to hover on the edge of Alleyn's christian name and to funk it at the last second. "Yes, that's it. He's a very stupid sort of man, is Bernie Noggins. There's the station. The colonel will be along presently. He's in a shocking mood over this affair, but you may be able to cope with him. I thought that before we moved on to Ottercombe, you might like to see the files and have a tell," said Harper whose speech still held a tang of West Country.

"Splendid. Where are we to stay?"

"That's as you like, of course, Mr. Alleyn, but I've told that old blatherskite Pomeroy to hold himself in readiness. I thought you might prefer to be on the spot. I've warned him to say nothing about it and I think he'll have the sense to hold his tongue. No need to put anybody on the alert, is there? This car's at your service."

"Yes, but look here——"

"It's quite all right, Mr. Alleyn. I've a small two-seater we can use here."

"That sounds perfectly splendid," said Alleyn and followed Harper into the police station.

They sat down in Harper's office while he got out his files. Alleyn looked at the photographs of past superintendents, at the worn linoleum and varnished wood-work, and he wondered how many times he had sat in country police stations waiting for the opening gambit of a case that, for one reason or another, had been a little too much for the local staff. Alleyn was the youngest chief-inspector at the Central Branch of New Scotland Yard, but he was forty-three. "I'm getting on," he thought without regret. "Old Fox must be fifty, he's getting quite grey. We've done all this so many times together." And he heard his own voice as if it was the voice of another man, uttering the familiar phrases.

"I hope we won't be a nuisance to you, Nick. A case of

this sort's always a bit tiresome isn't it? Local feeling and so on."

Harper clapped a file down on his desk, threw his head back and looked at Alleyn from under his spectacles.

"Local feeling?" he said. "Local stupidity! I don't care. They work it out for themselves and get a new version every day. Old Pomeroy's not the worst, not by a long chalk. The man's got something to complain about or thinks he has. It's these other experts, George Nark and Co., that make all the trouble. Nark's written three letters to the Illington *Courier*. The first was about finger-printing. He called it the Bertillion system, of course, ignorant old ass, and wanted to know if we'd printed everyone who was there when Watchman died. So I got him round here and printed him. So he wrote another letter to the paper about the liberty of the subject and said the South Devon constabulary were a lot of Hitlers. Then Oates, the Coombe P.C., found him crawling about outside Pomeroy's garage with a magnifying glass and kicked him out. So he wrote another letter saying the police were corrupt. Then the editor, who ought to know better, wrote a damn-fool leader, and then three more letters about me appeared. They were signed, 'Vigilant,' 'Drowsy' and 'Moribund.' Then all the pressmen who'd gone away came back again. I don't care. What of it? But the C.C. began ringing me up three times a day and I got fed up and suggested he asked you and he jumped at it. There's the file."

Alleyn and Fox hastened to make sympathetic noises.

"Before we see the file," Alleyn said, "we'd very much like to hear your own views. We've looked up the report on the inquest so we've got the main outline or ought to have it."

"My views?" repeated Mr. Harper moodily. "I haven't got any. I don't think it was an accident."

"Don't you, now!"

"I don't see how it could have been. I suppose old Pomeroy bleated about his injuries when he went screeching up to the Yard. I think he's right. Far as I can see the old man did take reasonable precautions. Well, perhaps not that, the stuff ought never to have been left on the premises. But I don't see how, twenty-four hours after he'd stowed the bottle away in the cupboard, he could have infected that dart accidentally.

We've printed the cupboard. It's got his prints on it and nobody else's."

"Oh," said Alleyn, "then it isn't a case of somebody else having tampered with the bottle and been too scared to own up."

"No."

"How many sets of Pomeroy's prints are on the cupboard door?"

"Several. Four good ones on the knob. And he turned the key in the top cupboard when he put the cyanide away. His print's on the key all right and you can't do the pencil trick, for I've tried. It's a fair teaser."

"Any prints on the bottle?"

"None. But he explained he wore gloves and wiped the bottle."

"The cupboard-door's interesting."

"Is it? Well, when he opened the parcel of darts he broke the seals. I got hold of the wrapping and string. The string had only been tied once and the seals have got the shop's mark on them."

"Damn good, Nick," said Alleyn. Mr. Harper looked a little less jaundiced.

"Well, it goes to show," he admitted. "The dart was O.K. when old Pomeroy unpacked it. Then young Will and Parish handled the darts, and then Legge tried them out. Next thing—one of 'em sticks into deceased's finger and in five minutes he's a corpse."

"The inference being——?"

"God knows! They found cyanide on the dart but how the hell it got there's a masterpiece. I suppose old Pomeroy's talked Legge to you."

"Yes."

"Yes. Well, Legge had his coat off and his sleeves rolled up. Cubitt and young Pomeroy swear he took the darts with his left hand and held them point outward in a bunch while he tried them. They say he didn't wait any time at all. Just threw them into the board, said they were all right, and then waded in with his trick. You see, they were all watching Legge."

"Yes."

100

"What about the other five, Super?" asked Fox. "He used six for the trick, didn't he?"

"Meaning one of them might have contrived to smear cyanide on one dart, while they looked at the lot?"

"It doesn't make any sort of sense," said Alleyn. "How was Cubitt or young Pomeroy to know Legge was going to pink Watchman?"

"That's right," agreed Harper, relapsing. "So it must be Legge but it couldn't be Legge; so it must be accident but it couldn't be accident. Funny, isn't it?"

"Screamingly."

"The iodine bottle's all right and so's the brandy bottle."

"The brandy glass was broken?"

"Smashed to powder except the bottom and that was in about thirty pieces. They couldn't find any cyanide."

"Whereabouts on the dart was the trace of cyanide?"

"On the tip and half-way up the steel point. We've printed the dart, of course. It's got Legge's prints all over it. They've covered Abel's or anybody else's who touched it except Oates, and he kept his head and only handled it by the flight. The analyst's report is here. And all the exhibits."

"Yes. Have you fished up a motive?"

"The money goes to Parish and Cubitt. Two-thirds to Parish and one-third to Cubitt. That's excepting one or two small legacies. Parish is the next-of-kin. It's a big estate. The lawyer was as close as an oyster, but I've found out it ought to wash up at something like fifty thousand. We don't know much beyond what everybody knows. Reckon most folks have seen Sebastian Parish on the screen, and Mr. Cubitt seems to be a well-known artist. The C.C. expects the Yard to tackle that end of the stick."

"Thoughtful of him! Anyone else?"

"They've found a bit already. They've found Parish's affairs are in a muddle and he's been to the Jews. Cubitt had money in that Chain Stores Unlimited thing, that bust the other day. There's motive there all right."

"Anyone else? Pomeroy's fancy? The mysterious Legge?"

"Him? Motive? You've heard Pomeroy, Mr. Alleyn. Says deceased behaved peculiar to Legge. Chaffed him like. Well, what is there in that? It seems there was a bit of a collision between them, the day Mr. Watchman drove into the

Coombe. Day before the fatality that was. Legge's a bad driver anyway. Likely enough Mr. Watchman felt kind of irritated, and let Legge know all about it when they met again. Likely, Legge's views irritated Mr. Watchman."

"His views?"

"He's an out-and-out communist is Legge. Secretary and treasurer of the Coombe Left Movement and in with young Will and Miss Moore. Mr. Watchman seems to have made a bit of a laughing stock of the man but you don't do murder because you've been made to look silly."

"Not very often I should think. Do you know anything about Legge? He's a newcomer, isn't he?"

Harper unhooked his spectacles and laid them on his desk.

"Yes," he said, "he's foreign to these parts. We've followed up the usual routine, Mr. Alleyn, but we haven't found much. He says he came here for his health. He's opened a small banking account at Illington, three hundred and fifty pounds. He came to the Feathers ten months ago. He gets a big lot of letters, and writes a lot to all parts of the West Country and sends away a number of small packages. Seems he's agent for some stamp collecting affair. I got the name, 'Phillips Philatelic Society,' and got one of our chaps to look up the headquarters in London. Sure enough, this chap Legge's the forwarding agent for the west of England. Well, he chummed up with young Will, and about three months ago they gave him this job with the Coombe Left business. I don't mind saying I don't like the looks of the man. He's a funny chap. Unhealthy, I'd say. Something the matter with his ears. We've searched all their rooms and I found a chemist's bottle and a bit of a squirt in his. Had it tested, you bet, but it's only some muck he squirts into his beastly lug. So I returned it. Cubitt's room was full of his painting gear. We found oil, and turpentine and varnish. Went through the lot. Of course we didn't expect to find anything. Parish," said Harper in disgust, "uses scent. Well, not to say scent, but some sort of toilet water. No, I don't mind saying I don't like the looks of Legge, but there again Miss Moore says Mr. Watchman told her he'd never set eyes on the man before."

"Well," said Alleyn, "let's go through the list while we're at it. What about young Pomeroy?"

"Will? Yes. Yes, there's young Will." Harper opened the file and stared at the first page, but it seemed to Alleyn that he was not reading it. "Will Pomeroy," said Harper, "says he didn't like Mr. Watchman. He makes no bones about it. Mr. Parish says they quarrelled on account of this chap Legge. Will didn't like the way Mr. Watchman got at Legge, you see, and being a hot-headed loyalist kind of fellow, he tackled Mr. Watchman. It wasn't much of an argument, but it was obvious Will Pomeroy had taken a scunner on Mr. Watchman."

"And—what is the lady's name? Miss Decima Moore. What about her?"

"Nothing. Keeps company with Will. She's a farmer's daughter. Old Jim Moore up to Cary Edge. Her mother's a bit on the classy side. Foreigner to these parts and can't forget she came down in society when she married Farmer Moore. Miss Decima was educated at Oxford and came home a red leftist. She and deceased used to argufy a bit about politics, but that's all."

Alleyn counted on his long thin fingers.

"That's five," he said, "six counting old Pomeroy. We're left with the Honourable Violet Darragh and Mr. George Nark."

"You can forget 'em," rejoined Harper. "The Honourable Violet's a rum old girl from Ireland, who takes views in paints. She was there writing letters when it happened. I've checked up on her and she's the genuine article. She'll talk the hind leg off a donkey. So'll George Nark. He's no murderer. He's too damned silly to kill a woodlouse except he treads on it accidental."

"How many of these people are still at Ottercombe?"

"All of 'em."

"Good Lord!" Alleyn exclaimed, "didn't they want to get away when it was all over? I'd have thought——"

"So would anybody," agreed Harper. "But it seems Mr. Cubitt had started off on several pictures down there and wants to finish them. One's a likeness of Mr. Parish so he's stayed down-along too. They waited for the funeral which was here. Deceased had no relatives nearer than Mr. Parish and Mr. Parish said he thought his cousin would have liked to be put away in the country. Several legal gentlemen came

103

down from London and the flowers were a masterpiece. Well, they just stopped on, Mr. Cubitt painting as quiet as you please. He's a cool customer, is Mr. Cubitt."

"How much longer will they be here?"

"Reckon another week. They came for three. Did the same thing last year. It's a fortnight to-night since this case cropped up. We've kept the private bar shut up. Everything was photographed and printed. There was nothing of interest in deceased's pockets. He smoked some outlandish kind of cigarettes. Daha—something, but that's no use. We've got his movements taped out. Arrived on Thursday night and didn't go out. Friday morning, went for a walk, but don't know exactly where, except it was through the tunnel. Friday afternoon, went upstairs after lunch and was in his room writing letters. Seen in his room by Mrs. Ives, the housekeeper, who went up at 3.30 to shut windows and found him asleep on his bed. Also seen at four o'clock by Mr. Cubitt who looked in on his way back from painting down on the wharf. Came downstairs at 5.15 or thereabouts and was in the private bar from then onwards till he died. I don't think I missed anything."

"I'm sure you didn't."

"You know," said Harper warming a little, "it's a proper mystery, this case. Know what I mean, most cases depend on routine. Boil 'em down and it's routine that does the trick as a general rule. May do it here, but all the same this is a teaser. I'm satisfied it wasn't accident but I can't prove it. When I'm told on good authority that there was cyanide on that dart, and that Mr. Watchman died of cyanide in his blood, I say 'well, there's your weapon,' but alongside of this there's six people, let alone my own investigation, that prove to my satisfaction nobody could have tampered with the dart. But the dart was poisoned. Now, the stuff in the rat hole was in a little china jar. I've left it there for you to see. I got another jar of the same brand. They sell some sort of zinc ointment in them and Abel had several; he's mad on that sort of thing. Now the amount that's gone from the bottle, which Noggins says was full, is a quarter of an ounce more than the amount the jar holds and Abel swears he filled the jar. The jar was full when we saw it."

"Full?" said Alleyn sharply. "When did you see it?"

"The next morning."

"Was the stuff in the jar analysed?"

Harper turned brick-red.

"No," he said. "Abel swore he'd filled it and the jar's only got his prints on it. And, I tell you, it *was* full."

"Have you got the stuff?"

"Yes. I poured it off and kept it. Seeing there's a shortage the stuff on the dart must have come from the bottle."

"For how long was the bottle uncorked?"

"What? Oh, he said that when he used it he uncorked the bottle and put it on the shelf above the hole, with the cork beside it. He was very anxious we should know he'd been careful, and he said he didn't want to handle the cork more than was necessary. He said he was just going to pour the stuff in the jar when he thought he'd put the jar in position first. He did that and then filled it, holding the torch in his other hand. He swears he didn't spill any and he swears nobody touched the bottle. The others were standing in the doorway."

"So the bottle may have been uncorked for a minute or two?"

"I suppose so. He plugged up the hole with rag before he did anything else. He had the bottle on the floor beside him."

"And then?"

"Well, then he took up the bottle and corked it. I suppose," said Harper, "I should have had the stuff analysed but we've no call to suspect Abel Pomeroy. There was none missing from the jar and there are only his prints on it, and there's the extra quarter ounce missing from the bottle. No, it's gone from the bottle. Must have. And, see here, Mr. Alleyn, the stuff was found on the dart and nowhere else. What's more, if it was the dart that did the trick and it's murder, then Legge's our bird because only Legge controlled the flight of the dart."

"Silly sort of way to kill a man," said Fox, suddenly. "It'd be asking for a conviction, Super, now wouldn't it?"

"Maybe he reckoned he'd get a chance to wipe the dart," said Harper.

"He had his chance," said Alleyn quickly. "Wasn't it

brought out that Legge helped the constable—Oates isn't it?
—to find the dart? He had his chance, then, to wipe it."

"And if he was guilty, why didn't he?" ended Fox.

"You're asking *me*," said Superintendent Harper. "Here's
the colonel."

III

The chief constable was an old acquaintance of Alleyn's.
Alleyn liked Colonel Brammington. He was a character, an
oddity, full of mannerisms that amused rather than irritated
Alleyn. He was so unlike the usual county-minded chief
constable that it was a matter for conjecture how he ever got
the appointment, for he spent half his life in giving offence
and was amazingly indiscreet. He arrived at Illington Police
Station in a powerful racing car that was as scarred as a
veteran. It could be heard from the moment it entered the
street and Harper exclaimed agitatedly :

"Here he comes! He knows that engine's an offence
within the meaning of the Act and he doesn't care. He'll get
us all into trouble one of these days. There are complaints
on all sides. On all sides!"

The screech of heavy tyres and violent braking announced
Colonel Brammington's arrival and in a moment he came in.
He was a vast red man with untidy hair, prominent eyes, and
a loud voice. The state of his clothes suggested that he'd
been dragged by the heels through some major disaster.

He shouted an apology at Harper, touched Alleyn's hand
as if it was a bomb, stared at Fox, and then hurled himself
into a seagrass chair with such abandon that he was like to
break it.

"I should have been here half an hour ago," shouted
Colonel Brammington, "but for my car, my detestable, my
abominable car."

"What was the matter, sir?" asked Harper.

"My good Harper, I have no notion. Fortunately I was
becalmed near a garage. The fellow thrust his head among
her smoking entrails, uttered some mumbo-jumbo, performed
suitable rites with oil and water, and I was enabled to
continue."

He twisted his bulk in the creaking chair and stared at Alleyn.

"Perfectly splendid that you have responded with such magnificent celerity to our *cri du cœur*, Alleyn. We shall now resume, thankfully, the upholstered leisure of the not too front, front stall."

"Don't be too sure of that, sir," said Alleyn. "It looks as if there's a weary grind ahead of us."

"O God, how insupportably dreary! What, hasn't the solution been borne in upon you in a single penetrating flash? Pray expect no help from me. Have you got a cigarette, Harper?"

Alleyn offered his case.

"Thank you. I haven't even a match, I'm afraid. Ah, thank you." Colonel Brammington lit his cigarette and goggled at Alleyn. "I suppose Harper's given you the whole tedious rigmarole," he said.

"He's given me the file. I suggest that Fox and I take it with us to Ottercombe and digest it."

"O Lord! Yes, do. Yes, of course. But you've discussed the case?"

"Yes, sir. Mr. Harper has given me an excellent survey of the country."

"It's damned difficult country. Now, on the face of it, what's your opinion, accident or not?"

"On the face of it," said Alleyn, "not."

"O Lord!" repeated Colonel Brammington. He got up with surprising agility from his tortured chair, and moved restlessly about the room. "Yes," he said, "I agree with you. The fellow was murdered. And of all the damned unconscionable methods of despatching a man! An envenom'd stuck, by God! How will you hunt it home to this fellow?"

"Which fellow, sir?"

"The murderer, my dear man. Legge! A prating soap-box orator of a fellow, I understand; some squalid little trouble-hatcher. Good God, my little Alleyn, of course he's your man! I've said so from the beginning. There was cyanide on the dart. He threw the dart. He deliberately pinked his victim."

"Harper," said Alleyn with a glance at the superintendent's shocked countenance, "tells me that several of the others agree that Legge had no opportunity to anoint the dart with cyanide or anything else."

"Drunk!" cried Colonel Brammington. "Soaked in a damn' good brandy, the lot of 'em. My opinion."

"It's possible, of course."

"It's the only answer. My advice, for what it's worth is, haul him in for manslaughter. Ought to have been done at first only that drooling old pedagogue Mordant didn't put it to the jury. However, you must do as you think best."

"Thank you, sir," said Alleyn gravely. Brammington grinned.

"The very pine-apple of politeness," he quoted. "Come and dine with me to-morrow. Both of you."

"May I ring up?"

"Yes, yes," said Colonel Brammington impatiently. "Certainly."

He hurried to the door as if overcome by an intolerable urge to move on somewhere. In the doorway he turned.

"You'll come round to my view," he said, "I'll be bound you will."

"At the moment, sir," said Alleyn, "I have no view of my own."

"Run him in on the minor charge," added Colonel Brammington, raising his voice to a penetrating shout as he disappeared into the street, "and the major charge will follow as the night the day."

A door slammed and in a moment the violence of his engines was reawakened.

"Well now," said Alleyn. "I wonder."

CHAPTER NINE

ALLEYN AT THE FEATHERS

I

THE sun had nearly set when Alleyn and Fox drove down Ottercombe Road towards the tunnel. As the car mounted a last rise they could see Coombe Head, a quarter of a mile away across open hills. So clear was the evening that they caught a glint of gold where the surf broke into jets of foam against the sunny rocks. Alleyn slowed down and they saw the road sign at the tunnel entrance.

"Ottercombe. Dangerous corner. Change down."

"So I should think," muttered Alleyn, as the sheer drop appeared on the far side. He negotiated the corner and there, at the bottom of the steep descent, was the Plume of Feathers and Ottercombe.

"By George," said Alleyn, "I don't wonder Cubitt comes here to paint. It's really charming, Fox, isn't it? A concentric design with the pub as its axis. And there, I fancy, is our friend Pomeroy."

"On the lookout, seemingly," said Fox.

"Yes. Look at the colour of the sea, you old devil. Smell that jetty-tar-and-iodine smell, blast your eyes. Fox, murder or no murder, I'm glad we came."

"As long as you're pleased, sir," said Fox, dryly.

"Don't snub my ecstasies, Br'er Fox. Good-evening, Mr. Pomeroy."

Abel hurried forward and opened the door.

"Good-evening, Mr. Alleyn, sir. We'm glad to see you. Welcome to the Feathers, sir."

He used the same gestures, almost the same words as those with which he had greeted Watchman fourteen days ago. And Alleyn, if he had realised it, answered as Watchman had answered.

"We're glad to get here," he said.

"Will!" shouted old Abel. "Will!"

And Will, tall, fox-coloured, his eyes screwed up in the sunlight, came out and opened the back of the car. He was followed by a man whom Alleyn recognised instantly. He was nearly as striking off the stage as on it. The walk was unmistakable; the left shoulder raised very slightly, the long graceful stride, imitated, with more ardour than discretion, by half the young actors in London.

The newcomer glanced at Alleyn and Fox and walked past the car.

"Another marvellous evening, Mr. Pomeroy," he said airily.

"So 'tis, then, Mr. Parish," said Abel.

Alleyn and Fox followed Will Pomeroy into the Feathers. Abel brought up the rear.

"Show the rooms, sonny. There are the gentlemen we're expecting. They're from London. From Scotland Yard," said Abel.

Will Pomeroy gave them a startled glance.

"Move along, sonny," said Abel. "This way, sir. Us'll keep parlour for your private use, Mr. Alleyn, in case so be you fancy a bit of an office like."

"That sounds an excellent arrangement," said Alleyn.

"Have you had supper, sir?"

"Yes, thank you, Mr. Pomeroy. We had it with Mr. Harper."

"I wonder," said Abel unexpectedly, "that it didn't turn your stomachs back on you, then."

"This way, please," said Will.

They followed Will up the steep staircase. Abel stood in the hall looking after them.

The Feathers, like all old buildings, had its own smell. It smelt of wallpaper, driftwood smoke, and very slightly of beer. Through the door came the tang of the waterfront to mix with the house-smell. The general impression was of coolness and seclusion. Will showed them two small bedrooms whose windows looked over Ottercombe Steps and the chimney-tops of Fish Lane, to the sea. Alleyn took the first of these rooms and Fox the second.

"The bathroom's at the end of the passage," said Will from Alleyn's doorway. "Will that be all?"

"We shall be very comfortable," said Alleyn, and as Will moved away he added: "You're Mr. Pomeroy's son?"

"Yes," said Will stolidly.

"I expect Mr. Harper has explained why we are here."

Will nodded and said nothing.

"I'd be very glad," added Alleyn, "if you could spare me a minute or two later on."

Will said, "I'll be serving in the bar all the evening."

"I'll see you there, then. Thank you."

But Will didn't move. He stared at the window and said, "This affair's upset my father. He takes it to heart, like; the talk that goes on."

"I know."

"I reckon he's right about it being no accident."

"Do you?"

"Yes. Nobody touched the bottle by mistake—'tisn't likely."

"Look here," said Alleyn, "can you spare a moment now to show me the rat-hole in the garage?"

Will's eyelashes flickered.

"Yes," he said, "reckon I can do that." He shifted his weight from one foot to the other, and added with a kind of truculence. "Reckon when the police come in, there's not much use in refusing. Not unless you've got a pull somewhere."

"Oh come," Alleyn said mildly, "we're not as corrupt as all that, you know."

Will's face turned scarlet but he said doggedly, "It's not the men, it's the system. It's the way everything is in this country."

"One law," suggested Alleyn amiably, "for the rich, and so on?"

"It's true enough."

"Well, yes. In many ways I suppose it is. However, I'm not open to any bribery at the moment. We always try to be honest for the first few days, it engenders confidence. Shall we go down to the garage?"

"It's easy enough," Will said, "to make the truth look silly. A man never seems more foolish-like than he does when he's speaking his whole mind and heart. I know that."

"Yes," agreed Alleyn, "that's quite true. I dare say the

apostles were as embarrassing in their day, as the street-orator with no audience is in ours."

"I don't know anything about that. They were only setting up a superstition. I'm dealing with the sober truth."

"That's what I hope to do myself," said Alleyn. "Shall we join the rats?"

Will led Alleyn across the yard to the old stables. A small evening breeze came in from the sea, lifting Alleyn's hair and striking chill through his tweed coat. Gulls circled overhead. The sound of men's voices drifted up from the waterfront.

"It'll be dark in-along," said Will.

"I've got a torch."

"The rat-hole's not in the proper garage, like. It's in one of the old loose-boxes. It's locked and we haven't got the key. Harper's men did that."

"Mr. Harper gave me the key," said Alleyn.

The old loose-box doors had been padlocked, and sealed with police tape. Alleyn broke the tape and unlocked them.

"I wonder," he said, "if you'd mind asking Mr. Fox to join me. He's got a second torch. Ask him to bring my case."

"Yes," said Will, and after a fractional pause, "sir."

Alleyn went into the stable. It had been used as an extra garage but there was no car in it now. Above the faint reek of petrol oozed another more disagreeable smell, sweetish and nauseating. The cyanide, thought Alleyn, had evidently despatched at least one rat. The place was separated from the garage-proper, an old coach-house, by a semi-partition; but the space between the top of the partition and the roof had recently been boarded up, and Alleyn awarded Harper a good mark for attention to detail. Harper, he knew had also taken photographs of the rat-hole and tested the surrounding walls and floor for prints. He had found dozens of these.

Alleyn flashed his torch round the bottom of the walls and discovered the rat-hole. He stooped down. Harper had removed the rag and jar, tested them for prints, and found Abel's. He had then drained off the contents of the jar and replaced it. There was the original rag stuffed tight in the hole. Alleyn pulled it out and the smell of dead rat became very strong indeed. The ray of light glinted on a small jar.

112

It was less than an inch in diameter and about half an inch deep.

Fox loomed up in the doorway. He said:

"Thank you, Mr. Pomeroy, I'll find my way in."

Will Pomeroy's boots retreated across the cobble-stones.

"Look here, Br'er Fox," said Alleyn.

A second circle of light flickered on the little vessel. Fox peered over Alleyn's shoulder.

"And it was full," said Fox.

"Yes," said Alleyn. "That settles it, I fancy."

"How d'you mean, sir."

"It's a case of murder."

II

The parlour of the Feathers is the only room in the house that is generally uninhabited. For the usual patrons, the private tap is the common room. The parlour is across the side passage and opposite the public tap-room. It overlooks Ottercombe Steps and beneath its windows are the roofs of the Fish Lane houses. It has a secret and deserted life of its own. Victoria's Jubilee and Edward the Seventh's wedding face each other across a small desert of linoleum and plush. Above the mantelpiece hangs a picture of two cylindrical and slug-like kittens. Upon the mantelpiece are three large shells. A rag-rug, lying in front of the fireplace, suggests that in a more romantic age Harlequin visited the Feathers and sloughed his skin before taking a leap up the chimney.

For Alleyn's arrival the parlour came to life. Someone had opened the window and placed a bowl of flowers on the plush-covered table. Abel Pomeroy hurriedly added a writing pad, a pencil, a terrible old pen and a bottle of ink. He surveyed the arrangements with an anxious smile, disappeared for a minute, and returned to ask Alleyn if there was anything else he needed.

"Two pints of beer, Mr. Pomeroy," said Alleyn, "will set me up for the rest of the evening."

Abel performed a sort of slow-motion trick with his right hand drawing away his apron to reveal a thickly cobwebbed bottle.

113

"I wonder, sir," he said, "if you'd pleasure me by trying a drop of this yurr tipple. 'Twurr laid down by my old Dad, many a year back. Sherry 'tis. 'Montillady. I did use to call 'er Amadillo afore I knew better."

"But my dear Mr. Pomeroy," said Alleyn, "this is something very extra indeed. It's a wine for the gods."

"Just what the old colonel said, sir, when I told him us had it. It would pleasure the Feathers, sir, if you would honour us."

"It's extraordinarily nice of you."

"You wurr 'straordinary nice to me, sir, when I come up to London. If you'll axcuse me, I'll get the glasses."

"It should be decanted, Mr. Pomeroy."

"So it should, then. I'll look out a decanter to-morrow, sir, and in the meanwhile us'll open the bottle."

They opened the bottle and took a glass each.

"To the shade of Edgar Allan Poe," murmured Alleyn, and raised his glass.

"The rest is yours, gentlemen," said Abel. "'Twill be set aside special. Thurr's a decanter in the Private. If so be you bain't afeard, same as George Nark, that all my bottles is full of pison, to-morrow I'll decant this yurr tipple in your honour."

Alleyn and Fox murmured politely.

"Be thurr anything else I can do, gentlemen?" asked Abel.

"We'll have a look at the private bar, Mr. Pomeroy, if we may."

"Certainly, sir, certainly, and terrible pleased us'll be to have her opened up again. 'Tis like having the corpse itself on the premises, with Private shuttered up and us chaps all hugger-mugger of an evening in Public. Has His Royal Highness the Duke of Muck condescended to hand over the keys, sir?"

"What? Oh—yes I have the keys."

"Nick Harper!" said Abel, "with his fanciful blown-up fidgeting ways. Reckon the man laces his boots with red tape. This way if you please, gentlemen, and watch yourselves for the step. 'Dallybuttons, Nick,' I said to him, 'You've aimed your camera and blowed thicky childish li'l squirter over every inch of my private tap, you've lain on your belly and scraped the muck off the floor. What do 'ee want,' I said! 'Do 'ee fancy the corpse will hant the place and write murderer's name in the dust?' I axed him. This is the door, sir."

Alleyn produced his bunch of keys and opened the door.

The private tap had been locked up by Oates a fortnight ago, and reopened by Harper and his assistants only for purposes of investigation. The shutter over the bar counter had been drawn down and locked. The window shutters also were fastened. The place was in complete darkness.

Abel switched on the light.

It was a travesty of the private tap that Alleyn saw. The comfort and orderliness of its habitual aspect were quite gone. It had suffered such a change as might overtake a wholesome wench turned drab in a fortnight. Dust covered the tables, settles, and stools. The butt ends of cigarettes strewed the floor, tobacco ash lay everywhere in small patches and trails. The open hearth was littered with ashes of the fire that had warmed Watchman on the night he died. Five empty tumblers were stained with the dregs of Curvoisier '87, two with the dregs of the ginger-beer. Of the eighth glass such powdered fragments as had escaped Harper's brush, crunched jarringly underfoot. The room smelt indescribably stale and second-rate.

"It do gall me uncommon," said Abel, "for my private taproom to display itself in thicky shocking state."

"Never mind, Mr. Pomeroy," said Alleyn, "we're used to it, you know."

He stood just inside the door with Fox at his shoulder. Abel watched them anxiously but it is doubtful if he remarked the difference in their attitudes. Fox's eyes, light grey in colour, brightened and sharpened as he looked about the room. But Alleyn might have been a guest in the house, and with no more interest than politeness might allow his gaze shifted casually from one dust-covered surface to another.

After a few minutes, however, he could have given a neat drawing, with nice attention to detail, of the private taproom. He noticed the relative positions of the dart-board, the bar and the settle. He paid attention to the position of the lights, and remarked that the spot, chalked on the floor by Oates, where Legge had stood when he threw the darts, was immediately under a strong lamp. He saw that there was a light switch inside the door and another by the mantelpiece. He walked over to the corner cupboard.

"Nick Harper," said Abel, "took away that theer cursed pison bottle. He took away the bits of broken glass and brandy bottle and iodine bottle. He took away the new darts, all six on 'em. All Nick Harper left behind is dirt and smell. Help yourself to either of 'em."

"Don't go just yet," said Alleyn. "We want your help, Mr. Pomeroy, if you'll give it to us."

"Ready and willing," Abel said with emphasis. "I'm ready and willing to do all I can. By my way of thinking you two gentlemen are here to clear my name, and I be mortal set on that scheme."

"Right. Now will you tell me, as well as you can remember, where everybody stood at the moment when you poured out the second round of brandies. Can you remember? Try to call up the picture of this room as it was a fortnight ago to-night."

"I can call it to mind right enough," said Abel slowly. "I been calling it to mind every night and a mighty number of times every night, since that ghassley moment. I was behind bar——"

"Let's have those shutters away," said Alleyn.

Fox unlocked the shutters and rolled them up. The private tap proper was discovered. A glass door, connecting the two bars, was locked and through it Alleyn could see into the Public. Will Pomeroy was serving three fishermen. His shoulder was pressed against the glass door. He must have turned his head when he heard the sound of the shutters. He looked at Alleyn through his eyelashes and then turned away.

Alleyn examined the counter in the private tap. It was stained with dregs fourteen days old. Abel pointed to a lighter ring.

"Thurr's where brandy-bottle stood," he said. "'Ess fay, thurr's where she was, sure enough."

"Yes. Now, where were the people? You say you stood behind the bar?"

"'Ess, and young Will was in corner 'twixt bar and dartboard. Rest of 'em had just finished round-the-clock. Bob Legge had won. They used the old darts and when he ran home he put 'em back in that thurr wooden rack by board.

116

Yurr they be. Nick Harper come over generous," said Abel with irony, "and left us they old darts. He collared the new 'uns."

"Ah yes," said Alleyn hurriedly. "What about the rest of the party?"

"I'm telling you, sir. Chap Legge'd won the bout. Mr. Watchman says, 'By God it's criminal, Legge. Men have been jailed for less,' he says in his joking way. 'Come on,' he says, 'Us'll have t'other half,' he says, 'and then, be George, if I don't let 'ee have a go at my hand.' He says it joking, sir, but to my mind Mr. Watchman knew summat about Legge and to my mind Legge didn't like it."

Abel glanced through the glass door at Will, but Will's back was turned. The three customers gaped shamelessly at Alleyn and Fox.

"Well now," Abel went on, lowering his voice, "Legge paid no 'tention to Mr. Watchman 'cept to say casual-like 'I'll do it all right, but don't try it if you feel nervous,' which wurr very wittest manner of speech the man could think of to egg on Mr. Watchman, to set his fancy hellbent on doing it. 'Ess, Legge egged the man on, did Legge. That's while he was putting away old darts. Then he moved off, tantalising, to t'other end of room. T'other ladies and gentlemen was round bar, 'cepting Miss Darragh, who was setting with her writing in ingle-nook. Thurr's her glass on 't old settle, sir. Stone-ginger, she had. Miss Dessy, that's Miss Moore, sir, she was setting on the bar, in the corner yurr swinging her legs. That'll be her glass on the ledge thurr. Stone-ginger. The three gentlemen, they wurr alongside bar. Mr. Cubitt next Miss Dessy, then Mr. Watchman and then Mr. Parish. I 'member that, clear as daylight, along of Miss Darragh making a joke about 'em. 'Three graces,' she called 'em, being a fanciful kind of middle-aged lady."

"That leaves Mr. George Nark."

"So it does then, the silly old parrot. 'Ess. George Nark wurr setting down by table inside of door, laying down the law as is the foolish habit of the man. Well now, I poured out the second tots beginning with Mr. Cubitt. Then Mr. Watchman and then Mr. Parish. Then George Nark brings his glass over with his tongue hanging out and insults t'murdered gentleman by axing for soda in this masterpiece

117

of a tipple, having nigh-on suffercated hisself with first tot, golloping it down ferocious. No sooner does he swallow second tot than he's proper blind tipsy. 'Ess, so soused as a herring wurr old George Nark. Lastly, sir, Mr. Watchman gets Legge's glass from mantelshelf and axes me to pour out the second tot."

"Leaving his own glass on the bar between Mr. Parish and Mr. Cubitt?"

"'Ess. Legge wurr going to wait till after he'd done his trick. Us knows what wurr in the evil thoughts of the man. He wanted to keep his eye in so's he could stick Mr. Watchman with thicky murderous dart."

"Mr. Pomeroy," said Alleyn, "I must warn you against making statements of that sort. You might land yourself in a very pretty patch of trouble, you know. What happened next? Did you pour out Mr. Legge's brandy for him?"

"'Ess, I did. And Mr. Watchman tuk it to him saying he'd have no refusal. Then Mr. Watchman tuk his own dram over to table by dart-board. He drank 'er down slow and then says he, 'Now for it!'"

"And had Mr. Legge been anywhere near Mr. Watchman's glass?"

Abel looked mulish. "No, sir, no. Not azacly. Not at all. He drank his over in ingle-nook opposite Miss Darragh. 'Twasn't then the mischief wurr done, Mr. Alleyn."

"Well," said Alleyn, "we shall see. Now for the accident itself."

The story of those few minutes, a story that Alleyn was to hear many times before he reached the end of this case, was repeated by Abel and tallied precisely with all the other accounts in Harper's file, and with the report of the inquest.

"Very well," said Alleyn. He paused for a moment and caught sight of Will's three customers staring with passionate interest through the glass door. He moved out of their range of vision.

"Now we come to the events that followed the injury. You fetched the iodine from that cupboard?"

"Sure enough, sir, I did."

"Will you show me what you did?"

"Certainly. Somebody—Legge 'twas—out of the depths of his hypocrasy, says, 'put a drop of iodine on it,' he says.

118

Right. I goes to thicky cupboard which Nick Harper has played the fool with, mucking round with his cameras and squirts of powder. I opens bottom door this way, and thurr on shelf is my first-aid box."

Alleyn and Fox looked at the cupboard. It was a double corner cabinet, with two glass doors one above the other. Abel had opened the bottom door. At the back of the shelf was a lidless tin, containing the usual first-aid equipment, and a very nice ship's decanter. Abel removed the decanter.

"I'll scald and scour 'er out," he said. "Us'll have your sherry in this yurr, gentlemen, and I'll join you to-morrow in fust drink to show there's no hanky-panky."

"We'll be delighted if you'll join us, Mr. Pomeroy, but I don't think we need feel any qualms."

"Ax George Nark," said Abel bitterly. "Have a tell with George Nark and get your minds pisened. I'll look after your stomachs."

Alleyn said hurriedly: "And that's the first-aid equipment?"

"That's it, sir. Bottle of iodine was laying in empty slot yurr," Abel explained. "I tuk it out and I tuk out bandage at same time."

"You should keep your first-aid box shut up, Mr. Pomeroy," said Alleyn absently.

"Door's airtight, sir."

Alleyn shone his torch into the cupboard. The triangular shelf forming the roof of the lower cupboard and the floor of the top one was made of a single piece of wood and fitted closely.

"And the bottle of prussic acid solution was in the upper cupboard?" asked Alleyn.

"'Ess, tight-corked. Nick Harper's taken——"

"Yes, I know. Was the upper door locked?"

"Key turned in lock same as it be now."

"You said at the inquest that you had used the iodine earlier in the evening."

"So I had, then. Bob Legge had cut hisself with his razor. He said he wurr shaving hisself along of going to Illington. When storm came up—it wurr a terror that thurr storm—us told Legge he'd better bide home-along. I reckon that's the only thing I've got to blame myself for. Howsumdever

119

the man came in for his pint at five o'clock, and I give him a lick of iodine and some sticking plaster."

"Are you certain, Mr. Pomeroy? It's important."

"Bible oath," said Abel. "Thurr y'are, sir. Bible oath. Ax the man hisself. I fetched out my first-aid box and give him the bottle. Ax him."

"Yes, yes. And you're certain it was at five o'clock?"

"Bob Legge," said Abel, "has been into tap for his pint *at* five o'clock every day 'cepting Sunday fur last ten months. Us opens at five in these parts and when I give him the iodine I glanced at clock and opened up."

"When you put the bottle in the top cupboard on the Thursday night you wore gloves. Did you take them off before you turned the key?"

"'Ess fay, and pitched 'em on fire. Nick Harper come down off of his high horse furr enough to let on my finger marks is on key. Don't that prove it?"

"It does indeed," said Alleyn.

Fox, who had been completely silent, now uttered a low growl.

"Yes, Fox?" asked Alleyn.

"Nothing, Mr. Alleyn."

"Well," said Alleyn, "we've almost done. We now come to the brandy Miss Moore poured out of the Courvoisier bottle into Watchman's empty glass. Who suggested he should have brandy?"

"I'm not certain-sure, sir. I b'lieve Mr. Parish first, and then Miss Darragh, but I wouldn't swear to her."

"Would you swear that nobody had been near Mr. Watchman's glass between the time he took his second nip and the time Miss Moore gave him the brandy?"

"Not Legge," said Abel thoughtfully. And then with that shade of reluctance with which he coloured any suggestion of Legge's innocence, "Legge wurr out in middle o' floor afore dart-board. Mr. Watchman stood atween him and table wurr t' glass stood. Mr. Parish walked over to look at Mr. Watchman spreading out his fingers. All t'others stood hereabouts behind Legge. No one else went anigh t' glass."

"And after the accident? Where was everybody then?"

"Crowded round Mr. Watchman. Will stepped out of corner. I come through under counter. Miss Darragh stood anigh us and Dessy by Will. Legge stood staring where he wurr. Reckon Mr. Parish did be closest still to glass, but he stepped forward when Mr. Watchman flopped down on settle. I be a bit mazed-like wurr they all stood. I disremember."

"Naturally enough. Would you say anybody could have touched that glass between the moment when the dart struck and the time Miss Moore poured out the brandy?"

"I don't reckon anybody could," said Abel, but his voice slipped a half-tone and he looked profoundly uncomfortable.

"Not even Mr. Parish."

Abel stared over Alleyn's head and out of the window. His lower lip protruded and he looked as mulish as a sulky child.

"Maybe he could," said Abel, "but he didn't."

CHAPTER TEN

THE TUMBLER AND THE DART

I

"WE may as well let him have this room," said Alleyn, when Abel had gone. "Harper's done everything possible in the way of routine."

"He's a very thorough chap, is Nick Harper."

"Yes," agreed Alleyn. "Except in the matter of the rat-hole jar. However, Fox, we'll see if we can catch him out before we let the public in. Let's prowl a bit."

They prowled for an hour. They kept the door locked and closed the bar shutters. Dim sounds of toping penetrated from the public taproom. Alleyn had brought Harper's photographs and they compared these with the many chalk marks Harper had left behind him. A chalk mark under the settle showed where the iodine bottle had rolled. The plot of the bottle of Scheele's Acid was marked in the top cupboard. The shelves of the corner cupboard were very dusty and the trace left by the bottle showed clearly. Alleyn turned to the fireplace.

"He hasn't sifted the ashes, Br'er Fox. We may as well do that, I think."

Fox fetched a small sieve from Alleyn's case. The ashes at first yielded nothing of interest, but in the last handful they found a small misshapen object which Alleyn dusted and took to the light.

"Glass," he said. "They must have had a good fire. It's melted and gone all bobbly. There's some more. Broken glass half melted by the fire."

"They probably make the fire up on the old ashes," said Fox. "It may have lain there through two or three fires."

"Yes, Fox. And then again it may not. I wonder if those fragments of the brandy glass were complete. This has been a thickish piece, I should say."

"A bit of the bottom?"

"We'll have to find out. You never know. Where was the broken glass?"

The place where most of the broken glass had been found was marked on the floor.

"O careful Mr. Harper!" Alleyn sighed. "But it doesn't get us much farther, I'm afraid. Fox, I'm like to get in a muddle over this. You must keep me straight. You know what an ass I can make of myself. No"; as Fox looked amiably sceptical. "No, I mean it. There are at least three likely pitfalls. I wish to heaven they hadn't knocked over that glass and trampled it to smithereens."

"D'you think there was cyanide in the glass, Mr. Alleyn?"

"God bless us, Fox, I don't know. I don't know, my dear old article. How can I? But it would help a lot if we *could* know one way or the other. Finding none on those tiny pieces isn't good enough."

"At least," said Fox, "we know there was cyanide on the dart. And knowing that, sir, and ruling out accident, I must say I agree with old Pomeroy. It looks like Legge."

"But how the devil could Legge put prussic acid on the dart with eight people all watching him? He was standing under the light, too."

"He felt the points," said Fox without conviction.

"Get along with you, Foxkins. Prussic acid is extremely volatile. Could Legge dip his fingers in the acid and then wait a couple of hours or so—with every hope of giving himself a poisoned hand? He'd have needed a bottle of the stuff about him."

"He may have had one. He may be a bit of a conjurer. Legerdemain," added Fox.

"Well—he may. We'll have to find out."

Alleyn lit a cigarette and sat down.

"Let's worry it out," he said. "May I talk? And when I go wrong, Fox, you stop me."

"It's likely then," said Fox, dryly, "to be a monologue. But go ahead, sir, if you please."

Alleyn went ahead. His pleasant voice ran on and on and a kind of orderliness began to appear. The impossible, the possible, and the probable were sorted into groups, and from the kaleidoscopic jumble of evidence was formed a pattern.

"Imperfect," said Alleyn, "but at least suggestive."

"Suggestive, all right," Fox said. "And if it's correct the case, in a funny sort of way, still hinges on the dart."

"Yes," agreed Alleyn. "The bare bodkin. The feathered quarrel and all that. Well, Fox, we've wallowed in speculation and now we'd better get on with the job. I think I hear Pomeroy senior in the public bar so presumably Pomeroy junior is at liberty. Let's remove to the parlour."

"Shall I get hold of young Pomeroy?"

"In a minute. Ask him to bring us a couple of pints. You'd better not suggest that he joins us in a drink. He doesn't like us much, and I imagine he'd refuse, which would not be the best possible beginning."

Alleyn wandered into the ingle-nook, knocked out his pipe on the hearthstone and then stooped down.

"Look here, Fox."

"What's that, sir?"

"Look at this log-box."

Fox bent himself at the waist and stared into a heavy wooden box in which Abel kept his pieces of driftwood and the newspaper used for kindling. Alleyn pulled out a piece of paper and took it to the light.

"It's been wet," observed Fox.

"Very wet. Soaked. It was thrust down among the bits of wood. A little pool has lain in the pocket. Smell it."

Fox sniffed vigorously. "Brandy?" he asked.

123

"Don't know. Handle it carefully, Br'er Fox. Put it away in your room and then get Pomeroy junior."

Alleyn returned to the parlour, turned on the red-shaded lamp and settled himself behind the table.

Fox came in followed by Will Pomeroy. Will carried two pint pots of beer. He set them down on the table.

"Thank you," said Alleyn. "Can you spare us a moment?"

"Yes."

"Sit down, won't you?"

Will hesitated awkwardly, and then chose the least comfortable chair and sat on the extreme edge. Fox took out his note-book and Will's eyes flickered. Alleyn laid three keys on the table.

"We may return these now, I think," he said. "I'm sure you'll be glad to see the Plume of Feathers set right again."

"Thanks," said Will. He stretched out his hand and took the keys.

"The point we'd like to talk about," said Alleyn, "is the possibility of the dart that injured Mr. Watchman being tainted with the stuff used for rat poison—the acid kept in the corner cupboard of the private tap. Now, your father——"

"I know what my father's been telling you," interrupted Will, "and I don't hold with it. My father's got a damn' crazy notion in his head."

"What notion is that?" asked Alleyn.

Will looked sharply at him, using that trick of lowering his eyelashes. He did not answer.

"Do you mean that your father's ideas about Mr. Robert Legge are crazy."

"That's right. Father's got his knife into Bob Legge because of his views. There's no justice nor sense in what he says. I'll swear, Bible oath, Bob Legge never interfered with the dart. I'll swear it before any judge or jury in the country."

"How can you be so positive?"

"I was watching the man. I was in the corner between the dart-board and the bar. I was watching him."

"All the time? From the moment the darts were unpacked until he threw them?"

"Yes," said Will doggedly. "All the time."

124

" Why?"

" Eh?"

" Why did you watch him so closely?"

" Because of what the man was going to do. We all watched him."

" Suppose," said Alleyn, "that for the sake of argument I told you we knew positively that Mr. Legge, while he held the darts in his left hand, put his right hand in his pocket for a moment——"

" I'd say it was a lie. He didn't. He never put his hand in his pocket."

" What makes you so positive, Mr. Pomeroy?"

" For one thing he was in his shirt sleeves."

" What about his waistcoat and trousers' pockets?"

" He hadn't a waistcoat. His sleeves was rolled up and I was watching his hands. They never went near his trousers' pockets. He held the darts in his left hand and I was watching the way he felt the points, delicate like, with the first finger of his other hand. He was saying they was right-down good darts; well made and well balanced." Will leant forward and scowled earnestly at Alleyn.

" Look 'ee here, sir," he said. "If Bob Legge meant any harm to they darts would he have talked about them so's we all looked at the damn' things? Would he, now?"

" That's a very sound argument," agreed Alleyn. "He would not."

" Well, then!"

" Right. Now the next thing he did was to throw all six darts, one after the other, into the board. He had six, hadn't he?"

" Yes. There were six new 'uns in the packet. Usual game's only three, but he took all six for this trick."

" Exactly. Now, what did he do after he'd thrown them?"

" Said they carried beautiful. He'd thrown the lot round the centre very pretty. Mr. Watchman pulled 'em out and looked at 'em. Then Mr. Watchman spread out his left hand on the board and held out the darts with his right. ' Fire ahead,' he says, or something like that."

Alleyn uttered a short exclamation and Will looked quickly at him.

" That wasn't brought out at the inquest," said Alleyn.

"Beg pardon? What wasn't?"

"That Mr. Watchman pulled out the darts and gave them to Mr. Legge."

"I know that, sir. I only thought of it to-day. I'd have told Mr. Harper next time I saw him."

"It's a little odd that you should not remember this until a fortnight after the event."

"Is it then?" demanded Will. "I don't reckon it is. Us didn't think anything at the time. Ask any of the others. Ask my father. They'll remember all right when they think of it."

"All right," said Alleyn. "I suppose it's natural enough you should forget."

"I know what it means," said Will quickly. "I know that, right enough. Mr. Watchman handled those darts, moving them round in his hands like. How could Bob Legge know which was which after that?"

"Not very easily, one would suppose. What next?"

"Bob took the darts and stepped back. Then he began to blaze away with 'em. He never so much as glanced at 'em, I know that. He played 'em out quick."

"Until the fourth one stuck into the finger?"

"Yes," said Will doggedly, "till then."

Alleyn was silent. Fox, note-book in hand, moved over to the window and stood looking over the roofs of Ottercombe to the sea.

"I'll tell you what it is," said Will suddenly.

"Yes?" asked Alleyn.

"I reckon the poison on those darts's a blind."

He made this announcement with an air of defiance, and seemed to expect it would bring some sort of protest from the other two. But Alleyn took it very blandly.

"Yes," he said, "that's possible, of course."

"See what I mean?" said Will eagerly. "The murderer had worked it out he'd poison Mr. Watchman. He'd worked it out he'd put the stuff in his drink, first time he got a chance. Then when Bob Legge pricks him by accident, the murderer says to himself, 'There's a rare chance.' He's got the stuff on him. He puts it in the brandy glass and afterwards, while we're all fussing round Mr. Watchman, he smears it on the dart. The brandy glass gets smashed to pieces but they find

126

poison on the dart. That's how I work it out. I reckon who-ever did this job tried, deliberate, to fix it on Bob Legge."

Alleyn looked steadily at him.

"Can you give us anything to support this theory?"

Will hesitated. He looked from Alleyn to Fox, made as if to speak, and then seemed to change his mind.

"You understand, don't you," said Alleyn, "that I am not trying to force information. On the other hand if you do know of anything that would give colour to the theory you have yourself advanced it would be advisable to tell us about it."

"I know Bob Legge didn't interfere with the dart."

"After it was all over and the constable looked for the dart, wasn't it Legge who found it?"

"Sure-ly! And that goes to show. Wouldn't he have taken his chance to wipe the dart if he'd put poison on it?"

"That's well reasoned," said Alleyn. "I think he would. But your theory involves the glass. Who had an opportunity to put prussic acid in the glass?"

Will's fair skin reddened up to the roots of his fox-coloured hair.

"I've no wish to accuse anybody," he said. "I know who's innocent and I speak up for him. There won't be many who'll do that. His politics are not the colour to make power-ful friends for him when he's in trouble. I know Bob Legge's innocent but I say nothing about the guilty."

"Now, look here," said Alleyn amiably, "you've thought this thing out for yourself and you seem to have thought it out pretty thoroughly. You must see that we can't put a full-stop after your pronouncement on the innocence of Mr. Legge. The best way of establishing Legge's innocence is to find where the guilt lies."

"I don't know anything about that?"

"Really?"

"Yes, sir," said Will. "Really."

"I see. Well, can you tell us if Mr. Legge stood anywhere near the brandy glass before he threw the darts?"

"He was nowhere near it. Not ever. It was on the table by the board. He never went near it."

"Do you remember who stood near that table."

Will was silent. He compressed his lips into a hard line.

"For instance," Alleyn paused, "was Mr. Sebastian Parish anywhere near the table?"

"He might have been," said Will.

II

"And now, Fox," said Alleyn, "we'll have a word with Mr. Sebastian Parish, if he's on the premises. I don't somehow think he'll have strayed very far. See if you can find him."

Fox went away. Alleyn took a long pull at his beer and read through the notes Fox had made during the interview with Will Pomeroy. The light outside had faded and the village had settled down for the evening. Alleyn could hear the hollow sounds made by men working with boats, the tramp of heavy boots on stone, a tranquil murmur of voices, and, more distantly, the thud of breakers. Within the house he heard sounds of sweeping and of quick footsteps. The Pomeroys had lost no time cleaning up the private bar. In the public bar, across the passage, a single voice seemed to drone on and on as if somebody made a speech to the assembled topers. Whoever it was it came to an end. A burst of conversation followed and then a sudden silence. Alleyn recognised Fox's voice. Someone answered clearly and resonantly, "Yes, certainly."

"That's Parish," thought Alleyn.

The door from the public taproom into the passage was opened and shut. Sebastian Parish and Fox came into the parlour.

The evening was warm and Parish was clad in shorts and a thin blue shirt. He wore these garments with such an air that the makers might well have implored him to wear their shorts and shirts, free of cost, in and out of season for the rest of his life. His legs were olive brown and slightly glossy, the hair on his olive brown chest was golden brown. He looked burnished and groomed to the last inch. The hair on his head, a darker golden brown, was ruffled, for all the world as if his dresser had darted after him into the wings, and run a practised hand through his locks. There was something almost embarrassing in so generous a display of masculine

128

beauty. He combined in his appearance all the most admired aspects of a pukka sahib, a Greek god, and a wholesome young Englishman. Fox came after him like an anti-climax in good serviceable worsted.

"Ah, good-evening, Inspector," said Parish.

"Good-evening," said Alleyn. "I'm sorry to worry you."

Parish's glance said, a little too plainly: "Hallo, so you're a gentleman." He came forward and, with an air of manly frankness, extended his hand.

"I'm very glad to do anything I can," he said.

He sat on the arm of a chair and looked earnestly from Alleyn to Fox.

"We hoped for this," he said. "I wish to God they'd called you in at once."

"The local men," Alleyn murmured, "have done very well."

"Oh, they've done what they could, poor old souls," said Parish. "No doubt they're very sound at bottom, but it's rather a long way before one strikes bottom. Considering my cousin's position I think it was obvious that the Yard should be consulted."

He looked directly at Alleyn and said: "But I know you!"

"Do you?" said Alleyn politely. "I don't think——"

"I know you!" Parish repeated dramatically. "Wait a moment. By George, yes, of course. You're the—— I've seen your picture in a book of famous trials." He turned to Fox with the air of a Prince Regent.

"What *is* his name?" demanded Parish.

"This is Mr. Alleyn, sir," said Fox, with the trace of a grin at his superior.

"Alleyn! My God, yes, of course; Alleyn!"

"Fox," said Alleyn austerely, "be good enough to shut the door." He waited until this was done and then addressed himself to the task of removing the frills from the situation.

"Mr. Parish," Alleyn said, "we have been sent down here to make inquiries about the death of your cousin. The local superintendent has given us a very full and explicit account of the circumstances surrounding his death but we are obliged to go over the details for ourselves."

Parish made an expressive gesture, showing them the palms of his hands. "But, of course," he said.

"Yes. Well, we thought that before we went any further we should ask to see you."

"Just a moment," interrupted Parish. "There's one thing I must know. Mr. Alleyn, was my cousin murdered?"

Alleyn looked at his hands which were joined together on the table. After a moment's thought he raised his eyes.

"It is impossible to give you a direct answer," he said, "but as far as we have gone we can find no signs of accident."

"That's terrible," said Parish, and for the first time his voice sounded sincere.

"Of course something that will point to accident may yet come out."

"Good God, I hope so."

"Yes. You will understand that we want to get a very clear picture of the events leading up to the moment of the accident."

"Have you spoken to old Pomeroy?"

"Yes."

"I suppose he's talked about this fellow Legge?"

Alleyn disregarded the implication and said: "About the position of everybody when Mr. Legge threw the darts. Can you remember——"

"I've thrashed the thing out a hundred times a day. I don't remember particularly clearly."

"Well," said Alleyn, "let's see how we get on."

Parish's account followed the Pomeroys' pretty closely, but he had obviously compared notes with all the others.

"To tell you the truth," he said, "I'd had a pint of beer and two pretty stiff brandies. I don't say I've got any very clear recollection of the scene. I haven't. It seems more like a sort of nightmare than anything else."

"Can you remember where you stood immediately before Mr. Legge threw the darts?"

Alleyn saw the quick involuntary movement of those fine hands and he thought there was rather too long a pause before Parish answered.

"I'm not very certain, I'm afraid."

"Were you, for instance, near the table that stands between the dart-board and the settle?"

"I may have been. I was watching Legge."

"Try to remember. Haven't you a clear picture of Legge as he stood there ready to throw the darts?"

Parish had a very expressive face. Alleyn read in it the reflection of a memory. He went on quickly.

"Of course you have. As you say, you were watching him. Only in the medley of confused recollections that picture was, for a time, lost. But, as you say, you were watching him. Did he face you?"

"He—yes."

Alleyn slid a paper across the table.

"Here, you see, is a sketch plan of the private bar." Parish looked at it over his shoulder. "Now there's the dart-board, fairly close to the bar counter. Legge must have stood there. There isn't room for more than one person to stand in the corner by the bar counter, and Will Pomeroy was there. So to face Legge you must have been by the table."

"All right," said Parish restively. "I don't say I wasn't, you know. I only say I'm a bit hazy."

"Yes, of course, we understand that perfectly. But what I'm getting at is this. Did you see Legge take the darts after the trial throw?"

"Yes. My cousin pulled them out of the board and gave them to Legge. I remember that."

"Splendid," said Alleyn. "It's an important point and we're anxious to clear it up. Thank you. Now standing like that as we've agreed you were standing, you would see the whole room. Can you remember the positions of the other onlookers?"

"I remember that they were grouped behind Legge. Except Abel who was behind the bar-counter. Oh, and Will. Will was in the corner as you've said. Yes."

"So that it would have been impossible, if any of the others came to the table, for their movement to escape your notice?"

"I suppose so. Yes, of course it would. But I can't see why it matters."

"Don't you remember," said Alleyn gently, "that Mr. Watchman's glass was on that table? The glass that was used afterwards when Miss Moore gave him the brandy?"

Parish was not a rubicund man but the swift ebbing of what colour he had was sufficiently startling. Alleyn saw the pupils of his eyes dilate; his face was suddenly rather pinched.

"It was the dart that was poisoned," said Parish. "They found that out. It was the dart."

"Yes. I take it nobody went to the table?"

"I don't think anybody—Yes, I suppose that's right."

"And after the accident?"

"How d'you mean?"

"What were your positions?"

"Luke—my cousin—collapsed on the settle. I moved up to him. I mean I stooped down to look at him. I remember I said—oh, it doesn't matter."

"We should like to hear, if we may."

"I told him to pull himself together. You see I didn't think anything of it. He's always gone peculiar at the sight of his own blood. When we were kids he used to faint if he scratched himself."

"Did anybody but yourself know of this peculiarity?"

"I don't know. I should think Norman knew. Norman Cubitt. He may not have known but I rather think we've talked about it quite recently. I seem to remember we did."

"Mr. Parish," said Alleyn, "will you focus your memory on those few minutes after your cousin collapsed on the settle. Will you tell us everything you can remember?"

Parish got to his feet and moved restlessly about the room. Alleyn had dealt with people of the theatre before. He had learnt that their movements were habitually a little larger than life, and he knew that in many cases this staginess was the result of training and instinct and that it was a mistake to put it down to deliberate artifice. He knew that, in forming an opinion of the emotional integrity of actors, it was almost impossible to decide whether their outward-seeming was conscious or instinctive; whether it expressed their sensibility or merely their sense of theatre. Parish moved restlessly as though some dramatist had instructed him to do so. But he may not, thought Alleyn, know at this moment how beautifully he moves.

"I begin to see it," said Parish suddenly. "Really it's rather as if I tried to recall a dream, and a very bad dream, at that. You see the lights kept fading and wobbling, and then one had drunk rather a lot, and then afterwards all that happened makes it even more confused. I'm trying to think about it as a scene on the stage, a scene of which I've had to memorise the positions."

"That's a very good idea," said Alleyn.

The door opened and a tall man with an untidy head looked in.

"I beg your pardon. Sorry!" murmured this man.

"Mr. Cubitt?" asked Alleyn. Parish had turned quickly. "Do come in, please."

Cubitt came in and put down a small canvas with its face to the wall. Parish introduced him.

"I'd be glad if you'd stay," said Alleyn. "Mr. Parish is going to try and recall for us the scene that followed the injury to Mr. Watchman's hand."

"Oh," said Cubitt and gave a lopsided grin. "All right. Go ahead, Seb. Sorry I cut in."

He sat on a low chair near the fireplace and wound one thin leg mysteriously round the other. "Go ahead," he repeated.

Parish, at first, seemed a little disconcerted, but he soon became fortified by his own words.

"Luke," he said, "is lying on the settle. The settle against the left-hand wall."

"Actors' left or audience's left?" asked Cubitt.

"Audience's left. I'm deliberately seeing it as a stage setting, Norman."

"So I understand."

"—and Inspector Alleyn knows the room. At first nobody touches Luke. His face is very white and he looks as if he'll faint. I'm standing near his head. Legge's still out in front of the dart-board. He's saying something about being sorry. I've got it now. It's strange, but thinking of it like this brings it back to me. You, Norman, and Decima, are by the bar. She's sitting on the bar in the far corner. Will has taken a step out into the room and Abel's leaning over the bar. Wait a moment. Miss Darragh is farther away near the ingle-nook, and is sitting down. Old George Nark, blind

133

tight, is teetering about near Miss Darragh. That's the picture."

"Go on, please," said Alleyn.

"Well, the lights waver. Sometimes it's almost dark, and then the figures all show up again. Or——" Parish looked at Cubitt.

"No," said Cubitt. "That wasn't the brandy, Seb. You're quite right."

"Well, I can't go any further," said Parish petulantly. "The rest's still a filthy nightmare. Can you sort it out?"

"Please do, if you can, Mr. Cubitt," said Alleyn.

Cubitt was filling his pipe. His fingers, blunt-ended, were stained as usual with oil paint.

"It's as everybody described it at the inquest," he said. "I think Seb and I both had the same idea, that Watchman was simply upset at the sight of his own blood. It's true about the lights. The room seemed to—to sort of pulse with shadows. I remember Luke's right hand. It groped about his chest as if he felt for a handkerchief or something. Legge said something like 'My God! I'm sorry. Is it bad?' Something like that. And then Legge said something more. 'Look at his face! My God, it's not lockjaw, is it?' And you, Seb, said, 'Not it,' and trotted out the old story about Luke's sensibilities."

"How was I to know? You make it sound——"

"Of course you weren't to know. I agreed with you, but Legge was very upset and, at the mention of lockjaw, Abel went to the cupboard and got out the iodine and a bandage. Miss Darragh came to life and took the bandage from Abel. Abel dabbed iodine on the finger and Luke sort of shuddered like you do with the sting of the stuff. Miss Darragh said something about brandy. Decima Moore took the bottle off the bar and poured some into Luke's glass. His glass was on the table."

"The table by the dart board close to Mr. Parish?"

Cubitt looked up from his pipe.

"That's it," he said. "Decima gave Luke the brandy. He seemed to get worse just about then. He had a sort of convulsion." Cubitt paused. "It was beastly," he said and his voice changed. "The glass went flying. Miss Darragh pressed forward with the bandage and then—then the lights went out."

"That's very clear," said Alleyn. "I take it that, from the time Abel Pomeroy got the iodine and bandage until Mr. Watchman died, you were all gathered round the settle?"

"Yes. We didn't really change positions much, not Legge, or Will, or Seb here, or me. Abel and the two women came forward."

"And when the lights went up again," said Alleyn, "were the positions the same?"

"Pretty much. But——"

"Yes?"

Cubitt looked steadily at Alleyn. His pipe was gripped between his teeth. He felt in his pockets:

"There was a devil of a lot of movement while the lights were out," said Cubitt.

CHAPTER ELEVEN

ROUTINE

I

"WHAT sort of movement?" asked Alleyn.

"I know what you mean," said Parish, before Cubitt could answer. "It was Luke. He must have had a sort of attack after the lights went out. It was appalling."

"I don't mean that," said Cubitt. "I know Luke made a noise. His feet beat a sort of tattoo on the settle. He flung his arms about and—he made other noises."

"For God's sake," Parish burst out, "don't talk about it like that! I don't know how you can sit there and discuss it."

"It looks as if we've got to," said Cubitt.

"I'm afraid it does," agreed Alleyn. "What other movements did you notice, beyond those made by Mr. Watchman?"

"Somebody was crawling about the floor," Cubitt said.

Parish made a gesture of impatience. "My dear old Norman," he said, "'Crawling about the floor!' You're giving Mr. Alleyn a wrong impression. Completely wrong!

I've no doubt one of us may have stooped down in the dark, knelt down perhaps, to try and get hold of Luke."

"I don't mean that at all," said Cubitt calmly. "Someone was literally crawling about the floor. Whoever it was banged his head against my knees."

"Where were you standing?" asked Alleyn.

"By the foot of the settle. I had my back to the settle. The backs of my knees touched it."

"How do you know it was a head?" demanded Parish. "It might have been a foot."

"I can distinguish between a foot and a head," said Cubitt, "even in the dark."

"Somebody feeling round for the brandy glass," said Parish.

"It was after the brandy glass was broken." Cubitt looked at Alleyn. "Somebody trod on the glass soon after the lights went out. There's probably nothing in it, anyway. I've no idea at all whose head it was."

"Was it Legge's head?" demanded Parish suddenly.

"I tell you, Seb," said Cubitt quite mildly, "I don't know whose head it was. I merely know it was there. It simply butted against my knees and drew away quickly."

"Well, of course!" said Parish. "It was Abel."

"Why Abel?"

Parish turned to Alleyn.

"Abel dropped the bottle of iodine just before the lights went out. I remember that. He must have stooped down to try and find it."

"If it was Abel he didn't succeed," said Alleyn. "The bottle was found under the settle, you know."

"Well, it was dark."

"So it was," agreed Alleyn. "Why did you think it might be Mr. Legge's head?"

Parish at once became very solemn. He moved to the hearthrug. He thrust his hands into the pockets of his shorts, pulled in his belly, and stuck out his jaw.

"God knows," he began. "I don't want to condemn any man, but Norman and I have talked this thing over."

"Come off it, Seb," said Cubitt. "We haven't a blessed thing against the fellow, you know. Nothing that would be of any interest to Mr. Alleyn. I'm very well aware that my own ideas are largely self-protective. I suppose you know, Mr. Alleyn, that Watchman left me some of his money."

"Yes," said Alleyn.

"Yes. It's as good a motive as any other. Better than most. I don't fancy I'm in a position to make suggestions about other people."

He said this with a sort of defiance, looking out of the window and half-smiling.

"This sort of thing," added Cubitt, "finds out the thin patches in one's honesty."

"If you can admit as much," said Alleyn quickly, "perhaps they are not so very thin."

"Thanks," said Cubitt dryly.

"Well," began Parish with the air of running after the conversation, "I don't altogether agree with you, Norman. I make no secret about dear old Luke leaving the rest of his money to me. In a way it was the natural thing for him to do. I'm his next-of-kin."

"But I," said Cubitt, "am no relation at all."

"Oh, my dear old boy!" cried Parish in a hurry, "you were his best friend. Luke said so when he——" Parish stopped short.

"To revert," said Alleyn, "to Mr. Legge. You were going to talk about Mr. Legge, weren't you?"

"I was," said Parish. "I can't help what you think, Norman, old boy. It seems to me that Legge's hand in this ghastly business is pretty obvious. Nobody but Legge could have known the poisoned dart would take effect. I must say I don't see that there's much mystery about it."

"And the motive?" asked Cubitt.

Alleyn said, "I understand your cousin told you that he and Mr. Legge were strangers to each other."

"I know he did," said Parish, "but I don't believe it was true. I believe Luke recognised Legge. Not at first, perhaps, but later. During that first evening in the bar. I suppose you know that Legge smashed into my cousin's car before ever he got here? That's a bit funny, too, when you come to think of it."

"What," asked Cubitt, "is the dark inference, Seb? Why was it funny? Do you suppose that Legge lurked round Diddlestock corner in a two-seater, and that every time he heard a powerful car coming down Ottercombe Road, he hurled his baby out of cover in the hopes of ramming Luke?"

"Oh, don't be an ass. I simply mean it was a coincidence."

"About the first evening in the bar?" suggested Alleyn, who had decided that there was a certain amount to be said for allowing Parish and Cubitt plenty of rein.

"Yes. Well, I was going to tell you," said Parish. "I talked to Luke while he had his supper in the bar. He told me about this business with the cars and rather let off steam on the subject of the other driver. Well, it turned out that Legge was sitting in the settle—the—actually it was the settle where Luke—where it happened. When Luke realised Legge must have heard he went across and sort of made the *amende honorable,* if you know what I mean. He didn't make much headway. Legge was rather stuffy and up-stage."

"Was all this while the poison-party was going on in the stable?"

"What? Yes. Yes, it was."

"So that Mr. Legge did not attend the party in the stables?"

"I suppose not. But he knew all about it. When Abel came in he warned everybody in the place about what he'd done."

Parish hesitated. "It's hard to describe," he said. "But if you'd known my cousin you'd understand. He seemed to be getting at Legge. Even you'll agree to that, Norman."

"Yes," said Cubitt. "I put it down to Luke's vanity."

"His vanity?" asked Alleyn.

"Parish doesn't agree with me," said Cubitt with a faint smile, "on the subject of Watchman's vanity. I've always considered he attached importance to being on good terms with people. It seemed to me that when Legge snubbed his advances Watchman was at first disconcerted and put out of countenance, and then definitely annoyed. They had a bet on that first night about Legge's dart-throwing and Legge won. That didn't help. Then, Watchman chipped Legge about his politics and his job. Not very prettily, I thought. It was then, or about then, that the trick with the darts was first mentioned."

"By Legge," Parish pointed out.

"I know, but Luke insisted on the experiment."

"Mr. Cubitt," said Alleyn, "did you not get the impression that these two men had met before?"

Norman Cubitt rumpled his hair and scowled.

"I don't say that," he said. "I wondered. But I don't think one should attach too much importance to what Watchman said." And like Parish, he added, "if you'd ever met him you'd understand."

Alleyn did not think it necessary to say that he had met Watchman. He said, "Can you remember anything definite that seemed to point to recognition?"

"It was more the way Luke spoke than what he actually said," explained Parish. "He kept talking about Legge's job and sort of suggesting he'd done pretty well for himself. Didn't he, Norman?"

"I seem to remember a phrase about leading the people by the nose," said Cubitt, "which sounded rather offensive. And the way Luke invited Legge to play round-the-clock was not exactly the glass of fashion *or* the mould of form. He asked Legge if he'd ever done time."

"Oh," said Alleyn.

"But it all sounds far too solemn and significant when you haul it out and display it like this."

"Any one would think," said Parish, "that you were trying to protect Legge. I thought it was all damned odd."

"I'm not trying to protect Legge but I've no particular wish to make him sound like a man of mystery. 'Who is Mr. X?' As far as we know Mr. X is a rather dreary little Soviet fan who combines philately with communism and is pretty nippy with the darts. And what's more I don't see how he could have infected the dart. In fact I'm prepared to swear he didn't. I was watching his hands. They're ugly hands and he's a clumsy mover. Have you noticed he always fumbles and drops his money when he pays for his drinks? He's certainly quite incapable of doing any sleight-of-hand stuff with prussic acid."

Alleyn looked at Fox. "That answers your question," he said.

"What question?" asked Cubitt. "Or aren't we supposed to know?"

"Fox wondered if Mr. Legge could be an expert at legerdemain," said Alleyn.

"Well, you never know. That's not impossible," said Parish. "He might be."

"I'll stake my oath he's not," said Cubitt. "He's no more likely to have done it than you are——"

Cubitt caught his breath and for the first time looked profoundly uncomfortable.

"Which is absurd," he added.

Parish turned on Cubitt. His poise had gone and for a moment he looked as though he both hated Cubitt and was afraid of him.

"You seem very sure of yourself, Norman," he said. "Apparently my opinion is of no value. I won't waste any more of Mr. Alleyn's time."

"My dear old Seb——" Cubitt began.

Alleyn said, "Please, Mr. Parish! I'm sure all this business of questions that seem to have neither rhyme nor reason is tedious and exasperating to a degree. But you may be sure that we shall go as carefully as we go slowly. If there is any link between this man and your cousin I think I may promise you that we shall discover it."

"I suppose so," said Parish, not very readily. "I'm sorry if I'm unreasonable, but this thing has hit me pretty hard."

"Oh dear," thought Alleyn, "he *will* speak by the book!" And aloud he said, "Of course it has. I've nearly done for the moment. There are one or two more points. I think you looked at the new darts before they were handed to Mr. Legge."

Parish froze at that. He stood there on the dappled hearthrug and stared at Alleyn. He looked like a frightened schoolboy.

"I only picked them up and looked at them," he said. "Anyone will tell you that." And then with a sudden spurt of temper. "Damnation, you'll be saying I killed my cousin next!"

"I wasn't going to say that," said Alleyn peacefully. "I was going to ask you to tell me who handled the darts before and after you did."

Parish opened his mouth and shut it again. When he did speak it was with a kind of impotent fury.

"If you'd said at first—you've got me all flustered."

Cubitt said, "I think I can tell you that, Alleyn. Abel unpacked the darts and laid them on the counter. Parish simply picked two or perhaps three of them up and poised them. That's right, isn't, Seb?"

"I don't know," said Parish sullenly. "Have it your own way. *I* don't know. Why should I remember?"

"No reason in the world," said Alleyn cheerfully.

"Well," said Cubitt, "Sebastian put them down and Will Pomeroy took them up. I remember that Will turned away and held them nearer the light. He said something about the way they were made with the weight in the brass point and not in a lead band. He said that the card flights were better than feathers. Abel fitted the darts with card flights." Cubitt hesitated and then added, "I don't suppose it's relevant but I'm prepared to say definitely that Parish did nothing more than pick them up and put them down."

"Thank you, Norman," said Parish. "Is that all, Mr. Alleyn?"

"My last question for the moment—did you see Miss Moore pour out the brandy for Mr. Watchman?"

Dead silence. And then Parish, wrinkling his forehead, looking half-peevish, half-frightened, said, "I didn't watch her, but you needn't go probing into all that. Decima Moore had nothing to do with——"

"Seb," interrupted Cubitt quietly, "you would do better to answer these questions as they are put to you. Mr. Alleyn will meet Decima. He will find out for himself that, as far as this affair is concerned, she is a figure of no importance. You must see that he's got to ask about these things." He turned to Alleyn with his pleasant lop-sided grin, "I believe the word is 'routine'," said Cubitt. "You see I know my detective fiction."

"Routine it is," said Alleyn. "And you're perfectly correct. Routine is the very fibre of police investigation. Your novelist too has now passed the halcyon days when he could ignore routine. He reads books about Scotland Yard, he swots up police manuals. He knows that routine is deadly dull and hopelessly poor material for a thriller; so, like a wise potboiler, he compromises. He heads one chapter 'Routine,' dismisses six weeks of drudgery in as many phrases, cuts the cackle and gets to the 'osses. I wish to the Lord we could follow his lead."

"I'll be bound you do," said Cubitt. "Well, if it's any help, I didn't notice much when Decima poured out the brandy except that she was very quick about it. She stood with the rest of us round the settle, someone suggested brandy, she said something about his glass being empty, and went to the bar for the bottle. I got the impression that she simply slopped some brandy in the glass and brought it straight to Watchman. If I may, I should like to add that she was on the best of terms with Watchman and, as far as I know, had no occasion in the world to wish him dead."

"Good God!" said Parish in a hurry, "Of course not. Of course not."

"Yes," said Alleyn. "I see. Thank you so much. Now then, Mr. Parish until the accident stood by the table where Mr. Watchman had left his empty glass. I take it that Mr. Parish would have noticed, would have been bound to notice, if anyone came near enough to interfere with the glass. He tells me that the rest of the party were grouped behind Legge. Do you agree to that, Mr. Cubitt?"

"Yes. Except Will. Will was in the corner beyond the dart-board. He couldn't have got at the glass. Nobody——"
Again Cubitt caught his breath.

"Yes?"

"In my opinion," said Cubitt, "nobody touched the glass, could have touched it, either before or after Decima fetched the brandy bottle. Nobody."

"Thank you very much," said Alleyn. "That's all for the moment."

11

"What's the time, Fox?" asked Alleyn, looking up from his notes.

"Half-past nine, sir."

"Has Legge come in yet?"

"Not yet, Mr. Alleyn," said Fox. He stooped slightly and closed the parlour door. Fox always closed doors like that, inspecting the handle gravely as if the turning of it was a delicate operation. He then straightened up and contemplated his superior.

"Legge," said Fox, advancing slowly, "is only here on sufferance as you might put it. I've just had one in the public tap. They're not opening the Private till to-morrow. So I had one in the Public."

"Did you, you old devil!"

"Yes. This chap Nark's in there and I must say he suits his name."

"In the Australian sense? A fair nark?"

"That's right, sir. I don't wonder old Pomeroy hates the man. He wipes out his pint-pot with a red cotton handkerchief before they draw his beer. To be on the safe side, so he says. And talk!"

"What's he talk about?"

"The law," said Fox with an air of the deepest disgust. "As soon as he knew who I was he started on it, and a lot of very foolish remarks he made. You ought to have a chat with him, Mr. Alleyn, he'd give you the pip."

"Thanks," said Alleyn. "About Legge. Why's he here on sufferance?"

Fox sat down.

"Because of old Pomeroy," he said. "Old Pomeroy thinks Legge's a murderer and wanted him to look for other lodgings, but young Pomeroy stuck to it and they let him stay on, and got his way. However, Legge's given notice and has found rooms in Illington. He's moving over on Monday. He seems to be very well liked among the chaps in the bar, but they're a simple lot, taking them by and large. Young Oates, the Ottercombe P.C.'s in there. Very keen to see you."

"Oh! Well, I'll have to see him sooner or later. While we're waiting for Legge, why not? Bring him in."

Fox went out and returned in half a minute.

"P.C. Oates, sir," said Fox.

P.C. Oates was brick-red with excitement and as stiff as a poker from a sense of discipline. He stood inside the door with his helmet under his arm and saluted.

"Good-evening, Oates," said Alleyn.

"Good-evening, sir."

"Mr. Harper tells me you were on duty the night Mr. Watchman died. Are you responsible for the chalk marks in the private taproom?"

P.C. Oates looked apprehensive.

"Furr some of 'em, sir," he said. "Furr the place where we found the dart, like, and the marks on the settle, like. I used the chalk off the scoring-board, sir."

"Is it your first case of this sort?"

"'Ess, sir."

"You seem to have kept your head."

Wild visions cavorted through the brain of P.C. Oates. He saw in a flash all the keen young P.C.s of his favourite novels and each of them, with becoming modesty, pointed out a tiny detail that had escaped the notice of his superiors. To each of them did the Man from Higher Up exclaim, "By thunder, my lad, you've got it," and upon each of them was rapid promotion visited, while chief constables, the Big Four, yes, the Man at the Top himself, all told each other that young Oates was a man to be watched. For each of these P.C.s was the dead spit and image of P.C. Oates himself.

"Thank you, sir," said Oates.

"I'd like to hear about your appearance on the scene," said Alleyn.

"In my own words, sir?"

"If you please, Oates," said Alleyn.

Dick Oates took a deep breath, mustered his wits, and began.

"On the night of Friday, August 2nd," he began, and paused in horror. His voice had gone into the top of his head and had turned soprano on the way. It was the voice of a squeaking stranger. He uttered a singular noise in his throat and began again.

"On the night of Friday, August 2nd, at approximately 9.16 p.m.," said Oates in a voice of thunder, "being on duty at the time, I was proceeding up South Ottercombe Steps with the intention of completing my beat. My attention was aroused by my hearing the sound of my own name, viz., Oates, being called repeatedly from a spot on my left, namely the front door of the Plume of Feathers, public-house, Abel Pomeroy, proprietor. On proceeding to the said front door, I encountered William Pomeroy. He informed me that there had been an accident. Miss Decima Moore came into the entrance from inside the building. She said, 'There is no doubt about it, he is dead.' I said, to the best of my knowledge and belief, 'My Gawd, who is dead?' Miss Moore then said 'Watchman.' I then proceeded into the private tap-room."

Oates paused. Alleyn said, "Yes, Oates, that's all right, but when I said your own words I meant your own words. This is not going to be taken down and used in evidence against you. I want to hear what sort of an impression you got of it all. You see, we have already seen your formal report in the file."

"'Ess, sir," said Oates, breathing rather hard through his nostrils.

"Very well, then. Did you get the idea that these men were tight, moderately tight, or stone-cold sober?"

"I received the impression, sir, that they had been intoxicated but were now sobered."

"All of them?"

"Well, sir, when I left the tap at nine o'clock, sir, to proceed—to go round the beat, they was not to say drunk but bosky-eyed like. Merry like."

"Including Mr. Legge?"

"By all means," said Oates firmly. "Bob Legge, sir, was sozzled. Quiet like, but muddled. Well, the man couldn't find his way to his mouth with his pipe, not with any dash as you might say."

"He was still pretty handy with the darts, though," observed Fox.

"So he was then, sir. But I reckon, sir, that's second nature to the man, drunk or sober. He smelt something wonderful of tipple. And after I left, sir, he had two brandies. He must have been drunk."

"But sobered by shock?" suggested Alleyn.

"That's what I reckoned, sir."

"Did you notice anything in Legge's manner or in the manner of any of the others that led you to think the thing wasn't an accident?"

Oates flexed his knees in the classic tradition and eased his collar.

"Legge," he said, "was rather put about. Well, sir, that's natural, he having seemingly just killed a man and got over a booze in one throw of a dart if you want to put it fanciful. Yes, he was proper put out, was Bob Legge. White as a bogey and trembling. Kept saying the deceased gentleman had taken tetanus. Now that," said Oates, "might of been a blind, but it looked genu-ine to me. That's Legge. There wasn't anything unusual in Abel Pomeroy. Worried, but there again, who isn't with a fresh corpse on the premises? Young Will had his eye on Miss Dessy Moore. Natural again. She's so pretty as a daisy and good as promised to Will. Staring at him, with eyes like saucers, and ready to swoon away. Kind of frightened. Bore up all right, till she'd told me how she give the deceased brandy, and then seemed, in a manner of speaking, to cave in to it, and went off with Will, scared-like and looking at him kind of bewildered. Will give me the clearest answers of the lot, sir. Kept his head, did Will."

"And the two friends?"

"Two gentlemen, sir? Mr. Parish looked scared and squeamish. Very put out, he was, and crying too, something surprising. Answered by fits and starts. Not himself at all. Mr. Cubitt the straight out opposite. Very white and didn't go near the body while I was there. Wouldn't look at it, I noticed. But cool and collected, and answered very sensible. It was Mr. Cubitt fetched the doctor. I got the idea he wanted to get out into the open air, like. Seemed to me, sir, that Mr. Parish kind of let himself go and Mr. Cubitt held himself in. Seemed to me that likely Mr. Cubitt was the more upset."

"Yes," said Alleyn. "I see. Go on."

"The rest, sir? I didn't see The Honourable Darragh till the morning. The Honourable Darragh, sir, behaved very sensible. Not but what she wasn't in a bit of a quiver, but being a stout lady, you noticed it more. Her cheeks jiggled something chronic when she talked about it, but she was very sensible. She's a great one for talking, sir, and it's my belief that when she got over the surprise she fair revelled in it."

"Really? And now we're left as usual with Mr. George Nark."

"Nothing but vomit and hiccough, sir. Drunk as an owl."

"I see. Well, Oates, you've given us a clear enough picture of the actors. Now for the dart. Where was the dart when you found it?"

"Legge found it, sir. I asked for it almost immediate, sir,

146

but they was all that flustered they paid no heed to me.
'Cepting Legge who had been going on about, 'was it the dart that did it?' and, 'had he killed the man?' and, 'wasn't it lockjaw?' and, 'he must have shifted his finger,' and so forth; and so soon as I asked for the dart he stooped down and peered about and then he says, 'there it is!' and I saw it and he picked it up from where it had fallen. It was stained and still looked damp, sir. Blood. And I suppose, sir, the poison."

Oates paused and then said, "If I may take the liberty, sir."

"Yes, Oates?"

"They all says, sir, that Mr. Watchman threw that there dart down, sir. They say he threw it down 'tother side of the table."

"Yes."

"Well, now, sir, *it was laying on the floor.*"

"What?" exclaimed Fox.

"It was," repeated Oates, "*a-laying* on the floor. I saw it. Ax Legge, he'll bear me out."

"Whereabouts?" asked Alleyn sharply.

"Behind the table, sir, like they said, and well away from where they had been standing. The table was betwixt the settle and the board."

"I see," said Alleyn. And then the wildest hopes of Dick Oates were realised. The words with which he had soothed himself to sleep, the words that he heard most often in his dearest dreams, were spoken unmistakably by the Man from Higher Up.

"By George," said Chief Detective-Inspector Alleyn, "I believe you've got it!"

CHAPTER TWELVE

CURIOUS BEHAVIOUR OF MR. LEGGE

I

ON that first night in Ottercombe, from the time Oates left them until half-past eleven, Alleyn and Fox thrashed out the case and debated a plan of action. Alleyn was now quite certain that Watchman had been murdered.

"Unless there's a catch, Br'er Fox, and I can't spot it if there is. The rat hole, the dart, the newspaper, and the general evidence ought to give us 'who,' but we're still in the dark about 'how.' There are those bits of melted glass, now."

"I asked old Pomeroy. He says the fireplace was cleared out the day before."

"Well, we'll have to see if the experts can tell us if it's the same kind as the brandy glass. Rather, let us hope they can say definitely that it's not the same. Oh Lord!"

He got up, stretched himself, and leant over the window-sill. The moon was out, and the sleeping roofs of Otter-combe made such patterns of white and inky black as woodcut draughtsmen love. It was a gull's-eye view Alleyn had from the parlour window, a setting for a child's tale of midnight wonders. A cat was sitting on one of the crooked eaves. It stared at the moon and might have been waiting for an appointment with some small night-gowned figure that would presently lean, dreaming, from the attic window. Alleyn had a liking for old fairy tales and found himself thinking of George Macdonald and the Back of the North Wind. The Coombe was very silent in the moonlight.

"All asleep," said Alleyn, "except us, and Mr. Robert Legge. I wish he'd come home to bed."

"There's a car now," said Fox, "up by the tunnel."

It was evidently a small car and an old one. With a ramshackle clatter it drew nearer the pub, and then the driver must have turned his engine off and coasted down to the garage. There followed the squeak of brakes. A door slammed tinnily. Someone dragged open the garage door.

"That's him," said Fox.

"Good," said Alleyn. "Pop into the passage, Fox, and hail him in."

Fox went out, leaving the door open. Alleyn heard slow steps plod across the yard to the side entrance. Fox said, "Good-evening, sir. Is it Mr. Legge?"

A low mumble.

"Could you spare us a moment, sir? We're police officers. Chief Inspector Alleyn would be glad to have a word with you."

A pause, another mumble, and then approaching steps.

"This way, sir," said Fox, and ushered in Mr. Robert Legge.

Alleyn saw a medium-sized man who stooped a little. He saw a large head, white hair, a heavily-lined face and a pair of callused hands. Legge, blinking in the lamplight, looked a defenceless, a rather pathetic figure.

"Mr. Legge?" said Alleyn. "I'm sorry to bother you so late in the evening. Won't you sit down?"

Fox moved forward a chair and, without uttering a word, Legge sat in it. He was under the lamp. Alleyn saw that his clothes, which had once been good, were darned and faded. Everything about the man seemed bleached and characterless. He looked nervously from Alleyn to Fox. His lips were not quite closed and showed his palpably false teeth.

"I expect," said Alleyn "that you have guessed why we are here."

Legge said nothing.

"We're making inquiries about the death of Mr. Luke Watchman."

"Oh, yes?" said Legge breathlessly.

"There are one or two points we would like to clear up and we hope you will be able to help us."

The extraordinarily pale eyes flickered.

"Only too pleased," murmured Legge and looked only too wretched.

"Tell me," said Alleyn, "have you formed any theory about this affair?"

"Accident."

"You think that's possible?"

Legge looked at Alleyn as if he had said something profoundly shocking.

"Possible? But of course it's possible. Dreadfully possible. Such a way to do things! They should have bought traps. The chemist should be struck off the rolls. It's a disgrace."

He lowered his voice and became conspiratorial.

"It was a terrible, virulent poison," he whispered mysteriously. "A shocking thing that they should have it here. The coroner said so."

He spoke with a very slight lisp, a mere thickening of sibilants caused, perhaps, by his false teeth.

"How do you think it got on the dart you threw into Mr. Watchman's finger?"

Legge made a gesture that disconcerted and astonished Alleyn. He raised his hand and shook a finger at Alleyn as if he gently admonished him. If his face had not spoken of terror he would have looked faintly waggish.

"You suspect me," he said. "You shouldn't."

Alleyn was so taken aback by this old-maidish performance that for a moment he could think of nothing to say.

"You shouldn't," repeated Legge. "Because I didn't."

"The case is as wide open as the grave."

"He's dead," whispered Legge, "and buried. *I* didn't do it. I was the instrument. It's not a very pleasant thing to be the instrument of death."

"No. You should welcome any attempt to get to the bottom of the affair."

"So I would," muttered Legge eagerly, "if I thought they would get to the truth. But I'm not popular here. Not in some quarters. And that makes me nervous, Chief Inspector."

"It needn't," said Alleyn. "But we're being very unorthodox, Mr. Legge. May we have your full name and address?"

Fox opened his notebook. Legge suddenly stood up and, in an uncertain sort of fashion, came to attention.

"Robert Legge," he said rapidly, "care of the Plume of Feathers, Ottercombe, South Devon. Business address: Secretary and Treasurer, The Combe Left Movement, G.P.O. Box 119, Illington."

He sat down again.

"Thank you, sir," said Fox.

"How long have you been here, Mr. Legge?" asked Alleyn.

"Ten months, My chest is not very good. Nothing serious, you know. I needn't be nervous on *that* account. But I was in very low health altogether. Boils. Even in my ears. Very unpleasant and painful. My doctor said it would be as well to move."

"Ah, yes. From where?"

"From Liverpool. I was in Liverpool. In Flattery Street, South, Number 17. Not a very healthy part."

"That was your permanent address?"

"Yes. I had been there for some little time. I had one or two secretaryships. For a time I was in vacuums."

"What!"

"In vacuum cleaners. But that did not altogether agree with my chest. I got very tired and you wouldn't believe how rude some women can be. Positively odious! So I gave it up for stamps."

His voice, muffled and insecure though it was, seemed the voice of an educated man. Alleyn wondered if he had been born to vacuum cleaners and philately.

"How long were you in Liverpool, Mr. Legge?"

"Nearly two years."

"And before that?"

"I was in London. In the City. I was born in London. Why do you ask?"

"Routine, Mr. Legge," said Alleyn and thought of Cubitt. "What I was going to ask you was this. Had you ever met Mr. Watchman before he arrived at Ottercombe?"

"Yes, indeed."

Alleyn looked up.

"Do you mind telling us where you met him? You need not answer any of these questions, of course, if you don't want to."

"I don't in the least object, Chief Inspector. I met him in a slight collision at Diddlestock corner. He was very nice about it."

Alleyn stared at him and he blinked nervously. Fox, Alleyn noticed, was stifling a grin.

"Was that the first time you saw him?"

"Oh, no. I'd *seen* him before. In court."

"What?"

"I used to go a great deal to the courts when I was in London. I always found it very absorbing. Of course, Mr. Watchman didn't know *me*."

"I see."

Alleyn moved Abel's best inkpot from one side of the table to the other and stared thoughtfully at it.

"Mr. Legge," he said at last, "how much did you have to drink on that Friday night?"

"Too much," said Legge quickly. "I realise it now. Not so much as the others, but too much. I have a good head as a rule, a very good head. But unless he moved his finger, which I still think possible, I must have taken too much." He gave Alleyn a sidelong glance.

"I usually play my best," said Mr. Legge, "when I am a little intoxicated. I must have overdone it. I shall never forgive myself, never."

"How long was it," Alleyn asked, "before you realised what had happened?"

"Oh, a very long time. I thought it must be tetanus. I've seen a man with tetanus. You see, I had forgotten about that dreadful stuff. I had forgotten that Mr. Pomeroy opened the cupboard that afternoon."

"That was for——"

"I know what you're going to say," Legge interrupted, again with that gesture of admonishment. "You're going to remind me that he opened it to get the iodine for my face. Do you suppose that I can ever forget that? I was doubly the instrument. That's what upsets me so dreadfully. He must have done something then, and accidentally got it on his fingers. I don't know. I don't pretend it's not a mystery." His face twitched dolorously. "I'm wretchedly unhappy," he whispered. "Miserable!"

People with no personal charm possess one weapon, an occasional appeal to our sense of pathos. There was something intolerably pitiable in Legge; in his furtiveness, his threadbare respectability, his obvious terror, and his little spurts of confidence. Alleyn had a violent desire to get rid of him, to thrust him away as something indecent and painful. But he said, "Mr. Legge, have you any objections to our taking your fingerprints?"

The chair fell over as Legge got to his feet. He backed towards the door, turning his head from side to side and wringing his hands. Fox moved to the door but Legge seemed unaware of him. He gazed like a trapped animal at Alleyn.

"O God!" he said. "O dear! O dear me! O God, I *knew* you'd say that!" and broke into tears.

11

"Come now, Mr. Legge," said Alleyn at last, "you mustn't let the affair get on your nerves like this. If, as you think, Mr. Watchman's death was purely accidental, you have nothing to fear. There's nothing very terrible in having your fingerprints taken."

"Yes, there is," contradicted Legge in a sort of fury. "It's a perfectly horrible suggestion. I resent it. I deeply resent it. I most strongly object."

"Very well, then," said Alleyn placidly, "we won't take them."

Mr. Legge blew his nose violently and looked over the top of his handkerchief at Alleyn.

"Yes," he said, "that's all very well, but I know what tricks you'll get up to. You'll get them by stealth, I know. I've heard of the practices that go on in the police. I've studied the matter. It's like everything else in a state governed by capitalism. Trickery and intimidation. You'll give me photographs to identify and take my fingerprints from them."

"Not now you've warned us," said Alleyn.

"You'll get them against my will and then you'll draw false conclusions from them. That's what you'll do."

"What sort of false conclusions?"

"About me," cried Legge passionately, "about me."

"You know that's all nonsense," said Alleyn quietly. "You will do yourself no good by talking like this."

"I won't talk at all. I will not be trapped into making incriminating statements. I will not be kept in here against my will!"

"You may go whenever you wish," said Alleyn. "Fox, will you open the door?"

153

Fox opened the door. Legge backed towards it, but on the threshold he paused.

"If only," he said with extraordinary intensity, "if only you'd have the sense to see that I couldn't have done anything even if I'd wanted to. If only you'd realise that and leave me in peace. You don't know *what* damage you may do, indeed you don't. If only you would leave me in peace!"

He swallowed noisily, made a movement with his hands that was eloquent of misery and defeat, and went away.

Fox stopped with his hand on the door knob.

"He's gone back to the garage," said Fox. "Surely he won't bolt."

"I don't think he'll bolt, Fox. Not in that car."

Fox stood and listened, looking speculatively at Alleyn.

"Well," he said, "that was a rum go, Mr. Alleyn, wasn't it?"

"Very rum indeed. I suppose you're thinking what I'm thinking?"

"He's been inside," said Fox. "I'll take my oath that man's done his stretch."

"I think so too, and what's more he had that suit before he went in. It was made by a decent tailor about six years ago, or more, and it was made for Mr. Legge. It fits him well enough and he's too odd a shape for reach-me-downs."

"Notice his hands?"

"I did. And the hair, and the walk, and the eyes. I thought he was going to sob it all out on my bosom. Ugh!" said Alleyn, "it's beastly, that furtive, wary look they get. Fox, ring up Illington and ask Harper to send the dart up to Dabs. It's got his prints. Not very nice ones, but they'll do to go on with."

Fox went off to the telephone, issued cryptic instructions, and returned.

"I wonder," said Fox, "who he is, and what they pulled him in for."

"We'll have to find out."

"He behaved very foolish," said Fox austerely. "All that refusing to have his prints taken. We're bound to find out. We'll have to get his dabs, sir."

"Yes," agreed Alleyn, "on the sly, as he foretold."

"I wonder what he's *doing* out there," said Fox.

"Wait a moment," said Alleyn. "I'll have a look."

He stole into the passage. Legge had left the side door ajar and Alleyn could see the yard outside, flooded with moonshine. He slipped out and moved like a cat, across the yard and into the shadow of the garage door. Here he stopped and listened. From inside the garage came a rhythmic whisper interrupted at intervals by low thuds and accompanied by the sound of breathing. A metal door opened and closed stealthily, a boot scraped across stone. The rhythmic whisper began again. Alleyn stole away and recrossed the yard, his long shadow going fantastically before him.

When he rejoined Fox in the parlour, he was grinning broadly.

"What's he up to?" asked Fox.

"Being one too many for the infamous police," said Alleyn. "He's polishing his car."

"Well, I'll be blooming well blowed," said Fox.

"He must have nearly finished. Switch off the light, Fox. It'd be a pity to keep him waiting."

Fox switched off the light. He and Alleyn sat like shadows in the bar parlour. The Ottercombe town clock struck twelve and, a moment later, the same dragging footsteps sounded in the yard. The side door was shut and the steps went past the parlour. The staircase light clicked and a faint glow showed underneath the door.

"Up he goes," whispered Alleyn.

Legge went slowly upstairs, turned the light off, and moved along the passage above their heads. A door closed.

"Now then," said Alleyn.

They went upstairs in the dark and slipped into Alleyn's room, the first on the top landing. The upstairs passage was bright with moonlight.

"His is the end one," murmured Alleyn. "He's got his light on. Do you suppose he'll set to work and wipe all the utensils in his room?"

"The thing's silly," whispered Fox. "I've never known anything like it. What's the good of it? We'll *get* his blasted dabs."

"What do you bet me he won't come down to breakfast in gloves?"

"He's capable of anything," snorted Fox.

"Sssh! He's coming out."

"Lavatory?"

"Possibly."

Alleyn groped for the door and unlatched it.

"What are you doing, sir?" asked Fox rather peevishly.

"Squinting through the crack," Alleyn whispered. "Now he's come out of the lavatory."

"I can hear that."

"He's in his pyjamas. He doesn't look very delicious. Good Lord!"

"What?"

"He's crossed the passage," breathed Alleyn, "and he's stooping down at another door."

"What's he up to?"

"Can't see—shadow. Now he's off again. Back to his own room. Shuts the door. Light out. Mr. Legge finished for the night."

"And not before it was time," grumbled Fox. "They've got a nice sort of chap as secretary and treasurer for their society. How long'll we give him, Mr. Alleyn? I'd like to have a look what he's been up to."

"I'll give him ten minutes and then go along the passage."

"Openly?"

"Yes. Quickly but not stealthily, Fox. It's the room on the right at the end. It looked almost as if he was shoving a note under the door. Very odd."

"What age," asked Fox, "is the Honourable Violet Darragh?"

"What a mind you have! It was probably young Pomeroy's door."

"I hadn't thought of that, sir. Probably."

Alleyn switched on the light and began to unpack his suitcase. Whistling soundlessly he set his room in order, undressed, and put on his pyjamas and dressing-gown.

"Now then," he said. He picked up his towel and sponge-bag and went out.

Fox waited, his hands on his knees. He heard a tap turned on. Water pipes gurgled. In a distant room someone began to snore in two keys. Presently Fox heard the pad of feet in the passage and Alleyn returned.

His towel was round his neck. His hair was rumpled and

156

damp and hung comically over his eyes. He looked like a rather distinguished faun who had chosen to disguise himself in pyjamas and a dressing-gown. Between thumb and forefinger he held a piece of folded paper.

"Crikey, Fox!" said Alleyn.

"What have you got there, sir?"

"Lord knows. A threat? A *billet doux*? Find my case, please, Fox, and get out a couple of tweezers. We'll open it carefully. At least it may have his prints. Thank the Lord I brought that camera."

Fox produced the tweezers. Alleyn dropped his paper on the glass top of the washstand. Using the tweezers, he opened it delicately. Fox looked over his shoulder and read ten words written in pencil.

"Implore you usual place immediately. Most important. *Destroy at once.*"

"Crikey again," said Alleyn. "An assignation."

"Where did you get it, Mr. Alleyn?"

"Under the door. I fished for it with a hairpin I found in the bathroom. Luckily there was a good gap."

"Will Pomeroy's door?"

"Does Will Pomeroy wear high-heeled shoes, size four and a half, made by Rafferty, Belfast?"

"Lor'," said Fox. "The Honourable Violet."

CHAPTER THIRTEEN

MISS DARRAGH STANDS FIRM

I

THE summer sun shines early on the Coombe, and when Alleyn looked out of his window at half-past five it was at a crinkled and sparkling sea. The roofs of Fish Lane were cleanly pale. A column of wood smoke rose delicately from a chimney-pot. Someone walked, whistling, down Ottercombe Steps.

Alleyn had been dressed for an hour. He was waiting for Mr. Robert Legge. He supposed that the word "immediately" in the note for Miss Darragh might be interpreted as "the moment you read this," which no doubt would be soon after Miss Darragh awoke.

Fox and Alleyn had been very industrious before they went to bed. They had poured iodine into a flat dish and they had put Mr. Legge's letter into the dish but not into the iodine. They had covered the dish and left it for five minutes, and then set up an extremely expensive camera by whose aid they could photograph the note by lamplight. They might have spared themselves the trouble. There were no fingerprints on Mr. Legge's note. Fox had gone to bed in high dudgeon. Alleyn had refolded the note and pushed it under Miss Darragh's door. Four minutes later he had slipped peacefully into sleep.

The morning smelt freshly. Alleyn leant over the window-sill and glanced to his left. At the same moment three feet away Fox leant over his window-sill and glanced to his right. He was fully dressed and looked solidly prepared to take up his bowler hat and go anywhere.

"Good-morning, sir," said Fox in a whisper. "Pleasant morning. He's just stirring, I fancy."

"Good-morning to you, Br'er Fox," rejoined Alleyn. "A very pleasant morning. I'll meet you on the stairs."

He stole to the door of his room and listened. Presently

the now familiar footsteps sounded in the passage. Alleyn waited for a few seconds and then slipped through the door. Fox performed a similar movement at the same time.

"Simultaneous comedians," whispered Alleyn. "Come on."

Keeping observation is one of the most tedious of a detective officer's duties. Laymen talk of shadowing. It is a poetic term for a specialised drudgery. In his early days at Scotland Yard, Alleyn had hated keeping observation and had excelled at it, a circumstance which casts some light on his progress as a detective. There are two kinds of observation in the police sense. You may tail a man in such a manner that you are within his range of vision but unrecognised or unremarked by him. You may also be obliged to tail a man in circumstances that forbid his seeing you at all. In a deserted hamlet, at half-past five on a summer's morning, Mr. Legge could scarcely fail to recognise his tormentors of the previous evening. Alleyn and Fox wished to follow him without being seen.

They reached the entrance lobby of the pub as Mr. Legge stepped into the street. Alleyn moved into the private tap and Fox into a sort of office on the other side of the front entrance. Alleyn watched Mr. Legge go past the window of the private tap and signalled to Fox. They hurried down the side passage in time to see Mr. Legge pass the garage and make for the South Steps. Alleyn nodded to Fox who strolled across the yard, and placed himself in a position where he could see the South Steps, reflected handily in a cottage window. When the figure of Mr. Legge descended the steps and turned to the left, Fox made decent haste to follow his example.

Alleyn opened the garage and backed the police Ford into the yard. He then removed his coat and hat, let a good deal of air out of his spare tyre and began, in a leisurely manner to pump it up again. He had inflated and replaced the spare tyre and was peering into the engine, when Miss Darragh came out of the pub.

Alleyn had not questioned the superintendent at all closely about Miss Darragh, nor was her appearance dwelt upon in the files of the case. He was therefore rather surprised to see how fat she was. She was like a pouter-pigeon in lavender print. She wore an enormous straw hat, and carried a haversack and easel. Her round face was quite inscrutable but Alleyn thought she looked pretty hard at him. He dived farther inside the bonnet of the car and Miss Darragh passed down the South Steps.

Alleyn gave her a good start and then put on his coat and hat.

When he reached the foot of the steps he looked cautiously round the corner of the wall to the left. Miss Darragh had reached the south end of Fish Lane and now plodded along a stone causeway to the last of the jetties. Alleyn crossed Fish Lane and followed under the lee of the houses. At the end of Fish Lane he behaved with extreme caution, manœuvring for a vantage point. There was nobody about. The fishing fleet had gone out at dawn and the housewives of Ottercombe were either in bed or cooking breakfast. Alleyn paused at Mary Yeo's shop on the corner of Fish Lane and the causeway. By peering diagonally through both windows at once, he had a distorted view of the jetty and of Miss Darragh. She had set up a camp-stool and had her back to Ottercombe. Alleyn saw her mount her easel. A sketching block appeared. Presently Miss Darragh began to sketch.

Alleyn walked down an alley towards the jetty, and took cover in an angle of one of the ramshackle cottages that sprawled about the waterfront. This is the rough quarter of Ottercombe. Petronella Broome has a house of ill-repute, four rooms, on the south waterfront; and William Glass's tavern was next door until Superintendent Harper made a fuss and had the licence cancelled. This stretch of less than two hundred yards is called the South Front. At night it takes on a sort of glamour. It's lamps are reflected redly in the water. Petronella's gramophone advertises her hospitality, bursts of laughter echo over the harbour, and figures move dimly to and fro across the lights. But at ten to six in the morning it smells of fish and squalor.

Alleyn waited for five minutes before Legge appeared from behind a bollard at the far end of the jetty. Legge crossed the end of the jetty and stood behind Miss Darragh who continued to sketch.

"Damn," said Alleyn.

The tide was out and three dinghies were beached near the jetty. A fourth was made fast to the far end and seemed to lie, bobbing complacently, directly under Miss Darragh. Alleyn thought the water looked fairly shallow for at least half-way down the jetty. He groaned and, with caution, moved towards the front. Miss Darragh did not turn, but from time to time Legge glanced over his shoulder. Alleyn advanced to the foreshore under cover of boats, fishing gear, and the sea wall. To an observer from one of the windows, he would have seemed to be hunting for lost property. He reached the jetty.

For half-way along the jetty the water was about two feet deep. Alleyn, cursing inwardly, rolled up his trousers and took to it, keeping under the jetty. The water was cold and the jetty smelt. Abruptly the bottom shelved down. Alleyn could now hear the faintest murmur of voices and knew that he was not so very far from his objective. The dinghy was hidden by posts but he could hear the glug-glug of its movement and the hollow thud it made when it knocked against the post to which it was made fast. Just beyond it was a flight of steps leading up to the jetty. Alleyn mounted a cross-beam. It was slimy and barnacled but he found handholds to the end. If he could reach the dinghy! His progress was hazardous, painful, and maddeningly slow, but at last he grasped the post. He embraced it with both arms, straddled the cross-beams and wriggled round until he reached the far side.

Underneath him was the dinghy and lying full-length in the dinghy was Inspector Fox. His notebook lay open on his chest.

Fox winked at his superior and obligingly moved over. Alleyn pulled the dinghy closer, and not without difficulty lowered himself into the bows.

"Two minds with but a single thought," he whispered. "Simultaneous comedy again."

He took out his notebook and cocked his ears.

From the jetty above, the voices of Miss Darragh and Mr. Legge sounded disembodied and remote. For a second or two Alleyn could hear nothing distinctly, but, as his concentration sharpened, words and phrases began to take form. Miss Darragh was speaking. She spoke in little bursts of eloquence broken by pauses that fell oddly until he realised that while she talked she painted.

"——and haven't I gone sufficiently far, coming down here, to meet you? I go no farther at all. I'm sorry for the nasty pickle you're in . . . terribly cruel the way . . . haunts you . . . compromised myself . . . can't expect . . ." Her voice died into a mysterious murmur. Alleyn raised his eyebrows and Fox shook his head. Miss Darragh droned on. Suddenly she said very distinctly, "It's no good at all asking, for I'll not do ut."

Legge began to mumble quite inaudibly. She interrupted him with a staccato, "Yes, yes, I realise all that." And a moment later, "Don't think I'm not sorry. I am." And then, incisively, "Of course, I know you're innocent of ut, but I can't——"

For the first time Mr. Legge became intelligible.

"My blood be on your head," said Mr. Legge loudly.

"Ah, don't say that. Will you be quiet, now? You've nothing to fear."

Legge's voice dropped again but Alleyn's hearing was now attuned to it. He heard isolated phrases. "Hounded to death . . . just when I was . . . expiated my fault . . . God knows . . . never free from it."

Footsteps padded across the beams overhead, and when Miss Darragh spoke, it was from a different place. She had moved, perhaps to look at the sketch, and now stood near the edge of the jetty. Her voice, seeming very close, was startlingly clear.

"I promise you," she said, "that I'll do my best, but I'll not commit perjury——"

"Perjury!" said Legge irritably. He had followed her.

"Well, whatever it is. I'll do my best. I've no fear at all of their suspecting you, for they'll have their wits about them and will soon see it's impossible."

"But don't you see—they'll think—they'll tell every one——"

"I can see it's going to be hard on you and I've got my— you know well enough why I feel bound to help you. That'll do now. Rest easy, and we'll hope for the best."

"Don't forget how I came to my trouble."

"I do not and I will not. Be off, now, for it's getting late. I've finished me little peep and it's nothing better than a catastrophe; me mind was not on ut. We'd best not be seen walking back together."

"I'm at your mercy," said Legge. And they heard him walk away.

II

Alleyn and Fox breakfasted in the dining-room. Cubitt and Parish were nowhere to be seen, but Miss Darragh sat at a corner table and gave them good-morning as they came in. Alleyn knew that from behind the paper she watched them pretty closely. He caught her at it twice, but she did not seem to be at all embarrassed and the second time twinkled and smiled at him.

"I see you've no paper," said Miss Darragh. "Would you like to have a look at the Illington *Courier*?"

"Thank you so much," said Alleyn, and crossed over to the table.

"You're Mr. Roderick Alleyn are ye not?"

Alleyn bowed.

"Ah, I knew you from your likeness to your brother George," said Miss Darragh.

"I am delighted that you knew me," said Alleyn, "but I've never thought that my brother George and I were much alike."

"Ah, there's a kind of a family resemblance. And then, of course, I knew you were here, for the landlord told me. You're a good deal better-looking than your brother George. He used to stay with me cousins, the Sean O'Darraghs for Punchestown. I met 'um there. I'm Violet Darragh so now you know who 'tis that's so bold with you."

"Miss Darragh," said Alleyn, "would you spare us a moment when you have finished your breakfast?"

"I would. Is it about this terrible affair?"

"Yes."

"I'll be delighted. I'm a great lover of mysteries myself, or I was before this happened. They're not such grand fun when you're in the middle of 'um. I'll be in the private taproom when you want me. Don't hurry now."

"Thank you," said Alleyn. Miss Darragh rose and squeezed past the table. Alleyn opened the door. She nodded cheerfully and went out.

"Cool," said Fox, when Alleyn joined him. "You'd never think she had anything up her sleeve, sir, now would you?"

"No, Fox, you wouldn't. I wonder what line I'd better take with her. She's as sharp as a needle."

"I'd say so," agreed Fox.

"I think, Fox, you had better ask her, in your best company manners, to walk into our parlour. It looks more official. I must avoid that friend of the family touch——" Alleyn stopped short and rubbed his nose. "Unless, indeed, I make use of it," he said. "Dear me, now, I wonder."

"What's the friend-of-the-family touch, sir?"

"Didn't you hear? She has met my brother George who is physically as unlike me as may be. Mentally, too, I can't help hoping. But perhaps that's vanity. What do you think?"

"I haven't had the pleasure of meeting Sir George, Mr. Alleyn."

"He's rather an old ass, I'm afraid. Have you finished?"

"Yes, thank you, sir."

"Then I shall remove to the parlour. My compliments to Miss Darragh, Foxkin, and I shall be grateful if she will walk into my parlour. Lord, Lord, I hope I don't make a botch of this."

Alleyn went to the parlour. In a minute or two Fox came in with Miss Darragh.

Ever since he entered the detective service, Alleyn has had to set a guard against a habit of instinctive reactions to new acquaintances. Many times has he repeated to himself the elementary warning that roguery is not incompatible with charm. But he has never quite overcome certain impulses towards friendliness, and his austerity of manner is really a safeguard against this weakness, a kind of protective colouring, a uniform for behaviour.

When he met Violet Darragh he knew that she would amuse and interest him, that it would be easy to listen to her and pleasant to strike up a sort of friendship. He knew that he would find it difficult to believe her capable of double-dealing. He summoned the discipline of a system that trains its servants to a high pitch of objective watchfulness. He became extremely polite.

"I hope you will forgive me," he said, "for suggesting

164

that you should come in here. Mr. Pomeroy has given us this room as a sort of office, and as all our papers——"

"Ah, don't worry yourself," said Miss Darragh. She took the arm-chair that Fox wheeled forward, wriggled into the deep seat, and tucked her feet up.

"It's more comfortable here," she said, "and I'm a bit tired. I was out at the crack of dawn at me sketching. Down on the front, 'twas, and those steps are enough to break your heart."

"There must be some very pleasant subjects down there," murmured Alleyn. "At the end of the jetty, for instance."

"You've a good eye for a picture," said Miss Darragh. "That's where I was. Or perhaps you saw me there?"

"I think," said Alleyn, "that you passed me on your way out. I was in the garage yard."

"You were. But the garage yard does not overlook the jetty."

"Oh, no," said Alleyn vaguely. "Now, Miss Darragh, may we get down to what I'm afraid will be, for you, a very boring business. It's about the night of this affair. I've seen your statement to the police, and I've read the report of the inquest."

"Then," said Miss Darragh, "I'm afraid you'll know all I have to tell you and that's not much."

"There are one or two points we'd like to go over with you if we may. You told the coroner that you thought the wound from the dart had nothing to do with Mr. Watchman's death."

"I did. And I'm positive it hadn't. A little bit of a puncture no bigger than you'd take from a darning-needle."

"A little bigger than that surely?"

"Not to make any matter."

"But the analyst found cyanide on the dart."

"I've very little faith in 'um," said Miss Darragh.

"In the analyst? It went up to London, you know. It was the very best analyst," said Alleyn with a smile.

"I know 'twas, but the cleverest of 'um can make mistakes. Haven't I read for myself how delicate these experiments are with their fractions of a grain of this and that and their acid tests, and their heat tests and all the rest of it? I've always thought it's blown up with their theories and speculations these fine chemists must be. When they're told to look for prussic acid they'll be determined to find it. Ah, well, maybe they did find poison on the dart, but that makes no difference at all to me theory, Mr. Alleyn. If there was prussic acid or cyanide, or somebody's acid on the dart (and why, for pity's sake, can't they find one name for ut and be done with ut), then 'twas put on in the factory or the shop, or got on afterwards for 'twas never there at the time."

"I beg your pardon?" asked Alleyn apologetically. "I don't quite——"

"What I mean is this, Mr. Alleyn. Not a soul there had a chance to play the fool with the darts, and why should they when nobody could foretell the future?"

"The future? You mean nobody could tell that the dart would puncture the finger?"

"I do."

"Mr. Legge," said Alleyn, "might have known, mightn't he?"

"He might," said Miss Darragh coolly, "but he didn't. Mr. Alleyn, I never took my eyes off 'um from the time he took the darts till the time he wounded the poor fellow, and that was no time at all, for it passed in a flash. If it's any help I'm ready to make a sworn statement, an affidavit, isn't it? that Legge put nothing on the dart."

"I see," said Alleyn.

"Even Mr. Pomeroy who is set against Mr. Legge, and Mr. Parish too, will tell you he had no chance to infect the dart."

Miss Darragh made a quick nervous movement with her hands, clasping them together and raising them to her chin.

"I know very well," she said, "that there are people here will make things black for Mr. Legge. You will do well to let 'um alone. He's a delicate man and this affair's racking his nerves to pieces. Let 'um alone, Mr. Alleyn, and look elsewhere for your murderer, if there's murder in ut."

"What's your opinion of Legge?" asked Alleyn abruptly.

"Ah, he's a common well-meaning little man with a hard life behind 'um."

"You know something of him? That's perfectly splendid. I've been trying to fit a background to him and I can't."

For the first time Miss Darragh hesitated, but only for a

second. She said, "I've been here nearly three weeks and I've had time to draw my own conclusions about the man."

"No more than that?"

"Ah, I know he's had a hard time and that in the end he's come into harbour. Let 'um rest there, Mr. Alleyn, for he's no murderer."

"If he's no murderer he has nothing to fear."

"You don't know that. You don't understand."

"I think perhaps we are beginning to understand. Miss Darragh, last night I asked Mr. Legge if, as a matter of routine, he would let us take his fingerprints. He refused. Why do you suppose he did that?"

"He's distressed and frightened. He thinks you suspect 'um."

"Then he should welcome any procedure that is likely to prove our suspicions groundless. He should rather urge us to take his prints than burst into a fit of hysterics when we ask for them."

A faint line appeared between Miss Darragh's eyes. Her brows were raised and the corners of her mouth turned down. She looked like a disgruntled baby.

"I don't say he's not foolish," she said. "I only say he's innocent of murder."

"There's one explanation that sticks out a mile," Alleyn said. "Do you know the usual reason for withholding fingerprints?"

"I do not."

"The knowledge that the police already have them."

Miss Darragh said nothing.

"Now if that should be the reason in this case," Alleyn continued, "it is only a matter of time before we arrive at the truth. If, to put it plainly, Legge has been in prison, we shall very soon trace his record. But we may have to arrest him for manslaughter to do it."

"All this," exclaimed Miss Darragh with spirit, "all this to prove he didn't kill Watchman. All this disgrace and trouble! And who's to pay the cost of ut? 'Twould ruin him entirely."

"Then he would be well advised to make a clean breast and tell us of his record, before we find it out for ourselves."

"How do you know that he has a record?"

"I think," said Alleyn, "I must tell you that I was underneath the south jetty at six o'clock this morning."

She opened her eyes very wide indeed, stared at him, clapped her fat little hands together, and broke into a shrill cackle of laughter.

"Ah, what an old fule you've made of me," said Miss Darragh.

III

But although she took Alleyn's disclosure in good part she still made no admissions. She was amused and interested in his exploit of the morning, didn't in the least resent it, and exclaimed repeatedly that it was no use trying to keep out of his clutches. But she did elude him, nevertheless, and he began to see her as a particularly slippery pippin, bobbing out of reach whenever he made bite at it.

Alleyn was on difficult ground and knew it. The notes that he and Fox had made of the conversation on the jetty were full of gaps and, though they pointed in one direction, contained nothing conclusive.

Detective officers are circumscribed by rules which, in more than one case, are open to several interpretations. It is impossible to define exactly the degrees of pressure in questions put by the detective. Every time an important case crops up he is likely enough to take risks. If he is lucky his departure from rule of thumb comes off, but at the end of every case, like a warning bogey, stands the figure of defending counsel, ready to pounce on any irregularity and shake it angrily before the jury.

Miss Darragh had not denied the suggestion that Legge had a police record, and Alleyn decided to take it as a matter of course that such a record existed and that she knew about it.

He said, "It's charming of you to let me down so lightly.'"

"For what, me dear man?"

"Why, for lying on my back in a wet dinghy and listening to your conversation."

"Isn't it your job? Why should I be annoyed? I'm only afraid you've misinterpreted whatever you heard."

"Then," said Alleyn, "I shall tell you how I have interpreted it, and you will correct me if I am wrong."

"So you say," said Miss Darragh good-humouredly.

"So I hope. I think that Legge has been to gaol, that you know it, that you're sorry for him, and that as long as you can avoid making a false statement you will give me as little information as possible. Is that right?"

"It's right in so far as I'll continue to hold me tongue."

"Ugh!" said Alleyn with a rueful grin. "You *are* being firm with me, aren't you? Well, here we go again. I think that if Mr. Legge had not been to gaol you would laugh like mad and tell me what a fool I was."

"You do, do you?"

"Yes. And what's more I do seriously advise you to tell me what you know about Legge. If you won't do that, urge Legge to come out of the thicket, and tell me himself. Tell him that we've always got the manslaughter charge up our sleeves. Tell him that his present line of behaviour is making us extremely suspicious." Alleyn paused and looked earnestly at Miss Darragh.

"You said something to this effect this morning, I know," he added. "Perhaps it's no good. I don't see why I should finesse. I asked Legge to let me take impressions of his finger-prints. Good prints would have been helpful but they're not essential. He picked up the dart, it has been tested and we've got results. I asked him for impressions because I already suspected he had done time and I wanted to see how he'd respond. His response convinced me that I was right. We've asked the superintendent at Illington to send the dart to the Fingerprint Bureau. To-morrow they will telephone the result."

"Let 'um," said Miss Darragh cheerfully.

"You know, you're withholding information. I ought to be very stiff with you."

"It's not meself I mind," she said. "I'm just wishing you'd leave the poor fellow alone. You're wasting your time, and you're going to do 'um great harm in the end. Let 'um alone."

"We can't," said Alleyn. "We can't let any of you alone."

She began to look very distressed and beat the palms of her hands together.

169

"You're barking up the wrong tree," she said. "I'll accuse no one; but look farther and look nearer home."

And when he asked her what she meant she only repeated very earnestly, "Look farther and look nearer home. I'll say no more."

CHAPTER FOURTEEN

CRIME AND MR. LEGGE

I

"Fox," said Alleyn, "get your hat. We'll walk to Cary Edge Farm and call on Miss Moore. Miss Darragh says it's a mile and a quarter over the downs from the mouth of the tunnel. She says we shall pass Cubitt painting Parish on our way. An eventful trip. Let us take it."

Fox produced the particularly rigid felt hat that appears when his duties take him into the country. Will Pomeroy was in the front passage and Alleyn asked him if he might borrow one of a collection of old walking-sticks behind the door.

"Welcome," said Will shortly.

"Thank you so much. To get to Cary Edge Farm we turn off to the right from the main road, don't we?"

"Cary Edge?" repeated Will and glared at them.

"Yes," said Alleyn. "That's where Miss Moore lives, isn't it?"

"She won't be up-along this morning."

"What's that, sonny?" called old Abel from the private taproom. "Be the gentlemen looking for Miss Dessy? She's on her way over by this time for Saturday marketing."

Will moved his shoulders impatiently.

"You know everyone's business, Father," he muttered.

"Thank you, Mr. Pomeroy," called Alleyn. "We'll meet her on the way, perhaps."

"'Less she do drive over in old car," said Abel, coming to the door. "But most times her walks."

170

He looked apprehensively at Will and turned back into the bar.

"We'll risk it," said Alleyn. "Back to lunch, Mr. Pomeroy."

"Thank 'ee, sir."

Alleyn and Fox walked up to the tunnel mouth. When they reached it Alleyn glanced back at the Plume of Feathers. Will stood in the doorway looking after them. As Alleyn turned, Will moved back into the pub.

"He will now telephone Cary Edge in case Miss Moore has not left yet," observed Alleyn. "No matter. She'll have been expecting us to arrive sooner or later. Come on."

They entered the tunnel.

"Curious, Fox, isn't it?" said Alleyn, and his voice rang hollow against the rock walls. "Ottercombe must have been able to shut itself up completely on the landward side. I bet some brisk smuggling went forward in the old days. Look out, it's slippery. Miss Moore must be an intrepid driver if she motors through here in all weathers."

They came out into the sunshine. The highway, a dusty streak, ran from the tunnel. On each side the downs rolled along the coast in a haze of warmth, dappled by racing cloud shadows. Farther inland were the hills and sunken lanes, the prettiness of Devon; here was a sweep of country where Englishmen for centuries had looked coastwards, while ships sailed across their dreams and their thoughts were enlarged beyond the seaward horizon.

"Turn to the right," said Alleyn.

They climbed the bank and rounded a furze bush in a sunken hollow.

"Good spot for a bit of courting," said Fox, looking at the flattened grass.

"Yes, you old devil. You may invite that remarkably buxom lady who brought our breakfast to stroll up here after hours."

"Mrs. Ives?"

"Yes. You'll have to get in early, it's a popular spot. Look at those cigarette butts, squalid little beasts. Hallo!"

He stooped and picked up two of them.

"The cigarette butt," he said, "has been derided by our detective novelists. It has lost caste and now ranks with the Chinese and datura. No self-respecting demi-highbrow will

171

use it. That's because old Conan Doyle knew his job and got in first. But you and I Br'er Fox, sweating hacks that we are, are not so superior. This cigarette was a Dahabieh, an expensive Egyptian. Harper said they found some Egyptian cigarettes in Watchman's pockets. Not many Dahabieh-smokers in Ottercombe, I imagine. Parish and Cubitt smoke Virginians. This one has lipstick on it. Orange-brown."

" Not Miss Darragh," said Fox.

" No, Fox. Nor yet Mrs. Ives. Let's have a peer. There's been rain since the Dahabiehs were smoked. Look at those heelmarks. Woman's heels. Driven into the bank."

" She must have been sitting down," said Fox. " Or lying. Bit of a struggle seemingly. What had the gentleman been up to?"

" What indeed? What did Miss Darragh mean by her 'look further and look nearer home?' We've no case for a jury yet, Fox. We mustn't close down on a theory. Can you find any masculine prints? Yes. Here's one. Not a very good one."

" Watchman's?"

" We may have to find out. May be nothing in it. Wait a bit, though. I'm going back to the pub."

Alleyn disappeared over the ridge and was away for some minutes. He returned with two stones, a bit of an old box, and a case.

" Better," he said, " in your favourite phrase, Br'er Fox, to be sure than sorry."

He opened the case. It contained a rubber cup, a large flask of water, some plaster-of-Paris, and a spray-pump. Alleyn sprayed the footprints with shellac, and collected twigs from under the furze bushes, while Fox mixed plaster. They took casts of the four clearest prints, reinforcing the plaster with the twigs and adding salt to the mixture. Alleyn removed the casts when they had set, covered the footprints with the box, weighted it with stones, and dragged branches of the furze bush down over the whole. The casts he wrapped up and hid.

" You never know," he said. " Let's move on."

They mounted the rise and away on the headland saw Cubitt, a manikin, moving to and fro before his easel.

" We'll have to join the infamous company of gapers," said

172

Alleyn. "Look, he's seen us. How eloquent of distaste that movement was! There's Parish beyond. He's doing a big thing. I believe I've heard Troy* speak of Norman Cubitt's work. Let's walk along the cliffs, shall we?"

They struck out to the right and hadn't gone many yards before they came to a downward slope where the turf was trampled. Alleyn stooped and examined it.

"Camp-stool," he muttered. "And here's an empty tube. Water-colour. The Darragh spoor, I imagine. An eventful stretch of country, this. I wonder if she was here on that Friday. You can't see the other place from here, Fox. You might hear voices, though."

"If they were raised a bit."

"Yes. Angry voices. Well, on we go."

As they drew nearer Cubitt continued to paint, but Parish kept turning his head to look at them. When they came within earshot, Cubitt shouted at them over his shoulder.

"I hope to God you haven't come here to ask questions. I'm busy."

"All right," said Alleyn. "We'll wait."

He walked beyond them, out of sight of the picture. Fox followed him. Alleyn lay on the lip of the headland. Beneath them, the sea boomed and thudded against a rosy cliff. Wreaths of seaweed endlessly wove suave patterns about Coombe Rock. A flight of gulls mewed and circled in and out of the sunlight.

"What a hullabaloo and a pother," said Alleyn. "How many thousands of times before they come adrift, do these strands of seaweed slither out and swirl and loop and return? Their gestures are so beautiful that it is difficult to realise they are meaningless. They only show us the significance of the water's movements but for themselves they are helpless. And the sea is helpless too, and the winds it obeys, and the wider laws that rule the winds, themselves ruled by passive rulers. Dear me, Fox, what a collection of ordered inanities. Rather like police investigations. I can't look over any more, I've no head for heights."

"Here comes Mr. Cubitt, sir," said Fox.

Alleyn rolled over and saw Cubitt, a vast figure against the sky.

* Mrs. Roderick Alleyn, R.A.

173

"We're resting now," said Cubitt. "Sorry to choke you off, but I was on a tricky bit."

"We are extremely sorry to bother you," said Alleyn. "I know it is beyond a painter's endurance to be interrupted at a critical moment."

Cubitt dropped down on the grass beside him.

"I'm trying to keep a wet skin of paint all over the canvas," he said. "You have to work at concert pitch for that!"

"Good Lord!" Alleyn exclaimed. "You don't mean you paint right through that surface in three hours?"

"It keeps wet for two days. I've got a new brand of slow-drying colours. Even so, it's a bit of an effort."

"I should think so, on a thing that size."

Parish appeared on the brow of the hill.

"Aren't you coming to see my portrait?" he cried.

Cubitt glanced at Alleyn and said, "Do, if you'd like to."

"I should, enormously."

They walked back to the easel.

The figure had come up darkly against the formalized sky. Though the treatment was one of extreme simplification, there was no feeling of emptiness. The portrait was at once rich and austere. There was no bravura in Cubitt's painting. It seemed that he had pondered each brushmark gravely and deeply, and had then laid it down on a single impulse and left it so.

"Lord, it's good," said Alleyn. "It's grand, isn't it?"

Parish stood with his head on one side and said, "Do you like it?" but Cubitt said, "Do you paint, Alleyn?"

"No, not I. My wife does."

"Does she exhibit at all?"

"Yes," said Alleyn. "Her name is Troy."

"O God!" said Cubitt. "I'm sorry."

"She's good, isn't she?" said Alleyn humbly.

"To my mind," answered Cubitt, "the best we've got."

"Do you think it's like me?" asked Parish. "I tell Norman he hasn't quite got my eyes. Judging by my photographs, you know. Not that I don't like it. I think it's marvellous, old boy, you know that."

"Seb," said Cubitt, "your price is above rubies. So long as you consider it a pretty mockery of nature, I am content."

174

"Oh," said Parish, "I'm delighted with it, Norman, really. It's only a suggestion about the eyes."

"How long have you been at it?" asked Alleyn.

"This is the sixth day. I had two mornings before the catastrophe. We shelved it for a bit after that."

"Naturally," added Parish solemnly. "We didn't feel like it."

"Naturally," agreed Cubitt dryly.

"Tell me," said Alleyn, "did you ever pass Mr. Watchman on your way to or from this place?"

Cubitt had laid a streak of blue across his palette with the knife. His fingers opened and the knife fell into the paint. Parish's jaw dropped. He looked quickly at Cubitt as if asking him a question.

"How do you mean?" asked Cubitt. "He was only here one day. He died the night after he got here."

"That was the Friday," said Alleyn. "Did you work here on the Friday morning?"

"Yes."

"Well, was Mr. Watchman with you?"

"Oh, no," said Cubitt quickly, "he was still in bed when we left."

"Did you see him on the way home?"

"I don't think we did," said Parish.

"In a little hollow this side of a furze bush and just above the main road."

"I don't think so," said Parish.

"No," said Cubitt, a little too loudly. "We didn't. Why?"

"He was there some time," said Alleyn vaguely.

Cubitt said, "Look here, do you mind if I get going again? The sun doesn't stand still in the heavens."

"Of course," said Alleyn quickly.

Parish took up the pose. Cubitt looked at him and filled a brush with the colour he had mixed. He raised the brush and held it poised. Alleyn saw that his hand trembled.

"It's no good," said Cubitt abruptly, "we've missed it. The sun's too far round."

"But it's not ten yet," objected Parish.

"Can't help it," said Cubitt and put down his palette.

"For pity's sake," said Alleyn, "don't go wrong with it now."

"I'll knock off, I think."

"We've been a hell of a nuisance. I'm sorry."

"My dear chap," said Parish, "you're nothing to the modest Violet. It's a wonder she hasn't appeared. She puts up her easel about five yards behind Norman's and brazenly copies every stroke he makes."

"It's not as bad as that, Seb."

"Well, personally," said Parish, "I've had quite as much as I want of me brother Terence and me brother Brian and me unfortunate cousin poor Bryonie."

"What!" exclaimed Alleyn.

"She has a cousin who is a noble lord and got jugged for something."

"Bryonie," said Alleyn. "He was her cousin, was he?"

"So it seems. Do you remember the case?"

"Vaguely," said Alleyn. "Vaguely. Was Miss Darragh anywhere about on that same morning?"

"She was over there," said Parish. "Back in the direction you've come from. She must have stayed there for hours. She came in, drenched to the skin and looking like the wrath of heaven, late in the afternoon."

"An enthusiast," murmured Alleyn. "Ah, well, we mustn't hang round you any longer. We're bound for Cary Edge Farm."

Something in the look Cubitt gave him reminded Alleyn of Will Pomeroy.

Parish said, "To call on the fair Decima? You'll be getting into trouble with Will Pomeroy."

"Seb," said Cubitt, "pray don't be kittenish. Miss Moore is out on Saturday mornings, Alleyn."

"So Will Pomeroy told us, but we hoped to meet her on her way to Ottercombe. Good luck to the work. Come along, Fox."

II

A few yards beyond the headland they struck a rough track that led inland and over the downs.

"This will take us there, I expect," said Alleyn. "Fox, those gentlemen lied about Watchman and the furze bush."

"I thought so, sir. Mr. Cubitt made a poor fist of it."

"Yes. He's not a good liar. He's a damn' good painter. I must ask Troy about him."

Alleyn stopped and thumped the point of his stick on the ground.

"What the devil," he asked, "is this about Lord Bryonie?"

"He's the man that was mixed up in the Montague Thringle case."

"Yes, I know. He got six months. He was Thringle's cat's-paw. By George, Fox, d'you know what?"

"What, sir?"

"Luke Watchman defended Bryonie. I'll swear he did."

"I wouldn't remember."

"Yes, you would. You must. By gum, Fox, we'll look up that case. Watchman defended Bryonie, and Bryonie was Miss Darragh's cousin. Rum. Monstrous rum."

"Sort of fetched her into the picture by another route."

"It does. Well, come on. We've lots of little worries. I wonder if Miss Moore uses orange-brown lipstick. I tell you what, Fox, I think Cubitt is catched with Miss Moore."

"In love with her?"

"Deeply, I should say. Did you notice, last night, how his manner changed when he talked about her? The same thing happened just now. He doesn't like our going to Cary Edge. Nor did Will Pomeroy. I wonder what she's like."

He saw what Decima was like in thirty seconds. She came swinging over the hilltop. She wore a rust-coloured jumper and a blue skirt. Her hair was ruffled, her eyes were bright, and her lips were orange-brown. When she saw the two men she halted for a second and then came on towards them.

Alleyn took off his hat and waited for her.

"Miss Moore?"

"Yes."

She stopped, but her pose suggested that it would be only for a moment.

"We hoped that we might meet you if we were too late to find you at home," said Alleyn. "I wonder if you can give us a minute or two. We're police officers."

"Yes."

"I'm sorry to bother you, but would you mind——?"

"You'd better come back to the farm," said Decima. "It's over the next hill."

"That will be a great bore for you, I'm afraid."

"It doesn't matter. I can go into the Coombe later in the morning."

"We shan't keep you long. There's no need to turn back."

Decima seemed to hesitate.

"All right," she said at last. She walked over to a rock at the edge of the track and sat on it. Alleyn and Fox followed her.

She looked at them with the kind of assurance that is given to women who are unusually lovely and sometimes to women who are emphatically plain. She was without self-consciousness. Nobody had told Alleyn that Decima was beautiful and he was a little surprised. "It's impossible," he thought, "that she can be in love with young Pomeroy."

"I suppose it's about Luke Watchman," said Decima.

"Yes, it is. We've been sent down to see if we can tidy up a bit."

"Does that mean they think it was murder?" asked Decima steadily, "or don't you answer that sort of question?"

"We don't," rejoined Alleyn, smiling, "answer that sort of question."

"I suppose not," said Decima.

"We are trying," continued Alleyn, "to trace Mr. Watchman's movements from the time he got here until the time of the accident."

"Why?"

"Part of the tidying-up process."

"I see."

"It's all pretty plain sailing except for Friday morning."

Alleyn saw her head turn so that for a second she looked towards Ottercombe Tunnel. It was only for a second and she faced him again.

"He went out," said Alleyn, "soon after breakfast. Mr. Pomeroy saw him enter the tunnel. That was about ten minutes before you left Ottercombe. Did you see Mr. Watchman on your way home?"

"Yes," she said, "I saw him."

"Where, please."

178

"Just outside the top of the tunnel by some furze bushes. I think he was asleep."

"Did he wake as you passed him?"

She clasped her thin hands round her knees.

"Oh, yes," she said.

"Did you stop, Miss Moore?"

"For a minute or two, yes."

"Do you mind telling us what you talked about?"

"Nothing that could help you. We—we argued about theories."

"Theories?"

"Oh, politics. We disagreed violently over politics. I'm a red rebel, as I suppose you've heard. It rather annoyed him. We only spoke for a moment."

"I suppose it was apropos of the Coombe Left Movement?" murmured Alleyn.

"Do you?" asked Decima.

Alleyn looked apologetic. "I thought it might be," he said, "because of your interest in the movement. I mean it would have been a sort of natural ingredient of a political argument, wouldn't it?"

"Would it?" asked Decima.

"You're quite right to snub me," said Alleyn ruefully. "I'm jumping to conclusions and that's a very bad fault in our job. Isn't it, Fox?"

"Shocking, sir," said Fox.

Alleyn pulled out his notebook.

"I'll just get this right, if I may. You met Mr. Watchman at about what time?"

"Ten o'clock."

"At ten o'clock or thereabouts. You met him by accident. You think he was asleep. You had a political argument in which the Coombe Left Movement was not mentioned."

"I didn't say so, you know."

"Would you mind saying so or saying not so? Just for my notes?" asked Alleyn, with such a quaint air of diffidence that Decima suddenly smiled at him.

"All right," she said, "we did argue about the society, though it's nothing to do with the case."

"If you knew the numbers of these books that I've filled

179

with notes that have nothing whatever to do with the case
you'd feel sorry for me," said Alleyn.

"We'll manage things better when we run the police,"
said Decima.

"I hope so," said Alleyn gravely. "Was your argument
amicable?"

"Fairly," said Decima.

"Did you mention Mr. Legge?"

Decima said, "Before we go any further there's something
I'd like to tell you."

Alleyn looked up quickly. She was frowning. She stared
out over the downs, her thin fingers were clasped together.

"You'd better leave Robert Legge alone," said Decima.
"If Watchman was murdered it wasn't by Legge."

"How do you know that, Miss Moore?"

"I watched him. He hadn't a chance. The others will
have told you that. Will, Norman Cubitt, Miss Darragh.
We've compared notes. We're all positive."

"You don't include Mr. Parish?"

"He's a fool," said Decima.

"And Mr. Abel Pomeroy?"

She blushed unexpectedly and beautifully.

"Mr. Pomeroy's not a fool but he's violently prejudiced
against Bob Legge. He's a ferocious Tory. He thinks we—
he thinks Will and I are too much under Bob's influence. He
hasn't got a single reasonable argument against Bob. He
simply would rather it was Bob than anyone else and has
hypnotised himself into believing he's right. It's childishly
obvious. Surely you must see that. He's an example in
elementary psychology."

Alleyn raised an eyebrow. She glared at him.

"I'm not disputing it," said Alleyn mildly.

"Well, then——"

"The camp seems to be divided into pro-Leggites and anti-
Leggites. The funny thing about the pro-Leggites is this:
they protest his innocence and, I am sure, believe in it. You'd
think they'd welcome our investigations. You'd think they'd
say, 'Come on, then, look into his record, find out all you
like about him. He's a decent citizen and an innocent man.
He'll stand up to any amount of investigation.' They don't.
They take the line of resenting the mildest form of question

about Legge. Why's that, do you suppose? Why do you warn us off Mr. Legge?"

"I don't——"

"But you do," insisted Alleyn gently.

Decima turned her head and stared searchingly at him.

"You don't look a brute," she said doubtfully.

"I'm glad of that."

"I mean you don't look a complete robot. I suppose, having once committed yourself to a machine, you have to tick over in the appointed manner."

"Always providing someone doesn't throw a spanner in the works."

"Look here," said Decima. "Bob Legge had an appointment in Illington that evening. He was just going; he would have gone if Will hadn't persuaded him not to. Will told him he'd be a fool to drive through the tunnel with the surface water pouring through it."

She was watching Alleyn and she said quickly, "Ah! You didn't know that?"

Alleyn said nothing.

"Ask Will. Ask the man he was to meet in Illington."

"The local police have done that," said Alleyn. "We won't question the appointment. We only know Mr. Legge didn't keep it."

"He couldn't. You can't drive through that tunnel when there's a stream of surface water pouring down it."

"I should hate to try," Alleyn agreed. "We're not making much of an outcry over Mr. Legge's failure to appear. It was you, wasn't it, who raised the question?"

"I was only going to point out that Bob didn't know there would be a thunderstorm, did he?"

"Unless the pricking of his thumbs or something——"

"If this was murder I suppose it was premeditated. You won't deny that?"

"No. I don't deny that."

"Well, then! Suppose he was the murderer. He didn't know it would rain. It would have looked pretty fishy for him to put off his appointment for no reason at all."

"It would. I wonder why he didn't tell me this himself."

"Because he's so worried that he's at the end of his tether.

Because you got hold of him last night and deliberately played on his nerves until he couldn't think. Because——"

"Hallo!" said Alleyn. "You've seen him this morning, have you?"

If Decima was disconcerted she didn't show it. She blazed at Alleyn:

"Yes, I've seen him, and I scarcely recognized him. He's a mass of overwrought nerves. His condition's pathological. The next thing will be a confession of a crime he didn't commit."

"How about the crime he did commit?" asked Alleyn. "It would be more sensible."

And that did shake her. She caught her breath in a little gasping sigh. Her fingers went to her lips. She looked very young and very guilty.

"So you knew all the time," said Decima.

CHAPTER FIFTEEN

LOVE INTEREST

I

ALLEYN had expected that Decima would hedge, rage, or possibly pretend to misunderstand him. Her sudden capitulation took him by surprise and he was obliged to make an embarrassingly quick decision. He plumped for comparative frankness.

"We expect," he said, "a report on his fingerprints. When that comes through we shall have official confirmation of a record that we suspected from the first and of which we are now certain."

"And you immediately put two and two together and make an absurdity."

"What sort of absurdity?"

"You will say that because he didn't come forward and announce 'I'm a man with a police record,' he's a murderer. Can't you see how he felt? Have you the faintest notion what it's like for a man who's been in prison to try to get back, to try to earn a miserable pittance? Have you ever thought about it at all or wondered for two seconds what becomes of the people you send to gaol? To their minds? I know you look after their bodies with the most intolerable solicitude. You are there always. Every employer is warned. There is no escape. It would be better, upon my honour, I believe it would be better, to hang them outright than—than to tear their wings off and let them go crawling out into the sun."

"That's a horrible analogy," said Alleyn, "and a false one."

"It's a true analogy. Can't you see why Legge was so frightened? He's only just stopped having to report. Only now has he got his thin freedom. He thought, poor wretch, that we wouldn't keep him on if we knew he'd been to gaol. Leave him alone! Leave him alone!"

"How long have you known this about him?" asked Alleyn.

She stood up abruptly, her palm against her forehead as though her head ached.

"Oh, for some time."

"He confided in you? When?"

"When he got the job," said Decima flatly.

Alleyn did not believe this, but he said politely, "That was very straightforward, wasn't it?" And as she did not answer he added, "Do you know why he went to prison?"

"No. I don't want to know. Don't tell me. He's wiped it out, God knows, poor thing. Don't tell me."

Alleyn reflected, with a certain amount of amusement, that it was as well she didn't want to know what Legge's offence had been. Some image of this thought may have appeared in his face. He saw Decima look sharply at him and he said hurriedly: "All this is by the way. What I really want to ask you is whether, on the morning you encountered Mr. Watchman by the furze bush, you were alone with him all the time."

He saw that now she was frightened for herself. Her eyes widened, and she turned extremely pale.

"Yes. At least—I—no. Not at the end. I rather think Norman Cubitt and Sebastian Parish came up."

"You rather think?"

"They did come up. I remember now. They did."

"And yet," said Alleyn, "when I asked them if they saw
183

Watchman that morning, they said definitely that they did not."

"They must have forgotten."

"Please! You can't think I'll believe that. They must have been over every word that was spoken by Watchman during the last hours of his life. They have told me as much. Why, they must have walked back to the inn with him. How could they forget?"

Decima said, "They didn't forget."

"No?"

"It was for me. They are being little gents."

Alleyn waited.

"Well," she said, "I won't have it. I won't have their chivalry. If you must know, they surprised their friend in a spirited attempt upon my modesty. I wasn't pleased and i was telling him precisely what I thought of him. I suppose they were afraid you would transfer your attentions from Bob Legge to me."

"Possibly," agreed Alleyn. "They seem to think I am a sort of investigating chameleon."

"I imagine," said Decima in a high voice, "that because I didn't relish Mr. Watchman's embraces and told him so, it doesn't follow that I set to work and murdered him."

"It's not a strikingly good working hypothesis. I'm sorry to labour this point but we've no sense of decency in the force. Had he shown signs of these tricks before?"

The clear pallor of Decima's face was again flooded with red. Alleyn thought, "Good Lord, she's an attractive creature. I wonder what the devil she's like." He saw, with discomfort, that she could not look at him. Fox made an uneasy noise in his throat and stared over the downs. Alleyn waited. At last Decima raised her eyes.

"He was like that," she murmured.

Alleyn now saw a sort of furtiveness in Decima. She was no longer tense, her pose had changed and she offered him no challenge.

"I suppose he couldn't help it," she said, and then with a strange look from Alleyn to Fox she added, "It's nothing. It doesn't mean anything. You needn't think ill of him. I was all right."

In half a minute she had changed. The educational

amenities provided by that superior mother had fallen away from her. She had turned into a rustic beauty, conscious of her power of provocation. The rumoured engagement to Will Pomeroy no longer seemed ridiculous. And, as if she had followed Alleyn's thought, she said, "I'd be very glad if you wouldn't say anything of this to Will Pomeroy. He knows nothing about it. He wouldn't understand."

"I'll sheer off it if it can be done. It was not the first time you'd had difficulty with Watchman?"

She paused and then said, "We hadn't actually—come to blows before."

"Blows? Literally?"

"I'm afraid so."

She stood up. Alleyn thought she mustered her self-assurance. When she spoke again it was in a different key, ironically and with composure.

"Luke," she said, "was amorous by habit. No doubt it was not the first time he'd miscalculated. He wasn't in the least disconcerted. He—wasn't in the least in love with me."

"No?"

"It's merely a squalid little incident which I had rather hoped to forget. It was, I suppose, very magnificent of Seb and Norman to lie about it, but the gesture was too big for the theme."

"Now she's being grand at me," thought Alleyn. "We are back in St. Margaret's Hall."

He said: "And Watchman had never made himself objectionable before that morning?"

"I did not usually find him particularly objectionable."

"I intended," said Alleyn, "to ask you if he had ever made love to you before?"

"I have told you he wasn't in the least in love with me."

"I'm unlucky in my choice of words, I see. Had he ever kissed you, Miss Moore?"

"This is very tedious," said Decima. "I have tried to explain that my acquaintance with Luke Watchman was of no interest or significance to either of us, or, if you will believe me, to you."

"Then why," asked Alleyn mildly, "don't you give me an answer and have done with it?"

"Very well," said Decima breathlessly. "You can have
185

your answer. I meant nothing to him and he meant less to me. Until last Friday he'd never been anything but the vaguest acquaintance." She turned on Fox. "Write it down. You'll get no other answer. Write it down."

"Thank you, miss," said Fox civilly. "I don't think I've missed anything. I've got it down."

"Well, have you finished?" demanded Decima, who had succeeded in working herself up into a satisfactory temper. "Is there anything else you want to know? Do you want a list in alphabetical order of my encounters with any other little Luke Watchmans who have come my way?"

"No," said Alleyn. "No. We limit our impertinences to the police code. Our other questions are, I hope, less offensive. They concern the brandy you gave Mr. Watchman, the glass into which you poured it, and the bottle from which it came."

"All right. What about them?"

"May we have your account of that particular phase of the business?"

"I told Oates and I told the coroner. Someone suggested brandy. I looked round and saw Luke's glass on the table, between the settle where he lay and the dart-board. There wasn't any brandy left in it. I saw the bottle on the bar. I was very quick about it. I got it and poured some into the glass. I did not put anything but brandy in the glass. I can't prove I didn't, but I didn't."

"But perhaps we can prove it. Was anyone near the table? Did anyone watch you pour the brandy?"

"Oh, God!" said Decima wearily, "how should I know? Sebastian Parish was nearest to the table. He may have noticed. I don't know. I took the glass to Luke. I waited for a moment while Abel Pomeroy put iodine on Luke's finger, and then I managed to pour a little brandy between his lips. It wasn't much. I don't think he even swallowed it, but I suppose you won't believe that."

"Miss Moore," said Alleyn suddenly, "I can't tell you how pathetically anxious we are to accept the things people tell us." He hesitated and then said, "You see, we spend most of our working life asking questions. Can you, for your part, believe that we get a kind of sixth sense and sometimes feel very certain indeed that a witness is speaking the truth, or, as the case may be, is lying? We're not allowed to recognize our sixth sense, and when it points a crow's flight towards the truth we may not follow it. We must cut it dead and follow the dreary back streets of collected evidence. But if they lead us anywhere at all it is almost always to the same spot."

"Eminently satisfactory," said Decima. "Everything for the best in the best of all possible police forces."

"That wasn't quite what I meant. Was it after you had given him the brandy that Mr. Watchman uttered the single word ' poisoned '?"

"Yes."

"Did you get the impression that he spoke of the brandy?"

"No. I don't know if your sixth sense will tell you I'm lying, but it seemed to me he *tried* to take the brandy, and perhaps did swallow a little, and that it was when he found he couldn't drink that he said—that one word. He said it between his clenched teeth. I had never seen such a look of terror and despair. Then he jerked his hand. Miss Darragh was going to bandage it. Just at that moment the lights went out."

"For how long were they out?"

"Nobody knows. It's impossible to tell. I can't. It seemed an age. Somebody clicked the switch. I remember that. To see if it had been turned off accidentally, I suppose. It was a nightmare. The rain sounded like drums. There was broken glass everywhere—crunch, crunch, squeak. And his voice. Not like a human voice. Like a cat mewing. And his heels, drumming on the settle. And everybody shouting in the dark."

Decima spoke rapidly and twisted her fingers together.

"It's funny," she said, "I either can't talk about it at all, or I can't stop talking about it. Once you start, you go on and on. It's rather queer. I suppose he was in great pain. I suppose it was torture. As bad as the rack, or disembowelling. I've got a terror of physical pain. I'd recant anything first."

"Not," said Alleyn, "your political views?"

"No," agreed Decima, "not those. I'd contrive to commit suicide or something. Perhaps it was not pain that made him cry like that and drum with his heels. Perhaps it was only reflex something. Nerves."

"I think," said Alleyn, "that your own nerves have had a pretty shrewd jolt."

"What do you know about nerves?" demanded Decima with surprising venom. "Nerves! These things are a commonplace to you. Luke Watchman's death-throes are so much data. You expect me to give you a neat statement about them. Describe in my own words the way he clenched his teeth and drew back his lips."

"No," said Alleyn. "I haven't asked you about those things. I have asked you two questions of major importance. One was about your former relationship with Watchman and the other about the brandy you gave him before he died."

"I've answered you. If that's all you want to know you've got it. I can't stand any more of this. Let me——"

The voice stopped as if someone had switched it off. She looked beyond Alleyn and Fox to the brow of the hillock. Her eyes were dilated.

Alleyn turned. Norman Cubitt stood against the sky.

"Norman!" cried Decima.

He said, "Wait a bit, Decima," and strode down towards her. He stood and looked at her and then lightly picked up her hands.

"What's up?" asked Cubitt.

"I can't stand it, Norman."

Without looking at Alleyn or Fox he said, "You don't have to talk to these two precious experts if it bothers you. Tell 'em to go to hell." And then he turned her round and, over her shoulder, grinned, not very pleasantly, at Alleyn.

"I've made a fool of myself," whispered Decima.

She was looking at Cubitt as though she saw him for the first time. He said, "What the devil are you badgering her for?"

"Just," said Alleyn, "out of sheer wanton brutality."

"It's all right," said Decima. "He didn't badger, really. He's only doing his loathsome job."

Her eyes were brilliant with tears, her lips not quite closed,

nd still she looked with a sort of amazement into Cubitt's
ace.

"Oh, Norman!" she said, "I've been so inconsistent and
fluttery and feminine. Me!"

"You!" said Cubitt.

"In a moment," thought Alleyn, "he'll kiss her." And he
said, "Thank you so much, Miss Moore. I'm extremely sorry
to have distressed you. I hope we shan't have to bother you
again."

"Look here, Alleyn," said Cubitt, "if you do want to see
Miss Moore again I insist on being present, and that's flat."

Before Alleyn could answer this remarkable stipulation
Decima said, "But, my dear man, I'm afraid you can't insist
on that. You're not my husband, you know."

"That can be attended to," said Cubitt. "Will you marry
me?"

"Fox," said Alleyn, "what are you staring at? Come back
to Ottercombe."

III

"Well, Mr. Alleyn," said Fox when they were out of earshot, "we see some funny things in our line of business, don't
we? What a peculiar moment now, for him to pick on for
a proposal. Do you suppose he's been courting her for a fair
while, or did he spring it on her sudden?"

"Suddenish, I fancy, Fox. Her eyes were wet and that, I
suppose, went to his head. I must say she's a very lovely
creature. Didn't you think so?"

"A very striking young lady," agreed Fox. "But I thought
the super said she was keeping company with young
Pomeroy?"

"He did."

"She's a bit on the classy side for him, you'd think."

"You would, Fox."

"Well, now, I wonder what she'll do. Throw him over
and take Mr. Cubitt? She looked to me to be rather inclined
that way."

"I wish she'd told the truth about Watchman," said Alleyn.

"Think there'd been something between them, sir? Relations? Intimacy?"

"Oh Lord, I rather think so. It's not a very pleasant thought."

"Bit of a *femme fatale*," said Fox carefully. "But there you are. They laugh at what we used to call respectability, don't they? Modern women——"

Alleyn interrupted him.

"I know, Fox, I know. She is very sane and intellectual and modern, but I don't mind betting there's a strong dram of rustic propriety that pops up when she least expects it. I think she's ashamed of the Watchman episode, whatever it was, and furious with herself for being ashamed. What's more, I don't believe she knew until Friday that Legge was an old lag. All guesswork. Let's forget it. We'll have an early lunch and call on Dr. Shaw. I want to ask him about the wound in the finger. Come on."

They returned by way of the furze bush, collecting the casts and Alleyn's case. As they disliked making entrances with mysterious bundles, they locked their gear in the car and went round to the front of the Feathers. But here they walked into a trap. Sitting beside Abel Pomeroy on the bench outside the front door was an extremely thin and tall man with a long face, a drooping moustache, and foolish eyes. He stared very fixedly at Fox, who recognised him as Mr. George Nark and looked the other way.

"Find your road all right, gentlemen?" asked Abel.

"Yes, thank you, Mr. Pomeroy," said Alleyn.

"It's a tidy stretch, sir. You'll be proper warmed up."

"We're not only warm but dry," said Alleyn.

"Ripe for a pint, I dessay, sir?"

"A glorious thought," said Alleyn.

Mr. Nark cleared his throat. Abel threw a glance of the most intense dislike at him and led the way into the private bar.

"'Morning," said Mr. Nark, before Fox could get through the door.

"'Morning, Mr. Nark," said Fox.

"Don't know but what I wouldn't fancy a pint myself," said Mr. Nark firmly, and followed them into the Private.

Abel drew Alleyn's and Fox's drinks.

"'Alf-'n-'alf, Abel," said Mr. Nark grandly.

Somewhat ostentatiously Abel wiped out a shining pint-pot with a spotless cloth. He then drew the mild and bitter.

"Thank 'ee," said Mr. Nark. "Glad to see you're acting careful. Not but what, scientifically speaking, you ought to bile them pots. I don't know what the law has to say on the point," continued Mr. Nark, staring very hard at Alleyn. "I'd have to look it up. The law may touch on it, and it may not."

"Don't tell us you're hazy on the subject," said Abel bitterly. "Us can't believe it."

Mr. Nark smiled in an exasperating manner and took a pull at his beer. He made a rabbit-like noise with his lips, snapping them together several times with a speculative air. He then looked dubiously into his pint-pot.

"Well," said Abel tartly, "what's wrong with it? You'm not pisoned this time, I suppose?"

"I dessay it's all right," said Mr. Nark. "New barrel bain't it?"

Abel disregarded this inquiry. The ship's decanter that they had seen in the cupboard now stood on the bar counter. It was spotlessly clean. Abel took the bottle of Amontillado from a shelf above the bar. He put a strainer in the neck of the decanter and began, carefully, to pour the sherry through it.

"What jiggery-pokery are you up to now, Abel?" inquired Mr. Nark. "Why, Gor'dang it, that thurr decanter was in the pison cupboard."

Abel addressed himself exclusively to Alleyn and Fox. He explained the various methods used by Mrs. Ives to clean the decanter. He poured himself out a glass of the sherry and invited them to join him. Under the circumstances they could scarcely refuse. Mr. Nark watched them with extraordinary solicitude and remarked that they were braver men than himself.

"Axcuse me for a bit if you please, gentlemen," said Abel elaborately to Alleyn and Fox. "I do mind me of summat I've got to tell Mrs. Ives. If you'd be so good as to ring if I'm wanted."

"Certainly, Mr. Pomeroy," said Alleyn.

Abel left them with Mr. Nark.

"Fine morning, sir," said Mr. Nark.

Alleyn agreed.

"Though I suppose," continued Mr. Nark wooingly, "all

weathers and climates are one to a man of your calling. Science," continued Mr. Nark, drawing closer and closer to Alleyn, "is a powerful high-handed mistress. Now, just as a matter of curiosity, sir, would you call yourself a man of science?"

"Not I," said Alleyn, good-naturedly. "I'm a policeman, Mr. Nark."

"Ah! That's my point. See? That's my point. Now, sir, with all respect you did ought to make a power more use of the great wonders of science. I'll give in your finger-prints. There's an astonishing thing, now! To think us walks about unconscious-like, leaving our pores and loops all over the shop for science to pick up and have the laugh on us."

It was a peculiarity of Mr. Nark's conversational style that as he drew nearer to his victim he raised his voice. His face was now about twenty inches away from Alleyn's and he roared like an infuriated auctioneer.

"I'm a reader," shouted Mr. Nark. "I'm a reader and you might say a student. How many printed words would you say I'd absorbed in my life? At a guess, now?"

"Really," said Alleyn. "I don't think I could possibly——"

"Fifty-eight million!" bawled Mr. Nark. "Nigh on it. Not reckoning twice overs. I've soaked up four hundred words, some of 'em as much as five syllable, mind you, every night for the last forty years. Started in at the age of fifteen. 'Sink or swim,' I said, 'I'll improve my brain to the tune of four hundred words per day till I passes out or goes blind!' And I done it. I don't suppose you know a piece of work called *The Evvylootion of the Spices?*"

"Yes."

"There's a tough masterpiece of a job. Took me a year and more, that did. Yes, I've tackled most branches of science. Now the last two years I've turned my eyes in the direction of crime. Trials of famous criminals, lives of murderers, feats of detection, all the whole biling of 'em. Can't get enough of 'em. I'm like that. Whole hog or nothing. Reckon I've sucked it dry."

Mr. Nark emptied his pint-pot and, perhaps as an illustrative gesture, sucked his moustache. He looked at Alleyn out of the corners of his eyes.

"This is a very pretty little case now," he said. "I don't say there's much in it but it's quite a pretty bit of an affair in its way. You'll be counting on knocking it off in a day or two, I suppose?"

"I don't know about that, Mr. Nark."

"I was a witness."

"At the inquest? I thought——"

"Not at the inquest," interrupted Mr. Nark in a great hurry. "No. Superintendent Nicholas Gawd-Almighty Harper had the running of the inquest. I was a witness to the event. More than that I've made a study of the affair and I've drew my own deductions. I don't suppose they'd interest you. But I've drew 'em."

Alleyn reflected that it was extremely unlikely that Mr. Nark's deductions would be either intelligible or interesting, but he made an agreeable noise and invited him to have another drink. Mr. Nark accepted and drew it for himself.

"Ah," he said. "I reckon I know as much as anybody about this affair. There's criminal carelessness done on purpose, and there's criminal carelessness done by accident, There's motives here and there's motives there, each of 'em making 'tother look like a fool, and all of 'em making the biggest fool of Nicholas Harper. Yes. Us chaps takes our lives in our hands when we calls in at Feathers for a pint. Abel knows it. Abel be too mortal deathly proud to own up."

"Carelessness, you said? How did it come about?"

If Mr. Nark's theory of how cyanide got on the dart was ever understood by himself he had no gift for imparting it to others. He became incoherent, and defensively mysterious. He dropped hints and, when pressed to explain them, took fright and dived into obscurities. He uttered generalisations of bewildering stupidity, assumed an air of huffiness, floundered into deep water, and remained there blowing like a grampus. Alleyn was about to leave him in this plight when, perhaps as a last desperate bid for official approval, Mr. Nark made a singular statement.

"The Garden of Eden," he said, "as any eddicated chap knows, is bunk. You can't tell me there's any harm in apples. I grow 'em. Us started off as a drop of jelly. We've come on gradual ever since, working our way up through slime and scales and tails to where we are. We had to *have* a female to do the job. Us knows that. Biological necessity. But she's been a poisonous snare and a curse to us as even the ignorant author of Genesis had spotted and noted down in his foolish fashion, under cover of a lot of clap-trap. She's wuss than a serpent on her own, and she's mostly always at the back of our troubles. Searchy la fem as the French detectives say and you ought to bear in mind. This ghastly affair started a year ago and there's three alive now that knows it. There was four."

Alleyn realised with a sinking heart that he would have to pay attention to Mr. Nark. He saw in Mr. Nark a desire for fame struggling with an excessive natural timidity. Mr. Nark hungered for the admiring attention of the experts. He also dreaded the law, to which he seemed to accord the veneration and alarm of a neophyte before the altar of some tricky and fickle deity. Alleyn decided that he must attempt to speak to him in his own language.

He said, "That's very interesting, Mr. Nark. Strange, isn't it, Fox? Mr. Nark has evidently—" he fumbled for the magic word—" evidently made the same deductions as we have from the evidence in hand."

Fox gave his superior a bewildered and disgusted glance. Alleyn said rather loudly, "See what I mean, Fox?"

Fox saw. "Very striking, sir," he said. "We'll have to get you into the force, Mr. Nark."

Mr. Nark buttoned his coat.

"What'll you take, gentlemen?" he asked.

But it was heavy going. To get any sense out of him Alleyn had to flatter, hint, and cajole. A direct suggestion threw him into a fever of incoherence, at a hint of doubt he became huffy and mysterious. As she seemed to be the only woman in the case, Alleyn attempted to crystalize on Decima.

"Miss Moore," he said at last, "is naturally very much upset by Mr. Watchman's death."

"Ah," said Mr. Nark. "Is she? She may be. P'raps! I don't know anything about women. She may be. Huh!"

Alleyn achieved a knowing laugh in which Fox joined.

"You look below the surface, I see," said Alleyn.

"I base my deductions on facts. Take an example," said Mr. Nark. His third drink, a Treble Extra, had begun to have a mellowing effect. His native burr returned to his usually careful utterance and he smiled knowingly. "Take an example. I don't say it's true to natur'. It's an illustration. A parrible. If I takes a stroll up along Apple Lane of a warm night and hears a courting couple 'tother side of hedge in old Jim Moore's orchard, I draws my own conclusions. Doan't I?"

"No doubt."

"'Ess. And *ef*," said Mr. Nark, "*ef* I do bide thurr not with idea of eavesdropping but only to reflect and ponder in my deep bitter manner on the wiles of females in gineral, and *ef* I yurrs a female voice I axpects to yurr, and a maskeline voice I doan't axpects to yurr, and *ef*," continued Mr. Nark fighting his way to the end of his sentence, "I says 'Hallo!' to myself and passes on a step, and *ef* I meets the owner of the maskuline voice I did axpect to yurr, standing sly and silent in hedge: what do I say? Wait a bit. Doan't tell me. I'll tell you. I says 'Durn it!' I says, 'thurr'll be bloodshed along of this yurr if us doan't look out.' And *ef* I bides a twelve month or more and nothing happens and then something does happen, bloody and murderous, what do I say then?"

Mr. Nark raised his hand as a signal that this question also was rhetorical and paused for so long that Fox clenched both his fists and Alleyn had time to light a cigarette.

"I sez," said Mr. Nark loudly, "not a damn' thing."

"What!" ejaculated Alleyn.

"Not a damn' thing. But I thinks like a furnace."

"What do you think, Mr. Nark?" asked Alleyn with difficulty.

"I thinks 'tis better to yold my tongue ef I want to keep breath in my body. And I yolds it. 'Ess fay, I be mum and I stays mum."

Mr. Nark brought off a mysterious gesture with his right forefinger, leered knowingly at Alleyn, and tacked rapidly towards the door. Once there, he turned to deliver his last word.

"Doan't you go calling my words statements," he said. "They're a nallegory, and a nallegory's got nothing to do with the law. You doan't trip me up thicky fashion. I know natur' of an oath. Searchy la fem."

CHAPTER SIXTEEN

ALLEYN EXCEEDS HIS DUTY

I

AFTER they had lunched Alleyn brought his report up to date and Fox, sitting solemnly at the parlour table, typed it in duplicate. Alleyn had a brief interview with Abel Pomeroy and returned with three tumblers. One of these he smashed to splinters with the poker, keeping the pieces together, and emptying them into a tin. The other two he wrapped up and placed, with a copy of his report, in his case. He also spent some time throwing down darts and finding that they stuck in the floor. These employments at an end, they drove to Illington. The day had turned gloomy, heavy rain was falling, and the road was slimy.

Alleyn dropped Fox at Woolworths and went on to Dr. Shaw's house at the end of the principal street. He was shown into a surgery that smelt of leather, iodine, and ether. Here he found Dr. Shaw who was expecting him. Alleyn liked the look of Dr. Shaw. He had an air of authority and a pleasing directness of manner.

"I hope I'm not an infernal nuisance, coming at this hour," said Alleyn. "Your patients——"

"That's all right. Surgery doesn't start till two. Old trot sitting out there in the waiting-room. *Malade imaginaire.* Do her good to wait a bit, she plagues my life out. Sit down. What do you want to talk about?"

"Principally about the wound and the dart. I've read the police report of the inquest."

"Thought it rather full of gaps? So it is. Mordant, the coroner, you know, is a dry old stick, but he's got his wits about him. Respectable bacteriologist in his day. He and Harper got their heads together, I imagine, and decided just how much would be good for the jury. What about the wound?"

"Were there any traces of cyanide, prussic acid, or whatever the blasted stuff is?"

"No. We got a man from London, you know. One of your tame experts. Good man. Mordant and I were both there when he made his tests. We didn't expect a positive result from the wound."

"Why not?"

"Two reasons. He'd bled pretty freely and, if the stuff was introduced on the dart, what wasn't absorbed would be washed away by blood. Also, the stuff's very volatile."

"They found the trace on the dart."

"Yes. Oates kept his head and put the dart into a clean soda-water bottle and corked it up. Couldn't do that with the finger."

"Even so, wouldn't you expect the stuff to evaporate on the dart.'

Dr. Shaw uttered a deep growl and scratched his cheek.

"Perfectly correct," he said, "you would. Puzzling."

"Doesn't it look as if the Scheele's acid, or rather the fifty per cent prussic acid solution, must have been put on the dart a very short time before Oates bottled it up?"

"It does. Thought so all along."

"How long was it, after the event, that you got there?"

"Within half an hour after his death."

"Yes. Now, look here. For private consumption only, would you expect a cyanide solution, however concentrated, to kill a man after that fashion?"

Dr. Shaw thrust his hands in his pockets and stuck out his lower lip.

"I'm not a toxicologist," he said. "Mordant is, and we've taken the king-pin's opinion. Watchman, on his own statement, had a strong idiosyncrasy for cyanide. He told Parish and Cubitt about this the night before the tragedy."

"Yes. I saw that in the files. It's good enough, you think?"

"We've got no precedent for the affair. The experts seem to think it good enough. That dart was thrown with considerable force. It penetrated to the bone, or rather, it actually entered the finger at such an angle that it must have lain along the bone. It's good enough."

"There was no trace of cyanide in the mouth?"

"None. But that doesn't preclude the possibility of his having taken it by the mouth."

"O Lord!" sighed Alleyn, "nor it does. Did the room stink of it?"

"No, it stank of brandy. So did the body. Brandy, by the way, is one of the antidotes given for cyanide poisoning. Along with artificial respiration, potassium permanganate, glucose, and half a dozen other remedies none of which is much use if the cyanide has got into the bloodstream."

"Have you a pair of scales?" asked Alleyn abruptly. "Chemical scales or larger but accurate scales?"

"What? Yes. Yes, I have. Why?"

"Fox, my opposite number, will be here in a minute. He's calling at the police station for the fragments of broken tumbler. I've got a rather fantastic notion. Nothing in it, I dare say. We've a pair of scales at the pub, but I thought you might be amused if we did a bit of our stuff here."

"Of course I would. Wait a moment while I get rid of that hypochondriacal crone. Shan't be long. Don't move. She only wants a flea in her ear."

Dr. Shaw went into the waiting-room. Alleyn could hear his voice raised in crisp admonishment.

"——pull yourself together, you know. . . . sound as a bell . . . take up a hobby . . . your own physician . . . be a sensible woman."

A doorbell rang and in a moment Fox and Superintendent Harper were shown into the surgery.

"Hallo, hallo!" said Harper. "What's all this I hear? Thought I'd come along. Got an interesting bit of news for you." He dropped his voice. "I sent a chap up to London by the milk train. He's taken the dart to Dabs and they've just rung through. The prints are good enough. What do you think they've found?"

"I can see they've found something, Nick," said Alleyn, smiling.

"You bet they have. Those prints belong to Mr. Montague Thringle who did four years for embezzlement and came out of Broadmoor twenty-six months ago."

"Loud cheers," said Alleyn, "and *much* laughter."

"Eh? Yes, and that's not the best of it. Who do you think defended one of the accused and shifted all the blame on to Thringle?"

"None other than Luke Watchman, the murdered K.C.?"

"You're right. Legge's a gaolbird who owes, or thinks he owes, his sentence to Watchman. He's just dug himself in pretty, with a nice job and a lot of mugs eating out of his hand, and along comes the very man who can give him away."

"Now I'll tell you something you don't know," said Alleyn. "Who do you think was implicated with Montague Thringle and got off with six months?"

"Lord Bryonie. Big scandal it was."

"Yes. Miss Darragh's unfortunate cousin, the Lord Bryonie."

"You don't tell me that. Miss Darragh! I'd put her right out of the picture."

"She holds a watching-brief for Thringle-alias-Legge, I fancy," said Alleyn, and related the morning's adventure.

"By gum!" cried Harper, "I think it's good enough. I reckon we're just about right for a warrant. With the fact that only Legge could have known the dart would hit—what d'you think? Shall we pull him in?"

"I don't think we'll make an arrest just yet, Nick."

"Why not?"

"Well, I think the result would be what the high-brows call a miscarriage of justice. I'll tell you why."

II

But before he had finished telling them why, an unmistakable rumpus in the street announced the arrival of Colonel Brammington's car. And presently Colonel Brammington himself came charging into the room with Dr. Shaw on his heels.

"I saw your car outside," he shouted. "A galaxy of all the talents with Aesculapius to hold the balance. Aesculapius usurps the seat of justice, poetic justice with her lifted scale."

Dr. Shaw put a small pair of scales on the table and grinned. Colonel Brammington took one of Alleyn's cigarettes and hurled himself into a chair.

"Curiosity," he said, "was praised by the great Doctor as one of the permanent and certain characteristics of a vigorous intellect. His namesake, the rare Ben, remarked that he did love to note and to observe. With these noble precedents before me I shall offer no excuse, but, following the example of Beatrice, shall like a lapwing run, close to the ground, to hear your confidence. An uncomfortable feat and one for which my great belly renders me unfit. Have you any matches? Ah, thank you."

Harper, with his back to the chief constable, turned his eyes up for the edification of Fox. He laid a tin box on the table.

"Here you are, Mr. Alleyn."

"Good." Alleyn weighed the box speculatively in his hands and then emptied its contents into the scale.

"What is that?" demanded Colonel Brammington. "Glass? Ah, the orts and fragments of the brandy-glass, perhaps?"

"That's it, sir," said Alleyn.

"And pray why do you put them on the scales?"

"Sir," murmured Alleyn politely, "to find out their weight."

Colonel Brammington said mildly, "You mock me, by heaven. And what do they weigh?"

"Two ounces, forty-eight grains. That right, Dr. Shaw?"

"That's it."

Alleyn returned the fragments to their box and took a second box from his pocket.

"In this," he said, "are the pieces of an identically similar glass for which I gave Mr. Pomeroy one and sixpence. They are his best glasses. Now then."

He tipped the second shining heap into the scales.

"Yes, by George," said Alleyn softly. "Look. Two ounces, twenty-four grains."

"Here!" exclaimed Harper. "That's less. It must be a lighter glass."

"No," said Alleyn. "It's the same brand of glass. Abel took the glasses for the brandy from a special shelf. I've borrowed two more, unbroken. Let's have them, Fox."

Fox produced two tumblers. Each of them weighed two ounces, twenty-four grains.

"But look here," objected Harper. "We didn't get every scrap of that glass up. Some of it had been ground into the boards. Watchman's glass should, if anything, weigh less than the others."

"I know," said Alleyn.

"Well, then——"

"Some other glass must have fallen," said Colonel Brammington. "They were full of distempering draughts, red-hot with drinking. One of them may have let fall some other glass. A pair of spectacles. Didn't Watchman wear an eye-glass?"

"It was round his neck," said Dr. Shaw, "unbroken."

"There seems to have been no other glass broken, sir," said Alleyn. "I've asked. Did you find all the pieces in one place, Harper?"

"Like you'd expect, a bit scattered and trampled about. I dare say there were pieces in the soles of their boots. Damn it all," cried Harper in exasperation, "it *must* weigh lighter."

He weighed the glass again, peering suspiciously at the scales. The results was exactly the same. The fragments of Watchman's glass weighed twenty-four grains heavier than the unbroken tumbler.

"This is rather amusing," said Colonel Brammington.

Alleyn sat at the table and spread the broken glass over a sheet of paper. Fox gave him a pair of tweezers and he began to sort the pieces into a graduated row. The other men drew closer.

"It's the same tumbler," said Colonel Brammington. "There, you see, are the points of one of those loathsome stars."

Alleyn took a jeweller's lens from his pocket.

"Ah!" muttered Colonel Brammington, staring at him with a bulging and raffish eye. "He peers, He screws a glass into his orb and with enlarged vision feeds his brain."

"We always feel rather self-conscious about these things," said Alleyn, "but they have their uses. Here, I think, are three, no, four small pieces of glass that *might* be different from—well, let's weigh them."

He put them in the scales.

"Thirty-one grains. That, Harper, leaves a margin of eleven grains for the bits you missed. Any good?"

"Do you think these bits are a different class of stuff, Mr. Alleyn?" asked Harper.

"I think so. There's a difference in colour and if you look closely you can see they're a bit thicker."

"He has written a monograph on broken tumblers," cried Colonel Brammington delightedly. "Let me look through your lens."

He crouched over the table.

"They are different," he said. "You are quite right, my dear Alleyn. What can it mean? The iodine bottle? No, it was found unbroken beneath the settle."

"What did you discover at Woolworth's, Fox?" asked Alleyn.

"Nothing much, Mr. Alleyn. I tried all the other places as well. They haven't sold any and they say there's very little shop-lifting in Illington."

"Veil after veil will lift," remarked Colonel Brammington, "but there will be veil upon veil behind. What is this talk of shop-lifting?"

"I'll explain, sir," began Alleyn.

"On second thoughts, pray don't. I prefer, Alleyn, to be your Watson. You dine with me to-night? Very good. Give me the evidence, and let me brood."

"But don't you wish to hear Mr. Alleyn's case, sir?" asked Harper in a scandalised voice. "Your position——"

"I do not. I prefer to listen to voices in the upper air nor lose my simple faith in mysteries. I prefer to take the advice of the admirable Tupper and will let not the conceit of intellect hinder me from worshipping mystery. But nevertheless give me your plain plump facts. I will sing, with Ovid, of facts."

"You will not have Ovid's privilege of inventing them," rejoined Alleyn. "I have brought a copy of my report on the case. It's up to date."

Colonel Brammington took the file and seemed to become the victim of an intolerable restlessness. He rose, hitched up his shapeless trousers and said rapidly in a high voice, "Well, good-bye, Shaw. Come to dinner to-night."

"Oh, thank you very much, sir," said Dr. Shaw. "I'd like to. Black tie?"

"As the fancy takes you. I shall make some gesture. Broadcloth and boiled linen. You come, Harper?"

"Thank you, sir, I'm afraid I can't. I've got to——"

"All right. I see. Three then. You, Alleyn; Shaw, and —ah——"

"Fox," said Alleyn.

"Ah, yes. Splendid. Well, *au revoir.*"

"I was going to ask you, sir——" began Harper.

"O God! What?"

"It doesn't matter, sir, if you're in a hurry," Harper opened the door with emphasised politeness. "Good-afternoon, sir."

"Oh, good-bye to you, Harper, good-bye," said Colonel Brammington impatiently, and plunged out.

"If that," said Harper sourly, "is the modern idea of a chief constable it's not mine. You wouldn't credit it, would you, that when that gentleman's brother dies, he'll be a Lord? A Lord, mind you! Bawling hurricane. Where's he get the things he says, Doctor? Out of his head or out of books?"

"Not having his brains, his memory, or his library, I can't tell you," said Dr. Shaw.

III

Alleyn, Fox and Harper went to the police station. Here they had a long reiterative conversation. They compared Alleyn's casts with the shoes Watchman wore on the day of his death, and found that they tallied exactly. They went over the case step by step. Alleyn expounded, the others listened. They laid their collection of oddments on Harper's table; the brandy-bottle, the broken glass, the iodine bottle, the stained newspaper, the small china vessel from the rat-hole and the bottle of Scheele's Acid. Harper gave Alleyn a stoppered bottle.

"Ah," said Alleyn, "that's the stuff out of the rat-hole jar. I want you to get it analysed. Perhaps Dr. Mordant would do it. No, I suppose that would be too unofficial. It had better go up to London."

"You think our murderer got the stuff from the garage?" asked Harper.

"I do."

"But the thing was full."

"Because it was full," said Alleyn.

"You reckon that was water," asked Harper slowly.

"Yes, Nick."

"I see," said Harper.

"The poison-party," said Alleyn, "was attended by Abel, who put the prussic acid in the china pot and stopped the hole; by Will, by Miss Moore, by Legge, who only looked in for a moment, and by a couple of fishermen who were on their way to the public bar and who don't come into the picture. Subsequently Abel warned everybody in the place about what he had done, so that the actual attendance at the poison-party may not give us our answer. On the other hand it is possible that one of them lagged behind and pinched the poison. They all profess to have forgotten in what order they left. Now prussic acid in Mr. Noggins fifty per cent solution is a highly volatile liquid. Judging by the stench, its fumes have accounted for at least one rat, so probably it was not removed immediately. On the other hand it seems it would evaporate considerably in something under an hour. I'm not sure on this point. We'll experiment. The experts say in their report, under an hour. Very good. My contention is that the murderer must have nipped into the garage, within an hour after Abel left it, and taken the poison which would be kept in a tightly-corked bottle until it was needed."

"But how the hell would he get it? The jar had Abel's prints. It hadn't been touched."

"Do you remember——?"

"By God!" shouted Harper. "Don't tell me. I've got it." He broke into a stream of oaths through which his enlightenment struggled for expression.

"That's it," said Alleyn. "Looks like it, doesn't it?"

"Looks like it!" ejaculated Harper. "It blasted well shrieks of it. I'm a hell of a detective I am! Look at me! I missed the point about that evaporation business! Took Abel in to look at the pot and he said it was just the amount he'd poured in. Well, the damn thing was full. I never thought it might be water. I took photographs and sealed the place up just as it was. I did pour off this stuff and keep it. I'll say that for myself. I made sure the poison had come out of the bottle in the cupboard. Blast it!"

"Abel's prints," Alleyn said, "were still on the key of the cupboard and on the knob. You can't open the door without turning the key and the knob. Dr. Shaw saw that, when he looked at the cupboard and waited until it had been tested for prints. If anyone else had been to the cupboard they would either have left their own prints, used gloves and

204

smeared Abel's prints, or else wiped them off entirely. Nobody could have been to the cupboard."

"I knew that, but all the same—— Well, I suppose I thought they might have got at the bottle while—oh, hell!"

"Anybody might have missed it, Mr. Harper," said Fox. "I didn't pick it till Mr. Alleyn pointed it out."

"And I was lucky," said Alleyn. "I'd read Taylor on the cyanides during our trip down."

"Well," said Harper, "the coroner and Dr. Shaw missed the point. Oates gave evidence of discovery of the stuff in the rat-hole. Old Pomeroy deposed it was the same amount he'd poured in. Nobody said anything about evaporation."

"Oates," Alleyn pointed out, "saw it the first night with Dr. Shaw, before they knew the exact nature of the poison. Not much more than twenty-six hours after it was put there."

"He might have just dipped the dart in the stuff," said Harper. "I did think of that. But now——"

"Now we know the dart must have been doctored a very short time before Oates sealed it up. You see where we're heading?"

"Yes," said Harper unwillingly. "I see, all right. But suppose Legge had the stuff on him and put it on the dart just before he threw it——"

"He didn't," said Alleyn. "Believe me, he didn't. He's a clumsy man. He fumbles. His hands are coarse and his fingers are thick. To get cyanide on that dart with seven pairs of eyes watching him, he'd need the skill and the hands of a conjurer. Even Abel Pomeroy, who thinks or wants to think Legge did the job, can't offer an idea of how he did it. Parish, who has thrown Legge in my teeth every time I've seen him, hasn't an argument to offer. And on the other side we've got Will, Miss Moore, Miss Darragh and Cubitt all ready to swear with, I believe, perfect truth, that Legge, as he stood there under the light, had no chance of anointing the fourth or any other dart."

"But we can't explain the poison in any other way."

"Oh, yes," said Alleyn, "I think we can. This is our case——"

Five o'clock had struck and they were still at the police station. Alleyn had gone over every word of his report with Harper. He had described each interview and had sorted the scraps of evidence into two groups, the relevant and the irrelevant. He had poured prussic acid solution into Abel's little jar and, to reproduce rat-hole conditions, had placed it in a closed drawer. At the end of forty-six minutes half had evaporated.

"So you see," said Alleyn, "if the liquid you found in the tin is water, as I believe it is, it looks as if the murderer must have visited the garage within forty-six minutes. Now on that night—the night on which Watchman chipped Legge and Will Pomeroy lost his temper—Legge gave an exhibition of dart-throwing which lasted only a few seconds. This took place a few minutes after Abel had set the poison in the garage. The argument followed. Legge went into the public bar where he brought off the trick with the darts. He then returned and joined the others in a game of Round-the-Clock——"

"There you are," interrupted Harper. "He could—sorry. Go on."

"I know he could, Nick, but wait a bit. According to your report they all, with the exception of Miss Darragh, who had gone to bed, stayed in the private taproom until closing time. Our forty-five minutes have gone."

"I suppose," said Harper, "one of them might have gone out for a few minutes without being noticed."

"Yes, and that is a point that will be urged by counsel. All we can prove here is opportunity—possibility. We can't bring anything home. May we have the stuff you took from the rat-hole, Nick? Fox, would you get my bag? Mr. Noggins was generous with his prussic acid and there are at least three ounces of the water, if it is water. The analyst can lend us half. Let's poach on his preserves and find out for ourselves."

Fox opened Alleyn's bag. From it he took two open-mouthed vessels about two inches high, two watch glasses, and a small bottle. Alleyn squinted at the bottle.

"Silver nitrate. That's the stuff. Can you produce some warm water, Nick? Well, well, I *am* exceeding my duty to be sure."

Harper went out and returned with a jug of water and a photographic dish. Alleyn poured a little water into the dish, half-filled one of his tiny vessels with the fluid found in the rat-hole, and the other with acid from Abel's bottle. He wetted the underside of the watch-glasses with nitrate solution and placed them over the vessels. He then stood the vessels, closed by the watch-glasses, in the warm water.

"Fox now says the Lord's Prayer backwards," he explained. "I emit a few oddments of ectoplasm and Hi Cockalorum the spell is wound up! Take a look at that, Nick."

They stared at the dish. On the surface of the prussic acid a little spiral had risen. It became denser, it flocculated and the watch-glass was no longer transparent but covered with an opaque whiteness.

"That's cyanide, that was," said Alleyn. "Now, look at the other. A blank, my lord. It's water, Br'er Fox, it's water. Now let's pour them back into their respective bottles and don't give me away to the analyst."

"I suppose," said Harper, as Alleyn tidied up. "I suppose this means we needn't worry ourselves about the cupboard. The cuboard doesn't come into the blasted affair."

Alleyn held on the palm of his hand the three pieces of glass he had separated from the fragments of the broken brandy tumbler, and the small misshapen lumps he had found in the ashes of the fire.

"Oh, yes," he said. "Yes. We're not home yet, not by a long march, but the cupboard still comes into the picture. Think."

Harper looked from the pieces of glass to Alleyn's face and back again.

"Yes," he said slowly, "yes. But you'll have the devil of a job to prove it."

"I agree," said Alleyn. "Nevertheless, Nick, I hope to prove it."

CHAPTER SEVENTEEN

MR. FOX TAKES SHERRY

I

PARISH came downstairs singing "La Donna è Mobile." He had a pleasant baritone voice which had been half-trained in the days when he had contemplated musical comedy. He sang stylishly and one could not believe that he sang unconsciously. He swung open the door of the private tap and entered on the last flourish of that impertinent, that complacently debonair refrain.

"Good-evening, sir," said Abel from behind the bar. "'Tis pleasant to hear you'm back to your churruping ways again."

Parish smiled wistfully.

"Ah, Abel," he said with a slight sigh, "it's not as easy as it sounds; but my cousin would have been the last man to want long faces, poor dear old fellow."

"So he would, then," rejoined Abel heartily, "the very last."

"Ah," said Mr. Nark, shaking his head. Norman Cubitt looked over the top of his tankard and raised his eyebrows. Legge moved into the ingle-nook where Miss Darragh sat knitting.

"What'll you take, Mr. Parish?" asked Abel.

"A Treble Extra. I need it. Hallo, Norman, old man," said Parish with a sort of brave gaiety. "How's the work going?"

"Nicely, thank you, Seb." Cubitt glanced at the clock. It was a quarter past seven. "I'm thinking of starting a big canvas," he said.

"Are you? What subject?"

"Decima," said Cubitt. He put his tankard down on the bar. "She has very kindly said she'll sit to me."

"How'll you paint her?" asked Parish.

"I thought on the downs by Cary Edge. She's got a red sweater thing. It'll be life size. Full length."

"Ah, now," exclaimed Miss Darragh from the ingle-nook, "you've taken my advice in the latter end. Haven't I been at you, now, ever since I got here to take Miss Moore for your subject? I've never seen a better. Sure the picture'll be your masterpiece for she's a lovely young creature."

"But, my dear chap," objected Parish, "we're off in a day or two. You'll never finish it."

"I was going to break it gently to you, Seb. If you don't object I think I'll stay on for a bit."

Parish looked slightly hurt.

"That's just as you like, of course," he said. "Don't ask me to stay. The place is too full of memories."

"Besides," said Cubitt dryly, "you start rehearsals on to-day week, don't you?"

"As a matter of fact I do." Parish raised his arms and then let them fall limply to his sides. "Work!" he said. "Back to the old grind. Ah well!" And he added with an air of martyrdom, "I can go back by train."

"I'll drive you into Illington, of course."

"Thank you, old boy. Yes, I'd better get back to the treadmill."

"Keep a stiff upper lip, Seb," said Cubitt with a grin.

The door opened and Alleyn came in. He wore a dinner jacket and stiff shirt. Someone once said of him that he looked like a cross between a grandee and a monk. In evening clothes the grandee predominated. Parish gave him a quick appraising glance, Mr. Nark goggled, and Miss Darragh looked up with a smile. Cubitt rumpled his hair and said: "Hallo! Here comes the county!"

Mr. Legge shrank back into the ingle-nook. Upon all of them a kind of weariness descended. They seemed to melt away from him and towards each other. Alleyn asked for two glasses of the special sherry and told Abel that he and Fox would be out till latish.

"May we have a key, Mr. Pomeroy?"

"Us'll leave side-door open," said Abel. "No need fur key, sir. Be no criminals in this neighbourhood. Least-ways——" He stopped short and looked pointedly at Legge.

"That's splendid," said Alleyn. "How far is it to Colonel Brammington's?"

"'Bout eight mile, sir. Shankley Court. A great masterpiece of a place, sir, with iron gates and a deer-park. Carry on four miles beyond Illington and turn left at The Man of Devon."

"Right," said Alleyn. "We needn't leave for half an hour." Cubitt went out.

Alleyn fidgeted with a piece of rag round his left hand. It was clumsily tied and fell away, disclosing a trail of red.

He twitched the handkerchief out of his breast pocket, glanced at it and swore. There was a bright red spot on the handkerchief.

"Blast that cut," said Alleyn. "Now I'll have to get a clean one."

"Hurt yurrself, sir?" asked Abel.

"Tore my hand on a rusty nail in the garage."

"In the garage!" ejaculated Mr. Nark. "That's a powerful dangerous place to get a cut finger. Germs galore, I dessay, and as like as not some of the poison fumes still floating about."

"Aye," said Abel angrily, "that's right, George Nark. All my premises is stiff with poison. Wonder 'tis you come anigh 'em. Here, Mr. Alleyn, sir, I'll get 'ee a dressing fur that thurr cut."

"If I could have a bit of rag and a dab of peroxide or something."

"Doan't you have anything out of that fatal cupboard," said Mr. Nark. "Not if you value the purity of your blood-stream."

"You know as well as I do," said Abel, "that thur cup-board's been scrubbed and fumigated. Not that thurr's any-thing in it. Thurr baint. Nicholas Harper made off with my first-aid set, innocent though it wurr."

"And the iodine bottle," pointed out Mr. Nark, "so you can't give the inspector iodine, lethal or otherwise."

"Thurr's another first-aid box upstairs," said Abel. "In bathroom cupboard. Will!" He looked into the public bar. "Will! Get 'tother box out of bathroom cupboard, my sonny. Look lively."

"It doesn't matter, Mr. Pomeroy," said Alleyn. "Don't bother. I'll use this handkerchief."

"No trouble, sir, and you'll need a bit of antiseptic in that cut if you took it off of a rusty nail. I'm a terror fur iodine,

r. I wurr a surgeon's orderly in France, Mr. Alleyn, and earned hospital ways. Scientific ideas baint George Nark's rivate property though you might think they wurr."

Will Pomeroy came downstairs and into the private tap. He put a small first-aid box on the counter and returned to he public bar. Abel opened the box.

" 'Tis spandy-new," he said. "I bought it from a traveller only couple of days afore accident. Hallo! Yurr, Will!"

"What's up?" called Will.

"Iodine bottle's gone."

"Eh?"

"Where's iodine?"

"I dunno. It's not there," shouted Will.

"Who's had it?"

"I dunno. I haven't."

"It really doesn't matter, Mr. Pomeroy," said Alleyn. "It's led itself clean. If I may have a bit of this lint and an inch of the strapping. Perhaps there wasn't any iodine?"

" 'Course there wurr," said Abel. "Yurr's lil' bed whurr it ay. Damme, who's been at it? *Mrs. Ives!*"

He stumped out and could be heard roaring angrily about he back premises.

Alleyn put a bit of lint over his finger and Miss Darragh tuck it down with strapping. He went upstairs, carrying his own glass of sherry and Fox's. Fox was standing before the ooking-glass in his room knotting a sober tie. He caught ight of Alleyn in the glass.

"Lucky I brought my blue suit," said Fox, "and lucky you rought your dress clothes, Mr. Alleyn."

"Why didn't you let me tell Colonel Brammington that ve'd neither of us change, Foxkin?"

"No, no, sir. It's the right thing for you to dress, just s much as it'd be silly for me to do so. Well, it'd be an ffected kind of way for me to act, Mr. Alleyn. I never get black coat and boiled shirt on my back except at the Lodge neetings and when I'm on a night-club job. The colonel vould only think I was trying to put myself in a place where don't belong. Did you find what you wanted, Mr. Alleyn?"

"Abel bought another first-aid set, two days before Watch-man died. The iodine has been taken. He can't find it."

"Is that so?"

Fox brushed the sleeves of his coat and cast a final searching glance at himself in the glass. "I washed that razor blade," he said.

"Thank you, Fox. I was a little too free with it. Bled all over Abel's bar. Most convincing. What's the time? Half-past seven. A bit early yet. Let's think this out."

"Right oh, sir," said Fox. He lifted his glass of sherry. "Good luck, Mr. Alleyn," he said.

Decima had promised to come to Coombe Head at eight o'clock. Cubitt lay on the lip of the cliff and stared at the sea beneath him, trying, as Alleyn had tried, to read order in the hieroglyphics traced by the restless seaweed. The sequence was long and subtle, unpausing, unhurried. Each pattern seemed significant but all melted into fluidity, and he decided, as Alleyn had decided, that the forces that governed these beautiful but inane gestures ranged beyond the confines of his imagination. He fell to appraising the colour and the shifting tones of the water, translating these things into terms of paint, and he began to think of how, in the morning, he would make a rapid study from the lip of the cliff.

"But I must fix one pattern only in my memory and watch for it to appear in the sequence, like a measure in some intricate saraband."

He was so intent on this project that he did not hear Decima come and was startled when she spoke to him.

"Norman?"

Her figure was dark and tall against the sky. He rose and faced her.

"Have you risen from the sea?" he asked. "You are lovely enough."

She did not answer and he took her hand and led her a little way over the headland to a place where their figures no longer showed against the sky. Here they faced each other again.

"I am so bewildered," said Decima. "I have tried since this morning to feel all sorts of things. Shame. Compassion for Will. Anxiety. I can feel none of them. I can only wonder why we should so suddenly have fallen in love."

"It was only sudden for you," said Cubitt. "Not for me."

"But——? Is that true. How long——?"

"Since last year. Since the first week of last year."

Decima drew away from him.

"But, didn't you know? I thought last year that you had guessed."

"About Luke? Yes, I guessed."

"Everything?"

"Yes, my dear."

"I wish very much that it hadn't happened," said Decima. "Of that I am ashamed. Not for the orthodox reason but because it made such a fool of me; because I pretended to myself that I was sanely satisfying a need, whereas in reality I merely lost my head and behaved like a dairymaid."

"Hallo!" said Cubitt. "You're being very county. What's wrong with dairymaids in the proletariat?"

"Brute," muttered Decima and, between laughter and tears, stumbled into his arms.

"I love you very much," whispered Cubitt.

"You'd a funny way of showing it. Nobody ever would have dreamt you thought anything about me."

"Oh, yes, they would. They did."

"Who?" cried Decima in terror. "Not Will?"

"No. Miss Darragh. She as good as told me so. I've seen her eyeing me whenever you were in the offing. God knows I had a hard job to keep my eyes off you. I've wanted like hell to do this."

But after a few moments Decima freed herself.

"This is going the wrong way," she said. "There mustn't be any of this."

Cubitt said, "All right. We'll come back to earth. I promised myself I'd keep my head. Here, my darling, have a cigarette, for God's sake, and don't look at me. Sit down. That's right. Now, listen. You remember the morning of that day?"

"When you and Sebastian came over the hill?"

"Yes. Just as you were telling Luke you could kill him. Did you?"

"No."

"Of course you didn't. Nor did I. But we made a botch of things this morning. Seb and I denied that we saw Luke as we came back from Coombe Head, and I think Alleyn knew we were lying. I got a nasty jolt when he announced that he was going to see you. I didn't know what to do. I dithered round and finally followed him, leaving Seb to come home by himself. I was too late. You'd told him?"

"I told him that Luke and I quarrelled that morning because Luke had tried—had tried to make love to me. I didn't tell him—Norman, I lied about the rest. I said it hadn't happened before. I was afraid. I was cold with panic. I didn't know what you and Sebastian had told him. I thought, if he found out that I had been Luke's mistress and that we'd quarrelled, he might think—— They say poison's a woman's weapon, don't they? It was like one of those awful dreams. I don't know what I said. I lost my head. And that other man, Fox, kept writing in a book. And then you came and it was as if—oh, as if instead of being alone in the dark and terrified I had someone beside me."

"Why wouldn't you stay with me when they'd gone?"

"I don't know. I wanted to think. I was muddled."

"I was terrified you wouldn't come here to-night, Decima."

"I shouldn't have come. What are we to do about Will?"

"Tell him."

"He'll be so bewildered," said Decima, "and so miserable."

"Would you have married him if this hadn't happened?"

"I haven't said I would marry you."

"I have," said Cubitt.

"I don't know that I believe in the institution of marriage."

"You'll find that out when you've tried it, my darling."

"I'm a farmer's daughter. A peasant."

"The worst of you communists," said Cubitt, "is that you're such snobs. Always worrying about class distinctions. Come here."

"Norman," said Decima presently, "who do you think it was?"

"I don't know. I don't know."

Cubitt pressed her hands against him and, after a moment, spoke evenly. "Did Will ever guess about you and Luke?"

She moved away from him at arm's length. "You can't think Will would do it?"

"Did he guess?"

"I don't think I——"

"I rather thought he had guessed," said Gubitt.

III

When Alleyn had gone out, the atmosphere of the taproom changed. Parish began to talk to Abel, Miss Darragh asked Legge when he was moving into Illington, Mr. Nark cleared his throat and, by the simple expedient of shouting down every one else, won the attention of the company.

"Ah," he said. "Axing the road to Shankley Court, was he? Ah. I expected it."

Abel gave a disgruntled snort.

"I expected it," repeated Mr. Nark firmly. "I had a chat with the chief inspector this morning."

"After which, in course," said Abel, "he knew his business. All he's got to do is to clap handcuffs on somebody."

"Abel," said Mr. Nark, "you're a bitter man. I'm not blaming you. A chap with a turrible load on his conscience, same as what you've got, is scarcely responsible for his words."

"On his conscience!" said Abel angrily. "What the devil do you mean? Why doan't 'ee say straight out I'm a murderer?"

"Because you're not, Abel. Murder's one thing and negligence is another. Manslaughter is the term for your crime. If proper care had been took, as I told the chief inspector—though, mind you, I'm not a chap to teach a man his own business——"

"What sort of a chap did you say you wasn't?"

Miss Darragh intervened.

"I'm sure," she said, "we all must hope for the end of this terrible affair. Whether 'twas accident, or whether 'twas something else, it's been a dreadful strain and an anxiety for us all."

"So it has then, Miss," agreed Abel. He looked at Legge who had turned his back and was engaged, with the assistance of a twisted handkerchief, on an unattractive exploration of his left ear. "Sooner they catch the murderer the happier all of us'll be."

Parish caught Abel's eyes and he too looked at Legge.

"I can't believe," said Parish, "that a crime like this can go unpunished. I shall not rest content until I know my cousin is avenged."

"Ah now, Mr. Parish," said Miss Darragh, "you must not let this tragedy make the bitter man of you. Sure, you're talking like the Count of Monte Cristo if 'twas he was the character I call to mind."

"Do I sound bitter?" asked Parish in his beautiful voice. "Perhaps I do. Perhaps I am."

A shadow of something that might have been a twinkle flitted across Miss Darragh's face.

"A little too bitter," she said, and it was impossible to tell whether or not she spoke ironically.

On the floor above them there was a sudden commotion. A man's voice spoke urgently. They heard a scuffle of feet and then someone ran along the upstairs passage.

"What's wrong with the sleuths?" asked Parish.

No one answered. Miss Darragh took up her knitting. Mr. Nark picked his teeth. Parish finished his beer.

"We all want to see the man caught," said Legge suddenly. He spoke in his usual querulous, muffled voice. He looked ill and he seemed extremely nervous. Miss Darragh glanced at him and said soothingly:

"Of course."

"Their behaviour," said Legge, "is abominable. Abominable! I intend writing a letter to the Commissioner of Scotland Yard. It is disgraceful."

Parish planted his feet apart, put his head on one side, and looked at Legge with the expression he used in films of the Bulldog Drummond type. His voice drawled slightly.

"Feelin' nervous, Legge?" he asked. "Now isn't that a pity."

"Nervous! I am not nervous, Mr. Parish. What do you mean by——"

"Gentlemen," said old Abel.

There was a brief silence broken by an urgent clatter of footsteps on the stairs.

The door into the private tap swung open. Alleyn stood on the threshold. When Miss Darragh saw his face she uttered a sharp cry that was echoed, oddly, by Parish.

Alleyn said:

"Nobody is to move from this room. Understand? What's Dr. Shaw's telephone number?"

Abel said, "Illington 579, sir."

Alleyn kicked the door wide open and moved to the wall telephone just outside. He dialled a number and came into the doorway with the receiver at his ear.

"You understand," he said, "none of you is to move. Where's Cubitt?"

"He's gone out," said Parish. "What's the matter, Mr. Alleyn, for God's sake."

Alleyn was speaking into the receiver.

"Dr. Shaw? At once, please, it's the police." He eyed them all as he waited.

"There has been an accident," he said. "Where's that decanter of sherry?"

"Here, sir," said Abel.

"Take it by the end of the neck, lock it in the cupboard behind you, and bring the key to me. That you, Shaw? Alleyn. Come at once. Same trouble as last time. I've given an emetic. It's worked, but he's half-collapsed. I'll do artificial respiration. For God's sake be quick."

He clicked the receiver and took the key Abel brought him. He dialled another number and spoke to Abel as he dialled it.

"Lock the shutters and all the doors. Both bars. Bring the keys here. Illington Police Station? Oates? Inspector Alleyn. I want Mr. Harper and yourself at once at the Plume of Feathers. Jump to it."

He hung up the receiver. Abel was clattering round the public bar. Alleyn slammed the shutters in the private bar.

"If any one opens these shutters or tries to leave this room," he said, "there will be an arrest on a charge of attempted murder. Bring those others through here."

"But, look here——" said Parish.

"Quiet!" said Alleyn and was obeyed. Abel shepherded a couple of astonished fishermen into the private bar. Will Pomeroy followed. Abel slammed down the bar shutter and locked it. He came to Alleyn and gave him the keys. Alleyn pushed him outside, slammed the door, and locked it.

"Now," he said, "come up here."

He ran up the stairs, taking three at a stride. Abel

followed, panting. The door of Alleyn's room was open. Fox sat on the bed with the wash-hand basin at his feet. His face was curiously strained and anxious. When he saw Alleyn he tried to speak, but something had gone wrong with his mouth. He kept shutting his jaw with a sharp involuntary movement and his voice was thick. He jerked his hand at the bowl.

"Thank God," said Alleyn. "Can you do yet another heave, old thing?"

Fox jerked his head sideways and suddenly pitched forward. Alleyn caught him. "Move that basin," he ordered. "I want to get him on the floor."

Abel moved the basin and together he and Alleyn lowered Fox. Alleyn had wrenched open Fox's collar and tie. He now loosened his clothes. Somewhere in the background of his conscious thoughts was an impression that it was strange to be doing these things to Fox whom he knew so well. He began the movements of resuscitation, working hard and rhythmically. Abel quietly cleared an area round Fox.

"When you'm tiring, sir," said Abel, "I'll take a turn."

But Alleyn scarcely knew he had a body of his own. His body and breath, precariously and dubiously, belonged to Fox. His thoughts were visited by hurrying pictures. He saw a figure that shoved and sweated and set the wheels of a great vehicle in motion. A figure turned and turned again at a crank handle. He was aware, at moments most vividly, of own glass of untouched sherry on the dressing-table. Fox's arms were heavy and stiff. Presently his eyes opened. The pupils had widened almost to the rim of the iris, the eyes had no expression. Alleyn's own eyes were half-blinded with sweat. Suddenly the body on the floor heaved.

"That's better," said Abel, stooping to the basin, "he'm going to vomit again."

Alleyn turned Fox on his side. Fox neatly and prolifically made use of the basin.

"Brandy," said Alleyn. "In a bag in the wardrobe."

He watched Abel fetch the flask. Alleyn unscrewed the top, smelt at the contents, and took a mouthful. He squatted on his haunches with the brandy in his mouth. The brandy was all right. He swallowed it, poured some into the cap of the flask, and gave it to Fox.

Downstairs the telephone was pealing.

"Go and answer it," said Alleyn.

Abel went out.

"Fox," said Alleyn. "Fox, my dear old thing."

Fox's lips moved. Alleyn took his handkerchief and wiped that large face carefully.

"Very inconvenient," said a voice inside Fox. "Sorry."

"You b—— old b——," said Alleyn softly.

CHAPTER EIGHTEEN

MR. LEGGE COMMITS A MISDEMEANOUR

I

"I'm better," said Fox presently. "I'd like to sit up."

Alleyn propped him against the bed.

A car pulled outside and in a moment Alleyn heard a clatter of steps and the sound of voices. Abel came in.

"Yurr be doctor," Abel said, "and Nick Harper with police. And colonel's on telephone roaring like proper grampus."

"O Lord!" Alleyn ejaculated. "Abel, tell him what's happened. He'll probably want to come over here. Apologise for me. Where's the doctor?"

"Here," said Dr. Shaw, and walked in. "What's the trouble? Hallo!"

He went to Fox.

"I'm better, doctor," said Fox. "I've vomited."

Dr. Shaw took his pulse, looked at his eyes, and nodded.

"You'll do," he said, "but we'll make a job of it. Come into the bathroom. You'd better keep that matter in the basin, Alleyn."

He opened his bag, took out a tube, and jerked his head at Fox.

"Here!" said Fox resentfully, eyeing the tube.

"How did it happen?" asked Dr. Shaw.

Harper came in.

"I've left Oates and another man downstairs," said Harper. "What's up?"

"Fox drank a glass of sherry," said Alleyn. "There's the glass. We'll detain all the crowd downstairs. You too, Mr. Pomeroy. Go down and join them."

"Move along, Abel," said Harper.

"I yurrd, I yurrd," grunted Abel irritably, and went out.

"You'd better go down with them, Nick," said Alleyn. "Tell Oates to watch our man like a lynx. Abel will show you a decanter. Bring it up here. Here's the key. Use my gloves. You'd better search them. You won't find anything but you'd better do it. Leave Miss Darragh for the moment."

Harper went out.

"Did you take any sherry, Alleyn?" asked Dr. Shaw sharply.

"I? No."

"Sure?"

"Perfectly. Why?"

"You look a bit dicky."

"I'm all right."

"Mr. Alleyn has just saved my life for me," whispered Fox.

"You come along," said Dr. Shaw, and led him out.

Alleyn took an envelope from his pocket and put it over the glass from which Fox had drunk. He weighted the envelope with saucer from his wash-hand stand. He got his bag and took out an empty bottle and a funnel. He smelt the sherry in his own glass and then poured it into the bottle, stoppered it, and wrote on the label. He was annoyed to find that his hands shook. His heart thumped intolerably. He grimaced and took another mouthful of brandy.

Harper came back.

"Oates and my other chap are searching them," said Harper. "They made no objections."

"They wouldn't. Sit down, Nick," said Alleyn, "and listen. Put Fox's sick out of the way first, for the Lord's sake. Give it to Shaw. I've got palsy or something."

Harper performed this office and sat down.

"Yesterday evening," said Alleyn, "Abel Pomeroy opened a bottle of a very sound sherry. Fox and I had a glass each. At a quarter to one to-day Abel decanted the sherry. He, Fox and I had a glass each after it was decanted. George Nark was

220

in the bar. Later on, Miss Darragh, Legge, Parish, Cubitt, and Will Pomeroy came in and we talked about the sherry. They all knew it was for our private use. Some forty minutes ago, Abel poured out two glasses. Fox drank his and within half a minute he was taken very ill. The symptoms were those of cyanide poisoning. I'll swear Abel didn't put anything in the glasses. There's Fox's glass. We'll do our stuff with what's left. I've covered it but we'd better get the dregs into an air-tight bottle. You'll find one in my bag there. There's a funnel on the dressing-table. D'you mind doing it? Clean the funnel out first. I used it for the stuff in my glass."

Harper did this.

"It's a bad blunder," he said. "What good would it do him? Suppose you'd both been killed? I mean, it's foolish. Is it panic or spite or both?"

"Neither, I imagine. I see it as a last attempt to bolster up the accident theory. The idea is that in the same mysterious way as cyanide got on the dart so it got into the decanter. The decanter, you see, was brought out from the corner cupboard. Mrs. Ives had washed it in about two dozen changes of boiling water. I don't think anybody but Nark and Abel were aware of this. We were no doubt supposed to think the decanter was tainted by being in the cupboard."

Superintendent Harper uttered a vulgar and incredulous word.

"I know," agreed Alleyn. "Of course it was. But if Fox and (or) I had popped off, you'd have had a devil of a job proving it was murder. Oh, it's a blunder, all right. It shows us two things. The murderer must have kept a bit of cyanide up his sleeve and he must have visited the private bar after Abel decanted the sherry at a quarter to one this afternoon. We will now search their rooms. We won't find anything, but we'd better do it. I'll just see how Fox is getting on."

Fox, white and shaken, was sitting on the edge of the bath. Dr. Shaw was washing his hands.

"He'll do all right now," said Dr. Shaw. "Better go to bed and take it easy."

"I'm damned if I do," said Fox. "Excuse me, sir, but I'm damned if I do."

Alleyn took him by the elbow.

221

"Blast your eyes," he said, "you'll do as you're told. Come on."

Fox consented with a bad grace to lying on his bed. Alleyn and Harper searched the rooms.

<h2 style="text-align:center">II</h2>

At first Harper said that the rooms, in all essentials, were as he had found them on the day after Watchman's death. In Cubitt's they found an overwhelming smell of studio and the painting gear that had engendered it. There were bottles of turpentine and oil, half-finished works, Cubitt's paint-box, and boxes of unopened tubes. Alleyn smelt the bottles and shook his head.

"We needn't take them," he said, "their stink is a lawful stink. You can't put turpentine or oil into vintage sherry and get away with it."

"What about prussic acid? It smells strong enough."

"Of almonds. A nutty flavour. Do you remember the account of the murder of Rasputin?"

"Can't say I do," said Harper.

"Youssoupoff put cyanide in the wine. Rasputin drank several glasses, apparently with impunity."

"But——"

"The theory is that the sugar in the wine took the punch out of the poison. That may account for Fox's escape. No doubt the sherry had a fine old nutty aroma. By God, I'll get this expert."

"What are we looking for?"

"For anything that could have held the stuff he put in the decanter. Oh, he'll have got rid of it somehow, of course. But you never know."

They went into the bathroom. In a cupboard above the hand-basin they found Abel's second first-aid outfit. Alleyn asked Harper if there had been a bottle of iodine there on the day after the murder. Harper said no. He had checked the contents of the cupboard. They separated and took the rest of the rooms between them, Alleyn going to Legge's and Parish's, Harper to the others. Alleyn took a small empty bottle from Parish's room. It had held pills and smelt of nothing at all. On Legge's dressing-table he found a phial half-full of a thick pinkish fluid that smelt of antiseptic. Mr. Legge's ear lotion. He kept it and searched all the drawers and pockets but found nothing else of interest. Abel's room was neat and spotless, Will's untidy and full of books. The wearisome and exacting business went on. Down below, in the private bar, Oates and his mate kept company with the patrons of the Plume of Feathers. They were very quiet. Occasionally Alleyn heard the voices of Parish and of Mr. Nark. Ottercombe clock struck ten, sweetly and slowly. There was a moment of complete quiet broken by a violent eruption of noise down in the bar. Alleyn and Harper met in the passage.

"Somebody cutting up rough," said Harper.

A falsetto voice screamed out an oath. A table was over-turned and there followed a great clatter of boots. Harper ran downstairs and Alleyn followed. Inside the private bar they found Legge, mouthing and gibbering, between Oates and a second uniformed constable.

"What's all this?" asked Harper.

"Misdemeanour, sir," said Oates whose nose was bleeding freely. "Assault *and* battery."

"I don't care what it is," screamed Legge. "I can't stand any more of this——"

"Shut up, you silly chap," admonished Oates. "He tried to make a breakaway, sir. Sitting there as quiet as you please, and all of a sudden makes a blind rush for the door and when we intercepts him he wades in and assaults and batters the pair of us. Won't give over, sir. You're under arrest, Robert Legge, and it is my duty to warn you that you needn't say anything, but what you do say may be used in evidence. Stop that."

"Persecuted," whispered Legge. "Persecuted, spied upon, driven and badgered and maddened. I know what it means. Let me go. Damn you, let me go!"

He kicked Oates on the shin. Oates swore and twisted Legge's arm behind his back. Legge screamed and went limp.

"You'll have to be locked up," said Harper sadly. "Now, are you going to behave or have we got to put the bracelets on you? Be a sensible chap."

"I'll resist," said Legge, "till you kill me."

"Oh, take him away," said Harper. "Put him in a room upstairs, both of you."

Legge, struggling and gasping horribly, was taken out.

"Ah, it's at his wits' end he is, poor wretch," said Miss Darragh.

Cubitt said, "Look here, this is ghastly. If he's not guilty why the hell——?"

Parish said, "Not guilty! I must say that for an innocent man his behaviour is pretty fantastic."

Will Pomeroy crossed the room and confronted Alleyn and Harper.

"Why's he arrested?" demanded Will.

"Assaulting a constable and interfering with the police in the execution of their duty," said Harper.

"My God, he was drove to it! If this is justice the sooner there's a revolution in the country the better. It's enough to send the man mad, the way you've been pestering him Haven't you the sense to see the state he's got into? Damme if I'm not nigh-ready to take on the lot of you myself. Let that man go."

"That'll do, Will," said Harper.

"'That'll do!' The official answer for every blasted blunder in the force. Bob Legge's my comrade——"

"In which case," said Alleyn, "you'll do well to think a little before you speak. You can hardly expect Mr. Harper to set up constables in rows for your comrade Legge to bloody their noses. While his mood lasts he's better in custody. You pipe down like a sensible fellow." He turned to Harper. "Stay down here a moment, will you? I'll take a look at Fox and rejoin you."

He ran upstairs and met Oates in the landing.

"My mate's put Legge in his own room, sir," said Oates.

"Good. He'd better stay with him and you'd better dip your nose in cold water before you resume duty. Then come and relieve Mr. Harper."

Oates went into the bathroom. Alleyn opened Fox's door and listened. Fox was snoring deeply and rhythmically. Alleyn closed the door softly and returned to the taproom.

It was the last time that he was to see that assembly gathered together in the private taproom of the Plume of Feathers. He had been little over twenty-four hours in Ottercombe but it seemed more like a week. The suspects in a case of murder become quickly and strangely familiar to the investigating officer. He has an aptitude for noticing mannerisms, tricks of voice and of movement. Faces and figures make their impression quickly and sharply. Alleyn expected, before he saw them, Cubitt's trick of smiling lopsidedly, Parish's habit of sticking out his jaw, Miss Darragh's look of inscrutability, Will Pomeroy's mulish blushes, and his father's way of opening his eyes very widely. The movement of Nark's head, slanted conceitedly, and his look of burning self-importance, seemed to be memories of a year rather than of days. Alleyn felt a little as if they were marionettes, obeying a few simple jerks of their strings and otherwise inert and stupid. He felt wholeheartedly bored with the lot of them, the thought of another bout of interrogation was almost intolerable. Fox might have been killed. Reaction had set in, and Alleyn was sick at heart.

" Well," he said crisply, " you may as well know what has happened. Between a quarter to one and five past seven somebody put poison in the decanter of sherry that was kept for our use. You will readily understand that we shall require a full account from each one of you of your movements after a quarter to one. Mr. Harper and I will see you in turn in the parlour. If you discuss the matter among yourselves it will be within hearing of Constable Oates who will be on duty in this room. We'll see you first if you please, Mr. Cubitt."

But it was the usual exasperating job that faced him. None of them had a complete alibi. Each of them could have slipped unseen into the taproom and come out again unnoticed. Abel had locked the bar shutter during closing hours, but every one knew where he kept his keys, and several times when the bar was open it had been deserted. Cubitt said he was painting from two o'clock until six when he returned for his evening meal. He had been one of the company in the taproom when Alleyn came in for the sherry but had left immediately to meet Decima Moore on Coombe Head. The others followed with similar stories, except old Pomeroy who frankly admitted he had sat in the taproom for some time, reading his paper. Each of them denied being alone there at any time after Abel had decanted the sherry. An hour's exhaustive inquiry failed to prove or disprove any of their statements. Last of all, Mr. Legge was brought down in a state of the profoundest dejection and made a series of protestations to the effect that he was being persecuted. He was a pitiful object, and Alleyn's feeling of nausea increased as he watched him. At last Alleyn said:

"Mr. Legge, we only arrived here last evening but, as you must realise, we have already made many inquiries. Of all the people we have interviewed, you alone have objected to the way we set about our job. Why?"

Legge looked at Alleyn without speaking. His lower lip hung loosely, his eyes, half-veiled, in that now familiar way by his white lashes, looked like the eyes of a blind man. Only his hands moved restlessly. After a moment's silence he mumbled something inaudible.

"What do you say?"

"It doesn't matter. Everything I say is used against me."

Alleyn looked at him in silence.

"I think," he said at last, "that it is my duty to tell you that a dart bearing your fingerprints was sent to the bureau early this morning. They have been identified and the result has been telephoned to us."

Legge's hands moved convulsively.

"They have been identified," Alleyn repeated, "as those of Montague Thringle. Montague Thringle was sentenced to six years imprisonment for embezzlement, a sentence that was afterwards reduced to four years and was completed twenty-six months ago." He paused. Legge's face was clay-coloured. "You must have known we'd find out," said Alleyn. "Why didn't you tell me last night who you were?"

"Why? Why?" demanded Legge. "You know why. You know well enough. The very sight and sound of the police! Anathema! Questions, questions, questions! At me all the time. Man with a record. Hound him out. Tell

226

verybody. Slam every door in his face. And you have the
mpertinence to ask me why I was silent. My God!"

"All right," said Alleyn, "we'll leave it at that. How did
ou spend your afternoon?"

"There you go!" cried Legge, half-crying but still with
hat curious air of admonishment. "There you go, you see!
traight off. Asking me things like that. It's atrocious."

"Nonsense," said Alleyn.

"Nonsense!" echoed Legge, in a sort of fury. He shook
is finger in Alleyn's face. "Don't you talk like that to me,
r. Do you know who I am? Do you know that before my
nisfortune I was the greatest power in English finance? Let
ne tell you that there are only three men living who fully
omprehended the events that brought about the holocaust of
?9 and '30, and I am one of them. If I had not put my
ust in titled imbeciles, if I had not been betrayed by a
kulking moron, I should be in a position to send for you
when I wished to command your dubious services, or dismiss
nem with a contemptuous fiddle-de-dee."

This astonishing and ridiculous word was delivered with
nch venom that Alleyn was quite taken aback. Into his
noughts, with the appropriate logic of topsy-turvy, popped
ne memory of a jigging line:

"To shirk the task were fiddle-de-dee.
    To shirk the task were fiddle-de, fiddle-de——"

He pulled himself together, cautioned and tackled Mr.
egge, and at last got a statement from him. He had spent
ne afternoon packing his books, papers and effects, and
utting them in his car. He had intended to take the first
ad into his new room that evening. He had also written
ome letters. He offered frantically to show Alleyn the letters.
lleyn had already seen them and they amounted to nothing.
le turned Legge over to Oates whose nose was now plugged
ith cotton-wool.

"You'd better take him to the station," said Alleyn.

"I demand bail," cried Legge in a trembling voice.

"Mr. Harper will see about that," said Alleyn. "You're
nder arrest for a misdemeanour."

"I didn't kill him. I know what you're up to. It's the beginning of the end. I swear——"

"You are under arrest for assaulting police officers," said Alleyn wearily. "I will repeat the caution you have already heard."

He repeated it and was devoutly thankful when Legge, in a condition of hysterical prostration, was led away. Harper with Oates and his mate, was to drive him to Illington and lodge him in the police station.

"The colonel's at the station," said Harper acidly. "That was him on the telephone while you were upstairs. His car's broken down again. Why, in his position and with all his money, he doesn't—oh, well! He wants me to bring him back here or you to come in. Which'll it be? The man'll talk us all dotty, wherever he is."

"I'll have another look at Fox," said Alleyn. "If he's awake, I'll get him into bed and then follow you into Illington. I'd like the doctor to see him again."

"There'll be no need for that, sir, thank you."

Alleyn spun round on his heel to see Fox, fully dressed and wearing his bowler hat, standing in the doorway.

CHAPTER NINETEEN

THE CHIEF CONSTABLE AS WATSON

I

"I've reported for duty, if you please, Mr. Alleyn," said Fox.

"You unspeakable old ninny," said Alleyn, "go back to bed."

"With all respect, sir, I'd rather not. I've had a very pleasant nap and am quite myself again. So if you'll allow me——"

"Br'er Fox," said Alleyn, "are we to have a row?"

"I hope not, sir, I'm sure," said Fox tranquilly. "Six years I think it is now, and never a moment's unpleasantness, thanks to your tact and consideration."

"Damn you, go to bed."

"If it's all the same to you, sir, I'd rather——"

"Mr. Fox," Alleyn began very loudly and stopped short. They stared at each other. Harper coughed and moved to the door. Alleyn swore violently, seized Fox by the arm, and shoved him into an arm-chair. He then knelt on the harlequin rug and lit the fire.

"I'd be obliged, Nick," said Alleyn over his shoulder, "if you'd bring Colonel Brammington here. Would you explain that circumstances over which I appear to have no control oblige me to remain at the Plume of Feathers?"

"I'm quite able to drive——" Fox began.

"You shut up," said Alleyn warmly.

Harper went out.

"Offences against discipline," said Alleyn, "are set forth in the Police Regulations under seventeen headings, including neglect of duty and disobedience to orders, together with a general heading covering discreditable conduct." He looked up from the fire. "Discreditable conduct," he repeated.

Fox was shaken with a soundless subterranean chuckle.

"I'm going into the taproom," said Alleyn. "If you move

out of that chair I'll damn well serve you with a Misconduct Form. See Regulation 13."

"I'll get the super in as my witness, sir," said Fox. "See Regulation 17." And at this pointless witticism he went off into an ecstasy of apoplectic mirth.

Alleyn returned to the taproom where Oates still kept guard. Miss Darragh was knitting in the ingle-nook, Parish stood near the shuttered windows, Cubitt was drawing in the battered sketch-book he always carried in his pocket. Abel Pomeroy sat disconsolately in one of his own settles. Will glowered in a corner. Mr. Nark wore the expression of one who has been made to feel unpopular.

Alleyn said, "You may open up again if you wish, Mr. Pomeroy. I'm sorry to have kept you all so long. Until you and your rooms had been searched, we had no alternative. To-morrow, you will be asked to sign the statements you have made to Mr. Harper. In the meantime, if you wish, you may go to your rooms. You will not be allowed to leave the premises until further orders. Mr. Nark may go home."

From the stairs came the sound of heavy steps. Harper and the second constable came down with Legge between them. Alleyn had left the taproom door open. Six pairs of eyes turned to watch Legge go out.

Miss Darragh suddenly called out, "Cheer up, now. It's nothing at all, man. I'll go bail for you."

Will started forward.

"I want to speak to him."

"Certainly," said Alleyn.

"I'm sorry it has turned out this way, mate," said Will. "Damned injustice and nothing less. It won't make any difference with the Party. You know that. We'll stick by you. Wish I'd bloodied 'tother nose and gone to clink along with you."

"They've got a down on me," said Legge desolately.

"I know that. Good luck!"

"Come along now," said Harper. "Get a move on. Ready, Oates?"

Oates went out to them and Alleyn shut the door.

"Well," said Parish. "I call that a step in the right direction, Mr. Alleyn."

"For God's sake, Seb, hold your tongue," said Cubitt.

"What d'you mean by that, Mr. Parish?" demanded Will. "You'd better be careful what you're saying, hadn't you?"

"That's no way to speak, sonny," said Abel.

"While I've a tongue in my head——" began Will.

"You'll set a guard on it, I hope," said Alleyn. "Good-night, gentlemen."

They filed out one by one. Parish was the only one who spoke. With his actor's instinct for an effective exit he turned in the doorway.

"I imagine," he said, looking steadily at Alleyn, "that I shan't be run in for contempt if I venture to suggest that this gentleman's departure marks the beginning of the end."

"Oh, no," said Alleyn politely. "We shan't run you in for that, Mr. Parish."

Parish gave a light laugh and followed the others upstairs.

Only Miss Darragh remained. She put her knitting into a large chintz bag, took off her spectacles and looked steadily at Alleyn.

"I suppose you had to take that poor fellow in charge," she said. "He behaved very foolishly. But he's a mass of nerves, you know. It's a doctor he's needing, not a policeman."

"Who? Mr. Montague Thringle?" asked Alleyn vaguely.

"So the cat's out of the bag is ut?" said Miss Darragh placidly. "Ah, well, I suppose 'twas bound to be. I've kept my end of the bargain."

"I'd very much like to know what it was," said Alleyn.

"Didn't you guess?"

"I wondered if by any chance Lord Bryonie's family had promised to keep an eye on Mr. Thringle."

"Ah, you'll end in a cocked hat with a plume in ut," said Miss Darragh, "if 'tis cocked hats they give to chief commissioners. That's it, sure enough. Me poor cousin Bryonie always felt he'd been responsible for the crash. He was very indiscreet, it seems, and might have helped to patch things up if he'd kept his wits about 'um. But he didn't. He'd no head for business and he only half-suspected there was anything illegal going on. But he said he'd only learned one kind of behaviour and, when it didn't fit in with finance, he was entirely at sea and thought maybe he'd better hold his peace. But it wasn't in his nature not to talk and that was the downfall of 'um. The jury saw that he'd been no more

231

than a cat's-paw, but when he got off with the lighter sentence there was a great deal of talk that 'twas injustice and that his position saved him. Thringle felt so himself and said so. Me cousin never lost his faith in Thringle who seemed to have cast a kind of spell over 'um, though you wouldn't think it possible, would you, to see Thringle now? But in those days he was a fine-looking fellow. Dark as night, he was, with a small imperial, and his own teeth instead of those dreadful china falsehoods they gave 'um in prison. It's no wonder at all you didn't know 'um from Adam when you saw 'um. Well, the long and short of ut 'twas that before he died the family promised poor Bryonie they'd look after Mr. Thringle when he came out of gaol. He was on their conscience, and I won't say he didn't know ut and make the most of ut. We kept in touch with 'um, and he wrote from here saying he'd changed his name to Legge and that he needed money. We've not much of that to spare but we had a family conference and, as I was planning a little sketching jaunt anyway, I said I'd take ut at Ottercombe and see for meself how the land lay. So that was what I did. Don't ask me to tell you the nature of our talks for they were in confidence and had nothing to say to the case. I wish with all me heart you could have left 'um alone but I see 'twas impossible. He fought those two big policemen like a Kilkenny cat, silly fellow. But if it's a question of bailing him out I'll be glad to do ut."

"Thank you," said Alleyn, "I'll see that the right people are told about it. Miss Darragh, have you done any sketching along the cliffs from the tunnel to Coombe Head?"

Miss Darragh looked at him in consternation. "I have," she said.

"In the mornings?"

"'Twas in the mornings."

"You were there on the morning after Mr. Watchman arrived in Ottercombe?"

She looked steadily at him. "I was," said Miss Darragh.

"We saw where you had set up your easel. Miss Darragh, did you, from where you were working, overhear a conversation between Miss Moore and Mr. Watchman?"

Miss Darragh clasped her fat little paws together and looked dismally at Alleyn.

232

"Please," said Alleyn.

"I did. I could not avoid it. By the time I'd decided I'd get up and show meself above the sky-line, it had gone so far I thought I had better not."

She gave him a quick look and added hurriedly, "Please, now, don't go thinking all manner of dreadful things."

"What am I to think? Do you mean it was a love-scene?"

"Not in—no. No, the reverse."

"A quarrel?"

"It was."

"Was it of that scene you were thinking when you told me this morning, to look further and look nearer home?"

"It was. I wasn't thinking of her. God forbid. Don't misunderstand me. I was not the only one who heard them. And that's all I'll say."

She clutched her bag firmly and stood up.

"As regards this searching," added Miss Darragh, "the superintendent let me off. He said you'd attend to ut."

"I know," said Alleyn. "Perhaps you won't mind if Mrs. Ives goes up with you to your room."

"Not the least in the world," said Miss Darragh.

"Then I'll send for her," said Alleyn.

While he waited for Harper and the chief constable, Alleyn brought his report up to date and discussed it with Fox who remained, weakly insubordinate, in his chair by the fire.

"It's an ill wind," said Fox, "that blows nobody any good. I take it that I've had what you might call a thorough spring-clean with the doctor's tube taking the part of a vacuum cleaner, if the idea's not too fanciful. I feel all the better for it."

Alleyn grunted.

"I don't know but what I don't fancy a pipe," continued Fox.

"You'll have another spring-clean if you do."

"Do you think so, Mr. Alleyn? In that case I'll hold off. I fancy I hear a car, sir. Coming through the tunnel, isn't it?"

Alleyn listened.

"I think so. We'll get the C.C. to fix up a warrant. Well, Br'er Fox, it's been a short, sharp go this time, hasn't it?"

"And you were looking forward to a spell in the country, sir."

"I was."

"We'll be here yet awhile, with one thing and another."

"I suppose so. Here they are."

A car drew up in the yard. The side door opened noisily, and Colonel Brammington's voice sounded in the passage. He came in with Harper and Oates at his heels. The colonel was dressed in a dinner suit. He wore a stiff shirt with no central stud. It curved generously away from his person and through the gaping front could be seen a vast expanse of pink chest. Evidently he had at some earlier hour wetted his hair and dragged a comb through it. His shoelaces were untied and his socks unsupported. Over his dinner jacket he wore a green tyrolese bicycling cape.

"I can't apologise enough, sir," Alleyn began, but the chief constable waved him aside.

"Not at all, Alleyn. A bore, but it couldn't be helped. I am distended with rich food and wines. Strong meat belongeth to them that are of full age. I freely confess I outdid the meat, outdid the frolic wine. It was, I flatter myself, a good dinner, but I shall not taunt you with a recital of its virtues."

"I am sure it was a dinner in a thousand," said Alleyn. "I hope you didn't mind coming here, sir. Fox was still——"

"By heaven!" interrupted Colonel Brammington, "this pestilent poisoner o'er tops it, does he not? The attempt, I imagine, was upon you both. Harper has told me the whole story. When will you make an arrest, Alleyn? May we send this fellow up the ladder to bed, and that no later than the Quarter Sessions! Let him wag upon a wooden nag. A pox on him! I trust you are recovered, Fox? Sherry, wasn't it? Amontillado, I understand. Double sacrilege, by the Lord!"

Colonel Brammington hurled himself into a chair and asked for a cigarette. When this had been given him, he produced from his trousers' pocket a crumpled mass of typescript which Alleyn recognised as the carbon copy of his report.

"I have been over the report, Alleyn," said Colonel Brammington, "and while you expended your energies so happily in resuscitating the poisoned Fox (and by the way, our murderer carries the blacker stigma of a fox-poisoner!) I read this admirable digest. I congratulate you. A masterly presentation of facts, free from the nauseating redundancies of most bureaucratic documents. I implored you to allow me to be your Watson. You consented. I come, full of my theory, ready to admit my blunders. Is there by any chance some flask of fermented liquor in this house to which cyanide has not been added? May we not open some virgin bottle?"

Alleyn went into the bar, found three sealed bottles of Treble Extra, chalked them up to himself and took them with glasses into the parlour.

"We should have a taster," said Colonel Brammington. "Some Borgian attendant at our call. What a pity the wretched Nark is not here."

"There are times," said Alleyn, "when I could wish that Mr. Nark had been the corpse in the case. I don't think we need blench at the Treble Extra and I washed the glasses."

He broke a paper seal, drew the cork, and poured out the beer.

"Really," said Colonel Brammington, "I do feel a little timid about it, I must say. Some fiendish device——"

"I don't think so," said Alleyn and took a pull at his beer. "It's remarkably good."

"You show no signs of stiffening limb or glassy eye. It is, as you say, good beer. Well, now, Alleyn, I understand from Harper that you have all arrived at a decision. I, working independently, have also made up my mind. It would delight me to find we were in agreement and amuse me to learn that I was wrong. Will you indulge me so far as to allow me to unfold the case as I see it?"

"We should be delighted, sir," said Alleyn, thinking a little of his bed.

"Excellent," said Colonel Brammington. He flattened out the crumpled report and Alleyn saw that he had made copious notes in pencil all over the typescript. "I shall relate my deductions in the order in which they came to me. I shall follow the example of all Watsons and offer blunder after blunder, inviting your compassionate scorn and remembering the observation that logic is only the art of going wrong with confidence. Are you all ready?"

"Quite ready, sir," said Alleyn.

"When first this case turned up," said Colonel Brammington, "it seemed to me to be a moderately simple affair. The circumstances were macabre, the apparent weapon unlikely, but I accepted the weapon and rejoiced in the circumstances. It was an enlivening murder."

He turned his prominent eyes on Harper who looked scandalised.

"After all," said Colonel Brammington, "I did not know the victim and I frankly confess I adore a murder. Pray, Mr. Harper, do not look at me in that fashion. I want the glib and oily art to speak and purpose not. I enjoy a murder and I enjoyed this one. It seemed to me that Legge had anointed the dart with malice afore-thought and prussic acid, had prepared the ground with exhibitions of skill, and had deliberately thrown awry. He had overheard Watchman's story of his idiosyncrasy for the cyanide. He had seen Pomeroy put the bottle in the cupboard. Cyanide had been found on the dart. What more did we need? True, the motive was lacking, but when I learnt that you suspected Legge of being a gaolbird, a sufficient motive appeared. Legge had established himself in this district in a position of trust, he handled monies, he acquired authority. Watchman, by his bantering manner, suggested that he recognised Legge. Legge feared he would be exposed. Legge therefore murdered Watchman. That was my opinion until this afternoon."

Colonel Brammington took a prodigious swig of beer and flung himself back in his tortured chair.

"This afternoon," he said, "I was astonished at your refusal to arrest Legge, but when I took the files away and began to read them I changed my opinion. I read the statements made by the others and I saw how positive each was that Legge had no opportunity to anoint the dart. I was impressed by your own observation that his hands were clumsy, that he was incapable of what would have amounted to an essay in legerdemain. Yet cyanide was found on the dart. Who had put it there It is a volatile poison, therefore it must have been put on the dart not long before Oates sealed it up. I wondered if, after all, the whole affair was an accident, if there was some trace of poison on Abel Pomeroy's clothes or upon the bar where he unpacked the darts. It was a preposterous notion and it was smashed as squat as a flounder by the fact that the small vessel in the rat-hole had been filled up with water. I was forced to believe the cyanide had been taken from the rat-hole immediately, or soon after, old Pomeroy put it there. Any of the suspects might have done this. But only four of the suspects had handled the darts; Legge, the Pomeroys, and Parish. Only Legge controlled the flight of the darts. Watchman took them out of the board after the trial throw and gave them to Legge. Now here," said Colonel Brammington with an air of conscious modesty, "I fancy I hit on something new. Can you guess what it was?"

"I can venture to do so," Alleyn rejoined. "Did you reflect that all the darts had been thrown into the board on the trial, and that if cyanide was on any one of them, it would have been effectively cleaned off?"

"Good God!" ejaculated the chief constable.

He was silent for some time, but at last continued with somewhat forced airiness.

"No. No, that was not my point, but by Jupiter it supports my case. I was going to say that since Watchman removed the darts and handed them to Legge, it would have been quite impossible for Legge to know which dart was tainted. This led me to an alternative. Either all the darts were poisoned or else, or else, my dear Alleyn, the dart that wounded Watchman was tainted after, and not before, the accident." He glanced at Alleyn.

"Yes, sir," said Alleyn. "One or the other."

"You agree? You had thought of it?"

"Will Pomeroy suggested the second alternative," said Alleyn.

"Damn! However! Legge, I had decided, was not capable of anointing one, much less six darts during the few seconds he held them in his hand before doing his trick. Legge would scarcely implicate himself by anointing the dart

237

after he had seen Watchman die. Therefore someone had tried to implicate Legge. I was obliged to bow to your wisdom, my dear Alleyn. I dismissed Legge. I finished your report and I considered the other suspects. Who, of these seven persons, for they are seven if we include Miss Darragh and Miss Moore, could most easily have taken cyanide from the small vessel in the rat-hole? One of the Pomeroys, since their presence in or about the outhouses would not be remarked. Abel Pomeroy's fingerprints and only his were found on the small vessel. Who of the seven had an opportunity to smear cyanide on the dart? Abel Pomeroy, since he unpacked the darts. Who, in the first instance, had cyanide brought into the premises? Abel Pomeroy. Putting motive on one side, I felt that Abel Pomeroy was my first choice. My second fancy—and don't look so wryly upon me, Harper, a chief constable may have fancies as well as the next man— my second fancy fell upon Will Pomeroy. Your interview with the unspeakable Nark, my dear Alleyn, was not barren of interest. Amidst a plethora of imbecilities, Nark seemed to make one disclosure of interest. He said, or rather from your report I understood him to hint, that he had, on the occasion of Watchman's first visit to Ottercombe, overheard an amorous encounter between Watchman and Miss Moore. He hinted, moreover, that as he crept farther along Apple Lane he came upon Will Pomeroy, lurking and listening in the hedge. Now, thought I, if this were true, here is the beginning of motive; for, in the interim, the courtship between young Pomeroy and Miss Moore ripened. Suppose, on Watchman's return, that the rustic lover thought he saw a renewal of attentions. Suppose Parish or Cubitt hinted at the scene they interrupted by the furze bushes? But ignoring motive, what of opportunity? Will Pomeroy handled the darts after they were unpacked by his father. Could he have had a phial of cyanide-solution in his pocket? Nobody watched Will Pomeroy with the close attention that they all gave to Legge. Your observation on the trial throw shatters this theory. Do I see another bottle of this superb beer? Thank you.

"On the whole I preferred Pomeroy senior. There seemed no reason to doubt young Pomeroy's violent defence of Legge. He would not have thrown suspicion on Legge and then vehemently defended him. Old Pomeroy, on the other hand, detests Legge and has, from the first, accused him of the murder. But I was determined to look with an equal eye upon the field of suspects. I turned, with I hope becoming reluctance, to the ladies. On Miss Darragh I need not dwell. Harper has told me of your discovery of her link with Legge, and it is obvious that she merely took what may be described as a family interest in him. The family tree in this instance being unusually shady. Ha! But Miss Moore, if Nark is to be believed, cannot be so dismissed. There had been amorous passages between Miss Moore and Watchman. Miss Moore denied this in the course of your interview. Could love have turned into the proverbial hatred? What happened when those ambiguous heelmarks were printed in the turf behind the furze bush? A quarrel? Was she afraid her lover would betray her to her fiancé? And opportunity? Could she have introduced poison into the glass? Who better, since she poured out the brandy? But here, as with young Pomeroy, I had to pause. Whoever poisoned Watchman took peculiar pains to implicate Legge, but, ever since the investigation began, Miss Moore has been ardent to the point of rashness in her defence of Legge. She has braved everything for Legge, and there is a ring of urgency in her defence that bears the very tinct of sincerity. I dismissed Miss Moore. I turned, at last, to Sebastian Parish and Norman Cubitt. Here it was impossible to ignore motive. Motive in the form of handsome inheritances was as conspicuous as a pitchfork in Paradise. What of fact? Cubitt did not handle the darts but, on my second alternative, he could have tainted the poisoned dart after Watchman threw it down. But if the dart was a blind and didn't kill Watchman, what did? The brandy? We are told that criminals repeat the manner of their crimes and this attempt upon you and Fox supports the theory. The murderer had killed Watchman by the method of putting cyanide in his brandy? The murderer hoped to kill you by putting cyanide in your sherry? To return. The fingerprint and rat-hole objection applies to Cubitt and Parish as it does to everyone but Pomeroy senior. Of course it is possible that the murderer drew the poison off with some instrument and without touching the vessel. This brings me to Parish."

Colonel Brammington darted a raffish glance at Alleyn and accepted a fresh cigarette.

"To Parish," he repeated. "And here we must not ignore a point that I feel is extremely important. Parish purchased the cyanide solution. It was he who suggested, to the certifiable Noggins, that it should be gingered up, as he put it. It was he who carried it back to the inn. Old Pomeroy said that the wretched Noggins' sealing-wax was unbroken when Parish gave him the bottle. It is possible to substitute one drop of sealing-wax by another? And if this had been done, why the interference with the rat-hole? But suppose the wrapping and seal were intact. Suppose that Parish made sure of obtaining a strong enough poison, delivered the bottle, sealed as he had received it, and later went to the rat-hole; why then he would be acting more wisely, he would be removing suspicion one step away from himself. His defence would be: 'If I had intended to use this damnable poison surely I would have taken the opportunity to extract it from the bottle when it was actually in my hands.' I began to think I had got on the trail at last. I inspected the notes made by our man, Oates, when the memory of the night's events were still fresh, or as fresh as the aftermath of Courvoisier would allow. It was Parish, equally with Watchman, who suggested they should have the brandy, Parish who applauded and encouraged the suggestion that Legge should try the experiment with the darts. I began to wonder if this was an opportunity Parish had awaited, if he had the cyanide concealed about him in readiness for use. Could he have reasoned that Legge, full of brandy, was likely to make a blunder in throwing the darts and that, if he did blunder, here was Parish's opportunity to bring off his plan? This was purely conjectural, my dear Alleyn, but before long I came upon a thumping fact. Up to the moment when Miss Moore poured out the brandy that failed to restore Watchman, Parish, and only Parish, had an opportunity of putting anything in Watchman's glass. Parish knew that if Legge wounded Watchman, Watchman would turn queasy. Parish encouraged the brandy-drinking and dart-throwing. Parish stood near the glass until it was used."

Colonel Brammington thumped the arm of his chair and pointed a hairy finger at Alleyn.

"Above all," he shouted, "Parish has done nothing but murmur against Legge. Suspicions, Bacon remarked, that are artificially nourished by the tales and whisperings of others, have stings. This, Parish foresaw. This he hoped would prove true. My case against Parish is that he took cyanide from the rat-hole as soon as he could after Abel Pomeroy put it there. Or, I offer it as an alternative, that he took cyanide from the original bottle, replaced the small amount with water, and contrived to rewrap and seal the bottle; and, as a blind, upset the vessel in the rat-hole without disturbing Pomeroy's prints, and filled it with water. This suggests a subtlety of reasoning which may or may not appeal to you. But to the burden of my tale. Parish had, that very evening, heard of Watchman's idiosyncrasy for cyanide, he had been reminded of Watchman's habit of turning faint at the sight of his own blood, he had heard Watchman baiting Legge and Legge's offer to perform his trick with Watchman's hand, he had heard Watchman half-promise to let him try. The following night, when the brandy was produced and drunk, he saw his chance. He encouraged the drinking and the projected experiment. When Legge wounded Watchman and Watchman turned faint, Parish stood near the glass. He had the cyanide about him. Brandy was suggested. Parish put his poison in the glass. The lights went out. Parish groped on the floor, bumped his head against Cubitt's legs, found the dart and infected it. He then ground whatever phial he had about him into powder together with the broken tumbler on the floor, and finding a more solid piece under his heel threw it into the fire. And from then onwards, gentlemen, I maintain that everything the fellow did or said is consistent with the theory that he murdered his cousin. I plump for Parish."

Colonel Brammington stared about him with an unconvincing air of modesty tinged with a hint of anxiety.

"Well," he said, "there you are. An essay in Watsoniana. Am I to be set down? Shall I perceive my mentor wafting his eyes to the contrary and a falling lip of much contempt?"

"No, indeed," said Alleyn. "I congratulate you, sir. A splendid marshalling of facts and a magnificent sequence of deductions."

If so large and red a man could be said to simper, Colonel Brammington simpered.

"Really," he said. "I have committed no atrocious blunder? My deductions march with yours?"

"Almost all the way. We shall venture to disagree on one or two points."

"I make no claim to infallibility," said the chief constable. "What are the points? Let us have them?"

"Well," said Alleyn apologetically and with an uncomfortable glance at Harper and at Fox, "there's only one point of any importance. I—in our view of the case you've—you've hit on the wrong man."

CHAPTER TWENTY

CONJECTURE INTO FACT

I

FOR a second or two Alleyn wondered if there would be an explosion or, worse, a retreat into heavy silence. Fearing that the expression of gloating delight upon Harper's face might turn the scales, Alleyn had placed himself between the chief constable and his superintendent. But Colonel Brammington behaved admirably. He goggled for a moment, he became rather more purple in the face, and he made a convulsive movement that caused his shirt-front to crackle sharply, but finally he spoke with composure.

"Your manners, my dear Alleyn," he said, "are, as always, worthy of a Chesterfield. I am pinked on the very point of a compliment. The wrong man? Indeed? Then I must be ludicrously at fault. I have made some Gargantuan error. My entire sequence of deductions——"

"No, no, sir. Your case against Parish is supported by facts, but not by all the facts. Parish might so nearly have murdered Watchman, by either of the two methods you've described."

"Then—— Well?"

"The circumstance that excludes Parish, excluded his only means of murder. If he did it, it was by poisoning the brandy, and he couldn't tell which glass would be used. Not ossibly. But we'll come to that in a minute. Our case, and m afraid it's a dubious one at the moment, is that there are ne or two scraps of evidence that only fit into the pattern they are allowed to point in one direction, and that is not wards Parish."

"What are they? More beer, I implore you."

"To begin with," said Alleyn, filling Colonel Brammington's lass, "the two iodine bottles."

"What!"

"Shall we take them, sir, as they turn up?"

"Let us, for God's sake."

"You, sir, ended with Sebastian Parish. I shall begin with im. If Parish was a murderer how lucky he was! How all ccasions did inform against Watchman and favour Parish! : was on the evening after his decision that the brandy was roduced, so *that* was pure luck. He didn't know Legge ould wound Watchman, he only hoped that under the ıfluence of brandy, he might miss his mark. When it so fell ut, he had to make up his mind very rapidly and plan a :ries of delicate and dangerous manœuvres. And how oddly e behaved! He risked his own immunity by handling the arts, and this, when his whole object was that Legge should em to be the poisoner. After the accident, instead of putting yanide in the brandy glass and moving away from it, he ood beside it, in a position that was likely to be remembered. nd again, how could he tell that Miss Moore would use aat glass? There were seven other glasses about the room. he might have taken a clean glass. Parish made no attempt force that glass upon her. She chose it. More stupendous ıck. Now, with the exception of Miss Moore, this objection pplies to the supposition that any of them put cyanide in ıe brandy-glass. They couldn't be sure it would be used. ɪnly Miss Moore could be sure of that for she chose it."

"You surely don't—— Go on," said Colonel Brammington.

"I entirely agree that, ruling out Legge and assuming that ıe whole arrangement of the business was an attempt to ıplicate Legge; Cubitt, Miss Darragh, Will Pomeroy, and Iiss Moore, must be counted out, since they have all declared ıat Legge was unable to meddle with the darts. Our case :sts on a different assumption."

"Here, wait a bit," cried the colonel. "No. All right. Go on."

"Abel Pomeroy and Parish were the only ones openly to accuse Legge. Abel Pomeroy was particularly vehement in his insistence that Legge deliberately killed Watchman. He came up to London to tell me about it."

"Old Pomeroy was my earlier choice."

"Yes, sir. To return to the brandy. For the reason I have given you, and for reasons that I hope to make clear, we are certain that cyanide was put on the dart after, and not before, it pierced Watchman's finger. Otherwise it would have been removed by the trial throw into the cork board or, if there was any trace left, possibly washed off by the blood that flowed freely from Watchman's finger and with which the dart was greatly stained. The cyanide was found on the point of the dart. Watchman, we think, was poisoned, not by the dart nor by the brandy. How, then?"

"But, my dear fellow, there was no cyanide in the iodine bottle. They found the bottle. There was no cyanide."

"None. Now here, sir, we have a bit of evidence that is new to you. I feel sure that if you'd had it earlier to-day it would have made a difference to your view of the case. We have found out that within a few hours of the murder, a bottle of iodine disappeared from the bathroom cupboard upstairs."

Colonel Brammington stared a little wildly at Alleyn, made as if to speak, and evidently thought better of it. He waved his hand.

"The bottle of iodine that was originally in the downstairs first-aid box," Alleyn continued, "was an entirely innocent bottle, with Abel's prints on it and only his. Legge's prints were added when he borrowed this bottle to doctor a cut on his chin. Abel gave it to him. Now that innocent and original bottle is, I consider, the one that was found under the settle. All that is left of the bottle Abel Pomeroy used when he poured iodine into Watchman's wound, is represented, or so we believe, by the surplus amount of glass Mr. Harper swept up from the floor and by the small misshapen fragments we found in the ashes."

"Hah!" ejaculated the colonel. "Now I have you. A lethal bottle, taken from the bathroom and infected, was substituted for the innocent bottle in the first-aid box. Only

Abel Pomeroy's prints were found on the cupboard door and so on. Abel Pomeroy himself took the bottle from the box and himself poured the iodine into the wound. Splendid!"

"Exactly, sir," said Alleyn.

"Well, Alleyn, I readily abandon my second love. I return, chastened, to my first love. How will you prove it?"

"How indeed! We hope that an expert will be able to tell us that the fragments of glass are, in fact, of the same type as that used for iodine bottles. That's not much but it's something and we *have* got other strings to our bow."

"What's his motive?"

"Whose motive, sir?"

"Old Pomeroy's."

Alleyn looked at him apologetically.

"I'm sorry, sir. I hadn't followed you. Abel Pomeroy had no motive, as far as I know, for wishing Watchman dead."

"What the hell d'you mean?"

"I didn't think Abel Pomeroy was strictly your first love, sir. May I go on? You see, once we accept the iodine theory, we must admit that the murderer knew Watchman would be wounded by the dart. Nobody knew that, sir, but Legge."

II

It took the second half of the last bottle of Treble Extra to mollify the chief constable, but he was mollified in the end.

"I invited it," he said, "and I got it. In a sense, I suppose I committed the unforgivable offence of failing to lead trumps. Legge was trumps. Go on, my dear Alleyn. Expound. Is it Locke who says that it is one thing to show a man he is in error and another to convince him of the truth? You have shown me my error. Pray reveal the whole truth."

"From the first," said Alleyn, "it seemed obvious that Legge was our man. Mr. Harper realised that, and so, sir, did you. This afternoon I told Harper that Fox and I had arrived at the same conclusion. You asked me not to give you our theory, but before and after you came into Illington we discussed the whole thing. Harper was for arresting him there and then, and I, mistakenly perhaps, thought that we should give him more rope. I thought that on our evidence, which rests so much upon conjecture, we would not establish a *primâ facie* case."

"What is your evidence beyond the tedious—well, go on."

"As we see it," said Alleyn, "Legge planned the whole affair to look like accident. No doubt he hoped that it would go no further than the inquest. His behaviour has been consistent with the theory of accident. He has shown us a man overwrought by the circumstance of having unwittingly killed someone. That describes his behaviour after Watchman died, at the inquest, and subsequently. He chanced everything on the accident theory. It is easy, now, to say he took an appalling risk, but he very nearly got away with it. If old Abel hadn't raised such a dust about the good name of his public-house, and if Mr. Nark and others had not driven Harper, here, to fury, you might very well have got no further. Legge's motive was the one we have recognised. It harks back to the days when he was Montague Thringle and stood his trial for large-sized embezzlement, and all the rest of it. At least three of the enormous number of people he ruined committed suicide. There was the usual pitiful list of old governesses and retired clerks. A shameful affair. Now, in defending Lord Bryonie, Watchman was able to throw almost the entire blame on Legge, or Thringle as I suppose we must learn to call him. Let him be Legge for the moment. Watchman made a savage attack on Legge, and it was in no small measure due to him that Legge got such a heavy sentence. He had an imperial and moustaches in those days and had not turned grey. His appearance was very greatly changed when he came out of gaol. After various vicissitudes in Liverpool and London, he came down here suffering from a weak chest and some complaint of the ear, for which he uses a lotion and a dropper. Harper found the dropper when he searched Legge's room on the morning after Watchman died. It's not there now."

"That's right," said Harper heavily.

"Legge got on well in Illington and Ottercombe. He'd got his philatelic job, and he was treasurer to a growing society. We shall inspect the books of the Coombe Left Movement. If he has not yet fallen into his old ways on a smaller scale, it is, I am sure, only because the funds at his disposal are not yet large enough. All was going like clockwork until, out of a clear sky, came Watchman in his car. That collision of theirs must have given Legge an appalling shock. Watchman didn't recognise him, though, and later while Legge sat unseen in the taproom, he overheard Watchman tell Parish of the collision and say, as Parish admitted he said, that he did not know the man who ran into him. But before Legge could go out that night, Watchman came across and tried to make friends with him. Legge doesn't seem to have been very responsive but he stuck it out. The rat-poisoning party returned and Legge's skill with darts was discussed. Legge took up Watchman's bet and won. I think it must have amused him to do that. Now, it was soon after this that Watchman began to twit Legge about his job and his political opinions. I've gone over the events of this first evening with the witnesses. Though they are a bit hazy, they agree that Watchman's manner was offensive. He ended by inviting Legge to a game of round-the-clock and the manner of the invitation was this: he said, 'Have you ever done time, Mr. Legge?' I think that throughout the whole evening Watchman, having recognised Legge, played cat-and-mouse with him. I knew Watchman. He had a curious feline streak of cruelty in him. I think it must have been then that Legge made up his mind Watchman had recognised him. Legge went into the public bar for a time. I believe he also went into the garage and sucked up cyanide in the little dropper he used for his ear lotion. Just, as they say, in case."

"Damned ingenious," said Colonel Brammington, "but conjectural."

"I know. We are only half-way through the case. It has changed its complexion with Oates's arrest of Legge for assault. We've only been here some thirty hours, you see. If we can check the time Legge appeared in the public bar with the time he left the private one, and all that dreary game, we shall be a step nearer. But dismiss all this conjecture and we still have the facts. We still know that only Legge controlled the flight of the dart."

"Yes."

"The next day was the fatal one. Legge stayed out of sight all day. Late in the afternoon, he left it as late as possible,

247

and just before the others came in, he went down to the bar with a razor-cut on his chin and asked Abel for some iodine. Abel got the box out of the corner cupboard and gave it to Legge. Legge returned it a few minutes later. He had dabbed iodine on his chin. He had also substituted for the iodine bottle in the box, the iodine bottle he had taken from the bathroom. This he had doctored with prussic acid from the rat-hole. By this really neat manœuvre he got Abel to do the dirty work and accounted for any prints of his own that might afterwards be found on the bottle. In the evening Legge had a perfectly genuine appointment in Illington. At about five o'clock the storm broke, and I think that like a good villain Mr. Legge made plans to the tune of thunder off-stage. The storm was a fair enough reason for staying indoors. The failing lights were propitious. The Pomeroys both told him he couldn't get through the tunnel. When Will Pomeroy went up to Legge's room in the evening, he found him rather thoughtful. However, he came down and joined the party in the bar. I think he had made up his mind that, if Watchman suggested the trick should be done that night, he would wound Watchman. Abel, so keen on antiseptic, would produce the first-aid set from the cupboard. So it worked out. Two points are interesting. The first is the appearance and the consumption of the brandy. That was an unexpected development but he turned it to good account. He sat in the ingle-nook and appeared to get quietly and thoroughly soaked. That would account nicely for his missing with the tricks. In the wood-basket beside his seat we found a newspaper into which liquid had been poured. The newspaper had been there since that night. Fox and I think we can detect a trace of the fruitful vine in the stains. But he must have watched the others anxiously. Would they be too tight to remember he had no chance to monkey with the darts? Luckily for him, Will, Abel, Miss Darragh, and Miss Moore, all remained sober. That brings us to the second point. Legge's great object was to provide himself with an alibi for doctoring the darts. That was why he fell in with Abel's suggestion that he should use the new darts. Legge stood under the central light and waited for the darts to be handed to him. He was in his shirt sleeves and they were rolled back like a conjurer's. Parish, Will, Abel, and Watchman, all handled the darts.

When Legge got them he at once threw them one by one into the board, as a trial. That was his first mistake but it would have looked odd for him not to do it. Then Watchman pulled them out and gave them to him. Watchman spread out his hand and the sequel followed. There were six people ready to swear Legge had done nothing to the darts."

Alleyn paused.

"I'm afraid this is heavy going," he said. "I won't be much longer. Watchman, when hit, pulled out the dart and threw it into the floor. When Oates called for the dart Legge obligingly found it on the floor behind the table but not before Oates, who's a sharp fellow, Nick, had, as he says, spotted it a-lying there. You throw those darts down as often as you like and I'll guarantee they stick in. And moreover we've statements from them all that it *did* stick in. All right. The lights had been wavering on and off throughout the evening. Before Watchman died they went off. There was a horrid interval during which Watchman made ghastly noises, everybody tramped about on broken glass, and Cubitt felt somebody's head butt against his legs. Miss Moore, she told me, heard somebody click the light to see if it would go on. Not very bright of Miss Moore. Legge clicked the light to make sure it would stay off. He then dived down to find the tell-tale iodine bottle and plant the innocent one under the bench. He must, as you say, have found the bottom of the bottle hard to smash and have thrown it in the fire. You remember he called out that he would throw wood on the fire in order to get a little light. Just as he did that the lights went on. There's a second switch in the ingle-nook, you know. He'd done another job of work in the dark. He'd picked up the dart and infected it with cyanide. The dart was sticking in the floor, well away from the others. He had only to feel for the table and then find the dart. Here he made the fatal mistake of adding a fancy-touch. We've proved that the dart was infected *after* the accident. Legge's fingerprints are all over it. If anyone else had pulled it out of the floor they would either have left prints of their own or smudged his. He should have left the dart alone, and we would have concluded that if it was ever poisoned the stuff was washed off by blood or had evaporated."

"I cannot conceive," said the colonel, "why he'd wanted to anoint the dart. Why implicate himself? Why?"

"In order that we should think exactly what we did think. 'Why,' we cried, 'there was Legge, finding the dart, with every opportunity to wipe it clean and he didn't! It couldn't be Legge!' Legge's plan, you see, depended on the theory of accident. He made it clear that he could have done nothing to the dart beforehand."

"Then," said the colonel, "if the rest of this tarradiddle, forgive me, my dear fellow, is still in the air, we yet catch him on the point of the dart."

"I think so. I explained to Harper this afternoon that I thought it better not to make an arrest at once. We realised that our case rested on a few facts and a mass of dubious conjecture. Fox and I pretend to despise conjecture, and we hoped to collect many more bits of evidence before we fired point-blank. We still hope to get them before Legge comes up for assault and battery. We hope, in a word, to turn conjecture into fact. Until this evening I also hoped to get more from Legge himself, and, by George, I nearly got a dose of prussic acid. He must have slipped into the taproom and put his last drop of poison in the decanter. He must also have had that last drop hidden away in a bottle somewhere ever since he murdered Watchman. Not on his person, for he was searched, and not in his room. Perhaps in his new room at Illington, perhaps in a *cache* somewhere outside the pub. Some time after Harper had searched his room, Legge got rid of a small glass dropper with a rubber top. If he used it to draw prussic acid from the rat-hole, he must have cleaned it and filled it with his lotion, emptied it and restored it to its place on his dressing-table. If he also used it to do his work with the decanter, he got rid of it this afternoon together with whatever vessel housed the teaspoonful of prussic acid. We'll search for them both."

Alleyn paused and looked round the circle of attentive faces. He raised a long finger.

"If we could find so much as the rubber top of that dropper," he said, "hidden away in some unlikely spot, then it would be good-bye conjecture and welcome fact."

III

"A needle," cried Colonel Brammington after a long pause, "a needle in a haystack of gigantic proportions."

"It's not quite so bad as that. It rained pretty heavily during the lunch-hour. Legge hasn't changed his shoes and he hasn't been out in them. They're slightly stained and damp. He crossed the yard several times, but he didn't get off cobble stones. The paths and roads outside the pub are muddy. He's therefore either thrown the bottle and dropper from the window or got rid of them in the house or garage."

"Lavatory," said Fox gloomily.

"Possibly, Br'er Fox. We may have to resort to plumbing. His whole object would be to get rid of them immediately. He didn't know when we mightn't take a glass of sherry. Now there's a valuable axiom which you, Colonel, have pointed out. The criminal is very prone to repetition. How did Legge get rid of the iodine bottle? He smashed it and threw the thick pieces into the fire. When he had more glass to get rid of in a hurry, wouldn't he at once think of his former method? He's a very unusual criminal if he didn't. There was no fire here, but during the afternoon he made several trips to the garage. He was packing some of his books in the car. I think our first move is to search the car and the garage. It's full of junk so it will be a delightful task."

Alleyn turned to Oates.

"Would you like to begin, Oates?"

"Yes, sir, thank you, sir."

"Search the car and garage thoroughly. I'll join you in ten minutes."

"Methodical, now," said Harper, "remember what I've told you."

"Yes, sir."

Oates went out.

"I think Mrs. Ives is still about," said Alleyn. "She works late."

"I'll see if I can find her, sir," said Fox.

"You'll stay where you are. I'll go," said Alleyn.

Mrs. Ives had gone to her room but had got no further

than her first row of curling pins. Alleyn interviewed her in Legge's room. She'd taken a cup of tea up to him in the afternoon when he was packing his books. She couldn't say exactly when, but knew it was after three and before four o'clock. She had noticed the ear-lotion and dropper on top of his dressing-table.

"Particular, I noticed it," said Mrs. Ives, "along of it being wet and marking wood. Usually, of a morning, it's all mucky with that pink stuff he puts in his ears. 'About time you washed that thing,' I said, 'and I see you've done it.' He seemed quite put-about. Well, you know, put-about, like, at my noticing."

"And did you go away soon after that, Mrs. Ives?"

"Well, sir, seeing I was not welcome," said Mrs. Ives, bridling a little, "I went. I offered to help him with his books but he seemed like he didn't fancy it, so I went on with my work upstairs. Polishing floor, I was."

"Which floor did you polish when you left Mr. Legge?"

"Passage, sir, and I might of saved myself the trouble, seeing he come and went to and fro from yard half a dozen times, stepping round me and dropping muck from his papers and passels."

"Did he go into the bathroom or any other room upstairs?"

Mrs. Ives blushed. "He didn't, then. He made two or three trips and after last trip he went into private tap. The gentlemen were down there, Mr. Parish and Mr. Cubitt. You come up here soon after that to change your clothes."

Alleyn thanked her, spent an uncomfortable quarter of an hour on the roof outside Legge's window, and returned to the parlour.

"We're in luck," he said, and gave them Mrs. Ives' story of the ear-dropper.

"That's why he didn't fill it with lotion again and leave it. He'd just washed it when Mrs. Ives walked in, and when she noticed it, he lost his nerve and decided to get rid of it."

"The dropper," said Harper, "had a rubber top."

"It'd float," said Fox.

"He didn't go there, Br'er Fox. Mrs. Ives would have seen him. And there isn't one downstairs. It's the garage or the yard. Hallo, here's Oates!"

Oates came in. He was slightly flushed with triumph.

"Well?" said Harper.

"In accordance with instructions, sir," said Oates, "I proceeded to search the premises——"

"A truce to these vain repetitions," began Colonel Brammington with some violence.

"Never mind all that, Oates," said Harper. "Have you found anything?"

"Smashed glass, sir. Powdered to scatters and under a bit of sacking. The sacking's been newly shifted, sir."

"We'll look at it," said Alleyn. "Anything else?"

"I searched the car, sir, without success. I noted she was low in water, sir, and I took the liberty of filling her up. When she was full, sir, this come up to the top."

He opened his great hand.

Lying on the palm was a small wet indiarubber cap such as is used on chemist's lotion droppers for the eye or ear.

"Good-bye conjecture," said Alleyn, "and welcome fact."

May 3rd, 1939,
  New Zealand.

THE END

Agatha Christie

The most popular and prolific writer of detective fiction ever known, her intricately plotted whodunits are enjoyed by armchair crime-solvers all over the world. How many of these have you read?

Hallowe'en Party *30p*

By the Pricking of My Thumbs *30p*

Endless Night *30p*

Third Girl *25p*

Murder at the Vicarage *25p*

One, Two, Buckle My Shoe *25p*

Lord Edgware Dies *30p*

After the Funeral *25p*

The Mystery of the Blue Train *25p*

The Pale Horse *25p*

Death in the Clouds *25p*

Three Act Tragedy *25p*

Death on the Nile *30p*

The Hollow *30p*

The Sittaford Mystery *25p*

Taken at the Flood *25p*

At Bertram's Hotel *25p*

4.50 From Paddington *25p*

A Caribbean Mystery *25p*

The ABC Murders *25p*

The Big Four *25p*

Hickory Dickory Dock *25p*

The Hound of Death *25p*

The Mirror Crack'd from Side to Side *25p*

Murder in the Mews *25p*

Partners in Crime *25p*

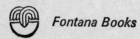 *Fontana Books*

Ngaio Marsh

'The finest writer in the English language of the pure, classical, puzzle whodunit. Among the Crime Queens, Ngaio Marsh stands out as an Empress.' *Sun.* 'Her work is as near flawless as makes no odds: character, plot, wit, good writing and sound technique.' *Sunday Times.* 'The brilliant Ngaio Marsh ranks with Agatha Christie and Dorothy Sayers.' *Times Literary Supplement*

When in Rome *30p*
Clutch of Constables *30p*
Death at the Bar *30p*
Final Curtain *30p*
Scales of Justice *30p*
Surfeit of Lampreys *30p*
Colour Scheme *30p*
Off With His Head *30p*
Vintage Murder *30p*
False Scent *30p*
Died in the Wool *30p*
Spinsters in Jeopardy *30p*
Death at the Dolphin *30p*
A Man Lay Dead *30p*
Death in a White Tie *30p*
Hand in Glove *30p*
Death in Ecstasy *30p*
Singing in the Shrouds *30p*
Artists in Crime *30p*
Enter a Murderer *30p*

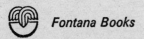 *Fontana Books*

Fontana Books

Fontana is best known as one of the leading paperback publishers of popular fiction and non-fiction. It also includes an outstanding, and expanding section of books on history, natural history, religion and social sciences.

Most of the fiction authors need no introduction. They include Agatha Christie, Hammond Innes, Alistair MacLean, Catherine Gaskin, Victoria Holt and Lucy Walker. Desmond Bagley and Maureen Peters are among the relative newcomers.

The non-fiction list features a superb collection of animal books by such favourites as Gerald Durrell and Joy Adamson.

All Fontana books are available at your bookshop or newsagent; or can be ordered direct. Just fill in the form below and list the titles you want.

FONTANA BOOKS, Cash Sales Department, P.O. Box 4, Godalming, Surrey. Please send purchase price plus 5p postage per book by cheque, postal or money order. No currency.

NAME (Block letters) _____

ADDRESS _____

_____

_____